ONE SNOWY KNIGHT

BOOK YOUR PLACE ON OUR WEBSITE AND MAKE THE READING CONNECTION!

We've created a customized website just for our very special readers, where you can get the inside scoop on everything that's going on with Zebra, Pinnacle and Kensington books.

When you come online, you'll have the exciting opportunity to:

- View covers of upcoming books
- Read sample chapters
- Learn about our future publishing schedule (listed by publication month *and author*)
- Find out when your favorite authors will be visiting a city near you
- Search for and order backlist books from our online catalog
- Check out author bios and background information
- Send e-mail to your favorite authors
- Meet the Kensington staff online
- Join us in weekly chats with authors, readers and other guests
- Get writing guidelines
- AND MUCH MORE!

**Visit our website at
http://www.kensingtonbooks.com**

ONE SNOWY KNIGHT

Deborah MacGillivray

ZEBRA BOOKS
Kensington Publishing Corp.
http://www.kensingtonbooks.com

ZEBRA BOOKS are published by

Kensington Publishing Corp.
119 West 40th Street
New York, NY 10018

All Kensington titles, imprints, and distributed lines are avail-
able at special quantity discounts for bulk purchases for sales
promotion, premiums, fund-raising, educational, or institu-
tional use.

Special book excerpts or customized printings can also be created to fit specific needs. For details, write or phone the office
of the Kensington Special Sales Manager: Attn. Special Sales
Department. Kensington Publishing Corp., 119 West 40th
Street, New York, NY 10018. Phone: 1-800-221-2647.

Zebra and the Z logo Reg. U.S. Pat. & TM Off.

ISBN-13: 978-1-4201-0450-9
ISBN-10: 1-4201-0450-0

First Printing: October 2009
10 9 8 7 6 5 4 3 2 1

Printed in the United States of America

Chapter One

Scotland, December 1296

Searing agony ripped through his back. The muscles of his right side screamed a plaint, warning he erred in pushing too far this day. Despite the spreading numbness, which always followed the intense burning, Noel de Servian struggled to stay upright in the saddle. The icy winds cut like daggers against his stiff back, and with each ragged breath the pain increased tenfold.

At this late juncture, he realized he should have stayed in Berwick until spring as King Edward had suggested. Even more to the point, mayhap he should not have rashly ridden on ahead of his small party. His edginess had pressed him to dismiss customary safety measures and recklessly spur Brishen to the forefront, hoping to scout out the way to the passes. Pulling off his helm, he looked about him and frowned. His troops were nowhere in sight. Clearly, he had ridden on too far ahead. Noel exhaled his frustration. Wagons traveled so slowly. He chafed, impatient to reach Craigendan Keep. *His new home*. He would finally, for the first time in his adult life, have a home to call his own.

Despite the snow swirling about him so thickly he could

barely see to the end of his horse's nose, or that fiery pain racked his poor muscles, the thought brought a smile to his lips. Though one of Edward's most trusted knights, Noel's reward had been long in coming. Too many battles. So much sacrifice. And it had nearly cost his life.

His mind cast back over a score year ago to when he had been a squire to the mighty King Edward, training alongside Julian Challon and Damian St. Giles. They had been proud to serve one of the most powerful monarchs England had ever seen. So naive they, little did any of them envision the horrors that lay ahead in their young lives, how bloody long the road to peace would be, the goal forevermore out of reach. His green mind had not counted on the brutal ugliness of warfare, not counted upon Edward's unquenchable thirst to be the king of the whole of Britain and beyond.

"I had *not* counted on being unable to find the bloody passes to Glen Shane," he groused to his steed, Brishen, as he reined him to a halt. Reaching under his mantle, he withdrew the crude map from an oilskin pouch at his waist and studied it once more. Blinking against the falling snow, he tried to shield the parchment with his heavy woolen cape to prevent the big flakes from hitting it and smearing the ink. "The passes *should* be here. We are close. We damn well have to be."

The horse gave him a tired nicker and shook his head up and down, the fittings of the bridle jingling like faery bells in the stillness; then he looked straight ahead as if saying, *right there, fool*. Noel wiped the snow from his eyes, squinting to see through the blinding storm. Was the gap in the hills really there and he simply lacked the wherewithal to spot the opening in this impenetrable whiteness?

Placing his hand behind him on the high cantle of the saddle, he turned to check his bearings. A spasm, white-hot, racked his muscles, nearly causing him to pass into blackness. The throbbing was that bad. That dangerous. He could not lose his awakening thoughts in this storm, or it might cost his life. After all these years of service to the English king, he had finally been granted the title of baron and the smallholding in this rugged Northland.

"It would be sad, indeed, if I died out here in this blizzard, never to lay eyes upon the fief that is finally mine." Noel chuckled at the irony, but then flinched, as even that caused his back to ache more.

Just four months past, Edward had convened Parliament in Berwick, a city once called 'the pearl of Scotland.' Of course, that had been before Edward's troops had invested the town in a three-day sack. The horrendous aftermath saw Noel waking in the deep of night, covered with sweat and unable to shake the ugly nightmares that plagued him. A foul miasma of half-rotted corpses still polluted the air come August when Edward Plantagenet had humbled all of Scottish nobility, forcing them to kneel to him—not as overlord of Scotland, but as their new ruler. After the rout of the Scottish army in April at the Battle of Dunbar, Edward had leisurely circled most of the conquered country. With an eye to seeing their defiant spirit crushed, the king demonstrated with redoubtable power, his wealth, his might, hoping to impress upon the Scots that he now held the country in his fist.

"I have doubts on that, Brishen. I see these Scotsmen watching Edward when the king is unawares. A steeled obduracy bespeaks these Highlanders are not cowered by the English, but merely bide their time. Already small pockets of resistance are causing mischief. Soon, someone—like young Andrew de Moray—will light the fires of rebellion, and the coming storm will roll across these untamed lands. There will be no stopping it, I fear."

Brishen's head bobbed up and down again, as if agreeing with the validity of his master's words. Noel gave a soft chuckle at the animal's behavior. Sometimes his horse was too bloody intelligent.

"Why I am eager to take control of the fief Edward conferred upon me, horse. I want everything settled before the impending madness erupts."

Slowing the transfer of the fief, in April he had taken a sword to his back in fierce single combat with the Baron Craigendan. The wound proved slow to heal. Oh, the muscles and flesh had mended. Vexing, the wound site remained tender, sore. The fever he battled after being injured had sapped his strength; he struggled still to regain it. Ten years ago he would have healed much faster.

He sighed. "Ten years ago I was a young man. This day I feel old, seven and thirty years *very* old, so tired it hurts to breathe." With an exhausted resolve, Noel nudged Brishen forward with his knees. "You are so bloody smart, horse, mayhap you can find the proper path into Glen Shane. The damn passes *have* to be near."

A strange racket arose, spooking the charger, causing him to bounce on his hooves and rear slightly. Ravens. Thousands and thousands of screeching ravens, their racket deafening. His horse had been through more battles than Noel cared to count, yet now stood trembling and refused to move any farther. The cacophony increased, as if a huge murder of ravens was taking flight. So peculiar, he had seen flocks of birds do this in autumn, but never in a snowstorm such as this. As the mount's fear increased, he began to back up. Noel tried to restrain the horse, but its alarm waxed out of control. The black mouth of hell opened before them. The birds came straight at them, pushing Brishen to rear high.

"Merde!" Noel's back slammed hard against the high cantle of his saddle, the helm falling from his grip. Agonizing pain lanced through his whole body, so intense he barely maintained his seat. Numbness possessed his right hand. He could not even flex his fingers. His left hand grasped the squared pommel and held on, all he could manage. The damn horse spun on his heels and fled, not responding to Noel's knee commands, the reins flapping uselessly just out of his reach.

Noel gritted his teeth. Tears poured down his face and mixed with the melting snowflakes until he was not sure how long the animal ran. And ran. There was no stopping him. Fighting waves of blackness that threatened to pull him into passing out, Noel lost all sense of direction as the horse galloped heedlessly along a narrow, steepening path, carrying him farther and farther away from the passes of Glen Shane and the shelter he hoped to seek with Julian Challon at his new fortress of Glenrogha. With the snow heavy, limbs of the pine trees bowed low, forcing him to dodge them. His mantle flapped each time he brushed one. The snow covered his surcoat and leathern hose and fell inside the edge of his cross-laced boots, the icy moisture leaching away his body heat. And still the crazed animal ran.

Darkness swirled through his mind, as his back jarred against the cantle with every jump the horse took, so savage the agony that he lost the function of his hand to clutch the leather pommel before him. Unable to focus, he was powerless to react fast enough when Brishen ran under a low limb. The heavy bough caught Noel across the chest, sending hot irons of torture through his muscles as he was knocked from the saddle, a second time when he landed hard, his hip hitting first, then his tender side.

He could not catch air. It was too much for his abused body; he simply lay there and, with a sense of detachment, watched the snow falling down upon him. At first it was cold. Deep shivers began to rack his body. Brishen came over and nudged his master's shoulder with his nose, trying to provoke Noel to stir. As the snow continued to cover him, the shuddering lessened, nor did he feel the freezing chill any longer. Little by little, he ceased to experience the bite of pain, just a strange soothing warmth.

Noel closed his eyes. "Brishen, have I traveled all these many miles, and fought so many ugly battles, only to have my fate meted out by falling snow?"

* * *

"Andrew! Annis!" Lady Skena MacIain lifted the fur-lined hood of the woolen mantle away from her face to listen, hoping to hear her children calling to her in response. There was only silence, that deep hush, which came when snow blankets the land, as if nothing stirred but wisely stayed huddled by fireside or in some cozy nest.

"Anyone with a thimble full of sense," she grumbled.

Trying not to give in to rising panic, she waited. For whatever harebrained reason, the twins had slipped off through the postern gate. Finding two sets of small footprints heading away from Craigendan, she followed, thinking that surely in this storm they had not wandered far. In hindsight, she should have turned back and fetched help in searching for them. Too late now. The blowing snow fell so thickly that it covered their trail, preventing her from pursuing them farther. Daylight was waning; night came early this time of the wheel. In this wonderland of white, losing one's sense of direction could happen too easily. It was imperative she find them before darkness descended completely.

"If wishes were candles I could light the way back to Craigendan," she said with growing despair.

The stour was heavy for this early in the season. The Yuletide celebrations were upon them—not that there would be much to celebrate. Still, this part of Scotland generally never saw snow like this until deep winter, sennights yet away. That worried her, as if wintertide had come early and would be a long, harsh one. Just what Craigendan did not need.

But then, this whole year had been nothing but one disappointment after another. First, everyone had lived with their hearts dark, anxious as the English had ridden north to invade Scotland. Word spread throughout the Highlands of the sack of Berwick, where a thousand score perished in three days of killing. Then the terror came closer—neighboring valleys of

Glen Shane and Glen Eallach had been given in charters by Edward Longshanks to English lords, men of Norman descent. Dragons of Challon, they called these warriors with whispered awe.

"Bloody English dragons," she spoke aloud, simply to hear some sound in this silent landscape. "At least Craigendan is too small of a holding for a wee beastie to want to come and claim. We have naught but a bunch of mouths to feed and damn little food."

She grimaced. And no men to protect Craigendan or hunt for meat come harshest winter. Nearly all their men had died on the field at Dunbar, her husband leading them. Without someone to fetch fresh meat regularly, Craigendan's people would be skin and bones come spring. Scots called winter "famine months." This year she worried it could be the worst her people had ever faced. The long summer had blistered the land; no rain for sennight upon sennight saw a drought grip the whole country, drying up burns and parching crops. Her stomach knotted at the last thought. Oh, Craigendan had enough food to eke by—for the nonce. Howbeit, if this snow came as a portend of the months ahead, things could become dangerous for her smallholding.

Her lord husband had been killed in the battle back in April. Aye, she had not spent long mourning his passing, for which she now struggled against profound guilt. Not that Angus had been a bad man. Well-respected by two Scottish kings, he had proven a good lord to Craigendan, protected it and saw that it prospered. He had been kind to her, after a fashion. Only, she had not married him for love, had not married by her choice either. She honored her lord husband, tried to please him and make him happy. Yet, in her naïve heart she always believed there was the other half of her soul out there waiting to find her. Silly mooncalf dreams of a young lass that refused to die. Angus was a score year older than she, and often treated her more like a daughter than a wife. Unlike those of her cousins, Tamlyn, Rowanne, Raven, and Aithinne, her lands were not part of the ancient charter that protected a female's rights going back to Pictish times; this charter entitled her kinswomen to hold their land and select their husbands. No choice had she when their king, Alexander III, had betrothed her to a stranger—Angus Fadden, a Lowlander. Still, as winter approached, she now missed Angus, missed the security he had meant to her people.

She shivered, thinking how the English king had sent knights to claim Glen Shane and Glen Eallach. Two of her cousins were now wed to Englishmen, two more were betrothed to Edward's warriors, and she walked as a widow. So much had altered in less than a year.

"Times change. Sometimes not for better." Combating the biting fear, she glanced around for telltale signs the children had come this way. "Andrew! Annis! Come. It grows late. Children, oh please answer me!"

Fearful they were lost out there in the endless white, she pushed on. Her wee ones were too small to survive long in this bitter storm. Wolf tracks had come nearer to the stronghold this fortnight past, driven closer to the holding in search of prey. People were not the only ones suffering after the dreadful summer.

"Children! Answer me this instant!" She attempted to sound stern, not panicked.

While she had never loved Angus the way a wife should a husband, she did love the children he had given her. Brother and sister born on the same night, Andrew and Annis were her whole world.

Another gust of spindrift swirled around her. The snow covered her long auburn hair, soaking it, but she dare not lift the hood for protection, as the fur lining muffled her hearing. The wind whistled through the pines, whispering voices of the Auld Ones.

She closed her eyelids, then pulled her mind to that dark

spot in her heart and listened, hoping her witch's sense could guide the path. Women of Ogilvie blood were oft touched with degrees of the kenning, a fey gift, the ability for the mind to reach beyond normal perceptions. Her mother's mother was an Ogilvie of the old line, thus she had inherited this power from their blood. The trait had never been strong in her, not like it was in her cousins Tamlyn or Aithinne, though she hoped this time it would serve her true.

Off to her right, far up ahead, she thought she perceived a voice. Opening her eyes she searched, but discerned naught in the blinding snow. Had her mind been playing tricks? Just as hope turned to disappointment, she heard it again.

"Mama!" So faint, she still did not trust the call to be real. Then it came once more. Louder. "Mama!"

Her heart leapt for joy as she gathered up her mantle, hurrying her steps through the deep snow. Though the response was repeated, she still could not see Andrew. But then, two small ghostly figures formed up ahead. She hated that the snowdrifts made it hard to reach them, and that with each step she sank all the way to the tops of her boots. The heavy wool of her kirtle saw the hem sodden and weighted. The chill was reaching her body, sapping its heat.

Then she noticed a pale form behind the children. A horse?

Her relief shifted back to apprehension. No steed would be out wandering in this. The animal could only mean a rider was near, yet none was on his back. As she drew close she saw it was a monstrous destrier, nearly as white as the snow, a beautiful stallion of power, an instrument of war, yet it followed behind her children with the mien of a puppy.

"Mama!" Annis cried and hurried toward her.

Skena leaned down to hug her darling daughter, though after that first rush of blessed relief that they were safe, she itched to take a hand to their backsides to ensure they would never do this again. "You two are in trouble, you ken?"

"Och, Mama, do not fash!" Andrew grinned, while petting

the mighty steed on its neck. "Is he not wonderful? The most valiant destrier in all of Scotland? He's a Kelpie, Mama."

"Nay, Kelpies are water horses, Andrew." She hugged him, and then ran her hands over his body to make sure he was unharmed.

"Is snow not frozen water? It tastes like water when I catch it on my tongue," he argued, crinkling his forehead. "I made a wish, Mama—my Yuletide wish—to the Cailleach, lady of winter. I asked her to send us a warrior, a knight to protect us."

"A knight to care for us . . . to love us," Annis added in her soft voice, lowering her lashes to hide the pain that her father had never loved her.

Skena's heart broke yet another time. Annis was such a pretty little girl. She had the same dark auburn hair and big brown eyes as Skena bore. People spoke of how her daughter was the spitting image of Skena when she was a child. How any man could not adore the bairn, she had never understood. Angus had doted on Andrew, his son and heir, but with 'the girl' he nearly denied her existence. Tossing her mind back over the past seven years, she could not recall Angus's ever calling their daughter by her given name. It was always 'the girl.'

Skena's trembling hand reached out and brushed the snow from Andrew's shoulders and hair. "Oh aye, a grand steed is he, too grand to be out in this winter storm. But he is no Kelpie."

"He *is*, Mama. He brought our knight, just as I asked," Andrew insisted, getting that stubborn look upon his countenance.

Skena sighed in exasperation, seeing Angus's face stamped upon their son's features. The lad was hard to deal with when he fixed on something. Oft losing the patience to deal with the willful child, Angus had wanted to foster him with his younger brother in the south on the Marches. Skena refused to allow it, begging to keep her son one more year before he was sent away for training. She did not want some man she had never met caring for her son. Though she little regretted she had bent her husband's resolve in this matter, she was apprehensive about Andrew's willful streak now there was no man to show him the way of the world.

Annis took her hand. "Come see, Mama. He is beautiful, a knight true, like some great warrior king of old that the *Seanchaidh* tells about around fireside."

"We need to get back to the *dun*—now. Dark surrounds us. You are aware night falls early now that the Solstice draws near. You are soaked. I am soaked. We'll catch our death if we do not get back and dry ourselves—"

"Mama!" Annis sobbed, tears streaming down her pale cheeks. "We leave him out in the stour. . . . The wolves will come . . . and get him."

Andrew took her other hand and tugged. "Come, we must fetch him back with us. He is ours now. I asked the Kelpie if he was, and he shook his head aye. Watch." He stroked the horse's velvety nose. "The warrior belongs to us now. You brought him for us, eh?"

The beast shook his head up and down, and then looked at Skena with soulful eyes. She blinked in shock. Was this warrior steed indeed one of the Fae?

"See, Mama?" Annis hopped back and forth on her feet. "Come, we must save the man. *Please . . .*"

Heaving a sigh, she saw the twins were in their obstinate mood and would refuse to listen to her. If she pushed them to obey, they might run off in different directions—a ploy they had used more than once when defiant. With the snow worsening, it was vital they get back to Craigendan quickly. "Very well, one should not doubt a Kelpie, I suppose."

Taking the reins of the beautiful steed, she turned him in the direction the children had come. Picking up Annis, she set the little girl in the saddle and then watched to make sure the horse would accept the small rider. Some destriers were trained never to permit anyone upon their backs but their masters, yet this animal turned his neck and merely observed as Skena settled Annis's hands on the high pommel. The horse's huge eyes seemed so gentle it was hard to believe this beast was trained to kill in war, was as valued a weapon as a lance or broadsword.

"Hold tight and grip with your knees as I taught you." Skena pulled the hood on the child's mantle about her small face.

"Aye, Mama." Annis's head bobbed in a nod.

Taking the reins, Skena allowed her son to tug her in the direction he wanted. Just as she feared this was a fool's errand, her eyes spotted an odd shape on the earth up ahead. As they neared, she grew alarmed some poor soul was on the ground covered by snow. Passing off the reins to Andrew, she rushed forward. By the length of the body she judged it to be a man.

"We tried to clean him off, Mama," Andrew said, "but the snow only covered him again."

"By the blessed lady, he must be the rider of the horse." Was he even alive? Skena knelt beside the still body, and with her freezing hands swept the snow from his face.

As she brushed off the slope of the second cheek, a small gasp came from her lips; she stared, transfixed by his beautiful countenance. Never had she seen a more perfect man. The wavy brown hair was not a dark shade, not light, though made a measure deeper from the wet snow. He had a beautiful chin, strong, yet not too square. Angus's face had been pleasant, but his jaw had looked as if it had been carved from a block of wood. This man's showed strength, character, yet there was a sensual curve that caused her to run her thumb over his nearly clean-shaven cheek. No face hair. Norman? Her hand stilled as a shiver crawled up her spine, one that had naught to do with the cold. Dismissing that concern, she swept the snow from his neck and shoulders. She rather liked that she could see his features; it allowed his perfection to show clearly. Nice strong brows, not bushy like Angus's. And lips . . . so carnal, a woman would wonder what it would feel like to taste them, crave to discover such mysteries for herself. Surely, this man was touched by the blood of the *Sidhe*; only one blessed by magic could be so lovely formed, a man possessed of the power to lure a woman into darkest sin, with nary a thought of the risk to her soul.

She jerked back slightly at the odd notions filling her mind, a yearning that had never come before. Still, there was no time to fritter away on such nonsense. Trembling in alarm, she feared he might be dead. Great anguish arose within her that one so beautiful would have his life cut short. As she touched his neck, she felt the throb of his blood. Faint. So very faint. Relief filled her heart at that small flicker of life. She had to get him to Craigendan and warm his blood or he might not survive. Even then, it would be a fight to save him. How long had he been lying in the snow? In the fading light it was clear his skin was grey, his lips tingeing blue.

Fretting at the urgency of the situation, Skena glanced up at her daughter. There was no way the children and she could get this man onto the horse's back. As well, waiting until they were missed and her people came searching for them was not a choice. Aid had to be summoned from the fortress. The warrior's life and theirs hung in the balance.

"If wishes were wings we could fly back to the *dun*," she muttered under her breath.

Rising to her feet, she tried to decide what the best course of action was. She could not abandon the man here alone, defenseless, while she went to fetch help, not with dark closing in. Nor could she leave the children with him. Grabbing Andrew by the waist, she swung him up behind his sister in the saddle.

"Andrew, you must ride for help. Do not run the horse. I know you love to do that. You must be careful he does not slip in the snow. Hie you to Craigendan and tell them to fetch a cart . . . and furs . . . any warming stones if they are ready. Tell Cook to heat water for baths and prepare hot broth for us all." She handed him the reins.

"Aye, Mama. I will be careful," he promised solemnly, assuming the responsibilities of a man upon his small shoulders.

"Our lives depend upon you, Andrew, my brave lad." She moved to the horse's head and rubbed his forelock. "My noble steed, carry my children safely to Craigendan. . . . Save us all and I shall see you get apples through the winter."

Closing her eyes tightly against the tears, she hugged the horse, and then said a silent prayer to the Auld Ones to keep her bairns safe. Hoping she was doing the right thing, she gave the horse a light slap on his haunch and set him in motion. With her heart pounding, she watched until the pale stallion disappeared in the blinding blizzard.

Turning back to the man on the ground, she once again had to wipe the gathering flakes from his face. She attempted to tug him to a sitting position, thinking she could wrap her mantle around them both and lend him what little body heat she still had. When she went to lift him, she realized he still had his broadsword lashed crosswise over his back. Finding the strap's buckle on the center of his chest, she released it.

Then froze as the howl came.

It was close by. The man groaned as she urgently rolled his dead weight, enough to drag the sword out from under him, and then dropped the leather sheath as she freed the blade. Holding the sword in her right hand, she used her left to release the clasp of her mantle. She would need her arms free to swing the sword. Keeping her eyes fixed upon the trees, she dragged her woolen cape over the man's unmoving body.

The deep growl sent a chill to her marrow as the threat of the snowstorm had failed to do. Low tree limbs rustled and then parted as the set of glowing yellow eyes peeked through the wintry foliage.

Swallowing hard, Skena brought the sword up, preparing to swing, and praying she had strength enough to wield the mighty sword true.

Chapter Two

Skena stood trembling, from the cold, aye, but more so from dread. With the specter of famine looming across the land, she feared wolves would soon be a threat they'd face. Foolishly, she had hoped the menace would not come this early in the season. Swallowing to moisten the dryness in her mouth, she watched the feral eyes narrow on her, judging how much a threat she presented holding the sword. Plainly, she posed nary a concern to the creature. Shoulders lowered, teeth bared, he edged forward, a low growl of intent rising deep in his throat. The animal scented her fear. Her weakness only emboldened him.

Keeping her attention on the black wolf, Skena quickly scanned to see if there were others coming up behind him or circling around. Where you found one, usually there lurked a pack. Her luck holding, thus far no other pairs of bright eyes appeared; no dark forms skulked through the unmoving undergrowth around the dense pine trees.

"Oh, please let him be a lone wolf," she offered her wish to the Auld Ones, before whispering dark words to weave the charm of protection, drawing upon what little powers she possessed to sustain her through this ordeal.

Skena was not a small woman. Her Ogilvie blood showed in her tall body and strong bones. Even so, to hold the heavy broadsword, which took years for a man to master, was wearing. Her arms vibrated; tremors racked her muscles. A mix of terror and cold. The winter storm slowly leached all the strength from her body. She fought against the quaking, still the sword wobbled in her grip.

Baring his fangs, the wolf crept slowly forward, more daring with each step. Skena had trouble keeping her vision clear. Falling flakes and those kicked up by the spindrift continued to stick to her long lashes, adding moisture to the tears she valiantly labored to hold at bay. It was vital to see the wolf when he leapt in order to time her swing.

"Off with you, evil *foal-chû*. You will not be making a meal of this warrior or me." She spoke her false courage, hoping the sound of her voice might frighten him into backing off. Instead, his body coiled, preparing to spring.

So intent was she upon the wolf, she hopped slightly when long arms enclosed about her. Startled and yet unwilling to take her eyes off the black creature. It was several heartbeats before she comprehended the stranger had awakened and was on his feet. Suddenly, in his strong embrace she was not so scared.

"Be still, my lady. I lend my strength to your swing." The warrior's cold hands closed over hers. He leaned heavily against her back; his powerful muscles caused her shaking to lessen.

Skena had little chance for the details of his nearness to filter through her thoughts, for with a feral snarl the wolf leapt for them. Frozen in terror she was unable to move, yet she felt the warrior wielding the sword. Bared teeth snapped close to her throat. She cried out and then flinched when the great blade caught the beast in the neck. Blood splattered across her clothing and face. Its heat shocked her. Numb with the horror, she stared at the animal writhing on the ground. In the gathering darkness, the pooling blood oddly appeared black upon the pristine snow. The coppery smell set her stomach to rolling; revolted, she choked back rising nausea. Her grip slackened about the hilt. The knight's fingers closed tighter about hers. "Nay, my lady, never leave a wounded animal alive . . . sometimes, not even a man. 'Tis when they are most dangerous. They risk all for they have naught to lose."

Standing before the wolf, he helped her raise the sword at an angle and plunge it into the animal's chest. The beast jerked thrice. Then no more. With a low, uttered groan, the warrior dropped his hands from the sword.

Her arms burning from the strain, Skena was unable to hold the blade tip up. It thumped to the ground. Still, she kept her grip on it. There might yet be more wolves to come; the scent of blood on the wind would now lure them. Skena turned to see the stranger reel on unsteady legs and then go down on his knees.

Grasping the sword with her right hand, she caught his upper arm with her left to steady him. "Och, Sir Knight. Please, do not fall in the snow. It saps your body of vital heat. Help comes soon. We must remain vigilant. The blood scent on the wind summons others."

He gave a faint nod of understanding, and then glanced up at her. Flakes hit his comely face, so pale from the cold. "Who . . . are you, demoiselle?" He reached up with a shaky hand and tenderly tried to swipe the splatters of blood from her cheek.

"I am Skena of Craigendan." Despite the residual terror and the chill racking her body, a fleeting smile curved her lips as she stared into his silvery eyes. So rare, there was a streak, almost a ring around the inner eye, but in the fading light she could not tell what shade it was.

"Craigendan? I am . . . near the fortress then?" He clearly struggled to remain in his thoughts. "I am lost . . . only to be found." He gave a faint laugh.

She was concerned. He was not shivering. People out in the cold shivered. Left in that condition too long they shuddered uncontrollably. If they stayed unwarmed beyond that, the quaking stopped as they pushed toward the threat of death. That he was confused, lacked good muscle control, and didn't tremble scared her.

Still dazed by killing the wolf, she tried to sound calm. "Not far from *Dun* Craigendan."

"Far for me, I fear. I sought the passes. . . . Glen Shane . . ." His words trailed off as his eyelids lowered.

Skena gave him a shake. "Stay awake. Fight it. Talk to me. You hunted for the passes of Glen Shane? Nary a stranger can find the passes. They are warded by an ancient spelling to keep outsiders away."

"Challon . . ." The word was barely audible. Another jerk from her saw his head snap up.

"You ken the Lord Challon?" she asked, with a touch of fear.

"Lady Skena . . . You are beautiful . . . so . . . beau—" He gave her a faint smile, but then it fell from his lips as he stopped speaking. Limp, he just rolled to the side.

"Beautiful, indeed," she scoffed. Struggling to pull him upright, she lost her grasp as he dropped back to his side. "Bloody man is daft. I am soaking, splashed with blood, and the *amadan* thinks me beautiful."

The weight of his muscular body was too much for her to control. Frowning at how weak a woman was compared to a man, she leaned the sword's hilt against his chest where she could snatch it up quickly if needed, and then set to straighten his poor legs. As she finished, she heard noises off in the distance in the direction of Craigendan. Soon, she spotted flickers of torches through the trees.

Upon his brown jennet, Andrew came first, leading the way for the others. "See, Mama, I fetched them."

She wanted to give her son a hug for his bravery, yet did not want to get blood on him. "You did well, Andrew. I am proud of you." Her teeth chattered so; it was hard to speak the words.

"My lady!" Galen called in concern as he halted the cart and climbed down. His ancient eyes took in her blood-splattered condition, the wolf, and the prostrate warrior. "You all right?"

"Aye." Skena nodded, but was too drained to say more.

"Here, wrap this around you," he said, flinging another mantle about her shoulders. "Jenna sent you another, fearing you would be soaked. You scatty female, you risk your death. You should not be so foolish. You ken all of Craigendan depends upon you."

"Galen, cease fashing. We need to be away from this place." Skena shivered, her eyes glancing about to make certain no wolves lurked in the low-hanging tree limbs.

"Oh, aye. And so we shall, afore the blood scent from that one lures his brethren. Warming stones and furs are in the cart. Snap to, lads," he spoke to Kenneth and Owen—boys barely four summers older than Andrew.

They hopped from the back of the cart and went to the fallen warrior. They were the nearest thing to 'men' at Craigendan, aside from Galen, who was four score if he was a day. Between the four of them they managed to lift the knight off the ground and into the straw-filled cart. The man screamed out as they placed him on his back, which set him to cursing in a tongue seldom heard by her.

"Norman." Galen's brow crinkled, as he looked to her. His face was etched with foreboding. "Lass, what sends one of the mighty leopard's knights all the way out here in this snowstorm? Bodes ill. Aught connected to Edward Longshanks only brings ravens and sorrow."

Skena saw fear reflected in the man's dark eyes. "No time to fret, old friend. Let us fetch him back to Craigendan. He has stopped shivering. That alarms me."

"Mayhap he will not live," the old man spoke, hope lacing his words.

"He *will* live," she countered, with determination she failed to fathom. She asked, "Is there a chance to send to Glen Shane to bid Auld Bessa, Evelynour or Oonanne to Craigendan?"

His head gave a faint shake. "Not in this, lass. You ken the Three Wise Ones of the Woods come when they are needed. But they grow old, their days short on this earth. To travel that distance in this storm would be too much to ask."

Skena grimaced, knowing her curing skills were not as strong as those of the three healers who cared for all in Glen Shane and beyond. Ignoring that apprehension, she placed the long sword by the warrior's side, noticing he had lapsed into a dark state of mind. Accepting Galen's hand, she hefted herself into the back of the wagon. Taking the heated stones from the sack, she placed them alongside the still man and then covered him with three bearskins.

"Take that sack and collect the wolf," Skena ordered, tossing the burlap to Galen. When everyone simply stared at her, she snapped, "Do it! 'Tis meat."

Andrew wrinkled up his nose. "I do not want to eat wolf meat, Mama."

Ignoring her son's sour face, she tucked a bearskin around the man's large body. "Meat is meat. In a stew you will not ken the difference."

As the cart pulled into the bailey, Skena hopped down from the bed of straw. They gently rolled the tall warrior onto a blanket to keep from jolting him about. Auld Bessa had warned her that a person left out in the cold too long might suffer heart seizures if they were bumped or handled too roughly.

"Each of you, take a firm grip on a corner of the *plaide*. We lift him at the same time. Slowly. No sudden jerks," she instructed.

Everyone in the fortress was in a pother, running up and asking questions. They wanted to ken who the stranger was and what was he doing on the road to Craigendan. A Norman knight on their lands raised dire concerns in all minds. Still,

Skena spared no time to fash over possible answers and what import they might hold for the future. Too worn down by the ordeal of looking for the children and then fighting the wolf, those disquiets would have to wait until the morrow. For the nonce, there were score of things to be done if they were to save this man's life.

"Where do we put him, Skena?" Galen asked.

She knew there was only one place. "Take him to the lord's chamber."

"But, my lady—" Galen began.

Skena cut him off, letting the elderly servant know she would brook no opposition. "'Tis hardly the time to fret over such trifles. He is a big man and should have room. With no healer, his care falls to me. I need him where I can tend to him and require a fireplace nearby. It will be a long night of the soul, mayhap several, until he rests safely out of harm's embrace."

Galen eyed her with misgiving, but held his tongue as they started up the winding stairs. Andrew ran ahead, opening the door to the large chamber, and then hurriedly pulled the covers back on the feather mattress.

"Place him down carefully. Do not jar him," she said, anxious. Once that was done she hugged Andrew and kissed his forehead. "Run along to Nessa. I want you and your sister to have a warm bath and be full of hot broth. Then to bed. I will come kiss you day's end when I am free."

Nessa came in to poke the fire, adding more peat bricks to raise the heat in the large chamber. "Who is he, my lady?"

"That remains a question unanswered at this point. Nessa, take Andrew and Annis. Bathe them in warm water. Keep adding hot water as it cools to make sure they are unburned by the cold. Fill them with hot broth and then tuck them up together with warming stones. Stay with them this night, please," Skena asked.

"Aye, my lady. See to the man. I will keep watch over your

lambs." The nursemaid took Andrew by the shoulder and turned him toward the door. "My nosy lad, you want to see if the warrior is all right. Never fear, young lordling, your mama will fetch him around. Come, you must do as your *màthair* bade."

"He is *my* warrior. I wished for him, and he came." Andrew dragged his feet, plainly wanting to stay. "The Kelpie fetched him for me."

"Oh aye, and you can tell him all about how he belongs to you—on the morrow." Nessa grabbed him by the sleeve of his sark and pulled him from the room.

Skena sat on the edge of the huge bed and then unbuckled the warrior's belt. Fortunately, he wore soft leathern hose, well treated with oil, so they were supple. That was a blessing. The oiled leather had turned away the snow, preventing the wetness from reaching the flesh of his legs. Galen could not work the frozen knots on the cross-laced boots; taking out his knife, he cut the lacings.

"Gently, Galen. Do not jostle him," she cautioned again.

The old man glared at her. "Lass, I have been caring for those who were exposed to bad weather long before your *màthair* was born. I ken we must keep him peaceful."

Jenna, her maidservant, came in carrying a stack of linens. "I ordered the big tub fetched. Cook has plenty of water on the fire. Is there aught else I should do, my lady?"

Skena nodded. "Aye, go to the stillroom and get my herb box. I need to make a tansy to ease his pains that will come with warming. Also, bring the large pot of healing ointment that Auld Bessa prepared for us back in the summer."

"Aye, my lady," Jenna nodded before scurrying off.

Galen examined the man's bare feet for cold burn. "Bluish, but not bad. He is cold inside more than out methinks. The flesh will be fine with care. His clothing served him well, protected him from the worst of the cold. His boots, like the hose, are well oiled, thus they turned away the wet. The children came upon him before he had been out there too long. Lucky for him." He added under his breath, "Mayhap not so lucky for Craigendan, eh?"

"By the Lady's blessing he lives. Remember that. Let us get him out of the mail and clothing." Skena worked in hurried silence, unlacing the sides of the dark green surcoat. Galen and Owen raised him to a sitting position to allow her to pull off the fine raiment. Her cold fingers had a hard time unbuckling the arming-points of the metal hauberk underneath, so Owen did it for her. "Help me turn him to his side. Methinks rolling off those hose would be easier in that way."

Skena gasped as she peeled the leather over his hips. "By the fires of Bel, what has harmed this man?"

This surely did not come from his fall and had naught to do with the cold. There was a palm-sized, reddish discoloration on his right side, curving around his lower back. She sucked in a harsh breath, fearing it was infected. In the dim candle-light she could not see clearly, but the patch of skin was crimson and puffy, likely why he cried out when they had placed him on his back in the wagon. She reached out and gingerly pressed the flesh with her fingertips. The marks remained white. Not a good sign. As she repeated the action, the knight moaned and started to awaken.

Skena was glad he roused; that he had remained unawake troubled her. Yet, in the same breath, she hoped his mind would stay cosseted in blackness while they finished the warming. She knew it would be painful as the skin and blood reacted to the warm water. Since the process had to be done slowly to protect his heart, she needed him as peaceful as possible.

Upon Jenna's return, Skena told Galen, "Help him sit while I mix the tansy to relieve his mind of the coming pain."

Hurrying to the table near the fireplace, she opened the large wooden box and quickly measured out pinches of St. John's wort, vervain, skullcap, valerian, chamomile, and crampbark into the wooden bowl and ground them with the pestle. The worts would work to relax the body and stop muscles from knotting. The ointment she had Jenna fetch also contained most of these in the special salve. It would ease his surface distress. Mixing the finely ground powder with water in a cup until dissolved, she then carried it to the bed.

"Sir Knight, please drink." She lifted the cup to his sensual lips, which were no longer tinged blue. Again, she was struck by just how handsome he was—nay, the man was beautiful.

The lids lifted on his eyes; their power hit her full force. Their paleness like liquid silver. That alone would be striking enough, but around the dark inner circle was a ring of amber. Never had she seen eyes such as his, so lovely she could lose herself in their shimmering depths. She had seen plenty of gray eyes before; they oft looked dull or flat. None had the special brilliance of this man's. The outer edge of the paleness had another ring, this time of black, which only made the eyes stand out. Arresting.

A razor to her soul.

Skena could not think, could hardly breathe. She stood enthralled by the stranger's spellbinding eyes. They were sleepy, softening their effect. A shiver slithered up her spine as she considered how it would be to see them alert, focused.

See the fires of hunger burn in them for her.

"Skena, I fetched broth," Muriel said, as she shuffled into the room. It broke the enchantment that held Skena frozen. The elderly woman put the small metal pot on the stand by the bed. "Enough for you both. Brought two spoons. Figure you will get more into him if you feed him, lass."

"Thank you, Muriel. Can you and Jenna please set more warming stones to heating? Then change the covers to dry once we move him? See the bed is as warm as we can get it."

After taking a swallow of the wort mixture, the knight scowled and pushed the cup away. "What foul poison do you feed me?" he grumbled.

"Oh aye, tastes like it was brewed with stump water, no doubt. Even so, you needs must choke it down, my braw warrior. Quickly."

He looked up at her, then offered her a lopsided smile. "Skena?"

"Aye, 'tis my name. You remembered." On impulse she reached out and brushed the three damp curls back from his high forehead. "And what is your name, *Sasunnach?*"

"Noel . . . de Servian," he managed to get out before a shiver racked his body. His eyelids fluttered, half-closing. She could see the gooseflesh on his skin. Not good, still better than his body ignoring the cold. The words were slurred as though he had a hard time concentrating. "I am at Glenrogha? Where is Brishen . . . my horse?"

"Leave it to a man to fash about his bloody horse. Your mighty steed is fine, well fed and safe within my stable. Come, drink up, and I will answer all your questions." She aided him in turning up the cup to drink the dark liquid. "Good. You can wash the horrid taste down with a wee bit of broth. It helps warm your blood as well."

She nearly jumped when he placed his arm about her back to help steady himself, and then scooted to the edge of the bed. It brought her in close contact with him, which in turn sent her heart to rocking. Well, it was not every day a man as bare as a newborn babe held on to her! And never one so pretty, so perfectly formed. That sort of excitement was not good for her, she knew. Chilled, too, she had to be careful about sudden jolts to her heart until she was warm once more. Forcing deep breaths, she tried to slow the pace. Her silly heart failed to pay heed. Her reaction to him was upsetting, frightening. No man had ever before caused such a flutter inside her, forced it to be hard to draw air.

And she paid for it. The increased pounding set her blood to speed up. Thick from being chilled, it ached coursing through her. Noticing he had not finished everything in the cup, she picked it up and drank the dregs. Pain came from the cold, yes, but more because of the effect he had upon her body.

"My lady, you hurt?" Muriel touched her right arm in concern.

Not capable of guising her feelings, Skena failed to meet her old nurse's stare. The woman held the power to discern her thoughts only too well. "Some. Being in the cold slowed my blood. The warming is always distressful. Like when you sit on your foot too long and try to stand."

"Drink some broth, lass. You must keep from taking ill," Muriel whispered the warning. "This warrior needs all your skills to save him. Auld Bessa taught you much, but it will take your strength to see him through this."

"I will drink it, soon. He needs it more." Skena fed him a spoonful of the hot broth. Then a second. So caught in the web of magic spun from his ensorcelling gaze, she was barely aware of Owen and Kenneth dragging in the wooden tub. De Servian's glimmering eyes watched her every move, her every reaction to him. By the fifth spoonful, the potion's effect was starting to hit his mind. She quickly gave him a bit more liquid, while they filled the tub. "Make sure the water is only warm. 'Tis too distressing to stand it hot at the start. Howbeit, put cloths into a pan and soak them with hot water. I need to put those on his neck and chest to heat the heart first."

Noel de Servian appeared alert, but Skena kenned that was often deceiving. Auld Bessa told how men too long out in the cold would go running around and actually yank off their clothing, their minds too numb to know the difference between hot and freezing. The blue tinge was leaving his lips, fingers, and ears. The shivering was more violent. Clearly, his muscles were not responding. His movements were slow, labored as he tried to push the spoon away. He frowned at his hand as if not understanding why it failed to respond as he wanted.

"Skena?" he asked again, puzzled. "Where am I?"

"At Craigendan. You told me you were going to Glenrogha, but became lost in the snowstorm." She hoped if he talked he might fight the lethargy.

"Challon . . . I sought him," he finally said.

She nodded. "You spoke that was your aim. When the storm lessens and is not dangerous, I will send word to Glenrogha to let the Earl Challon ken you are at Craigendan and safe."

"At Craigendan?" He tried to stand, so she jumped to support him by putting her arms around his waist.

Muriel clucked her tongue and rushed to wrap a sheet about his hips. "You are a braw and bonnie lad, Sir Noel, but my old heart cannot take all your fine splendor at once."

Bemused, he watched the elderly lady tuck the fabric in at his waist, plainly unawares he had been without any clothing. While that brought a fleeting smile to Skena, it showed how the cold still had him in its grip. She needed to get him into the tub without delay.

"Can you walk, Sir Noel? We have a warm bath prepared for you." She gave a nod to Galen, who took the knight's arm and wrapped it about his neck to help prop up the warrior.

De Servian's steps were uncontrolled, but they finally got him to the tub, and with a little maneuvering, into the warm water. It seemed to sap his remaining strength, so she permitted him to lean against the side of the tub and rest.

"Galen, you and the lads go *beek* yourselves by fireside. I will call you again if I need help getting him from the tub. I do not think I will. He will regain his strength as he shakes the cold from his flesh," she assured him. Recalling it was her night to keep watch on the wall, she fussed, "By Bel's fire!"

Galen turned at her exclamation. "My lady, what troubles you?"

"This night is my turn to hold watch upon the—" she started to explain only to have her retainer cut her off.

"Mind your tongue, Skena." His eyes jerked to the warrior and then back to her with a stern glare, silently admonishing her that their secrets were not for the man's ears. "Fash not, on this night few souls would be daft enough to venture out in this stour. Not even a bloody Campbell would be so mooncalf as to take the risk. One less doing their duty will matter little. You stay. You are needed here if you have your mind fixed upon saving this knight of King Edward. Though I would bend your ear on the wiseness of that path, I have doubt you would heed my words."

"You are right, my friend. Even a Campbell would not go aroaming in this whiteout, and right again, I will hear no discourse on withholding treatment that saves this man's life." She exhaled her trepidation. "I will deal with consequences of his coming soon. Too soon, I fear."

Jenna and Muriel finished changing the bed and then wadded up the damp bedclothes. Her maidservant glanced to the bowl by the bed and back to Skena. "You have not touched the broth, lass. Now it cools," she chided. "I will fetch you some more."

"You have my thanks, Jenna, but I am not hungry this eve," Skena replied.

Jenna placed her fists on her hips and frowned. "Do not try to pull the wool over these eyes, Skena MacIain. I ken you miss supper to see others have a full belly these past sennights. Stop that. We need you. Many depend upon you, lass. You require your strength to stay healthy and get through this winter. So you will be eating your supper, or I will get Galen and Owen to pin you while I pour it down your throat."

"Very well." Skena gave Jenna's arm a squeeze to let the woman know she appreciated the fussing over her.

Muriel held back, hesitating, but finally stepped closer as Jenna closed the door. "Skena, did you see the man's side?"

Skena gave a stiff nod. Taking the salve, she smeared it thickly across his neck and shoulders. "I meant to give it a closer look."

"My eyes are not as sharp as they used to be, but I have

seen many a man damaged in battle. That wound is not too old. He took a dirk or mayhap a sword to his side, likely through the seam of his mail shirt. I would say not a year gone either." Muriel appeared anxious.

Skena's movements stilled. Not a year gone? Dunbar? Or worse, Berwick? She did not know which would make her sicker. That she now worked to save an Englishman, when he likely had been killing her countrymen just months before, caused her empty stomach to roll.

"My fear, the wound is tainted and was not made pure before they allowed it to heal over. Something now inflames it. Oft when a man's skin is pierced, the weapon embeds small pieces of fabric or mail in the flesh. Injuries must be made clean before they allow the skin to seal. We needs must make a poultice, draw the impurity to the surface and then lance it. It will only grow worse and likely poison his blood. He will sicken otherwise. Mayhap die."

Skena knew the old woman spoke the truth. "Let us see if he makes it through this ordeal. Come morn, we can examine his side and what needs to be done. Go eat your meal."

"I will come back to see if you need help getting him to bed." Muriel smiled and touched Skena's shoulder for reassurance. "Though, seeing as he is a braw and bonnie lad, I doubt any woman would have trouble getting him in her bed."

Skena's insides twisted at the thought of her knight being in the bed of another woman. It was most odd. She was jealous. Silly nonsense. She did not even know this man. He was not *her* knight.

A lump rose in her throat, but she swallowed back the pain.

Chapter Three

Intending to rub more salve on the knight's chest, Skena stepped to the side of the wooden tub. She jerked upright as her gaze collided and locked with that of the handsome stranger. The stupor lifting, the silver eyes were clear, aware. They watched her with a feral intensity. Big cats or wolves had that same focus, the ability to single out prey and track it without blinking. The pale eyes robbed her of the capacity even to breathe, held her spellbound with their ascendancy. Never had she seen such dominant eyes, as if this man held the craft to look inside her deepest heart and ken her secrets, her longings, things she dare not admit even to herself.

Noel de Servian scared her in ways she scarcely understood, aside from the myriad questions summoned by his presence in the vale. Knights did not journey alone through Scotland, especially English ones. So why had this beautiful warrior been found in her small glen with nary a soul about him for support? Knights of the nobility had squires, men-at-arms, servants, and yet this man traveled with none? Skena shivered, from the chill of being out in the storm, true, but also from fear. His arrival heralded a change ahead for Craigendan.

No fool, she was aware the frisson was also provoked by those enthralling eyes, aware no male before had caused this fluttering in her chest. Barely able to remember why she held the pot of salve, she dipped her shaky fingers into the silky ointment again, and then smeared it across the other side of his chest.

De Servian glanced down at her hand rubbing his skin. His expression bemused, he asked, "Pray tell, what are you doing, Lady Skena?"

"The salve . . . is special," she stammered out. "Oils protect the skin from cold burn, salve to speed the healing. Also, the herbs calm pains your flesh feels from the heat of the water."

"But my chest is *above* the water." The weak smile he offered her faded when a shudder racked his body, so severe he seemed to lose what little strength he had regained. Eyelids half-closing, he slumped.

Panicked that he was not shedding the chill from his body quickly enough, she snatched up one of the cloths soaking in the pail of hot water. She spread it across the plane of his broad chest. When he flinched she jumped.

"God's wounds!" His lids flew up as he grabbed hold of the cloth and tried to fling it away.

Skena caught his wrist and stopped him. So odd, her strength did little to restrain this knight. Even in his weakened state, she felt the fearful might of his strong arm—his sword arm. It was her touch, naught more, which stilled him. His eyes looked to her hand where it gripped his wrist, then traveled slowly up to her face.

"Please, Sir Noel, you must allow me to place these hot cloths upon your chest . . . to warm your heart."

"Noel," he corrected.

"'Tis what I said." Skena relaxed when she felt resistance leave him.

"Nay, you said *Sir* Noel. I would have you address me in the familiar." He had said it as granting leave, but she did not miss that it held the ring of a command to it.

She offered him a shy smile, trying to hide the fact she still found it hard to draw air around him. "As you wish, I shall call you by your given name—provided you let me tend you without fashing. I promise all I do is necessary to haste to your recovery. You shall sicken with ague, mayhap chilblains . . . or worse, should I not care for you in a timely fashion."

His lids fluttered once more as if his mind was slipping away, but he finally nodded. Skena carefully spread the cloth over his chest. Satisfied he remained quiet, she laid another on top of that one. His jaw flexed and he ground his teeth, but they were his only reactions.

"You may curse if you wish," she suggested, reaching for a third rag. "Men seem to find comfort and release with such words."

"Too much effort . . ." He paused as another shudder shook his body, and then faintly recoiled when she put the rag to his chest. "I am having trouble keeping my thoughts together. . . . So explain, why do you scald me? Surely, this serves some purpose other than torture?"

Skena slowly poured warmer water into the tub. "For those left out in a storm too long, 'tis important to warm them in steps. Auld Bessa, a great healer, says blood thickens and will freeze, same as ice forms in water. The blood must be warmed to stave off chilblains, but foremost, you must heat the heart. She cautions a body can be taken in seizure if care is not used to do this painstakingly. These cloths applied to your chest shall set you on the path to it beating right. Then I can raise the water's heat gradually to thaw the rest of you. The tansy you drank will ease the pains which come. It will also make you sleepy. Once the warming is done, I will dry you, apply the salve to your skin, then put you in bed with heating stones— and pray you are not seized with lung sickness."

"So you do this to heat my blood, and you are not truly a Highland witch planning on cooking me . . . *eating me*." He chuckled, a smirk tugging at the corner of his mouth, though she was unsure why.

"Och, what a horrid thing to say!" Skena paused to consider this *Sasunnach*. "Is that what you Englishmen say about Scotswomen?"

"They speak of a pagan land with ancient ways, ways the church frowns upon. They say Auld Gods lurk in the shadows, calling Scots back to their heathen rituals, and warn of witches with strange powers that spellbind a man until he forgets his name." His right hand reached out and lifted her long hair away from her neck and shoulder, exposing her throat. The pale eyes moved over her body, watching her with that predator's intensity, which set her to an alarm she failed to understand. "'Tis warned Scotswomen have blue and green scales upon their belly and breasts. Tell me, Skena, do they speak truth?"

"Englishmen," she said in scorn. "Bloody fools who believe tales meant for wee bairns."

"Mayhap a man believes such things because he is tempted to search out the answers for himself." As he fingered the long strand of her dark auburn hair, a fire lit his unearthly eyes. "I always imagined a witch as a hag with black hair. I suppose they might be young, fair, and with hair the shade of fire."

"Fire, indeed," she scoffed, using it as a shield against the wildly skittering emotions ignited by his close scrutiny.

"Very well, 'tis truth your hair is dark. Only, the light from the flames plays around your tresses lending them a fiery glow." His words held a husky cant. "Your eyes lower when I look at you. Why is that, Skena?" He stroked the back of his hand against her throat, watching the shiver he conjured ripple along her skin.

Skena raised her shoulders in a faint shrug. "Because of the way you look at me, my lord. 'Tis very direct."

"You are a beautiful woman, Skena. Surely, men watch you all the time." His curled fingers cupped under her chin as he brushed the pad of his thumb back and forth over her jaw.

Applying the gentlest of pressure, he forced her to look up and meet his stare.

Skena blushed as heat flooded her face. "A fright is what I am. For you to say such things only tells me your blood is still slow and clouds your mind. Any lackwit can see my hair is caked with wolf's blood."

"What I see is a lady of valor who stood over me . . . saved my life. Not many women could have faced the charge of a wolf as resolute. Blood is my lady's badge of courage. It serves you well. Your attention in warming me shows you are a good woman, Skena. A caring woman." Noel de Servian dragged his thumb slowly over her cheek. "Howbeit, there are other ways for a woman to warm a man's blood. Faster ways . . ."

De Servian leaned forward, his mouth softly covering hers. Shocked, she tried to gasp 'oh,' but that merely gave him an opening to deepen the kiss. Trembling, she was lost to the flood of wild sensations. Left terrified by this magic he wielded so ruthlessly.

For so long, she had avoided kissing. Angus was a good man, kind in his treatment, but he had failed to elicit any desire in her. She assumed such was the way between men and women until she overheard servants talking about having relations with their husbands or men they fancied, heard their bawdy laughter, their joy. Then she had wondered in guilt if there was something wrong with her. Oddly, she had lain in the dark and done her wifely duty to give Angus an heir, yet kissing him had seemed to ask for something she was unwilling to surrender to the man who had been her lord husband.

Her reactions to this stranger were startling. First instinct had been to pull back from him, thinking him too bold, too reckless. But, when he sensed her resistance, his hand moved to clasp the back of her neck and allowed her no retreat from him. With the gentlest of pressure he held her captive and taught her that she knew nothing about kissing. His lips were cool, but soft, slowly forming hers, encouraging Skena to follow his lead. Her struggles faded as she found her will yielding to his tender assault.

Mayhap she should be vexed that this stranger dared such advances when he barely knew her name. Her mind failed to summon the outrage befitting a lady. Instead, she found herself leaning toward him, giving over to the wondrous flood of sensations. How his lips were warmer now, how his tongue brushed against the seam of hers, almost teasing them to open. Heat rushed through her body as if her blood boiled. A hard cramp lodged in the pit of her belly, twisting with a need so strong it was almost blinding. Flames licked at her mind, making her faint. Her hands clutched the backs of his arms, her fingers desperately curling around the smooth skin and hard muscles.

De Servian shivered, then a deeper quake racked his body, and his hand dropped from her neck. He leaned back and gave her an exhausted smile. "I thank you . . . for helping *warm* me, Skena." His head tilted to one side, as though he found it too hard to hold up.

When his lids started to close, she scooped up water and rubbed some on his cheeks. "Please stay awake, Sir Noel, for a wee bit longer. I must see you warmed, dried, and in bed."

"Noel," he corrected. "Call me Noel. I gave you leave to use my name."

"Aye, you did. 'Tis a lovely name, too." *Suiting a man with lovely eyes*, she thought. Skena swallowed back that bit of folly. If she encouraged him to talk he might not drift off to sleep, thus she prodded him about things he had spoken of before. "You said you were trying to reach the Lord Challon at Glenrogha? You are kin to the mighty Black Dragon?"

"Brothers . . . after a fashion. I believe you Scots call us foster brothers. When I was five my father was killed in a tournament. A freak accident. A lance splintered and a long shard got through the ocularium and was driven into his skull. The duke took our family's holding and gave it to another lord.

Unable to face existence without my father, my mother . . . took her own life . . . drowned herself in the lake."

Skena's heart squeezed at the thought of Noel de Servian as a child of five, smaller than Andrew, and losing both his father and mother. How any mother could have left her beautiful son to deal with life alone was more than she could understand. "I sorrow you faced such heartbreak when you were so young."

"'Tis a long time ago. Fortunately, Earl Michael took me in and gave me a home. I served as page at Castle Challon and was raised with Julian, his brothers, and their cousin, Damian St. Giles. When I was age eleven, we were sent to be squires for King Edward, and then later served as his knights."

He leaned his head back and shut his eyes, so he failed to see her still at the words, which brought darkness to her heart. This was no ordinary English knight. He had powerful friends. Though not through blood, he was bound to the men of Challon deeply. Scots knew foster brothers were often more devoted than true sons of the same blood. There was a chance he was merely coming to pay visit to the new overlord of Glen Shane. A chance. One she doubted. Well, no use begging for trouble. She took a steadying breath and turned to pick up another rag from the pail, adding it atop the others. He flinched slightly, but offered no further complaints.

"I sorrow to cause you distress. 'Tis important the warming be done in the right way." Skena took up another rag and wiped his face and neck. "You come to visit your foster brothers?"

His head gave a small shake no, his hands gripping the sides of the tub to keep himself upright. "How long does a proper warming take, my lady? I find I weary and wish to sleep. Mayhap if you were to kiss me again it shall speed haste to your methods."

"My lord, 'tis unseemly for a woman to permit a stranger to kiss her whilst they are alone in a bedchamber. I should not have allowed you to do so the first time, but you caught me unawares." Skena bit the corner of her mouth, telling herself she did not want him to kiss her again. Nay, a thousand times nay.

She frowned. She never used to lie, but with the passing days mendacity came too easily to her lips. Lies to her people about how precarious their situation was—a fortress with nary a male over ten and four summers to man the ramparts or to hunt for meat, more deceit covering how the drought left them with little in the way of supplies. All Craigendan's people looked to her for assurances they would come through this winter without their bellies rubbing their backbones.

So the lies came.

Now there would be more untruths, she feared. Lies to this man. Lies to her people about what his coming meant. So tired and hungry, she just wanted to curl up in bed and sleep, only she had a way to go before she could rest assured about his condition.

Skena misliked how he kept trying to fall asleep. Yes, the potion was relaxing him, pushing him to be drowsy. But he was too alert one breath, then slipped away from his thoughts the next. Scared, she wished Auld Bessa was here to guide her.

"But we are not strangers, Skena. I have given permission for you to address me as Noel. May I call you Skena?"

She chuckled. "I believe you already have. We Scots hold little keeping in the use of titles. Most call me Skena of Craigendan or Skena MacIain."

His eyelids lifting, a cautious glimmer flickered in his unusual eyes. "You do not call yourself Skena Fadden?" There almost seemed to be a guarded tone to the question, but she could not gather why.

For some reason, that he knew of her husband, knew his name, caused her heart to slow. "Did you ken Angus?"

"Know him? No, I did not *know* him." There was an odd flatness to his tone, but mayhap it was simply the tansy making him sleepy. "So you do not take his name as your own?"

"Nay. I keep the name of my father's clan. My mother's

family was of Clan Ogilvie. I bore her name in the Highland way until I was ten and six, then I assumed my father's name in order to inherit this holding from his clan. Scots do not put much stock in a woman taking a husband's name as theirs."

"Skena. 'Tis a very beautiful name. Does it have a meaning?"

Skena folded a cloth thrice and then wrapped it across the back of his neck. "Not that I ken. Some say it comes from Skene, a place near the coast, far to the east."

"'Tis still beautiful," he managed to say just before a big yawn hit him.

"Methinks you use that word too much. When a word is overused it loses its power." She stepped to the end of the tub. "Give me your foot."

"My foot? Why ever for? They are not beautiful." He chuckled lowly.

She had to smile. "Men's feet are ne'er beautiful. Even so, I wish to see it." When he failed to move, she reached into the tub and lifted his leg. Holding it up by the ankle with her left hand, she pinched his big toe.

"Oww. . . . That hurt," he complained, his brow furrowing.

"Good." Skena pinched the next toe, getting the same reaction. Then the next.

Grabbing the side of the tub he tried to lever himself out of the water, but could not because of his foot being up in the air. "God's wounds, woman, why do you torment my toes? I tell you that you are beautiful, and you set to bedevil me. I thought women liked to hear such things."

"Only when such words are truth." Skena stared at the handsome warrior, biting back the pain she felt for some inexplicable reason. Why did this man, a total stranger, find the way to wound her with simple words? Forcing down the lump in her throat, she finished checking his toes on his left foot, then allowed it to drop back into the water. "The other one, please."

As another deep yawn hit him, he flexed his arms, stretching them straight out. His arms were beautiful. She frowned. Now she was using the bloody word! Well, they were. Strong, muscular, taut. She had seen many a man's arms through the years; workers out in the fields would take off their shirts, or when they washed in the loch. Men training with swords or staffs oft removed their sarks. As she stared, she could not ever recall seeing anyone's so prettily formed. They were long, matching his height; muscular, but not too bulky.

"Skena?" He called her name and wiggled his right foot before her, snapping her attention back to her chore. "Be done with your toe tweaks. This is a hard position for my back to hold."

"Sorry. I merely check your toes to make certain you have feeling in them."

"So you make me scream out in agony to know I am well?" He laughed in mocking.

"Aye, if you did not cry out from the hurt, then I would fear damage was done."

"Since I howl, then I am fine? Be done, Skena, I suffered no harm."

She dropped the foot and then stepped to remove a cloth on his chest, intending to apply a fresh one. "Your toes are fine. I have not judged the rest of you though."

He glanced down at her hand, suppressing a smug grin, and then lifted the long, black lashes on his pale eyes. "Tell me, lovely Skena, shall you go to pinching *all* of me to make certain my flesh is fine? We might be at this the whole of the night, if that be your intent."

Placing two fingers against his neck where the blood pounded the strongest, she wanted to test how his heart beat. She tried not to look into his eyes, but he seemed to want her to meet them for he playfully wiggled his eyebrows. When she pretended not to see the way his sensual mouth curved into a sly smirk, he leaned forward and kissed the inside of her wrist.

"*Amadan*. Sit still. I try to see how your heart works," she fussed, flustered by his action and trying to guise it. "I am checking to see if you are warm enough."

"Warm and getting warmer all the time." Instead of obeying her, he reached out and placed two fingers on the pulse point at her throat. "What about you, Skena? Are you warm?"

"Methinks you are too playful for one who was nearly an icicle a short while ago." She dropped her hand. "Do you feel strong enough to stand, Sir Noel?"

"Noel. Remember? You said Scots set no store in titles, so why do you keep using mine?" Taking the cloth from his neck, he used it to wipe his face. "You also did not answer my question—are you warm?"

"You have not answered mine either."

He countered, "My question first."

"But I am worried about your condition. You are just being troublesome."

"Troublesome?" He grinned, passing her the rag. "You have not begun to see how *troublesome* I can be."

One by one, he removed the remaining cloths from his chest and tossed each to the floor, the whole time never taking that hungry predator's stare from her. Putting his hands on the side of the tub, he hefted himself upward. Water sluiced off his naked body, fascinating to watch as the rivulets snaked down his chest, hips, and thighs. Her lungs cried out for air as she sucked in a ragged breath. Finally, reason returned, and she thought to snatch up the drying linen.

As Muriel had pointed out, taking in Noel de Servian in the 'all together' was hard on a lass. He was tall, taller than most of the Scotsmen she was used to, and instead of their stockier build, often with skin heavy with freckles, de Servian was lean and unblemished, save for a small pale line across his upper left arm. She bit back the word bubbling up inside her, because she had scolded him for overusing it, yet as he stepped from the tub she could not help but believe she stared at the most comely of men her eyes had ever beheld.

"Here." She held out the long sheet of linen cloth between them. De Servian merely lifted his arms and waited for her to wrap it about his waist. She had to lean in to him to drape it around his hips, which brought her too near to that wonderful expanse of his broad chest. Her heart jumped and then painfully bounced against her ribs. She tried to step back, but he brought his arms down and encircled her.

De Servian gave her a half smile. "I am weak. I need something to lean on."

Skena slowly lifted her gaze. Standing in his embrace, she judged him strong enough. "You do not feel feeble to me, my lord," she whispered as their stares met and held. But *she* did. She trembled in his arms, scared of what this man's coming meant. Scared that he reached her as none other. A stranger, yet something seemed so familiar about him.

"You have no inkling just how weak I am." His words were slow, leaving her to assume the tansy was hitting him full force.

De Servian leaned forward slightly, so close she could not draw air. If she did she would inhale that scent of pure male. Worse, there was nary a space between them. That single draw of air would press her breast to his chest.

Dizziness swirled through her mind as she remained perfectly still, caught in his embrace.

Chapter Four

Noel bit the inside of his lower lip to keep from smiling like a fox singling out a lambkin from the flock. He was finding he had an instant fondness for this Scots lass. *Skena*. She had stood over him, ready to protect him from the wolf, yet she trembled like a fawn in his arms. There was intelligence to the soft brown eyes, a caring that touched his heart. A heart he'd almost forgotten he had. He could not ever recall a woman ready to fight for him. . . . Not even his mother. Primitive mating instincts stirred to life within him, setting loose the driving need to stake his claim. It lent new power to his blood.

Suddenly, he did not feel so old.

He wanted her. Wanted to take her here and now. Elemental, raw, the craving clawed at his skin. His senses already buffeted from the warm bath, this strong longing finally even blotted out the dull pains completely. There was nothing but the pulse of his blood, beating out a tattoo of *take her . . . take her . . . take her. . . .*

That she provoked such a violent response within him was staggering. He had not desired a woman this strongly since . . . Well, he could not recall when. *Mayhap never.* He considered if that dreadful potion she had fed him could be responsible for this violent reaction, some pagan love philter to stir his loins.

After a moment's hesitation, he dismissed it out of hand. This was too pure, too focused, and as wild and savage as a stallion scenting a mare in season.

He leaned toward her slightly, not enough to spook her, but in a testing of how she would react to his male threat. She stiffened and almost seemed to stop breathing; though she held still, she sought no retreat. He could not stop the slow smile from spreading over his lips. *His tender warrior.* Some people found courage naturally. They willfully charged into any situation and worried later about the backlash. True courage came when someone was scared, yet did not back down. She was frightened of him on several levels. He was male and bigger. He was English, the enemy in troubled times, a man who could be a threat to all she held dear. And most alarming to her, she was petrified of what he provoked her to feel. There was no hiding the response for it was written plainly on her lovely face.

She was so close her scent filled his mind. He tilted so his nose brushed the side of her hair, wanting to breathe in Skena. His muscles flexed to prevent him from nuzzling her cheek. That would be one step too far. The sharp coppery tang of the wolf's blood hit his senses first, but underneath was 'perfume' that was Skena. Intoxicating. Heady.

Oh aye, Skena MacIain saved his life this night. Only, he suddenly had the fey sense she could rescue him from the grayness of this world.

If only she would dare.

For his whole life, he had simply taken each day one at a time. He was humbled being favored as an honorary Challon brother, felt privileged, safe in that acceptance. He was devoted to Julian, Simon, and Damian, though likely he was a bit closer to Guillaume, mayhap because they were only months apart in age. Growing up with them held much sought after advantages. He had been envied by countless, feared by the rest. The mere whisper of the name Challon caused many a man's blood to turn to ice. He never resented that he was not a true son of Earl Michael, and was content to serve the man's sons, and later their king under the Challon pennon.

Still, the future was by no means his. He had never forgotten that everything had been taken from him merely because he was too young to hold the fief that had been his family's for centuries. He barely recalled details of that dark time. Just the pain. The pain of hearing his father had been killed in the lists, while waging mock battles with the hope of increasing the near empty coffers of Darkmoor. His mother's howls of anguish, echoing against the stone walls of the castle. Vague whispers of the servants. Their fearful glances. At age five he scarcely understood why. He soon learnt.

He recalled awaking in the middle of the night, breaking the dream of his father's death. So vivid, he almost felt as if he had traveled back in time and visited the horrible scene. He watched his father as the lance hit his chest, splintered into jagged shards, one flying up into his helm's visor, driving through the ocularium and into his brain through his eye. So detailed, he woke screaming. Terrified, barely able to breathe, he crawled from the high bed and went to seek out his lady mother, wanting her comfort, her soft words telling him that everything would be all right.

She had not been there. No soft words of reassurance. And *nothing* was all right.

The servants carried her into the castle shortly after dawn-break, her night rail and black hair sodden, her skin alabaster white. For a long held breath he merely stared at the woman they carried. Surely, this was some poor lost soul, a stranger to Darkmoor? Only his eyes spotted the scar on the back of her hand. Five months past, Mother had been using a dull knife and put too much pressure on it to make it cut. The blade had slipped and sliced across the back of the opposite hand. Clutching at straws, his mind even thought for a brief instant how odd this unfortunate woman had a mark exactly like his mother. He heard a deep keening and wondered who was making that horrible noise.

Then he understood. It was coming from him.

Sennights later, the Earl Michael arrived, telling him to pack his belongings, that he was to come to Castle Challon to live. He knew the handsome, commanding man. His father and Lord Challon had been close friends. It was not easy for Noel to accept; everything seemed to be taken from him. First Father, then Mother, and finally his heritage, Darkmoor. The black-haired man with the brilliant green eyes had smiled and said not to be scared, that at Castle Challon he would have brothers, a home . . . someplace safe.

Yes, he had been protected, permitted to grow alongside the men of Challon. Still, he had never had a future of his own. He had always fought for others, never for himself.

In all those years since, he remembered many women, women who wanted his body, wanted the power the Challon pennon afforded him. They paraded through his life, his bed, in their fine silks, velvets, and brocades, heavily bedecked with gold, pearls, or other precious jewels. Never had one been willing to give her own life to defend his.

Skena had. He'd heard her send the children off. She could have left him, ridden back to the fortress with the children to fetch help. Instead, she stayed behind to shield him from the threat of wolves. That choice could have cost her life, and she had known that. If she had it all to do over again, he'd be willing to bet Craigendan that Skena MacIain would make the same choice.

Something about that valiant, selfless act touched him in a way words failed to explain. It humbled him.

He wanted to flex his arms and pull her against his body, teach her how quickly she could heat his blood. His groin lurched hard, reminding him other parts of his body were also undamaged by the cold. He had to bite his tongue to keep from asking if she needed to tweak *that* as she had his toes.

Skena had let him kiss her before. That surprised him. From the expression on her lovely face, it had stunned her as well. He wanted to kiss her again, only he had a feeling she would put distance between them if he pushed her.

Finally, her fear of him shattered the strange spell. She feigned being unruffled. "Come, let me help you to the bench so I may dry your hair. I needs must get you to bed before you become too sleepy from the tansy or take a chill again."

"You want me to go to bed, Skena?" He did not guise his stressing of the word *bed*, and that seemed to break her lethargy.

Skena took a step away, but stopped as her back hit the resistance of his arms. He did not want to release her, but realized he had to. He saw her exhale relief when he lowered his arms. He gave her credit—she did not run, but turned and slid her arm about his waist for him to lean against her. He could have reached the bench on his own, but this allowed him to pull her closer, holding her in a less threatening way. *Step-by-step saw the deed accomplished*, he thought.

Just as he was breaking out in a grin, he jumped when her hand touched his inflamed side. He cursed through gritted teeth. Disgusted with the increasing pain, he knew the side bothered him long past when it should not. In the beginning, he had hoped since he was aging it was just slow to heal. Obviously, there was some shred of fabric or metal still embedded deep in his flesh, and it was festering, the pain a thousand red-hot needles.

"Sorry, I did not mean to contrary your sore spot. Here, sit on the bench before the fire. I do not want you to take chill."

Noel lowered himself onto the middle of the bench to keep it from toppling with him, instantly feeling the fire wash over his skin. The intense dry heat felt soothing. Skena picked up a woolen blanket and wrapped it around his shoulders. Only, with her standing in front of him, that put her breasts dead center of his eye level. He groaned.

"How do you feel, Sir Noel? If there is pain I can mix another tansy to ease your distress."

Almost without thought, she reached up and pushed several stray curls back from his forehead. Clamping his teeth together, he struggled to rein in his rampant desire. The maddening woman simply did not understand what a temptation she presented.

"You are gritting your teeth again. Please, do not try to be strong. The worts can take the pain away—"

Clamping his hands around her waist he intended to set her back to save his sanity. Instead, he stilled. He was shocked by how thin her hips were. He could feel her bones clearly defined under the woolen kirtle. That brought a frown to him. Skena was a big woman, full-breasted, thus he would have thought she carried more weight. He grew concerned she was not eating enough for some reason. Was she sick?

"You are too skinny, Skena." His big hands spanned her waist easily, too easily, as if he held a young girl. He flattened the material to outline her body.

Skena held rigid, then she strugggled to jerk away, clearly upset. "I thank you to keep your bloody opinions to yourself, Sir Noel."

"Noel," he reminded her.

"I am thinking you are too forward by half, *Sir* Noel. I did not ask you for your thoughts. Now let go, so I can dry your hair and then get you to bed." She tried to shove his hands away.

Stubbornly, Noel held her hips fast. "Why are you so thin, Skena? Are you sick? Some sort of wasting sickness? Tell me."

She remained silent.

Burning anguish pulsed through his blood, so blinding he could hardly think. The specter of something being wrong with Skena terrified him. He had just found this special woman, discovered there might be a possibility for something beyond the grayness of his existence. That it could be snatched away from him before he ever had a chance to find out the mystery of Skena MacIain scared him in a way that facing the hell of battles had failed to do.

Dread of this prospect opened that door on those long ago emotions from when he was a child and had learnt that the people he loved could suddenly be taken from him. He was a warrior, who had stood against a charge of twenty score heavy horse, monstrous animals with mighty hooves pounding the earth, drawing closer and closer, bearing riders with lances lowered. That terror paled beside the alarm that something was wrong with Skena.

How could this woman come to matter so much to him within this short span? Noel could not fathom the why, simply knew it as truth. He recalled kneeling in the snow and wiping the blood from Skena's cheek, wondering what magical creature had come to save him. Now, after watching her tenderly care for him, he grew convinced that fate had finally seen fit to give him a future of his own, that he had been sent to Craigendan for a purpose.

They say Christmastide is a season of miracles. Mayhap this was his chance for one. Living for so long apathetic, he now prayed 'twas so.

When his parents had died, he had been robbed of all. His coming to this fortress in this Northland seemed as if Lady Fate was balancing accounts, giving him the home and a family that had been taken from him. He could save Skena and her children from the same tragedy he had tasted, losing your home and all that was yours.

In the end, possibly he might find redemption for killing Angus Fadden.

Chapter Five

Skena trembled as she helped de Servian lie down; he was so exhausted, his eyes closed the instant his head touched the pillow. His tall frame with those long legs filled the huge bed, almost seeming to dwarf it. She settled him on his left side to keep pressure off his tender spot, and then set about to pull the bed curtains on the far side, blocking the draft in the large chamber. A bearskin covered the wooden shutters closed upon the narrow window, and a tapestry was on top of that, yet the winds still found a way inside around the edges. Wanting the heat from the fireplace to reach him, she left the curtains at the foot tied back.

Rounding the corner, she paused with her hand on the bedpost. Possibly she did not need the support. *Possibly she did*. Noel de Servian was stretched out the length of the bed, with a *plaide* pulled loosely across his hips.

"Have mercy!" she hissed lowly.

Never before had she looked upon a nearly naked man and found such perfection in his body. Men always appeared oddly created, to her way of thinking. Too hairy legs, ugly feet, some with chests that reminded her of a bear pelt, and strangely, longer through the torso than a woman. Noel de Servian was none of those things. There was a lean, animalistic elegance to his hard muscles; shadows folded around their curves defining their strength and form, shaped by his years of training as a warrior. The broad chest was nearly hairless, smooth, his belly rippled. A wave of flames roared through her blood as she stared at the most ravishing of men.

Three curls of the soft hair carelessly spilled across his high forehead. Her fingers itched to reach out and brush them back. His brown hair was not cut in the Norman style but longer, curling, as though he failed to assume their courtly ways, which reminded Skena of a bowl being placed on their heads. She was glad. This suited him. As she had dried the thick mass, the color had lightened and the waves increased. There was a razor sharp intelligence, a force of command that filled those grey eyes. Men would follow this warrior into battle, accept his orders without question. Die for him. Swallowing the bitter taste of jealousy, she did not want to think what women would do upon his bidding. Noel de Servian was such a handsome man.

Such a threat. In more ways than one.

She must remember that and never let down her guard. He was English, the invader. This man and his countrymen had crushed the army of forty thousand Scots on the fields of Spottsmuir, possibly even killed men of Craigendan in that rout. At all times she must hold tight to those truths; not for one breath could she ever drop her defenses with this knight who could only spell trouble for her.

Letting go of the bedpost, she went to fetch the small pot of ointment. As she lifted it, she hesitated. Helping him dry off had been upsetting in a way she was not prepared to handle. Her foolish heart pounded, her mouth went dry, and she actually found it hard to hold a single thought in her head. Sensations washed through her, crawled under her skin with a pagan fire, making her breasts feel heavier, fuller. A burning began at the base of her belly and throbbed like a second heartbeat. Not having experienced these disturbances before did not mean

she failed to recognize them for what they were: she desired
Noel de Servian with a power that was unholy. Most perplex-
ing, she had always assumed a woman had to fall in love with
a man before these intense feelings came to her, possessed her.
Never would she have suspected she could suffer such a craving for a warrior who was barely more than a stranger.

A stranger, yet his words had held the ability to wound
her pride. When he held her hips and declared she was too
skinny, that simple opinion was a knife rending her heart. She
saw concern in those all-seeing eyes. Yet, it failed to stop the
pain in that he found her woefully thin.

She had lost flesh these past months. Doing her chores and
that of a man, she worked too hard from dawn to dark, ate less
and less as she saw the supplies dwindle. That had taken a toll.
Still, to hear him declare her too lean nearly crumpled her
spirit. Sucking in a hard breath, she told herself to stop these
silly thoughts, to put them out of her mind. She had been wed
for years and came with two children. A man such as Noel de
Servian could have any woman he wanted at his beck and call.
He could never want her.

"Get on with the chore and be done with it," she whispered
the chide to herself.

Setting the pot down on the small table, she scooped up the
salve with her fingers, and then froze as she considered where
to start. There was . . . so much of him! He seemed to be resting so peacefully that she hated to disturb him.

Mayhap she would let him slumber. His body surely needed
sleep to heal. Wiping her fingers on the rim of the black pot,
she pulled the woolen blanket across his legs and over his
shoulder, and then went to clean the wolf's blood from her
body and hair.

Pausing to glance back she saw, poor man, he had not
stirred. With a plaint that could not be denied, she had wanted
to stroke him, give free rein to the urges pulsing within her
blood. Only, it would be the wrong thing to do. Skena feared

in touching him her soul would somehow form an unbreakable bond with this handsome warrior. A bond that could prove too costly in the future. Better not risk the pain. Not risk her soul.

"Coward," she muttered. Walking to the fireplace she added more peats to the fire. "Aye, a bloody coward I am."

Noel watched her.

With an air of utter exhaustion, Skena dropped down to the long bench and unlaced her boots. Clearly believing him asleep, she did not hesitate to stand and remove the brooch pinned at her shoulder, and then unbuckle the belt about her waist. She unwound the woolen material from her hips and dropped it on the long bench. Next came the long, linen sark, leaving her in nothing but a thin, sleeveless chemise.

He had been right in his opinion of her shape. Her breasts were high and full; the vision of Skena hit him like taking an arrow to his groin. Howbeit, the rest of her body bordered on painfully thin. The two traits usually did not go together, leading him to suspect the weight loss was recent. Again, the specter of fear clawed at his heart; he was alarmed that she was ill. The carriage of her body expressed fatigue, yet there was strength to this woman. There was no deformity or stooping to her bones. Skena was formed to perfection; square, proud shoulders, long graceful neck, and wide hips, formed for bearing babes, would make her a prize in any man's eyes. He failed to discern anything visibly wrong with this Scots lass outside of needing to eat more.

Unhurriedly, she moved to the fireplace to toss on more bricks of peat, and then stirred the fire to raise the flames. It had struck him odd, when he first came to this North Country, that dirt could be burnt, but he soon learnt this was one of the primary sources of fuel for the Scots. The chamber filled with its pungent, almost heady aroma. The bluish flames burned lower, not as bright as a wood fire, yet still threw off enough light to keep the deep shadows at bay and render her worn chemise nearly transparent.

His body flexed hard in a cramp of lust, so intense that it nearly blotted out thought, leaving him with the blinding, primitive drive to mate. His fingers flexed tightly in the woolen blanket to keep from acting on the overpowering urge. The situation did not ease as Skena turned back to the tub, her hands taking hold of the hem of the short rail, and with a quick skimming up her body, pulled it over her head. He drank in the image of Skena's naked beauty. She might scold him for using the word, but nothing else came to mind that fit so well.

Noel ached to go to her. He wanted to put his mouth on the crest of her rounded breast, swirl his tongue about the peak, stiff from the cool air of the room. Then he would draw it into his mouth and suck hard. He hungered to hear her gasp as she rode the razor's edge of pain-pleasure, to teach her just how strongly his desires ran. Claim her as a man claimed his mate. He wanted her, but he pined for more than ecstasies of the flesh. He yearned to believe there could be a Christmas miracle that could see them find a peace between them.

As she stepped into the tub, the door opened, and one of the maidservants came in carrying a tray. The aroma told him it was hot stew. Skena glanced up and offered a fleeting smile to the woman.

"I peeked in at your lambs. Nessa has them tucked up, snug in bed. I fear they may not sleep this night though, so excited are they. Andrew keeps insisting the Cailleach sent a Kelpie with that one," she jerked her head toward the bed, "because the lad wished it so. Such a fanciful tale, but the boy believes it, Skena."

"Oh, aye. I heard all about his Yule wish when we found the knight." She offered her a sad expression.

The woman chuckled. "Life would be so easy if we had the power to wish for something and it came true, eh?"

"Wishes are for fools," Skena said sourly. "If wishes were peafowl we would have a fancy supper this night fit for a king."

Setting the tray down and putting the bowls on the table-top, the maid said, "Well, 'tis naught as fancy as a peahen, but I brought cheese, bread, and some stew. The bread is stale, but you can sop it in the broth. No pieces big enough to be a trencher, but still enough to fill a belly."

"I thank you for your caring, Jenna, but I meant it when I said I was not hungry." Skena picked up a rag and scrubbed her face.

"Aye, what you always say of late. But I also told you that despite your protests you are going to eat, or I would get Galen and Owen to pin you while I pour it down your gullet. You cannot keep missing meals, Skena. It has to stop. One day you are going to push too hard and end up sick. Then where will we all be? I will not accept nay for an answer. I will stay 'til you eat." The woman moved to the tub, scooped up a chunk of soap from a bowl on the bench and began lathering Skena's long auburn hair.

Noel frowned. That bit of conversation merely reinforced his inkling that Skena's being thin was out of step. Such mis-givings led him to ponder if mayhap, instead of being sick, she grieved for her dead husband. It would not be the first time a widow fell into decline after such a loss. Had not the sorrow driven his mother to madness, resulting in her taking her own life? He gnawed at the corner of his lip as concern, resentment, and jealousy flared bright in the pit of his belly.

Noel had never known the Baron Craigendan, had not seen him at court, nor even heard his name until that fateful day that nearly cost Noel his life. Their first and only meeting had come in the bloody aftermath of Dunbar when Noel's troops had taken the baron and his men prisoner. Bloody stupid fool. The man had surrendered his sword, even ordered his men to lay down their pikes. A ragged-looking lot they were, half-covered in blood of their countrymen, some of the last men left, flanking Sir Patrick Graham, who had stood and valiantly fought to the death. There had been little choice for Fadden. Surrender and live, or fight on and be slaughtered to a man. The baron had showed common sense and ordered his men to yield. Noel commanded them to stack their weapons in a pile and then line up to be marched back to the main host of the English forces.

No, brave Skena should not waste sorrow on the knave who had slammed into Noel's squire, wrenched the sword from the young man's hands, and run the boy through. The crazed man had then attacked Noel, though he was still dismounting Brishen. That man had no shred of honor. That man had been unworthy of this Scottish lass. It was a shame if she were grieving so for Angus Fadden. That she possibly starved herself because of bereavement angered Noel.

Picking up the pail, the maidservant slowly rinsed the soap from Skena's long hair, the white foam sliding down her neck and then crawling over her breasts. Noel swallowed hard as desire thickened his blood. Part of the bedpost blocked his vision of Skena as she rose from the tub, water sluicing off her hard body in small streams. He fought the impulse to shift for a better view, having the feeling Skena would not have openly bathed with him in the room had she suspected he was awake. The wolf's blood had pushed her to the desire to be shed of it. The other woman hurriedly held up a drying sheet, shielding Skena from his hungry gaze.

"Who is the warrior, my lady? What was he doing in our glen? Why has he come?" Jenna, still holding up the linen sheet, moved with Skena to the fire.

"Sir Noel de Servian, he said his name was. He was on his way to Glenrogha to pay visit to the Earl Challon, his foster brother," Skena answered.

The other woman sucked in a breath. "This lord is foster brother to the Black Dragon? Oh, Skena—"

"Hush. No sense borrowing troubles, Jenna. We have

plenty enough already. Fetch me a chemise, please," she asked as she dried her arms.

The woman did as bid, going to the tall wardrobe to take out the shift for Skena. "He was a long ways from Glenrogha. Out there alone in the storm. Where were his men? Surely he did not travel through Scotland with nary a vassal for support? Most odd, indeed."

"Do not go spinning silly tales of a Kelpie fetching him to Craigendan because of a child's wish," Skena reproached, and then began vigorously toweling her hair.

Jenna came toward the bed, so Noel shut his eyes. He felt the corner of the blanket being partially lifted. Cool air touched his skin. "He is a braw and bonnie man, this one. Unharmed by the storm, I judge." She clucked her tongue. "Did you coat him with Auld Bessa's salve?"

"I will." A defensive tone filled Skena's answer.

"Methinks you are a coward, Skena MacIain." With a chuckle, she dropped the cover. "Of course, if you would rather . . . I could force myself to do the chore in your stead."

"I said I will," Skena snapped.

"Someday, Skena, you will learn the way of things. Stop hiding from yourself, lass," the woman said in gentleness.

"I hide from naught. Every bloody day I would like to lie in bed and ignore the situation facing us. And every damn bloody day I climb from the bed and stare harsh realities in the face. Let no one say I spurn aught," Skena rebuked.

"'Tis not what I speak of and you ken it."

The door opened again. Noel risked a peek through slitted eyes to see the girl child come in. Rubbing one eye with her fist, she made a sleepy face, and looked about for her mother. Spotting Skena, she rushed toward her.

Skena hurriedly snatched up a *plaide* and wrapped it about her naked body like a mantle. "Sweetling, you should be tucked up in bed, dreaming of Yuletide treats." Skena took hold of the child's frail shoulders and turned her toward the door, only to have the child willfully spin about.

"I want to see the warrior, *màthair*. I slept for a bit, but awoke, afraid he was ill and dying. He is ours now. You must not let him sicken," she choked on a sob.

"He but sleeps, Annis," Skena assured her daughter.

The child insisted with stubbornness, "I want to see."

"Very well." Skena exhaled in resignation. "But do not wake him. He needs his rest."

Noel closed his eyes tight, as mother and child came toward the bed. The mattress gave a small shift as the child began to climb onto the bedside.

"Annis, I said you may see him. I did not mean for you to crawl onto the bed to do it," Skena fussed at the child.

Ignoring her mother, she patted his shoulder with a small hand, and then she pushed against him to lean forward. The warm scent of child filled his nostrils as she placed her small mouth upon his cheek to plant a kiss. "Thank you, kind warrior, for coming to care for us. We need you. So very much. My *màthair* won't eat—"

"Annis! Enough!" Skena grabbed her daughter about the waist and swung her off the bed. "Jenna, see this littlelin gets back to Nessa and this time she stays where she is put."

"Mama, what is our warrior's name?"

Noel again risked looking through half-closed eyes. The little girl was clearly dragging her feet. He had to fight against the smile threatening to spread across his lips. She was a smaller version of Skena, little more than five summers old.

Kneeling before her daughter, Skena kissed the child's forehead. "Sir Noel de Servian is his name."

"Noel?" The child's face lit with a grin. "Does that not mean Christmas in the Norman, Mama? Father Malcolm said that was so in our lessons."

Skena nodded. "I believe that is the meaning of the name."

"Do you not see—he is our Christmas knight. See, Andrew

is right. We wished for him, and he came to save us," she insisted.

Rising, Skena gave the child a slight nudge, pushing Annis into the maid's arms. "Off with you." She stood watching until the door had closed on them.

"Why does everyone persist in placing faith in wishes? Wishes are naught but a bloody waste of breath. If wishes summoned warriors we would have a whole army at our beck and call," Skena grumbled. "Of course, then we would have to feed them, but surely we could just wish for a banquet fit for a bloody king. And mayhap if I wish for my tears to turn to gold then I could buy more cows and sheep. Wishes are for fools and children. Not for Skena MacIain." Dropping the blanket, she picked up the chemise from the bench and slid it over her head, then wrapped the *plaide* about her again.

After a long sigh, she walked back to the bed. Noel quickly feigned sleep again. The handle on the metal pot clanked, telling him she had pulled it closer to the bedside. There was a moment of silence, as if she hesitated, then she finally spoke. "I am no bloody coward."

Noel held still as she smeared the cream across his upper chest. Her hand worked slowly, moving in languid circles, first one side, and then the other. His body shifted to betrayal, responding to her caress on his skin. There was no stopping his blood. His erection pounded with a growing intensity against the woolen blanket. Willing the insistent movement to cease proved futile.

Her touch was soothing. Gentle strokes across his shoulders and arms soon had him relaxing. But then the minx grew bolder. Her thumb pad swiped the salve over his flat male nipple, paused, and then applied a stronger pressure as she became aware of his body's small changes.

Skena's words came as a ghostly whisper, "*Duine brèagha.*"

Beautiful man. The corner of his mouth tugged up. She called him beautiful after she had scolded him for using the word too much, by doing so diminishing its worth. Noel had a feeling Skena was careful with her words, which only made the spoken sentiment all the more intoxicating.

Then the vexing woman dragged her hand down the middle of his chest, over his belly, and showed no sign of slowing. Oh, he did not want her to stop! He craved for her to keep on snaking that strong hand down his body, lower and lower. Howbeit, if she knew he was awake she would never risk being so bold.

With the quickness of an adder, he opened his eyes as his hand shot out and locked hard about her wrist. "Stop."

Chapter Six

Skena jumped.

She had believed Lord de Servian to be sleeping peacefully, lulled by the worts of the tansy. She learnt differently. In a move so quick she had no time to blink let alone react, his left hand shot out and wrapped around her wrist. His strength was terrifying. The grip was not hurtful, just blocked her from shifting her arm in any direction. She gave a small tug. Useless. The man was not letting go of her.

The soft firelight cast flickering shadows across his handsome face, and illuminated those unearthly eyes. Their force, their magical ascendancy wove a spell, leaving her unable to move. All she could do was stare at his virile perfection and swallow back the desires clamoring inside her.

Her cheeks burned bright, though she doubted he could see her embarrassment with her standing in half shadows. And did she burn with shame! She had given in to her foolish longing to touch him and caressed his strong body as she wanted, enjoyed stroking his warrior hard muscles. Now she stood caught like a child filching a tart from the kitchen.

Her tongue swiped her lips to moisten them to speak. To cover for her brazen behavior she offered, "I merely wanted to apply the salve on your side, my lord. The worts will ease the distress you feel in the sore spot."

"Is that what you were doing?" Challenge flashed in de Servian's eyes. He did not believe her, gave no polite pretense otherwise. Lifting her arm, he placed her hand next to the red patch and then released it. "You mayhap forgot where the said *spot* was?"

She cautiously applied the ointment to the darker patch of skin. Not admitting any misdoing, she said, "'Tis hard to see in these long shadows."

A brash smile spread over his lips as his brows lifted. "Really? To the contrary, I found it quite easy to see."

Skena paused as her heart did a small roll, and then she sharply sucked in air. "You were never asleep? I . . . I . . . would not have bathed. . . . I thought the potion would see you resting deeply." Her eyes skimmed over his body from head to toes and then back. "There *is* a lot of you. You are taller than most men I ken. Mayhap I should have mixed the tansy stronger."

"Could be. Could be something more potent hit my blood, overpowering its effect."

His direct stare bore into her, leaving her to feel like a timid hare caught in the hunter's snare. Her heart dropped to the pit of her belly, slowing to a hard pagan throb. It was playing with fire, but she had to ask, "What is more potent?"

The corner of his mouth quirked up smugly. Instead of giving her an answer, he came back with a question of his own. "Why do you not eat, Skena?"

She glanced to the food growing cold on the table. "I . . . I was not hungry."

"Sometimes we are too tired to eat. When we have many responsibilities in our lives weighing down upon our shoulders, we must force ourselves to partake some nourishment in spite of our wishes. Oft, when I was tired from battle, I did not want food. Same as when I was recovering from my wound. The will to eat was just not present. Even so, I forced myself. It was the only way to regain my strength." His gaze traveled over her, making her glad she had the *plaide* about her, a shield against his hungry eyes. "You are not sick, are you, Skena?"

"Nay. There is naught wrong with me."

"Except that you refuse to eat. Even your child frets over that," de Servian pressed, not dropping the line of talk.

"Annis thinks she kens the way of things. But she is only a wee bairn. She does not understand. . . ." Skena allowed her words to trail off. She could think of no reason to give this man for her reticence to eat. "Do you feel like eating?"

The crooked half smile came again. "Aye, I find I am . . . *hungry.*"

Skena started to turn, but paused as she was once again caught by the power of his stare. The way he had stressed the word *hungry* caused her to wonder if he used it with another meaning. She was unsure how to deal with this commanding man. Giving a shrug, she went to the table and placed a bowl on the tray.

De Servian scooted up in the bed and pushed the pillow behind his back. He watched her with that disarming predator's intensity as she carefully placed the wooden tray across his lap, and then sat upon the bed next to him. Instead of picking up the spoon, he simply looked at her.

Feeling as if she were missing something, she asked, "Is aught wrong, my lord? I am sorry 'tis only small fare, but we are a poor holding."

"I find I tire. Would you mind feeding me? Please?"

Skena glared at this Norman warrior. He did not appear too weak to feed himself. His grip upon her wrist had been amazingly strong. She brooded if he were trying to trick her for some reason, yet failed to see a why for it. Mayhap he was suddenly feeling the toll upon his body from being out in the cold.

Edging nearer, she picked up the bread and broke the chunks into smaller pieces. Using the spoon, she pushed them down into the stew and allowed them to soak up the liquid. "'Tis a bit hard and crusty. I offer apologies."

He smiled. "None needed. It shan't be the first time I have eaten stale bread. The stomach does not seem to mind these things."

Skena scooped up a spoonful and carried it to his mouth. He opened and then closed around it. His eyebrows lifted in surprise as he chewed.

"Delicious. Your cook knows the secret to seasoning well."

Skena smiled. "I will tell him. He is a prideful man and will enjoy the praise." As she carried another spoonful to his mouth he shook his head no.

"You first," he insisted.

Vexed, she refused. "I am not hungry."

A stubborn look crossed de Servian's face. "Then I shan't eat either."

"But your body requires nourishment to fight the sickness, which still might try to claim you," she insisted.

His frowned deepened. "Why do you starve yourself, Skena?"

She inhaled slowly to control her spiraling temper. "Not that 'tis any of your concern, but I do not starve myself. I eat when I am hungry."

"Do you?"

The arrogant man saw too much. There was no screen for her against de Servian. She hated that he could so easily scry her thoughts in her eyes. Surely, with all the lying that she had been reduced to of late, she should have acquired the necessary skills to protect herself from a mere stranger. Clearly, he had fixed on the detail that she was too thin, and like a dog with a bone was going to worry it to the marrow. After a short exhale, she captured a spoonful of the stew and shoved it in her mouth.

The bloody man grinned over his victory, but wisely refrained from saying anything, aware he had pushed her as far as he could without angering her. He opened his mouth to the offer of more stew when she nearly shoved it at him, then impishly, refused another until she had eaten one, too.

"Some of the bread, please," he requested.

The broth had softened it, so she picked up a chunk and held it up for him, hesitating at the last instant as their eyes locked. When she remained unmoving, he leaned forward and closed his lips around the bread and her fingers holding it. Shocked by his boldness, she had not meant for him to do that. She pulled them back, but his tongue swiped her first finger and then he sucked on it, as though he intended to capture every morsel.

An odd sensation hit the back of her neck and then slammed downward with a blazing heat, causing a strange cramping at the base of her belly. It twisted like a knife, burned to where it was agonizing. The reaction doubled as he picked up another chunk of bread with the purpose of feeding it to her.

Eyes wide, she shook her head no. Her refusal set an obstinate look upon his face. She pleaded, "Please, my lord, I am too full. If I eat more I will feel ill."

"Eat. You feel pressure in your belly because you fail to eat enough. This bite, then I shall let you be," he insisted.

Skena was not lying. She did feel too full. And he was right—her going without food had caused her belly to draw up.

"Shall I pin you down and feed it to you? I shan't need a lad of barely ten and two and an old man to help me." He wiggled it before her mouth.

"I am not sure I like you Noel de Servian."

He shrugged as if he failed to believe her. "Very well. Methinks I shall enjoy pinning you to the bed, Skena MacIain," he said as he started to tilt toward her.

Giving a small yelp, she ate the bread piece from his fingers. As he removed them, he swiped a drop from her lower lip with his thumb pad. Skena had to fight herself from opening and sucking that wicked thumb back into her mouth. The wild reactions within her said these gestures had a meaning beyond merely feeding each other, which he understood only too well.

But she must not lose herself to these dark lures. Too much was at stake here. This man was naught but a foreigner. Worse—an Englishman. Until his purpose for coming to Glen Shane was unriddled, she had to keep hold of her reason.

Full of himself, de Servian leaned back. When she only sat there, he prompted, "More please."

She nearly threw the spoon at him. "If you can feed me, Lord de Servian, then you can bloody well feed yourself."

"True, but then we would miss the dance." He chuckled.

Skena blinked in confusion. "Dance? Does the fever rise?" She put the back of her hand to his forehead. "You burn to the touch. I fear you may still take lung sickness before the night wanes."

"I burn, but my mind does not wander. The dance I speak of is the dance of seduction. Surely, you know about seduction, Skena?" His voice was low, husky.

"Methinks, my lord, the fever addles your wits."

"Noel," he corrected.

"My lord will do just fine," she refused to do as he bid, holding on to that last small defense against him.

"If you will not feed me, you may take the rest away." He crossed his arms and closed his eyes in dismissal. Skena picked up the tray, but nearly dropped it as he spoke again. "Then you may finish applying the ointment."

The bowl rattled, but she managed to keep it from falling to the stone floor. "I ought to pick up the stew and dump it on his bloody head," she grumbled under her breath.

Placing the tray on the table, she set about to mix him another tansy. Despite his playful disposition, she feared he was not as well as he thought. A person who experienced a deep chill often failed to show any signs of a sore throat or lung congestion until hours after exposure. The rising fever was the first hint of coming sickness. His forehead was flushed to the touch, a clear signal all was not well. Measuring out pinches of the worts, she paused, glanced back to him, still sitting up in the bed, and added a bit more. She ground them and then dissolved them in the cider Jenna had fetched with the supper.

When she held the cup out to him, he took it. He tilted it to look inside. "More mud and stump water? Take this foul witch's potion away."

"Drink it. You may yet show illness in the hours of dawning. I have taken chills before and only later did my throat begin to ache and I had a hard time swallowing."

Arching a brow, he eyed the cup again and then her. "What do you give me in return for choking down this vile stuff?"

Skena chuckled at his question. "You sound like Andrew pandering for a treat for doing something I asked of him."

"And do you give Andrew a treat?"

"Lord de Servian, please drink the tansy so I may seek my bed. It has been a very long day for me."

"Seek your bed—" He patted the mattress beside his hip. "—which happens to be *my bed* at present."

Skena folded her arms across her middle, in a manner to protect herself from the emotions he caused her to feel. "My lord, methinks you are used to charming women with your smiles and a wiggle of your eyebrows. I assure you such contrivances are wasted upon me."

"'Tis good to know such things." His lips pursed as if he were keeping a laugh within.

"So if you will drink the potion . . ."

"Only if you give me something to rid my mouth of the taste afterward. I mean it, Skena, if you want me to down this sludge and twigs, I want a bribe." He lifted his brows and awaited her response. When she stood tongue-tied, he added, "You barter with an unwell man. Delay in giving me care and mayhap I shall sicken. You wish that sin upon your soul?"

"I delay in naught. You hold the bloody brew in your hand." Skena stomped her foot.

He shrugged and leaned to set the cup on the stand by the bed. "Upon your head . . ."

She slowly approached the bedside. "Very well, what is it you crave for a bribe, my lord?"

"First, call me Noel."

Skena stood locked in a staring contest, her inner voice telling her to keep her distance from this man, that he posed a threat to her, to Craigendan. But she was pulled toward him as a summer moth was to a balefire. "Foolish little moth," she whispered.

"Call me Noel," he insisted with a sterner tone.

Skena nearly growled, "You enjoy giving orders too much, Lord de Servian."

"Noel."

Skena threw up her hands in defeat. "Noel."

"That was not too hard, eh? Now I shall drink this—if you give me a reward." A shudder suddenly racked his body, draining the color from his face.

Skena nearly jumped to his side. "Please, you must drink the tansy, then lie down and rest."

"A kiss," he whispered.

She wondered if she heard him wrong. "A kiss?"

"Aye. I shall drink this dreadful stuff if you give me a kiss. Otherwise . . ." His shoulders lifted in a weak shrug.

The man was beyond vexing. Trying the voice she used on the children, she ordered, "Drink."

He lifted the cup to his mouth, and then paused to wink at her. The bloody man winked! "I'm drinking, but I expect a kiss." With that he tipped up the cup.

Skena watched the long column of his throat work, never having thought a man's neck was so . . . well . . . *beautiful*. She frowned at the word. Since de Servian had come into her life she found it applied too often to the annoying man. As she watched, she could envision crawling upon the bed, kissing the strong muscles of his throat, running her tongue over him. She shook her head, trying to rid it of the image that seemed only too real.

The cup empty, he stretched out his arm to hand it back to her. As she took it, he proved again just how fast he could move, grabbing her lower arm and pulling her across his lap. She opened her mouth to protest, but his closed upon hers, his lips quickly showing her how to follow his lead. She tasted the bitter worts from his mouth. Cared little. Slanting his head for a better angle, he let his mouth devour hers, deepening the contact as he issued the primitive male demand for her submission. And she would have given it, gladly, had another strong shiver not racked his body.

He slowly released her, his pale eyes roaming over her face with an expression of awe, similar to the emotions bubbling inside her. That look upon his countenance left Skena feeling as though someone had slammed a fist to her chest.

She slid off the bed, and with shaking hands, pulled the blankets up around him. "You should try to sleep."

He weakly nodded.

Skena went to the large, square basket in the corner and removed the blankets and pallet she planned to use. Carrying them to the bench, she set them on it and then unrolled the pallet on the floor before the fireplace.

"What are you doing, Skena?" de Servian called from the shadows.

She rose from her stooped over position. "It occurs to me, my lord—"

"Noel," he corrected.

"Methinks you are accustomed to giving orders and expect all souls to jump to your bidding. As to what I am doing . . . I am fixing my maid's pallet before the fire. You are too quick to use that tone of command with me, my lord." She picked up a blanket and spread it over the pallet.

"Aye, men are quick to follow my behest," he agreed.

Taking another blanket, she carried it to the bed. "And women? They, too, fall all over their feet just to please the Lord de Servian?"

He smiled with complete arrogance. "You sound jealous, Skena?"

"Me? I have nary a jealous bone in my whole body."

He laughed lowly. "And you are so honest as well."

"I used to be," Skena admitted in candor. "A lie never crossed my teeth."

"And now?"

She shrugged. "Now, hard times forced upon me by the ruthless, selfish, pigheaded ways of men see I do what I must to survive and protect my people." Skena took the cover and spread it over him.

"So you are truthful about lying."

"We take what we can get, my lord. May as well, because wishing gives us naught else."

"If one does not believe in wishes, how will they ever come true? Mayhap the wishes go unfulfilled because you place no faith in them. Open your heart, Skena, and make a wish with the trust of a child," he entreated.

"Lord de Servian, I am too tired to argue the point, or waste breath upon silly, useless wishes." She flipped the end of the blanket back from his feet and then set to rapidly covering them front and back with the salve, but only up to the knee. When finished, she tucked the covers in around them, and turned to face him. There was no getting around the chore. She could not ignore the care he needed. "You look tired. Why do you not lie down as I continue dressing your skin?"

He nodded and scooted down under the covers. With curious eyes he watched her pick up his left hand and start to apply the ointment, then work her way up his arm. "This is soothing, Skena. I cannot recall anyone ever caring for me like this."

His voice sounded wistful. Gone was the playful tone of

flirtation. His words made her believe that no one had ever taken care of him before. She sat on the edge of the bed to reach his right arm.

"I am sure your lady mother did so on many occasions. We tend to forget those memories of when we were smaller," she said, moving to cover the other arm.

Sadness flickered in his eyes as he gave a small shake of his head no. "I recall my mother very well. The few images I hold remain clear."

Her quick movements slowed. She was sorry she had spoken without thinking. Pain squeezed her heart as she recalled he had been younger than Andrew or Annis when he lost his lady mother, seeing him alone in the world at that tender age.

His chest expanded as he drew in air to fight deep emotions. De Servian sucked in his lower lip, as if he were gnawing on it, considering if he should say the words that obviously still caused him pain. Some things did not go away, but lingered in the heart, unhealed, visibly the case for this man. "I recall her gentleness, the scent of verbane and lavender that seemed to cling to her skin when she hugged me at night. My father was competing in a tournament, hoping for the riches it would bring. Instead, it cost his life. My mother loved him very much, rare in the nobility, I suppose. A true love match. She found life unbearable without him, so one moonlit night she walked her grief into the lake."

Skena's hand stilled on de Servian's neck as she 'saw' the images in his mind. Not just what his words provoked within her, but the kenning sang pure and true. With the force of a lightning strike, she actually saw his memories, 'walked in his mind,' as some spoke of the ability. Never had she experienced the gift with this clarity at any point in her life. Her cousin Aithinne always had. Her three brothers constantly complained that she could unfairly steal their thoughts. Skena had long ago accepted her Ogilvie blood was not strong enough. But now she saw everything. The small boy waking in the night, scared because his whole world had changed, seeking his mother's reassurance. Skena witnessed everything through his child's eyes as they carried his mother into the castle. Felt his loss, the desolation, the dread of being left alone.

"I understand her sorrow, but she should never have left you, Noel." Her voice was nearly a whisper.

"You called me Noel." He offered her a sad smile.

Skena swallowed the tears clogging her throat. "You scare me, Noel de Servian." Backing off the bed, she wanted to run away and hide from him. How could this man so turn her life upside down in such a short time? "Get some rest." Not waiting for his reply she rushed to the pallet.

Usually, she banked the fire before turning into bed. This night she wanted the room to stay as warm as possible; to see that it did, she added a couple more peats to the fire. Allowing her hair to fall over the side of her face, she swiped away a stray tear with the back of her hand. Sadness for the small child who had lost his parents and had been alone in the world, sadness that he felt no one had cared for him with tenderness since.

Sadness for herself because this man reached her in a way none ever had before.

Chapter Seven

"Skena!"

She stirred in her dark slumber, unsure who was calling her or why. It had been a struggle to find her rest. Images of Noel de Servian kissing her had taunted her into the wee hours of the night, left her foolishly wanting what she could never have. She finally drifted off with a passel of questions chewing at the pit of her belly.

"Skena!" The call came again. Harsh. Raspy.

A moan of protest rose in her throat as she tried to climb out of the blackness of her mind. Despite every muscle in her body complaining, she forced herself to awaken. Something about the cry caused alarm to speed her blood from its night thickness. Sitting up, she shivered. Her stiff back protested. A yawn came and finally went before she recalled she was on a sleeping pallet before the fireplace. A shudder racked her body, so she leaned over for a peat brick to place on the fire, making sure not to smother the low flames. Once it started to catch, she carefully added another.

"Skena . . ." This time the summons was weaker.

Pushing up, she realized her name had been called from the bed. *De Servian.* Her heart slammed up in her chest as she hurried to bedside. He had half-kicked the covers off, and even in the shadows she could see he was bathed with sweat. Clearly, he was not fully awake; his arms and legs thrashed against the covers.

"Skena . . ."

His calling her name when he was not in his awakening mind touched her in a way she could not unriddle. She reached out and placed the back of her hand to his forehead and nearly flinched at the heat off his flesh. Moving her hand down to his chest, she checked if the rest of him burned as strongly with fever. This level of heat was dangerous.

"Noel." Skena leaned over him and shook his shoulder.

The silver eyes popped open, but they looked up at her blankly, not really seeing her. This state terrified her. She had feared the sickness would come upon him. Now the fight for his life would begin.

Skena started to pull her hand back, but his shot out and grabbed her lower arm in a grip that was near bruising. His stare finally seemed to focus upon her.

"Do not leave me," came the harsh whisper.

With de Servian's expression glazed, she wondered if he spoke to her, or in his feverish torment this was the child Noel, wanting his mother not to abandon him. Once again, she achieved that rare oneness with this man, taking his pain within her heart and making it her own.

"Skena . . . do not leave me. I do not want to die alone," he gasped.

She placed her hand over his where he gripped her lower arm. "Noel, 'tis only the sickness. You are strong and not going to die. I will be here as long as you need. But I must get some help, call for things I can use to care for you. Do you understand?"

Noel did not respond for so long she feared the consuming heat possessed him too tightly in its grip. Auld Bessa spoke that if unchecked, the fever could burn out a man's mind. Though she had assured him otherwise, the dark specter of losing de Servian gripped her soul. Finally, he gave a nod, and his hand released her.

Skena stroked his cheek. "Rest easy, *mo cridhe.*" As the endearment was out of her mouth, she flinched. She had called him *my heart.* Holding her breath, she waited for his reaction, but only another shudder racked his body. Most likely, he would not recognize the words. "Try to keep the covers over you. Your sweating turns cold if you kick them off."

Rushing to the door, she jerked it open and nearly tripped over a body sleeping before the threshold. She righted herself by catching the doorframe before she fell. The large lump shifted as the covers rolled back.

"Galen?" she asked in surprise.

The old man tried to cough, nod, and yawn at the same time, while awkwardly reaching for the dirk in his boot. "What be the trouble, Skena?"

She put her hands on her hips. "Why are you sleeping before the door? The floor is too cold for your aching bones."

"Aye, 'tis truth. Only, I was not leaving you alone with that bloody *Sasunnach,*" he informed her. "He might split your gullet." His eyes traveled over her in the thin night rail, then he added, "Or worse."

"Thank you for your protectiveness, dear friend, but you spent half a night on the cold floor for naught. You will be sick as he is if you do not stop such nonsense. I need more bedding, drying sheets, hot water, honey, oilcloths, and send one of the lads out for a pail of snow and another to fetch up more peat bricks."

"Snow?" He rubbed his face. "Wha . . . Ah, the fever came upon the warrior."

Skena frowned. "Keep the faint tone of hopefulness out of your words, old man."

"Why, Skena? Mayhap it would be fortune's will." He folded up his pallet, his eyes never leaving her.

Helpless to explain, she turned her hands palms up. "I lack

the ability to tell you. De Servian is special in a way I cannot impart." Hesitating, she questioned revealing all to him, but then decided mayhap it was best. "Aye, he is English, and I ken not why he is here. . . . Only . . ."

"Only?"

"The kenning in me is strong with him. I saw his mind, his remembrances of when he was but a child," she confessed, confused by this vital connection between them.

Galen's head snapped back. "The kenning is weak in you, Skena. You have never before been able to reach out with the gift in that way. Why him? A bloody Englishman? This bodes ill. Mark my words."

"The future's path I cannot foresee. Nevertheless, the fey bond is there. *Keen*. I can only accept it to mean that in some manner de Servian is different from other men. Important," she defended.

Laying the rolled covers and pallet to the side of the wall, Galen gave a fatherly glower. "Are you sure you do not confuse the kenning with desire? Pretty men can turn a maid's head; few are e'er worthy of trust. Everything in life comes too easily to them, Skena. Especially women. Best you ponder upon that before you go fixing in your mind that the Lord de Servian is somehow above all others, lass. You only set yourself up for heartache."

Skena felt as if she had taken a hit to her heart when he brought up women coming to de Servian too easily. Had she not fashed over these very thoughts only a short time ago? Still, it wounded her to hear someone else speak the same qualms. Made her feel hopeless, a silly lass with dreams that refused to die.

"I fail to recall asking for your views on the English lord. I asked for several items and the peat, water, and snow to be fetched. Or shall I go do these things myself?"

Galen's brows lowered at her scolding. "Go ahead, Skena, take the hide off my back with that sharp tongue of yours. You ken I am right. You also ken I will follow your orders. And I will be here with a shoulder for you to cry upon, lass, the day this pretty adder plays you false." He shook his head at her as she opened her mouth to speak. "Hold the lady of the keep rebuke. 'Tis a waste of breath, and we both ken it. I am going. I am going."

Skena spared but a glance at her elderly servant shuffling down the hallway. It brought sadness that he disapproved of her actions concerning de Servian. Galen had always been so supportive of her in everything, first serving her lady mother and then her with complete loyalty. Worse, she knew the old man was being truthful, merely echoing her own worries about this English warrior and his coming to Craigendan.

Despite that, it did little to deter her from the path before her. De Servian's fate was now twined with hers in some strange manner; the kenning told her this to be a certainty. For good or ill, the coming of Noel de Servian was the will of the Auld Ones.

And there was naught to alter that.

Peat burned bright in the fireplace, doing its best to dispel the wintry wind howling outside. The cold walked through the stone walls as if they were not there. It seemed strange. He burned with fever, the internal heat ravaging his mind, yet she forced the fire to consume precious peat at a high rate to the point it was uncomfortable for her.

"Fighting fire with fire," she said under her breath.

As Skena looked down upon the handsome man, she shook, not from cold, but from fear her healing skills would not be enough to pull him back from the brink. Once a mind crossed over the bridge of Annwyn—the Otherworld of the Auld Ones—it took a strong witch to use the dark words to craft a spell to hold tight to the soul. She had seen one or two men alive, but not 'right' in their head. Their bodies in this world, their minds already moved on to the shadows of Annwyn; two halves of the same soul forever divided. She was not sure she was strong enough to fight for this man and win.

In a hastily tossed on kirtle with the sides still untied, Jenna hurried in with the oilcloths, extra bedding, rags, and honey. "Water is heating on the fire, despite Cook's grumbling about being awoken at this hour. Owen is fetching a bucket of snow as we speak." She put the items down on the bench and then came to Skena where she was dabbing a wet cloth over Noel's forehead. "How is he?"

"He worsens, I fear. When his calling awoke me, he still recognized me. Now . . ." Her shoulders gave a small shrug. "I am not so sure."

When he suddenly began coughing, Skena winced. Thick fluid was building up in his chest; his breathing was labored. Each passing breath saw de Servian growing sicker.

Weakly, he lifted his hand to touch her cheek. A feeble grin spread over his mouth. "Skena. I remember."

"Good. Struggle to stay with me. You must fight this," she begged, combating the tears threatening to overwhelm her. She could not give in to them. She needed all her wits to win this coming battle.

Skena's head whipped around as Owen came in with a large pail of snow. He carried the bucket to the table and set it on the floor beside it. "Hope this is enough, Skena. I will fetch more as you need it."

"Thank you. Go help Cook with the hot water."

"Aye, I will." He paused by her side. "Skena, I did not go outside the wall when I gathered the snow, but fetched it from beside the stable where it was clean. The horses were kicking up a fuss, especially that big white stallion belonging to your knight."

"Why?"

"Wolves. They were scratching at the postern gate, trying to dig their way in. Several. A pack from the sounds of it."

Owen stared at her with dark, worried eyes. "Mayhap we need to give them something to fight over. Kill one or two of them. Wait until they come close, then we could down them. Let the horde feast upon their own."

She almost echoed the 'we,' but as a question. What he suggested was that *she* would kill the wolves as the animals ventured close. None of Craigendan's women were good enough with the bow to hit a wolf and fell him. Galen no longer could pull the bowstring with enough force to bring a beast down, and Owen had trouble seeing well at distances.

Everything always fell upon her shoulders. Skena closed her eyes to hold tight against her rising fear. Not one wolf—she would be dealing with the pack. Too clearly, she could summon the image of the black wolf jumping for her throat, the smell of his blood as it splashed her face. A nightmare to face that horror again. Even so, she had no choice. If the wolves were digging their way into the compound, they would have to be stopped by one means or another.

Keeping her counsel, she did not want to tell the boy she had a similar idea, but with a different outcome. Mayhap they could create a blind and lure one or two wolves at a time into the outer ward, and drop them as they entered the pen. As she had told them before, meat was meat. Why should the wolves have a full belly and her people go hungry? Desperate times made for desperate deeds. Somehow, it seemed the only reasonable alternative. In one single effort, she would be removing the threat of the wolves, but in a manner that helped Craigendan's people as well. Another of life's hard choices she was forced to make.

Still, she was not going to reveal her forming thoughts to Owen. The lad could never keep a secret behind his teeth if he tried. Should she tell him she planned on luring the wolves inside the outer bailey with designs of seeing them in the stew pot, it would be on every set of lips in the whole bloody fortress before dawnbreak. Her way, the people would warm to the scent of a hot hash without fashing overly about where the meat came from.

"Let me get through this crisis. Then I will sort out marauding wolves. Tell Galen to set someone to guarding the gate. We cannot afford to have them dig their way under the door before I can address the matter. Alert those on the wall to keep a sharp eye and ear. The pack might find another corner to tunnel under since they have started looking for the weak spots."

"I will, Skena." He gave her a nod and hurried off.

Going to the table she took a large rag and folded it in half. She scooped two handfuls of snow from the bucket and piled them at the center of the material. Then, she laid the material over itself twice; thus it was cold, yet the ice would not touch his flesh. She had to drop his fever fast, but dare not apply the snow directly to his skin because of the earlier exposure. It could deepen any previous damage.

"De Servian, can you hold on to me and raise up just a bit?" She tried to help lift him. The man was a dead weight, so solid was his muscle.

The coughing halted as he offered her a weak grin. "Noel."

That brought a smile to Skena. "Ah, so your thoughts remain with me. I need you to sit up just a wee bit. I want to put an oil-cloth over the pillow so this will not soak the bedding. Then I will apply this cold press to the back of your neck. Can you lift up?"

He started coughing again, but nodded. Even as sick as he was, he showed amazing strength in holding on to her and pulling up as she asked. She quickly slid the oiled cloth over the pillow, and then formed the covered snow to his neck, finally easing him back.

"C-cold," he complained.

She patted his hand where he still clutched her. "Oh, aye. I will only keep it there for a short spell each time. It will help combat the fever."

He offered her a faint nod, but already she could see his teeth starting to chatter.

"Jenna, mix some snow with the water in the bowl on the table. Only a little. I don't want it too cold. Enough to see if we can break the fever. When that's done, you may leave."

His grip tightened on her arm. "Do . . . not . . . leave me."

De Servian's plea ripped through her heart. "I am here. Rest easy."

Skena worked until the first light of dawn broke over the *cnoc* of *Leith Crioch*. Her fingers grew stiff; her knuckles ached from wiping down his body with the frigid water. After the heat raging his flesh dropped, he would begin shivering again, and then slowly the fever would return to his body. To help with the chest rattle, she mixed a tansy of comfrey, white willow bark, mullen, elderberries, and angelica. Though he protested, he did drink it down. De Servian was still very sick, but she felt a spark of hope in that he was a strong man, a warrior used to hardships. He could fight this. He had to.

"Please let him battle this," she wished to the Auld Ones.

As exhaustion creaked through her body, she dried his chest and limbs, and then wrapped Noel in several blankets. He seemed more peaceful. The shudders were not as severe when they came. The fever failed to spike as high. His eyelids were shut, and he finally seemed to be resting, so she wanted to seize the chance to lie down for a short spell, before the fortress came alive with the day's activities. There was always so much to do, and everyone would come wanting her to solve each and every problem. She was so tired. She merely wanted to close her eyes for a short time.

As Skena turned to seek her pallet before the fire, de Servian's hand grabbed her arm again. His breathing was labored, raspy, but in a loose fashion that said he fought the illness. "Skena . . . do not leave me . . ."

"I am here, Noel." Skena took the cloth, dabbing at the sweat beaded on his brow.

"You called me Noel." He started to grin, but another round of coughing racked him, though the phlegm sounded moist, not dry and hacking. As long as that was the case, she knew his body was winning the battle against the ill humors.

Sighing, she looked longingly to the pallet and then shrugged. She crawled up on the bed and scooted to where she could sit next to him, reassure Noel she was still there. With her back against the bed's headboard, she pulled her knees to the side and then tugged a cover over them. "I will be here, as long as you wish."

"Talk . . . to . . . me," he said in gasps. "Tell me . . . about Craigendan. What 'tis . . . like come spring?"

"'Tis green. Most days the fog lifts and the sky is bright and clear, almost blinding. Other times the *haar* rolls in and hovers near the ground, almost as if they are old souls who have not made the journey to Annwyn."

"*Haar?*" he asked.

"'Tis what we call mist and fog."

Taking her hand, he gave it a squeeze. "Tell me more. . . ."

Skena spoke of how the land awakened after a wintry spell, of the beauty of the rugged countryside. Talked until she could not recall what she spoke of. Eventually, her legs grew stiff, and she stretched them out. Then later, her head drooped in exhaustion, and she slept, her arm curled around de Servian.

"Noel," she whispered on a soft sigh.

Chapter Eight

"Noel." His name came on a soft sigh.

Luxuriating in the toasty bedding, she wiggled her toes and stretched. Skena was so warm. Since she slept alone the big bed was always chilly on winter morns. Before dawn demanded she arise and attend her duties, she would burrow under the covers and move as little as possible to hold her body's warmth in the feathered mattress. Sometimes the children came in and cuddled. Those lazy morns were nice, the three of them sharing their heat. Never anything as snug as this. Fearful it was naught more than a pretty dream, she did not want to open her eyes and awaken to frigid bed ticking and covers. Unexpectedly, as she shifted, she bumped another body. A very warm body!

Forcing her eyelids open, she blinked several times because of sleep sand. When she could focus, she stared at the massive shoulders and hard back of a man. De Servian. She almost jumped back. *Almost.* That delicious warmth held her there. Surely, it was not a bad thing to borrow his heat on this cold, snowy morn? His breathing was shallow, his body barely moving as he slowly inhaled and then exhaled, showing he was sleeping deeply.

As her eyes traveled over the braw spine and the defined

muscles of his back, she bit back the word *beautiful.* Men were not supposed to be beautiful or comely or gorgeous. Those were terms applied to women. When folks spoke of men they said striking, handsome, or mayhap virile, and those things did apply to Noel de Servian. Even so, he seemed *more* than any of the men she had met, thus those simple words failed to pay him due homage.

She swallowed hard as the scent of his body filled her mind, provoking a strange reaction in her blood. Leaning forward, she nearly pressed her nose to his shoulder to breathe in the fragrance of his skin. A smile crossed her lips as she savored the delicious, heady tang of his flesh. Never before could she recall liking the way a man smelled; she was tempted to bury her face against his back and revel in the elemental essence that was Noel de Servian. He smelled good. He smelled *right.*

Decency should propel her back to the far side of the bed, instead of cuddling next to him. It was a big bed, after all, with plenty of room for four people. There was little need for her to be almost pressed up against his body. Evermore plagued with cold feet and hands, she supposed they had instinctively sought the radiant warmth de Servian offered. Now that she was awake, she should scoot over to her side, if not climb out of bed entirely.

Skena bit the corner of her lip, fighting a battle within herself. And losing. Gradually, she brought her hand up to his shoulder blade, brushing and yet not fully touching. She held still. Hesitating. She owned no right to stroke this man in any way other than as a healer. Shameful though it may be, she wanted to. So easily, she could story to herself that she merely sought to try out the kenning again, see if the connection was still there and as strong as she remembered. And in truth, that curiosity was a wee part of what was driving her. To experience the kenning so potent within her, when never before had she been able to draw on that fey gift, had been startling.

Though of late she had told endless untruths, she had never deceived herself. To offer that as an excuse for why she fondled his back would be naught but bald-faced mendacity.

She pressed her hand to his hot flesh. He still fought the fever, but the wracking cough had quieted, allowing him to slumber peacefully. When he showed no reaction to the gentle caress, she drew her palm downward to the small of his back. The old wound site burned, scorching. She lifted her hand and placed it on his hip.

Her palm tingled. The kenning.

Until Noel de Servian had come into her life she had never perceived its sense so clearly, so intensely. As she touched this warrior's flesh, she was overwhelmed by so many things. Emotions, yes. Desire—without doubt! Never had she craved to handle a man so intimately, yearned to feel those sword-roughened hands on her. Oh, she wanted him with a power that seized her whole being. Visions flooded her mind, of his hands sliding over her naked body, squeezing her breasts, pressing her down into the soft, feathered mattress. That was the hunger. There was more. So much more. Something about this man reached beyond the flesh, past the need to mate. It touched that spot within her no one had before, awoke dreams she had put away a long time ago when she had been forced to marry Angus.

Timidly, she snaked her fingers over the curve of his hard, round buttock. Straying too close to the festering spot, suddenly it felt as if she took a blow to her body, as though steel had pierced her side. Sucking in a deep breath, her mind swirled with pain. His pain. Pain she now shared. Through strength of will, she held her hand there and opened her heart, allowing the force to flow from him into her. It was almost too much to experience after the years of near silence from the kenning, but she closed her eyes and tried to shed the mortal shackles of this world, reach for Annwyn, into the Realm of Shadows where the Auld Ones resided. Immediately, darkness surrounded her, swallowed her. She might have panicked had she not known she was touching Noel. Her anchor.

Skena stood in a vast cavern on a narrow stone bridge with no sides. She moved ahead with hesitant, careful steps. Slowly light began to fill her mind. Then almost with the snap of a whip she was carried from there. She stood on a field, in a place unfamiliar to her. Taking a step, she recoiled. She had trod on a man's arm. A dead man. As she backed up, she stepped on another. Her head snapped around and around, seeing bodies everywhere. Men dead or dying, some places two and three deep. There was hardly a place to walk. She swallowed back the scream of horror, bubbling up in her throat.

A man on a snow white destrier galloped up the knoll toward her. Other knights on horses and soldiery afoot followed behind. He was covered in mail. The helm with the nose piece made it hard to recognize his face. Only as he rode near, he abruptly reined the stallion to a halt, the beautiful horse rearing. Then the unearthly eyes looked at her. A pale, liquid silver, with odd circles of amber, they widened and then focused upon Skena as if he could really see her in the midst of all the bodies.

A dread slammed into her, paralyzing her. She needed to warn him. Danger was near. Everything began to swirl and shift about her. Somehow, she had to fight to reach him, stop what evil that was going to happen.

"Skena . . ." he said.

The voice pulled her to him, but everything kept bending, twisting, to where she could see only Noel as he dismounted his horse. There were others about; they were nothing but blurs, their voices garbled. She had to reach him before it was too late. Pushing and shoving against the faceless bodies, not caring where her feet landed, she never saw the hand that wielded the sword, just witnessed as it plunged into Noel's back. Felt it enter her as if she had taken the blade in his stead.

"No!" The scream escaped as she saw blood gushing down his leg, the huge red stain soaking and spreading on the surcoat.

"Skena!" The urgent plea pulled her back into the darkness. "Awaken. Please awaken."

Her shoulders being shaken finally yanked her away from the place of dead and dying. She could only lie there and fight against the lingering images and emotions still crowding her mind. Fear over how close de Servian came to dying, not long ago. Finally, as movement returned, she lifted her hand and allowed her fingers to softly stroke his handsome face.

"Death brushed your soul. It was so close, you dying," she whispered, sorrow filling her that she might never have known this man. "I saw. . . ."

"Saw what? You were dreaming, Skena. Naught more than images our mind tries to sort through." Carefully, his hand pushed her hair away from the side of her face. "I do not pretend to understand why our minds torment us in such fashion. Sometimes, 'tis like stories created in our head. Other times, pieces of our lives are in there. These images soon fade if you allow it, or replace them with other thoughts."

She dropped her hand to the strong column of his neck and allowed her thumb to brush over the point where she felt the pulse of his blood. "I was not dreaming. I was there, saw you take the sword to your side." She choked on the sob welling in her throat.

"Dreams oft seem real to us, but are merely night visitations. Let them trouble you not," he assured her. His hand reached up to close over hers, where it still touched his neck, and then squeezed.

"Nay, truly I did not sleep. I was awake," she insisted.

He shook his head no. "You slept. I had a hard time calling you back from Morpheus's realm. You scared me."

Oddly, she wanted him to understand, to accept her as she was. "Nay, I am born of blood that has 'the sight.' Ogilvie blood. People oft speak of it as 'walking in another's thoughts.' That is what I was doing. I walked in your thoughts."

Leaning over her, Noel stilled. "What mean you? You 'walked' in my thoughts? No one can do that." His mouth gave a faint smile, slightly condescending as if she were a half-wit.

"Aye, there are a few who can. . . . Gifted ones. Highlanders are aware of some who possess powers, abilities. 'Tis called the kenning." Skena looked up into the silvery eyes, afraid, unsure how he would hear her confession. "Females of Ogilvie blood are fey. They sometimes see things in dreams, others in visions. If they are powerful enough, they can do this through touch, to know what you think, even see images from your past or what may come."

He snorted a derisive laugh. "'Tis daft. Do you lend belief to such childish folly, Skena?"

She tried not to let his immediate rebuff of the notion bother her. People had strong reactions when faced with the truth that women of Clan Ogilvie were *different*. They were witches. Some spoke of such with reverence; others in mistrust, fear, or even abhorrence. People outside of the clans preferred to believe witches did not truly exist. Others accepted their existence and either wanted to use their power for their own gain, or shunned them, and thus were scared of them.

As she looked up into his bespelling eyes, she wondered which path he would choose. Mayhap it was better for her to keep silent and not reveal these dark secrets to him, better than to explain and have him look at her in shock or loathing. A few could never accept that their thoughts were not their own; there was no way to shield themselves from this violation. Her heart would break if he turned away from her. Only here for such a short time and already he was coming to mean so much to her. Mayhap too much.

Skena wondered how Tamlyn and Aithinne were handling this same situation with their new English husbands. Had they kept their secrets, or were these Dragons of Challon men made of sterner stuff, powerful enough not to fear powers unseen in a woman? Her cousins were strong seers. Auld Bessa said likely they were the strongest in the clan since Evelynour, and her birth was so many years ago people had stopped counting the number of summers she had walked this earth.

For her cousins to conceal their nature, their special abilities, would be much harder than it would be for Skena, likely one of the weakest of the Ogilvie line. Hiding the craft in her would take little effort. Never had she been seized by the visions or dreams that came so easily to her cousins.

Until this man.

So many wondrous things stirred to life within Skena, summoned by Noel de Servian. Hope took seed in her heart. With the kenning this strong when she touched him, it had to be a sign. Mayhap the dreams of a young girl's heart, which had refused to die, had been answered with the coming of this one special man. She wanted to tell him of this wondrous magic, share it with him.

"I believe in many things since your coming," she confessed in a whisper.

Noel gave her a faint smile. "'Tis a magical season when wishes are answered, they say."

Skena lowered her lashes. "Wishes are a waste of time. They lead only to disappointment."

"Do they?" There was challenge in de Servian's voice as he leaned forward and brushed his lips to hers.

Just a gentle, fleeting touch between them, but her body nearly leapt, wanting to capture his kiss, deepen it. She rose to the primeval power of being under this virile warrior. Surrender clamored within her blood.

The chattering voices of children, growing louder, caused them to jerk apart. Skena scooted hurriedly off the bed, snatched up a cover, and swung it around her like a *ruanna*. She did not need Andrew and Annis seeing her in bed with de Servian. Already they cosseted hopes he was the knight of their Yule wish who had come to save them. That they believed in wishes was troublesome enough. She was not going to lose herself to the false magic, which would fade in bright sunshine.

The door pushed open and both children clattered in, not waiting for a well-come. Noel moved quickly to shove himself back under the covers. That set off a round of coughing from him.

Skena watched her son and daughter climb up on the bed and begin plaguing de Servian with questions. Her heart squeezed as she observed Annis putting her hand to his forehead to see how hot he was.

Nay, wishes were not for her.

"Bloody pathetic liar," she whispered under her breath.

Chapter Nine

"Skena, oh, come quick!" Elspeth called as she rattled into the hall, her frail frame scarcely able to bear the heavy mail and armaments she wore. The baldric about the girl's hips swung loosely, nearly causing her to trip in her rush forward. Shoving the sheath to her side, she removed the too-large helm and pushed her sandy-colored hair back from her worried face. "Riders come through the draw. Mayhap a score. What shall we do?"

"Och, not bloody Duncan Comyn again? You'd think the lackwit would stay by fireside with the snow up to his arse and leave us in peace." Skena exhaled irritation at the prospect of facing him again. "Just what I did not need this day."

She was tired, hungry, and short-tempered. Three days of tending de Servian saw her worn down and in little mood to deal with any man, especially one by the name of Comyn. She had come belowstairs to eat, and then hoped to curl up on her pallet and rest before she collapsed.

"Nor any other," Muriel said, setting aside the basket of wool she was preparing to spin. "The bloody *amadan* seizes upon the storm as a reason to come sniffing around Craigendan again. I mislike Comyn's so-called caring over your welfare, Skena. He watches you in a way that rubs against my grain."

"Like a half-starved wolf he prowls the border of late, conjuring excuses so he can turn up at the drop of a pebble. Always with a perfectly logical explanation for his visit, always so solicitous," Skena agreed with Muriel's opinion.

"Mark words, lass, a Comyn ne'er did aught to help another soul. Those wolf eyes view Craigendan and you as his next meal." Muriel clucked her tongue and shook her head. "He ain't the knave his brother Phelan was, true, but I still hold no shred of trust in the man. And neither should you."

Skena huffed a dry chuckle. "I would sooner cuddle an adder to my breast."

Muriel nodded. "Nary a tear was shed when Phelan Comyn drew his last breath nearly four months past, even if it were by an English hand, as some say. Not sure if many would spill ones for Duncan either. Still, best beware in handling that one, lass."

Duncan Comyn's continued interest in Craigendan unsettled Skena. She feared he had already twigged out how few men were within the curtain and merely waited for their female weakness to see them at their most vulnerable before he made his move. A shiver crawled up her spine at the image of that ever coming to pass.

"Nay, 'tis not The Comyn." Elspeth shook her head. "'Tis English—men bearing the standard of the Black Dragon. The snowdrifts see them moving slowly up the grade, but they will reach here anon."

"The Black Dragon?" Rattled by the news, Skena nearly dropped the earthen pitcher she held. With an unsteady hand she carefully placed it on the trestle table, next to the boughs of evergreens they were preparing as decorations for the Yuletide celebration. She could not let others see how the news troubled her. Biting back the flare of bile rising in her stomach, she asked with a calm she failed to feel, "The Earl Challon comes?"

"I cannot say if 'tis the earl, but his pennon—the green

dragon on a field of black—stands out clearly against the snow. Either he comes or sends a messenger in his stead." Elspeth set the helm down on the end of the table. "Oh, Skena, why now? Why does the dark lord come? Surely only something of great import would drag him out in these drifts. Earl Challon has paid little heed to Craigendan since he became the new lord of Glenrogha. Outside of the Dragon taking Angus's homage back in the spring—"

"And then my lord husband imprudently broke his troth nary a week later by going to fight the English at Dunbar." That fact had caused Skena deep misgivings, leaving her with many a sleepless night since May when word came of the Scottish defeat. Whispers of awe and fear told that even hard-bitten men dared not cross the Earl Challon. Few e'er tried and live to boast about it.

Well, Angus was dead; there would be no punishment to rain down upon his stubborn head. Craigendan, her children, and ultimately she would bear the backlash of his foolish choices. She had begged Angus to stay out of the coming fight, allow the nobles to carry on their heedless politics and war. Craigendan was best served by their men staying home and protecting what little they had. But nay, hardheaded Angus had to ride to the Comyn standard. Not listening to her, he argued the time had come for Scots to stop their petty clan squabbles and stand together to drive the English back over the border. He feared Longshanks intended to bleed the country dry with taxes, or worse, parcel out Scottish fiefs to his English lackeys.

Later, she learned that neither Phelan nor Duncan had ridden to the call of their mighty cousin until the last hour; both since had claimed they arrived too late to take part in the battle. It little surprised her. Skena knew Duncan never looked you square in the eye when he spoke of it. That had been the difference between the two brothers. Both were liars. Only, Phelan could stare you stone cold in the face, showing the countenance of an angel, while untruths spilled over his teeth. Duncan lied as easily as his older sibling had, but he was unable to meet your eyes. Skena figured knowing that quirk might someday work to her advantage.

Scant days after the Scottish defeat, Duncan had returned to deliver the tides that Angus had died in combat. Boasting that his brother and he were some of the few Scottish nobles left free in the aftermath, he said the biggest measure of the Scots' aristocracy were in irons and sent south to England or were dead. 'Tis spake upwards of five-hundred score Scots were killed on the field of Spottsmuir—a resounding rout, yes, yet it still drew the ire of the English king. Word came many prisoners had been sentenced to death by horse trampling.

Since that day, she awoke each morn fearful news would come that the new earl of Glenrogha had decided Craigendan needed a new lord, a loyal English one. This fate had not ensued, so after a time she figured the mighty Black Dragon had deemed her keep too small of a concern to bother with. Reports unquestionably had reached his ears that Craigendan had no master. Still, he had failed to pay the smallholding a visit during the summer months, not even after he and Tamlyn had returned from Parliament at Berwick, which the English king had called back in August.

Skena rubbed her forehead trying to keep the fears at bay, seeing all eyes in the Great Hall looking to her for reassurance. Well, she had none to spare. The summer months had been trying, seeing the harvest wither and die from the drought. For a time her people had carried water from the burn to see that the crops they needed to survive grew. The struggle had been a losing one. Too soon, it had turned to a desperate effort to fetch enough water just to see that the animals lived.

Summons had gone out for all Scots nobles and land-holders, commanded to show themselves before Edward Longshanks and to sign documents of fealty and homage, or face being attainted. The English now laughed and called the document "Ragman Roll." Luckily, Skena had received no such orders, possibly because her holding paid homage to the Earl Challon; he was already Edward's man. She had taken the coward's path and not travelled to the big city on the eastern coast. Her choice had been a gamble. Did she fail in not going, earning the English ire for it might be seen as an insult? The lesser of two evils was to stay and wait. If she had shown her face at Berwick, immediate attention would have been drawn to the fact that her lord husband was dead, killed in rebellion against the English king, thus ensuring he would set a new man in Angus's place. The powerful ruler would have sealed her fate then and there.

She had heard the monarch did not set much store in Scots females holding lands and titles. Had he not commanded Challon to come claim Tamlyn and her *honours*? Was not the Lord Guillaume betrothed to her cousin Rowanne and the other brother, Simon, to wed Rowanne's sister, Raven? Damian St. Giles, Lord Ravenhawke was now husband to cousin Aithinne. None of these ladies had e'er raised a hand against Edward Plantagenet, and yet their fate had been decreed according to his whims. How well would she have fared against this mighty ruler, when her husband had actually lifted his banner for the Scottish army and raised men to kill English soldiery?

Autumn had come, and still, no one made a move against Craigendan. As no dire fate from the English had befallen her and her people, she considered applying to the Earl Challon for men to protect the fortress and to hunt for meat in deep winter, making him awares of the grim circumstances facing all in her smallholding. Just a little aid would mean such a difference in getting through this season. After all, he was not only their overlord, but now kinsman, a cousin by marriage.

What stopped her were the children. She feared what would happen to her, to them. Challon would likely place a man of his choosing as governor of the keep, possibly force her to marry, thus putting in jeopardy the rights of Andrew and Annis to this land.

Mayhap it was only a matter of putting off the eventuality, but she had hoped they could muddle along until she came up with some acceptable solution to the predicament. Craigendan needed a lord, and a new lord it would soon get. She simply hoped this time to have a say in who would be her husband. She had always envied that right of the Ogilvie heiresses. She had Ogilvie blood in her veins, but was not of the line that held the ancient charter from old King Malcolm. Scottish and English kings alike had once honored that decree.

"The skein of time has unraveled," Skena said under her breath.

Tamlyn's new husband would view the fortress as virtually undefended. Skena glanced at Elspeth, rigged out in mail and armor so she would appear a man when she strolled upon the boulevard of the curtain wall. Her stomach tightened, staring at her too thin kinswoman. She had little hope the women of the keep would fool the trained eye of this mighty lord. Julian Challon would never accept the current situation. While Craigendan was small and insignificant compared to the three vast fortresses belonging to her cousins, the daughters of the Earl Kinmarch, it was a key to protecting the back of Glen Shane. The Black Dragon would not permit that to go without remedy once he ascertained the situation.

Skena's dread must have been reflected upon her face.

"Oh, Skena, what do we do?" The girl's huge eyes filled with fear.

"We?" Skena echoed, feeling faint. There was never a 'we' to help Skena bear the burdens or make decisions.

She fought the shudder snaking through her body. Mayhap she had been foolish to turn a blind eye to the realities of the bleak situation, waiting instead of taking the dilemma in hand and wedding a man of her choosing, before either the earl or his king could seal her fate. Only, facing the prospects of another marriage to a man she did not love held little lure for her.

Her mind instantly conjured the image of Noel de Servian. So clearly, it was almost as if he were standing there. Her insides twisted as the wanting slammed through her entire being.

"It does no good to make wishes as Andrew did. Fate has never been so kind to me," Skena muttered, then blinked to banish his vision. Drawing a ragged breath she forced a smile to bolster all watching her. "Elspeth, hie you to the wall. Alert our women on the curtain to keep their heads down and stay away from the men coming in. Especially Dorcas. Tell her I will take a switch to her back if she dares lift her head to one. All must be about their watch, just as our men would patrol. Leave me to deal with this bloody English dragon."

Skena gave Elspeth's arm a small squeeze as she sent her off, flinching at how thin the lass felt. Her cousin had never been a strong woman, and since losing her betrothed at Dunbar, the girl seemed to be wasting away. Selfishly, Skena had spent the summer hiding from the fact that marriages would need to be made for the women of her clan and for herself. There were no other alternatives. The crux of the problem came in that the nearest men were from Clans Comyn and Campbell, both having lands pushing up against the far border of Craigendan. Each clan had long craved to get their hands on Glen Shane and Glen Eallach. She feared they saw Craigendan as a means of getting a foothold into the Ogilvie lands.

Had not Duncan Comyn already come around repeatedly since his brother's death last August? Rumor said Lord Ravenhawke killed Phelan; others spoke of the Dragon himself dispatching Phelan Comyn. Most had shrugged and muttered it was no big loss. Phelan had not been popular with the men, since he oft dallied with married females. For some fool reason, the Scotsman had rashly led an attack on the Challon party as they returned from Parliament. As a result the second son, Duncan, was now the new chief of the Comyns of

Dunkeld. After claiming his brother's place in the clan, Duncan had turned his attention to Craigendan, claiming he wanted to pay court to Skena.

"Stuff and nonsense. Men and their foolish schemes think women none the wiser to their lies and ways." Skena dusted her hands on her apron and then untied it, attempting to make herself presentable. Her mother had not plucked her from a neep patch. She figured Duncan wanted Craigendan so he could turn it into a thorn at Lord Challon's back. She wanted no part of being caught in the middle of a power struggle between Duncan Comyn and Julian Challon.

Muriel stepped close as Elspeth hurried away. "Dangerous times, lass. Tread carefully with this English Dragon. Remember he is overlord here."

Skena sucked in a steadying breath. "I have nary a need for whispered warnings of things I already ken. I have heard how the mighty beastie's name is uttered in dread. Hard-nosed men pale when they speak of Julian Challon. Still, think on it— Tamlyn is no fool. Word travels back that she is well pleased with her new lord husband. Norman-English he may be, but they say my cousin warms to her dragon. I pray this is so. Mayhap it will give me an edge in dealing with him."

"I told you so—you should have taken matters into your hands and found a husband. Now you will be at the mercy of an Englishman." Muriel continued to upbraid her for her lax handling of the impasse.

"Hush blethering. You spoke such to me so many times this summer." Skena little needed everyone hanging on her elbow, telling her they were worried, or what she should have done. "'Tis too late. 'What ifs' and 'should haves' help no one. Cease the fashing. Let me find some measure of peace within myself before I have to face this arrogant and powerful male who holds the fate of all here in the palms of his hands."

Muriel looked contrite. "Beg pardon, Skena. In my panic I forget the burdens you carry." She paused, her eyes lifting upward to the tower. "What about the braw man in your bed? I have seen you tending him. You favor him. Aye, he needs care for the short term, but he is a fine man. You will find naught better if you search the breadth of this land. A proper lord he would make for Craigendan."

If only. Skena choked back the pain fisting around her heart and pointed out, "We truly ken little about the man. He might be an ogre by nature."

Muriel laughed mockingly. "Clutching straws, Skena? My eyes may not be as sharp as they were a score year ago, but that man is quality. Few like him about. You want him—do not deny this. Your eyes speak the story, lass. Cease waiting for life to happen. Take what you want before men fashion the path of your destiny."

"Shut your gub and let me gather my wits." She tried to sound stern, the lady of the keep. Muriel chuckled. Skena could not stop the blush spreading up her neck and to her cheeks as she noticed all eyes upon her. "Och, everyone, go about your chores. Fetch some bread and cheese. Warm some cider. They will be cold, weary from the long ride in the snow. We have guests acoming. Snap to."

Skena fisted her hands, thinking how the fare for these Englishmen would be food from the mouths of Craigendan's people. Well, there was naught for it. She had to treat this Englishman with all respect due to their overlord. Mayhap things would work out. With Earl Challon being kinsman, mayhap she could indeed apply for support.

"If wishes were cows we would not starve this winter," she muttered, and glanced down at her faded kirtle, disheartened she had no time to change. Well, they were a poor holding. No use to put on airs and pretend otherwise.

Galen hurried in, his face drawn. "Skena, I came as soon as I heard. 'Tis truth? The Black Dragon comes?"

"We learn shortly." Skena curled her fingers into her palms to hide the trembling.

Chapter Ten

Skena stood before the huge fireplace in the Great Hall, pretending to watch the blaze. There was beauty in the peat's flickering blue flames. Still, she found no solace in the warmth, instead fretted if there were enough peats to get them through the winter, knew they had not cut any to lay aside for next year. To keep de Servian cosseted, she had burned thrice the number of blocks that she would for herself alone. She had been so frugal with their rationing this past month. Worry gnawed at her mind. Everything seemed tainted with the specter of unease of late. Each time she swore things could not get worse, some trouble came along and increased her woes tenfold.

"Believing things cannot grow worse is like having faith in wishes. If wishes were wings, I would will them to carry this bloody English dragon back to his lair and leave me in peace," she spoke lowly to the fire.

The double doors were jerked open, causing her head to snap up. Her stomach tightened, preparing for the coming order. She was not a weak woman. Oh aye, she was stubborn, willful, mayhap *too* willful according to Angus. However, to face this Black Dragon was an ordeal she was not girded for. Never in her whole life had she fainted, but the prospect loomed in her mind as a very real possibility. Her blood jumped as her eyes locked on the tall man flanked by his entourage.

So this was the Earl Julian Challon.

He paused halfway to her and removed his leathern gloves, which he passed off to a smaller man behind him, likely his squire. Then he removed the helm and pushed back the mail coif, revealing a riot of black curls. If she had not gazed upon the countenance of Noel de Servian, she would instantly have said she stared into the face of the most handsome man she had ever seen. Clean-shaven in the Norman way, his strong jaw and sensual mouth were revealed in their perfection. As he neared, she saw the green eyes flecked with shards of dark amber returned the same scrutiny as hers. Skena's stomach muscles flexed hard, wondering about the opinion he was forming of her. She was not dressed in the finery of a lady of her station. She was tired, worn thin by work, fear, and nursing de Servian for three straight days. The face she presented to him was shadowed by the uncertainties she found harder and harder to hide.

"Good morrow, Earl Challon. I am Lady Skena MacIain. I bid you well-come to Craigendan. Please be at home in my humble keep. May I offer food and drink to you and your men after your cold, hard ride?" Where she found the ability to speak she did not know. Her throat was corded with tension.

He inclined his head slightly. "My men would appreciate something warm, aye."

"A mulled cider or mead?" she offered, motioning to the bench by the fire for him to sit and warm himself.

Instead, he stepped to the fire and held out his hands to it. "Either would be most well-come. Howbeit, I am not the earl. I am Guillaume Challon, Baron Lochshane." He offered her a gentle smile. "I fear I am still unaccustomed to the title as yet."

This man was one of the bastard half-brothers of the earl. Back in the spring, the Earl Challon had raised his brother,

Guillaume, to be the lord of Lochshane and set the betrothal to her cousin, Rowanne. That she was not dealing with the Black Earl, as Julian Challon was called, caused the faint trembling within her to lessen. The baron was an imposing man, mayhap even a shade taller than de Servian. A formidable warrior indeed, but the fact he was not his powerful brother eased the fretting a small measure. Likely this man would not rule upon the fate of Craigendan. That left the question of why he was here.

She nodded to a servant to bring in the food and drink for the Englishmen. She grit her teeth when several of the lasses began blushing around the men. Ah, a keep full of females and no men for months was a dangerous situation. She needed all of Craigendan's secrets shielded from prying eyes. Obviously, these Norman warriors would have to stay the night; it was too far for them to journey back to Lochshane with night falling so soon in the day. She would have a hard time seeing some of the keep's workers did not climb into the pallets of Baron Lochshane's men. It was too easy to let something slip when the mind was on matters of the flesh, she feared.

"My lord, pray what drives you out into the snow to pay a visit to Craigendan?" She tried to pose the question to sound as naught more than polite curiosity. "To be sure, you hardly enjoyed the ride here in the aftermath of the worst snowstorm we have ever seen."

"Sometimes demons drive men to extreme measures, my lady." He chuckled at some private jest. "In this circumstance, 'they' seized on the excuse of hunting for an old and very dear friend. Men from the party of Sir Noel de Servian were found wandering in the storm near the passes of Glen Shane. We took them back to Lochshane, but we failed to locate their master. This morn we turned our hunt in your direction after finding his helm on the road to Craigendan. I thought it possible that when he became lost he might have found shelter here. The *dun* is the nearest shelter to where the helm was discovered. Did my friend, perchance, make his way to your gate?"

Suppressing the urge to look at the ceiling, as if she could see through stone and mortar to where de Servian lay resting, she swallowed back the words that were eager to spring forth from her tongue. Oddly enough, her first impulse had been to answer with an untruth. Lies came too easily these strange days. Her heart cried out that this man would take her knight away, so urged her not to let him discover Noel was in the lord's chamber. Sheer folly. Despite the children making a wish, Noel de Servian was not summoned from the mists by a Kelpie. There would be no hiding him from Lord Challon.

She inhaled slowly to steady herself, realizing she danced on treacherous ground. It was folly to lie to this man any more than necessary. "Aye, we came upon Lord de Servian out in the snow. He had fallen from his horse."

Guillaume Challon's eyes were too sharp. He took note of her unease. What a fool she was. This man was a mighty warrior, used to dealing with his powerful brother, kings, and the nobility of three countries. A simple country lass unused to games of intrigue was no match for him. Instead of demanding to know where de Servian was, he merely gave her a faint smile and waited. There was a calm determination in this man of Challon that bespoke they could play games of staring all night and he would always come out the winner.

"Bloody dragon," she mumbled under her breath.

He arched a brow. "Beg pardon, my lady?" He had heard her. She saw the intelligence flicker in the hazel-green eyes.

"Lord de Servian is in the lord's chamber. Resting."

Concern filled his stare. "Night seems to come at midday in this land, but the hour is still early for Noel to be abed. Was he injured in the fall?"

"Nay, I fear an injury he sustained early this year distresses him." Noticing how her hands shook, she clasped one in the other, determined for him not to see how rattled she was.

Skena glanced up as the food and cider were placed on the table. "Come warm your innards and then I will take you to see Lord de Servian." She started to turn toward the table, but he caught her upper arm and restrained her with a firm though gentle touch.

"I prefer to see Noel now, my lady." It was a request, yet his soft tone was steel. He was not asking, but commanding.

She stiffened her spine, worried that he might think she had not been doing all she could to save his friend. "Very well, Baron. If you will follow me?"

As they passed, he nodded permission to his men to relax and partake of drink and food. They removed their mantles and sat at the long trestle table. At the great doors, she paused to look back, fearful her servants might do something to reveal how vulnerable Craigendan was. The men were smiling up at the women and—curse them—her ladies were watching these Englishmen with hungry eyes. She was glad Dorcas was on the wall, patrolling. Without doubt, the troublesome woman would prove a problem around these handsome Normans, in more ways than one. Skena really hated leaving the Great Hall. Under her watchful eye, her workers would behave. Without her there to herd them, she dreaded they would respond to attention from the men before giving true thought to Craigendan's precarious position. Muriel scurried in from the kitchen, pausing to pinch Fenella on the arm, a reminder to pay heed to her forward ways. Skena relaxed concerns. Muriel would see to things.

"Lady Skena . . ." Sir Guillaume motioned toward the stairs with his hand.

Lifting her kirtle so she would not trip on the steps, she started up. "Lord de Servian had lain on the ground long enough to become covered with snow. My children found him. He spoke his destrier was spooked by ravens."

"At the passes? Then he had been near to Glenrogha. His guard said they figured he had made it that far just before they lost sight of him." He shook his head. "He should have ridden his palfrey, not a tetchy destrier, in a winter storm and on terrain unfamiliar. They hold steady and are not so easily spooked. But you say 'tis the previous wound he suffered causing him trouble?"

"He was blae when we found him."

"Blae?" he echoed. "Beg pardon?"

"Aye, pale, blue from the cold. I took all care in warming him properly, and he seems to be a strong man, able to fight off the worst of being left in the snow. Still, he sickened with fever. I have battled that for three days and nights. He passed the crisis in the middle of the night. He is hoarse. I am giving him boiled vinegar and honey for that and a tansy to help fight the phlegm. Even so, I feel it will be days before he is ready enough to travel with you—"

"There will be no need for him to travel back with me."

"But he said he was trying to reach Glenrogha to seek out your brother."

"Aye, that was his plan, according to his men. He wanted to visit Julian before coming here."

Her hand stilled upon the latch to the lord's chamber. "Here? Why would he be coming to Craigendan?"

The clear green eyes skimmed over her. "He was coming to take possession of the fief. Noel de Servian is the new baron of Craigendan."

It took all her willpower for her legs not to collapse under her. She could not absorb the enormity of his statement. She had known from the start the man lying in the chamber represented change. Foolishly, she had failed to discern just how much.

"So, it seems Edward has sent a dragon after all. A foster dragon," she snapped.

Her hand trembled as she pushed open the door. Inside, a loud voice chattered away. Annis and Andrew were on the bed with Lord de Servian, Jenna nowhere in sight. Her son was telling the knight about Kelpies, while Annis dabbed a damp rag at the resting man's brow.

Guillaume Challon's glare nearly turned her stomach sour as he rounded on her. "This is the care you afford one of King Edward's most trusted knights?"

Skena could not stop from backing up before the angry man. "Baron, I assure you—"

"Here, you child, get away from him," Guillaume barked, motioning with his hand for the children to get away from de Servian.

Poor Annis, used to sharp commands from her father, almost seemed to shrink in upon herself. Her brown eyes went huge, fright filling them. Skena knew the feeling—the man was a force to behold. Had she not just quailed before the baron? Only, no one dared speak to her daughter in this manner. Skena feared if Annis knew only harsh tones from men of power that she might come to fear them and the marriage vows she would one day make.

Swallowing her trepidation, she took swift steps to block Guillaume from the bed. "While you are brother to the overlord here, I am baroness of Craigendan, and no man shall dare address my daughter in such a rude manner. Am I made clear?"

De Servian's hand weakly reached up, took the cloth off his forehead, and then flung it into Guillaume's face. Startled, the man snatched off the rag and tossed it back. Andrew burst out laughing, but quickly ducked out of sight on the far side of the bed. The top of his head popped back up as he peeked to see the baron's reaction.

"Rein in your temper on my behalf, Guillaume. You look just like Julian when you glower thusly. A dragon breathing fire terrifies small girls." Noel shifted slightly and caught Annis's small hand. Placing a kiss on her palm, he said, "I thank you, Lady Annis, for keeping watch over me whilst I sent your mother to finally eat something."

Skena's heart melted, watching her daughter experience

true tenderness from a man who was a figure of authority. Tears welled up in her throat. Lifting her hand to her mouth, she pressed her bent thumb to her lips, keeping back words wanting to spill forth.

Annis did not move, untrusting of de Servian's gentleness. Skena held her breath. Finally her daughter leaned forward and kissed Noel's hand as he had hers. Despite fears and questions that arose from learning that this man was the new lord of her holding, this gesture to reassure her small child touched her deeply.

"Skena, did you eat while you were belowstairs? You were not absented long enough." Noel spoke with the tone of the new lord here.

How could she have missed this before? Too unquestioning, she merely assumed he was used to giving commands to his men. Never once had it occurred to her that he could be expressing his possession of this keep.

"Nay, I barely got to the table when we were descended upon by a pesky dragon, *Baron Craigendan*." She did not take the edge off the chill in her voice, letting him know Guillaume had broken the tides that Noel was lord here now. Mayhap she should be more concerned about her fate and the children's and pretend to have no objections to the situation. Only, it scared her. This man would soon decide what would be her future, would steal the rights of her children.

De Servian watched her without moving, so still she could almost wonder if he even drew air. His silver eyes showed a touch of regret, then he shifted his gaze to his foster brother. "Skena, may I speak with Guillaume alone?"

"Aye, Baron. Of course, Baron. Whatever you want, Baron." She snapped her fingers as she spoke to the children, "Annis, Andrew, come. The baron wishes to speak to his foster brother without pesky Scots underfoot."

She could see the children were confused by the harsh sound of her voice, so laced with vehemence. Annis leaned over and kissed de Servian's hand again, then climbed down off the bed. Andrew pursed his mouth and was slow to come, not happy about leaving *his* knight.

"Come, children, hurry. We would not want to risk angering the baron." Skena grabbed the children's shoulders and pushed them to the door. She paused before closing it, looking at the two very handsome men, but really only seeing one.

"Bloody dragons." She slammed the door with her full fury.

Guillaume watched the lady of Craigendan herd her two small children out the door. With a parting glance back, she closed the door—noisily—leaving them alone. "By God, she is just like these other women of Ogilvie blood."

Noel weakly pushed up to lean his shoulder against the cross boards of the bed. "Oh, and pray tell, what are these Ogilvie women like?"

"Ready to cut your liver out and feed it to you in big pieces." But there was a smile on his friend's mouth.

"From that expression on your handsome face I would adjudge such is not entirely a bad fate."

"Not entirely, though there are times. They are headstrong, used to rule, resent the bloody hell out of English invaders—"

"And beautiful," Noel added. "I briefly met the Lady Tamlyn and the Lady Aithinne back in August. Both Julian and Damian pretended indifference toward them before Edward. I assumed that was merely for show. It would never do for the king to know that they value their ladies."

"Lady Skena does not exhibit open defiance quite so strongly. Likely, her being a widow sees her used to accepting a man's rule. Of course, Rowanne was married before, but I fear in this instance it only fostered her rebellious spirit. They speak my betrothed planted a knife in her lord husband's chest one night, then stood and watched him die."

Noel's head snapped back, startled by Guillaume's allegation. "Surely, you jest?"

"I warn you, my brother. These women of Clan Ogilvie are a breed rare, a law unto themselves. And take heed, there is little doubt they are witches."

Now Noel did laugh. "Trying to tweak my nose? This is a mischief I would expect from Simon, not you. He was always the one to enjoy a jest. You remained the rock for Julian."

"Nary a jape—a caveat. Be forewarned, these females are supposedly descended from a race of witchwomen who long time ago were said to have the ability to turn into catamounts. While I have not had chance to witness such, they do display the ability to know things beyond a normal range. You recall how Damian spoke of the kenning, a gift from his Scottish mother? Well, 'tis the same. His mother came from Ogilvie blood, likely where he gets it."

"I shall ponder about this later when I am not so tired and my head ceases this dull throb." Noel sighed in exhaustion.

Guillaume arched a questioning brow. "What are you going to do with the lady and her children?"

"I owe the children my life; I owe Skena," Noel said flatly. "Still, the situation is complicated, which sees many a pitfall ahead of me."

Guillaume pulled a chair next to the bed and sat. "How so?"

"A flock of ravens near the passes of Glen Shane spooked Brishen."

"Queer moody birds. They seem to guard the passes." Guillaume eyed him. "You will find Glen Shane . . . different, odd. The folk are good, but their beliefs, their ways can cause pause. Give the people a chance. While Edward sent us here as nary a blessing, we have been fortunate in making a home in this Northland. I was delighted to hear the news you were assuming control of Craigendan, as I know Julian is."

"I am pleased to have him as my overlord. We have been warriors too long, my friend," Noel said solemnly.

"So how did the children and Skena save your life?"

"Brishen ran. My back slapped against the cantle, hitting an old wound that is not healing right. Then I fell. I cannot say how long I lay there, unable to rise, with the snow covering me. The children slipped off from the fortress because they swear they heard someone they call The Cailleach whispering to them to follow."

"The Cailleach, a crone goddess, lady of winter to these Scots." Guillaume nodded, familiar with the lore.

"I may have to give an offering to their goddess then. Had the children not followed the call, they would never have found me. I was too off the beaten path; no one else would have come. My fate would have been a very cold end."

"Lady Skena mentioned there was a problem with your back. Pray what is it?"

"Near the end of the battle at Dunbar, I took a sword through the split in my mail. 'Tis not healing right. I lose the power to grip in my right hand." Noel held up his hand and flexed it, checking the numbness.

Guillaume pushed away from the chair. "Let me have a look see."

Noel turned so his back was to his friend, the muscles burning with each shift.

"*Merde!* That's blood red." Guillaume touched his fingers to the angry flesh. 'Tis hot. Noel, we need to deal with that without delay."

"Skena said the same thing. Methinks she was hoping to get me past the worst of being exposed to the cold before she went gouging on me."

"I notice you speak of her not as Lady Skena, but in the familiar." Guillaume prodded with his words and his fingers.

Noel hissed in pain. "Enough. Any fool can tell it festers. I rot from the inside out."

"Aye, it's clear something remains behind, poisoning your flesh. Sorry, my friend, we needs must draw the baneful corruption to the surface, lance it, and then cauterize it—done as soon as we can fetch the items needed. It shan't be merry. Of course, from that parting glance the Lady Skena gave you, she should enjoy taking a knife to your wound. I infer you failed to inform her you were the new lord here."

"You gather correctly."

Guillaume stopped his examination. "Why had you not told her?"

"There are complications that will have to be addressed. I was not feeling well enough to deal with the repercussions."

"And that being?"

"That the man who did a fair job of running me through at Dunbar was Angus Fadden, Baron Craigendan."

Guillaume sat down hard. "I can see where that might muddy the waters."

"But there is more."

"More?"

"Oh, aye. As the battle was winding down, we trapped a large group of Scots and disarmed them. Fadden slammed into one of my squires, grabbed his sword, and ran him through, then came at me from behind as I dismounted. The blade sought the seam in the mail, slicing into the side of my back."

Guillaume's face darkened as he showed comprehension. "Ah. You dispatched the coward in single combat."

Leaning back, Noel nodded. "Aye, I killed Angus Fadden."

Chapter Eleven

"Still, it was a fair fight. I know you too well. You are as a brother to me, a most honorable man and not one to attack a man from behind. The same cannot be said about the former baron, eh? Plus you were fighting wounded. He had the advantage," Guillaume pointed out.

Noel gave a weak nod, shifting in the bed to be more comfortable. "Howbeit, will that matter once they learn? I will be the murderer of her husband, the children's father, in their eyes."

"Stop such falsehoods. You murdered no one. The baron made his own choices, cork-brained though they were. He was likely too pigheaded to accept defeat. He knew if he attacked you, you would kill him. If he felled you before stopped, then he knew your men would cut him to pieces. One might view Fadden chose to take his own life, but was too cowardly and wanted it done by another's hand," Guillaume opined.

"Mayhap." Noel knew that no matter if it had been the baron's choice, the end results would be his to bear.

"Well, they say 'tis the season of miracles. The light is the shortest. End of one turn of the wheel, start of a new. Mayhap the blessings of Christmastide shall grant you a fresh beginning as well." Guillaume exhaled. "We shall get you healed, then I fear there are issues that need addressing here."

"Issues?" Noel echoed.

Guillaume nodded, rising and going to the fireplace to toss on a couple more blocks of peat. Using the poker, he jabbed at the half-burnt ones to stir the flames. "Most odd, Noel. Upon our arrival we were not challenged. I called out at the gate, demanding admittance in the name of Challon, and we were permitted entrance. No men came close to confront us."

"You rode under the standard of the Black Dragon. That tends to strike fear into the hearts of all men, not just Scots. They know Julian is their overlord."

Guillaume merely lifted his brow and shrugged. "Methinks very soon you need to get out of that bed, assume the title of baron, and do a head count of your men."

"What are you saying?" Noel reached for one of the covers and wrapped it around his shoulders.

"Cipher this. How many men of Craigendan did you take prisoner at Dunbar?"

Noel thought back on that dreadful day. So many dead or dying. One of the images he wished he could exorcize from his memory. The ugliness seemed forevermore burned into his soul. "Two score, mayhap a few over. Why?"

"And what happened to them?"

"Edward had them sent to Edinburgh Castle and then to England. Tides came most were trampled under horses as traitors. Why should their fate be of question to you?"

"Methinks the *men* on the boulevard are likely young boys, naught more. They seem pages and squires, not men-at-arms. You need to take complete stock of your new holding. If you require soldiery, we can pull some from Lochshane and Glenrogha until spring. Once we have a tally of Craigendan, then we can refit to see your holding is secure. The Comyns and Campbells both craved to get their hands on this place. Julian is keeping close eye on Duncan Comyn, after his brother

Phelan tried to kill all in the Challon party when they returned from Berwick."

"Rumors reached Berwick of the attack and that Phelan Comyn was left dead in the aftermath. Duncan had to do some tall talking and groveling at Edward's boot to keep control of the clan's holding of Dunkeld. What really happened?"

"Phelan and his men ambushed the party as they returned from Parliament. Damian took arrows in the battle."

Noel questioned, "Is he all right now?"

"Oh aye, doing very well. He is up and about, working to regain his strength. He will be a father in a few months. So will Challon. Hard to imagine, eh?" A grin spread over Guillaume's face.

"Methinks they are more than ready for a settled home, a family. So am I," Noel told him.

"Which brings me back to my original question, which you sidestepped—what are your plans for the widow and the children?"

"Once, long ago, Fate robbed me of my birthright," Noel admitted, feeling the pain of a loss that had never truly left him.

Guillaume leaned back in the chair. "It also gave you Julian, Simon, Damian, Dare, Redam, and me for brothers though."

"True, and not for one day did I draw breath without giving thanks for that twist of life. I have been blessed, I fully know." Noel paused, fighting back old emotions. Oddly, he had gone through much of his life without tasting the child's sorrow, the sense of losing everything. Being here in Craigendan seemed to have let loose the old demons. "Long ago Fate took a family from me. Mayhap it now returns what it stole. Skena is a fighter." He did not add the words *unlike my mother*. "She cares about her children, about the people of this keep. I hope . . . given time she will come to accept the paths of our destiny."

* * *

Skena tried to keep her emotions under control as she shepherded the children down to the Great Hall. With each step along the winding staircase, it became harder to keep everything reined in. Anger, resentment, and disappointment bubbled in her to the point it was hard to think. Of course, she had no right to feel let down. This knight was nothing to her. A Norman stranger that her children had come upon in the snow. He owed her naught. She would have tended any soul lost in a storm.

A stranger she had lain next to in bed, touched and desired.

Only now, he was the new lord of Craigendan. By the Auld Ones, where did that leave her? What would happen to her children? Panic surged white hot in the pit of her belly.

Trying to curb rising dread, she gently pushed the children through the bustle of activities in the Great Hall. Some of the workers were starting to decorate for Yuletide, coming in the passing of a few days. Somehow, that was jarring in the light that this might possibly be the last holiday she would witness as lady of this keep.

Her steps faltered as she noticed several of Challon's men were aiding the young women in tying the boughs of holly and evergreens to the columns of the hall. Mayhap she should not resent this. The women of Craigendan would need to take husbands soon. And she certainly could not cast the first stone over the fact that their gazes had fallen upon Englishmen. Had she not desired de Servian?

"That was before I knew he was the new baron," she muttered.

Seeing Jenna, she made a beeline to her. "Take the children to Nessa. Ask her to see they stay to their rooms for now."

Jenna frowned, her eyes worried. "What is it, Skena? Has something happened?"

"Could you please do as I ask?" Skena snapped, though she instantly regretted her harsh tone. "Forgive me, dear friend. I am . . . troubled."

Jenna nodded. "I see that. I will take the lambs to Nessa. You need not fret over them."

"Skena!" Owen rushed into the hall, and then pulled up seeing Challon's men all about. He hesitated, swallowed hard, but then came forward to her. "Skena, you needs must come."

Skena trembled as she tried to contain the emotions threatening to swamp her. The whole bloody summer she had worked so hard. And for what? For an English lord to come in and assume control of her keep? Glancing down at her shaking hands, she nearly grimaced at the rough skin. They appeared more the hands of a serf than a lady. She curled her fingers into fists to keep from rattling apart.

"Skena, are you well?" Owen asked.

She gave a short humorless laugh. "Oh aye, I could not possibly be better. Come, let me handle whatever needs sorting out so I may find a nice, dark corner in which to collapse."

Owen looked perplexed. "Are you tired?"

"Tired?" She nodded. "Tired of life, my young friend."

Hurrying to the tally room, Skena snatched up her work mantle and left the hall before anyone could stop her. She was at the end of her tether and was unsure she could handle much more without collapsing into a heap and crying. She was worn to a frazzle from nursing de Servian for three days. Now to learn this man she had cared for would rob her of Craigendan, steal her children's heritage, was beyond what she could deal with.

She followed Owen through the inner ward and then into the bailey. As she spied the stables, she had a sense of where he was heading. To the postern gate. She glanced around, searching for the guard set on the back entrance.

"Where is the sentry posted on the gate?" Skena asked in a cross tone, not intended for the lad, but for the woman who had abandoned her duty.

He paused before the metal-plated door and shrugged. "Dorcas."

The name was explanation enough. Skena's mouth set in a frown. Why had she not hazarded a guess? The bane of Skena's life, Dorcas was always at the heart of any problem in Craigendan. After Dorcas's husband died of a wasting sickness, nearly six years ago, Skena had been forced to take her in. There had been no turning her back on kin. At this late day, she was not sure if she regretted that rainy morn when Dorcas came to Craigendan, or had grown to accept it as an odd blessing. Within a fortnight of her coming, Dorcas had lured Angus into her bed. Skena misliked how Dorcas had single-mindedly set out to achieve that aim. As time passed, she had been silently relieved that Angus spent his nights elsewhere. Howbeit, it rankled he had chosen Dorcas for a leman. Worse, it undermined Skena's position. Dorcas felt she did not have to take orders from Skena, that her place in Angus's life furnished her privileges the other women of the keep were not afforded. Her insolence only grew with each passing year.

She should have found some villein from Clan Campbell or Clan Comyn to take Dorcas to wife by now and been done with her. One less headache she would have to deal with. That thought brought a smile to her lips. Oh aye, a husband from either would do well to unload Dorcas upon; then the aggravating woman could cause them mischief and leave Skena in peace. Would serve the troublemaker well if Skena wed her to a swine herder; see how the wench with airs above her station would fare then. Skena had never challenged the situation while Angus had been alive, and, at times, secretly was grateful that his interests had been fixed elsewhere. In a peculiar way she grudgingly felt Dorcas had earned her elevated status. Well, Angus was long gone. The protection he gave Dorcas's mischief-making ways had worn thin.

"The winds of change blow around us all, Dorcas. It may be the last thing I do as the lady of Craigendan, but I will find you a fitting husband. You can bloody well wager your silver buckle on that," Skena threatened under her breath with a dram of glee.

Owen's forehead crinkled in confusion. "Beg pardon, Skena. After that sickness last month made my ears swell, I do no' hear so well. Muriel said it takes a while for them to get better."

"Naught for you to concern yourself about, my fine lad. We need to build a narrow run, high enough the wolves cannot easily jump over, and with a blind to protect me. We will let in one or two, and I can pick them off, whittle the pack down. It needs to be out to about here." She drew a line in the snow with the heel of her boot. "Long, but tight, so they cannot turn around easily." As she came around his right, she spotted what had been his immediate concern.

"See," he pointed, "they made a big hole at the bottom corner, enough for a snout to push under. Much more, Skena, and they will get in."

"Oh aye, this night if they are not stopped." She looked around for something to prevent them from burrowing under the gate. "Owen, run to the armory. Fetch five older swords, a hammer, two pikes, and a length of rope."

"Swords? Whatever for?"

"Oh, hurry, Owen. Time's a wasting." She gave the lad a push to speed his steps.

Instead of waiting for his return, Skena went to the stairs, which led up to the boulevard. There her ladies patrolled. She grimaced at the weakness of the ruse. They looked precisely what they were—women barded in armor to appear as men. There would be little fooling the Lord Challon if he caught a good sight of them. Of course, mayhap it was no longer her problem, but could be dumped into de Servian's lap.

"Baron Craigendan, you have damn few supplies, too many mouths to feed, and nearly all belong to women. How do you like those apples, *Baron*?" she grumbled. Coming upon a woman on patrol, she asked, "Where is Dorcas? She was set to watch the postern gate."

Margaret's owlish brown eyes blinked from behind the too large helmet. Her shoulders lifted in a shrug. "She disappeared after the English warriors came. Said you were inside with an Englishman keeping you warm . . ." She lowered her lashes. "Sorry, Skena, her words not mine. You ken the sloven."

"Too well. Go back to patrolling. Keep watch along the walk. The wolves alarm me. They are too bold by half. Tell the ladies to enter through the kitchen tunnel, and change in the covey or the cleansing room. Do not enter the keep direct or the English might spot you for what you are."

"Aye, Skena."

"Thank you, Margaret."

Snowflakes hit Skena's face as she stared through the crenellation at the woods that ran toward the loch. The wolves would be in their den sleeping now, but soon they would come scratching at the gate. She had to be ready to act, but feared the pen could not be built this night. Risking peril, she would have to hold them at bay one more day.

"Skena!" Galen hurried across the ward at an uneven pace, struggling not to slip in the snow. Owen and Kenneth trailed behind him with their arms full of the items Skena had called for. "You scatty female, planning on going to war with the English?"

Skena descended the staircase and headed back to the gate. "Going to war? Aye, in a manner of speaking." Grabbing one of the swords stacked crosswise in Kenneth's arms, she drove it into the frozen ground to where the blade covered the small opening the wolves had dug in the snow. It went in only so far, as she suspected it would do, so she took the hammer and pounded it in deeper.

"Smart thinking, lass. Here let me." Galen grabbed a sword and planted it less than a hand's breadth from the first one.

They worked until all five were stuck halfway in the soil

against the door. It would stop the pack from digging under, or the gate from being pushed open. When that was done, she poked one of the pikes through the metal holder of the crossbar, and drove it in at an angle, slanting behind the swords. Galen saw what she was doing and speared the second pike in from the other side so they formed an X. To give it all strength, she wove the rope through the pikes and broadswords.

"Well done, lass. Now no worries the varmints will get in."

Skena nodded, pleased with her handiwork. "For this night. They will soon give up and seek another weak spot. Each day that passes will only see the threat growing worse. We needs must take other measures on the morrow."

"They need hunting down, true." Galen regarded her solemnly. "But we have no men. Mayhap, the Lord Challon and his . . ." His words trailed off under her scorching glare.

Skena reined in her spiraling temper, not ready to tell Galen that Noel de Servian was the new lord here. Craigendan was still hers. The instant the tides were spoken, she would cease to be the lady.

That was something she was unprepared to face just yet.

She stared at the makeshift barrier set to thwart the wolves from getting in. "Too bad I did not try the same tactic with the bloody English."

Chapter Twelve

"Lady Skena." The deep voice of Guillaume Challon spoke from behind her.

Taking off her mantle, Skena jumped. The man was daunting. Word had reached Craigendan that his brother, the earl, was even more unapproachable. In light of that, she should be happy she now dealt with him instead of the Black Dragon.

"Aye, my lord?" she replied coolly.

"Do you have a healer within the curtain?" he asked.

"Our healer died several years past. We depend upon Auld Bessa to help with miseries here. I am sure you know her to be the healer for Glenrogha. Of course, with the snow so deep there is no fetching her. She is too old to travel in this frigid cold. Fortunately, I was raised with her knowledge. Muriel is also adept in healing. Methinks you will find no fault in how I cared for the new baron," she tried to keep the sharp edge from her last word, but failed.

His brows lifted, but he said naught in reproof. "I am sure you did everything possible to aid Noel to shake off the exposure to the storm. Since I hold this man dear as a brother, I offer thanks for your vigilant nursing. My concern now is his old wound. I examined it and mislike the look. The poison festers and will pollute his blood. We needs must draw the corruption to the surface, lance and cauterize it before that dire fate happens. We dare not delay, but must do it this very night."

Skena nodded. "Very well. I will go prepare poultices. In the meantime, you should eat and take rest. You had a hard journey."

"I thank you for your kindness, Lady Skena." He gave her a faint smile.

Feeling tired, Skena motioned for Muriel to see to the baron's needs, and then left the room. At the archway, she glanced back at Guillaume Challon. He was a striking man, an imposing warrior. She wondered how her cousin, Rowanne, viewed this knight who would be her lord husband come spring. Gossip came that Tamlyn was pleased with Julian Challon, and already she bred with his babe. Only, Skena fretted about Rowanne. Her cousin's first marriage had not gone well. Did she view the changes in her life with anticipation and hope, or did dread fill her heart?

Barely aware of what she was doing, she headed down the long hall, winding past the kitchen. Her steps on the stone floor faintly echoed against the walls. At the door to the still-room, she lifted the ring that dangled from her belt. Her hand shook as she inserted the key into the lock. She frowned, not liking her weakness, wishing she were stronger.

"If wishes were faery lights we would need no tapers," she grumbled. From the box by the door, she picked up a precious candlestick and touched the wick to the hall torch. "Wishing never helped aught in my whole bloody life. I see no reason to keep wasting my breath."

Smoke from tallow cups fouled herbs, thus Skena used beeswax candles in the stillroom. She was careful to ration their use. Burdened with men's chores, her workers had little time to replenish supplies before cold weather had hit. Tilting the candle, she allowed three drops to hit the holder, and then jammed the stick's base into the melted wax. The wax contained ground bits of cedar wood; the cleansing scent with its magical properties wafted through the room.

Skena looked at the long rows of wooden boxes and vessels stored on the shelves, while sprays, garlands, and posies hung from the ceiling to dry. An island of quiet away from the chaos of the keep's everyday life. The enclosed room generally offered a respite. She loved the solace found here, relished the heady perfumes of plants and worts, their fragrant sensuality cosseting her mind and opening her senses. This time, those soothing scents brought no tranquility. Badly needing that gentle renewal of her spirit, she tried to reach out with the kenning and touch the room's fey enchantment that had always before calmed her soul.

She failed. Too much was pressing inward on her mind.

"I ken the right worts to rid the *dun* of fleas, but I neglected to learn the charm to cure a dragon infestation." Walking to the table, she told herself everything would be all right. "It has to be," she whispered in the stillness. No reply came from the shadows. "Nor did I expect one. The Auld Ones have better things to do than fash over the likes of this lass. 'Tis up to me to find my path in this life—and without the aid of wishes."

And for a moment she almost believed that. Then fierce emotions curled through her insides like a writhing snake. Flinging herself onto the table, she broke down, crying for the first time since this nightmare year had started. Tears were useless. They changed naught. Only, she was *so* weary. Not eating enough, rationing the food they would need for the coming months, she was worn down by all the burdens of seeing the fortress prepared for the long winter.

As the drought had scorched the land, crops shriveled and water dried up in the burn. Come harvest, they had not reaped enough to meet the tithe to their overlord, let alone sustain the people of Craigendan through the approaching months. Dread over what would come down upon their heads, due to Angus's rebellion against the English king, had haunted her every step.

As the daylight grew shorter, there had not been time to cut the full stores of peat. The apples were smaller, scarcely filling half their usual barrels. Sleepless nights followed. She rarely drew a breath without scores of misgivings.

Now those fears had become reality. There was a new lord of Craigendan. An English lord. This man would want a wife and heirs. What would happen to her and the children? Oh, she had no doubt Tamlyn or Aithinne would take her in and give them a home. Only, Craigendan was the birthright of Andrew and Annis. Her son should grow up to one day be lord here, Annis a lady instead of some poor relation.

Everything seemed to be closing in. Bubbling up inside her, the panic shredded her fragile resolve. Tears came and would not stop. She did not even try to stem their flow.

Worse, she was loath to admit, pain also came from the thought of Noel de Servian. He was sent here by his king. None of this was his doing. He was merely an instrument of his ruler's whims. Yet, that would not stop him from taking control of Craigendan. How silly, her foolish heart had looked at the handsome man and wanted him, and despite knowing better, had idiotically started spinning dreams.

"Dreams are as useful as wishes," she choked the words out.

The door pushed open, causing her to suck in her sobs. She swiped the tears away with the backs of her hands. Pretending to be working, she snatched open the lids on boxes of dried herbs.

Muriel shuffled in, closing the door behind her. "What are you about, lass?"

"Making poultices with ground calendula, Scots elm, prunella, and St. John's wort. I will mix that with myrrh tincture. The Baron Challon thinks we must draw the poison to the surface on Lord de Servian without delay." As the elderly woman shambled near, Skena turned her head away in a ruse of reaching for the mortar and pestle. She dare not meet Muriel's all-seeing eyes.

"Stop hiding your face, Skena MacIain. I ken you too well for you to pull the wool over these old eyes." With a mother's loving touch, she pushed one side of Skena's hair behind her shoulder. "This man of Challon upset you. You went upstairs with one expression and came down looking as if your whole life had been destroyed. What happened in those few breaths to set your spirit on this dark path?"

Skena pressed her palms to the table, leaning on it for support. The enormity of the situation slammed into her again, filling her with despair. "We wait no longer for the English king to send a new lord for Craigendan."

"I thought Sir Guillaume was given Lochshane, that he would wed Rowanne come Beltane?" Muriel asked.

"Not Guillaume Challon. The new lord of Craigendan is Noel de Servian." Skena fought gritting her teeth over the prospect.

Muriel's spine straightened at the tides. "So that was his purpose for being out in the storm. Och, Skena, has the man said aught about his plans? What about you and the children? We needed a new lord, aye. We could not go on as we have. You kenned that, lass. This knight will bring needed men—"

"Englishmen, mayhap paid mercenaries," Skena sneered.

Muriel nodded. "Oh, aye. Englishmen. But men still, Skena. Would you rather the Comyns or Campbells get their hands on this place? You have an English overlord now. You needs must keep peace with him. Times change. The specter of war and famine stalk this land. Make pax with de Servian. Seek out an advantage, thus ensuring our survival."

"Make pax? Pray tell how? I have naught to bargain with, Muriel. He will claim all, my heritage, that of my children. The only good thing of going through a loveless marriage with Angus was that Craigendan was protected, and that my son and daughter would one day rule here. Otherwise, all this, my whole life has been for *naught*."

Muriel stroked her hand over Skena's back, allowing her to

cry silently. "Angus was nay husband for you. He was a good man, most say, but he was none too smart. He never kenned what to make of you. He failed to recognize the rare gift he had been given. Or mayhap to the point, he did know how fine you were, too fine for the likes of him. You two never found a level ground. That is the past. Turn your eyes to the future. Your marriage to him gave you two perfect children you love very much. More so, it brought you to this point in time. What is behind us molds us, sees us who we are. You are made stronger because of your past, stronger than you suspect."

"Strong? I stand here rattling to pieces and crying like a bairn," she choked on her scoff.

"Hush this fashing. You are beyond weary. You have stayed up nursing Lord de Servian, and not been eating again. Stop that. 'Tis important to all here that you keep your wits about you. You must deal with this new lord—"

"You keep saying that. But how? There is naught left with which to bargain. He will turn me out to go begging to Tamlyn or Aithinne for a home for me and my children."

"And they would take you in without hesitation. I doubt that will come to pass. Bargain with what every woman always barters with." Muriel moved to the door, leaned out, and called for Jenna.

"Muriel, is aught a matter?" Jenna came in, looking from Muriel to Skena. "Oh, lass, what has happened?"

Muriel snapped, "Nevermind. No time to blether. Have some stew fetched for Skena. Then go to the lord's chamber and collect a fresh sark and kirtle—not her best, mind. No need to be too obvious about feminine wiles. Men always come faster to fate when they believe 'tis their own notion. Something comely. Also fetch her comb and a ribbon for her hair."

Skena held her tongue until Jenna left, and then rounded on her former nurse. "What games play you, my dear friend?"

"From the dawn of time men have waged wars upon these isles. They run stag mad, locking antlers, paying little heed to poor females who must stand by and deal with the aftermath. Women learn to wage war as well, though not with sword and lance, but with what the Auld Ones gifted them—their minds and bodies." Muriel glared back at her with quiet determination when Skena frowned. "Craigendan needed a new lord. You kenned that would happen. Well, we got one. He needs a little fixing, true, but that works to our betterment."

"Muriel, what are you saying?"

"Do not go simple on me, lass. The man has come to us. 'Tis up to you to bend him to your will," Muriel insisted.

"What if he has other notions?" Skena bit the corner of her lip to keep it from trembling.

"Give him no chance. His being sick means you are there caring for him, seeing to his needs. Use this time to speak to him, let him learn about you and Craigendan. Offer him something to fix his desires upon."

"He is a bloody *Sasunnach*." Skena threw up her hands.

"Tamlyn has accepted her English dragon for a mate. They speak that Aithinne actually had her brothers carry off Lord Ravenhawke and chain him in her bed. Your cousins are smart enough to learn the way of things. Follow their example."

Skena shrugged doubt. "I do not think I could ever be so bold as to chain a man in my bed."

"'Tis nary a need. He is already there, naked. Men can be shaped lass through touch, through longing. Those silver eyes watch you with a bottomless hunger."

Skena sighed in misgiving and dejection. "I could not shape the will of Angus."

"You ne'er really tried. Closing your eyes and doing your wife's duty is no way to control a man. I have a feeling with that one abovestairs you will want your eyes wide open. There's the difference. Trust me."

Skena felt ready to break down and cry again. Grabbing the sides of her kirtle, she spread the material. "Look at me. A fright these days, I appear like a serf. I would turn no man's head . . . let alone someone like him. He could have any woman he wants."

Muriel clucked her tongue and then smiled. "Then you admit you would like to turn that lord's head. A step in the right direction. Mayhap the children's wish was true. They yearned for a braw warrior to come protect us. We were in a sore need. The Auld Ones show you the path, but expect you to fight to make choices a reality."

Looking at her shaking hands, Skena felt defeat pressing down upon her shoulders. There was no way that beautiful man would want a tired mother with two pesky children. "Oh, how I wish the powers of my Ogilvie blood were stronger."

"You would witch him to your bidding?" Muriel seemed surprised. "There was a time you would deem such dishonorable."

"There was a time I ne'er lied either. These dark days call for drastic measures. As you say, a woman must make war with the few weapons granted her. I wish—"

"Take care. Sometimes the Auld Ones enjoy a wee laugh, giving you what you yearn for, but not quite in the manner you envision."

"If wishes were neeps we would not starve this winter. Och, I give up wishing! 'Tis only for children who still believe in magic." Putting a hand to her waist, she took a steadying breath. "Oh, Muriel, this is hopeless! I will make a bloody fool of myself trying to woo de Servian's favor. I have no skills in this."

Muriel shook her head as she plucked herbs out of the boxes. "You should not adjudge these things by past experiences. You had no desire for a trough-fisted husband, thus not inspired to learn about that side of your nature. Well, you have all the inspiration any woman should desire up there in your bed. Stop fashing and fix your mind on the chore ahead."

"I wish—"

"You just said you swore off wishes. Hold true, lass. This is nary a moment for wishes. 'Tis a time for deeds."

Skena lifted the dried sprig of verbane to her nose. Inhaling the fruity scent, she closed her eyes. Images of Noel de Servian filled her mind, the longing so acute she wondered if Muriel could be right. Had she not been able to walk in his mind? Never before had she achieved this. Did that not hold significance?

"Oh, bother." She frowned, running her hand through her long hair. "Lies and wishes. I have had enough of both to last a lifetime!"

"Both are our nature, lass. We seek hope for solutions, and when they do not come, we stoop to lies. Your body tells you one thing. Logic adds its own voice. Only, you feel duty too strongly. You are loyal to a fault, even to a husband you did not love. These are sinister days, Skena. Angus arrogantly followed his fate to Dunbar and paid the price. Loyalty to him cannot be put before devotion to your children, to the people of our clan. Forget the past. Time to face forward and do what you needs must." Muriel reached up and brushed her hair away from her cheek. "You ken the choices. Go live on the succor of others? Seek the veil and become a sister at some nunnery? Or take a husband. Longshanks was bound to send a man to replace Angus. If he had not, then the Earl Challon would place his own man in charge. Count your blessings, lass, that Noel de Servian is the new baron. Fix his desires upon you. Forge a new life for you both. Stop fashing about Fate being cruel, and count the blessings of the Auld Ones. They gave you the means to save your place here. If you but have the courage."

"I never had courage like Tamlyn or Aithinne. They could look a dragon in the eye. . . ." She caught herself, realizing her unintentional jest.

Muriel chuckled. "Aye, they have looked at dragons and tamed these English beasties. Do you not see how hard it must have been for them? Reared by a man who allowed them their heads, they ruled their holdings without benefit of a man's control or advice. You are accustomed to reining in, curbing your wants and needs to what Angus allowed. Compromise, lass."

Skena felt despair washing over her. "Oh, Muriel, I am scared."

"A woman's lot. But we face our fears. We use our wits," she winked at Skena, "and our bodies, and fashion our lives the best we can. Remember he is not even a real dragon, but a foster dragon."

"You make it sound simple."

"'Tis simple. You only seek to make it more complicated than it is." Muriel hugged her. "'Tis a matter of seeing what is good, and what can be changed, instead of bemoaning things that are not perfect. Nothing is ever perfect. Life is the best we can make of it. You are stronger than you ever see. A late bloomer, you grew up under Angus's iron will. Seize your inner power. Stop looking at your hands, Skena. Salve will heal them. Believe me, a man does not inspect a woman's hands when he wants her. You have the chance, lass, to turn fate, shape how things will go for Craigendan. Mayhap even find something more in life than you ever expected outside of dreams."

Open your heart, Skena, and make a wish with the trust of a child.

Forgetting her lack of faith in hoping, Skena closed her eyes and opened her heart, but wished with the trust of a woman wanting something she had never had.

Love.

Chapter Thirteen

Holding a wooden box full of everything she would need for lancing de Servian's back, Skena marched up the winding staircase. It rankled that Guillaume Challon had sent for her, ordered her immediate presence as if she were naught but a servant.

"Bloody dragons think they are special. The world trembles at their feet. Ha! I have a mind to give this one a proper set down," Skena grumbled to herself, trying to build her courage.

Muriel trailed behind her, carrying a stack of linen cloths. "Lass."

The woman's one word caution caused Skena to frown. Pausing on the step, she glanced over her shoulder. "Muriel, did you say aught?"

Muriel's laugh was mocking. "Cease the mummery. I am the one hard of hearing these days, not you. You are just hardheaded. Keep your eyes on the goal, Skena, not on your wounded pride. Men are an arrogant lot. Methinks these Norman lords of Challon are likely worse than most, a power unto themselves. Men such as them give orders offhand; comes natural to them, so they ne'er stop to think how they sound. If you were to beard this dragon about his brisk order, he would be flummoxed you took umbrage. Request or command—

'tis the same to them. They expect to be obeyed. Battle for the things that matter most; ignore what you cannot change or what has little true and lasting value."

"How did you get so wise, my friend?" Skena offered Muriel a smile.

Despite silver kissing her thick red hair, Muriel's soft brown eyes shone with an eternal beauty. "By making too many mistakes in my long life. I but try to save you from the same missteps."

Skena leaned over and placed a light kiss on the elderly woman's cheek. "Thank you, dear Muriel. I remain indebted to you for being my guide. You are a second mother to me."

"And you are the daughter I wish I bore instead of that ruddy slattern I gave life to. I swear she is a changeling, switched at birth. Dorcas cannot be of my blood." Muriel's mouth set as she thought of her only child, who she wished to perdition at least twice a sennight. "Remind yourself what is important and you will do right by us all."

With Muriel's sage advice ringing in her ears, Skena banked her temper and entered the lord's chamber. De Servian, with a *plaide* spread over his legs, sat propped up in bed. Across the room Guillaume Challon poked at the peat fire, stirring it to burn brighter. Skena's steps faltered. She had to bite her tongue when she saw the stack of extra peat and the pile of splinted boards next to the fireplace. He would need the high wood blaze to make the poker hot enough to properly sear flesh, but she fretted over how much fuel it would use, nearly a week's worth, she feared.

Muriel set the stack of linen on the end of the bench, har-rumphed a reminder to Skena, and then turned to leave. "If you need me, lass, I will be belowstairs playing shepherd." Her way of telling Skena not to be anxious about Craigen-dan's women and the English soldiers, that she would keep a watchful eye on everything.

"Ah, there you are, Lady Skena," Guillaume remarked

needlessly, simply so he could pass along the hint of rebuke in his voice.

At first, he barely spared her a glance. Then his head jerked back as he actually took her measure. Skena set her teeth to keep from replying, afraid he was going to scold her for taking time to change clothing and make herself more presentable while he waited. His eyes widened and slowly travelled down her body, then back to her face, taking in that she was now attired more in keeping with the lady of Craigendan. He inclined his head in approval, but offered no comment. There was an appreciative glint in his eyes, yet banked, as though he set her off limits. Since this man was to be her cousin Rowanne's husband come spring, Skena gave him high respect that he was holding to himself, instead of applying the usual 'out of sight, out of mind' morals. Men too oft thought they could do as they pleased when away from the watchful eye of their wives or betrotheds. This man of Challon was a riddle, but she pretended not to notice his reaction as she sorted out the herbs and worts, lining them up on the tabletop.

"You have everything needed in ready?" Guillaume inquired.

"Aye, poultices made for drawing, salve for healing and to stop pain, and the mixings for a strong anodyne." As she began measuring out the various dried leaves and barks into the bowl to grind, Guillaume moved to the table, closely observing everything she did.

His voice was challenging. "What are you plying Noel with, Lady Skena? You said you have no healer. Are you so certain you know what you are putting in the potion?"

"I am careful, my lord. I blend feverfew, willow bark, mandrake, and mawseed in mead as the anodyne for his pain. I have a salve with mawseed as well. We can apply it after the cautery."

"Mawseed? Poppy?" He lifted the vial and sniffed.

"What some call it. I add in a few drops to free his mind from the intense pain he will feel. 'Tis not enough to harm him." When he merely stared at her, Skena glared back, and then lifted the cup and drank a measure. "Satisfied?"

Guillaume frowned. "That was hardly necessary, Lady Skena."

"Lord Challon, poisoning the new baron would hardly serve me or my people well, think you not?" Skena brindled. "As he is foster brother to the Dragons of Challon I ken it would mean my life should harm befall de Servian. I am not a lackwit."

"Never would I adjudge you as such. Howbeit, people have been poisoned carelessly by measurements of poppy and mandrake."

"Guillaume, leave Skena be," de Servian called from the bed. "If you do not cease annoying her, I shall put my knee to your chest and allow her to pour the brew down your throat to prove to you that it's safe."

Lord Challon chuckled. "Not in the condition you are in, my friend. Damian took an arrow to the chest and a couple to his thigh in August and recovers still. Even he could best you in a fair fight."

"Allow Skena to care for me. I could not ask for better treatment than I have received at her hands." De Servian's words were soft spoken, but it was clear he would brook no opposition.

Skena added a little more mead to the cup and carried it to the bed. She held it out to de Servian and then waited for him to take it.

"More stump water?" Noel gave her a sensual smile.

Her heart did a slow roll as heat flared in the pit of her belly. The worts and the drink were already starting to affect her, she feared, but that was little compared to de Servian's sway over her. *Could be something more potent hit my blood, overpowering the drink's effect.* Oh aye, she was smart enough to recognize it was this man who set that erratic fluttering in her chest. She knew he was baron here now, but that reality did little to stem the desire she felt for the Norman.

"Nay, you should enjoy this. 'Tis mead—cider and honey. It will enhance the effect of the worts, take the edge off your pain. I want this to go as easy for you as possible."

"And do I get a reward for drinking this witch's potion?" One corner of his mouth pulled up higher.

Their eyes met as he took the goblet of mead; they were both remembering how he had kissed her the last time she gave him a tansy. He finally raised the cup in a salute, and then drank the contents in three swallows. As he passed it back to her, his pale eyes skimmed over her in the dark green sark. She had left off the shawl she often pinned at her left shoulder, allowing the low, square neck to go uncovered.

"Green becomes you, Skena." Fires of passion flashed in his smoldering gaze, as he reached out and took hold of her braid. Slowly, he unwound the plait and pulled the white ribbon from the thick mass. "I prefer it free."

Skena, dizzy and lost to the lure of the silvery depths with the ring of brilliant amber, had to force herself to remember Guillaume Challon watched them. Shrugging, she was now embarrassed she had fussed with her appearance in the hopes of pleasing him. "I merely wanted it out of the way while we worked."

De Servian's eyebrows lifted as he dangled the ribbon, silently saying he failed to believe her. His expression softened. Most grey eyes seemed cold, emotionless. Not this man's. Such concern flickered within their depths. It was hard to hold tight to her anger when she looked at him. Instead, she could only hear the words as he spoke about his mother's death, see the lingering vision of the battle where he had nearly lost his life.

"Skena, I regret you heard the tides of my being given

Craigendan from Guillaume instead of me," he offered his sincere apology.

Skena felt as if she took a blow to her middle, reminded of what was at stake here. "Oh aye, but then you never had the chance to tell me did you?" Three days and three nights and the bloody man had not seen fit to inform her that he was the new lord here.

"I bear the guilt. Only, I hoped you would come to know me before I had to tell you of the change," he explained softly.

Her hands trembled, so she hid them behind her hips. "Why? So we could become friends?" she countered.

Noel slid off the bed, taking the cover with him. He wrapped it around his waist, and then stepped to her. "Friends?"

His smile reflecting a jumble of emotions, he reached out and touched the backs of two fingers against her neck where her blood pulsed the strongest. He dragged them agonizingly downward, across her shoulder to the edge of the kirtle's top, and then along the drawstring, setting off ripples of goose-flesh across her skin.

Flames of desire roared through her. Everything about her receded to shadows as she could only see Noel. Anxious, she spared a quick glance toward Guillaume, to see what he made of de Servian's attention toward her, yet she could barely pay heed to the other man.

"We can be friends, Skena. I would like to hope for such. In time, mayhap more." He tilted his head in question. De Servian finally dropped his hand as the door opened.

Owen and Kenneth pushed through dragging a long bench, exactly like the one before the fireplace, followed by Galen. He glowered at the two Englishmen, but then looked to her. "Where do you want this thing, Skena?" The tone in his voice clearly bespoke he took orders from his lady, not these inter-lopers.

Guillaume ignored that and instructed, "Set it against the other bench so they make a long table."

Galen's mouth set as he met the Lord Challon's eyes, man-to-man, not as a servant to a nobleman. Finally, he turned back to Skena, making evident to all he obeyed no one but her. Skena gave him a brief nod, telling him to do as the Norman lord wanted.

After the benches were pushed together, she set about putting down two covers to make it more comfortable for de Servian. This would be a long process, and she wanted him as tranquil as possible. When she finished, she shooed the lads to the kitchen to fetch hot water. Galen wanted to stay and glower at the Englishman, but she sent him off as well. Ignoring the old man's set mouth, Skena set tallow cups about to give them more light to work by.

Stepping past her, Guillaume sat before the fire on a footstool, and began to sharpen a long thin blade. Skena watched him for an instant, revulsion spreading through the pit of her stomach, aware that blade would be cutting into de Servian.

Noel paused before lying facedown on the makeshift table, and said, "Wipe that fool's grin off your face, Guillaume, before I do it for you. Methinks you are too eager to prod me with that pig sticker."

"Another day's passing would see you begging me to split that wound open with a dull, rusty knife. 'Tis ugly, getting darker with streaks fanning out from it."

"Close your eyes and rest for now," Skena suggested, wanting to see him as comfortable as possible before they started the ordeal. "The potion will soon make you drowsy."

Pulling down the *plaide* to expose the tender site, she grimaced as she saw it was indeed much darker, the yellow-white pus center more pronounced. Skena swallowed back bile as she picked up the mawseed salve and began covering his lower back. He flinched when she neared the old wound, her fingers tracing the spidery marks radiating outward from it. Sir Guillaume was right. It had to be done now. There was no time to delay. The 'bloody fingers' reaching out from the wound site was the poison already migrating into his blood. It would soon kill him if not treated.

Trying to keep her mind focused on her task and not the feel of his hard muscles, how stroking him caused her whole body to knot in hunger, she spoke. "I know it will distress you as I cover the sensitive area, but this deadens the pain. It will help some when we place the hot pads over it."

Noel gave her a short nod. "Let us be done with the gouging. I have been in bed too many days. There is much that needs handling."

Guillaume observed as Skena placed the prepared poultices in a large bowl. She saw doubts about her abilities in the bracketed corners of his mouth. "Have you done anything like this before?" he voiced his concerns.

Skena shook her head. "We have not seen any major injury since our healer died. Even so, I assure you I am able to do what must be done." She met his level stare. "I am stronger than I appear, my lord."

As if girding himself with the inevitability, he exhaled. It was clear he was not satisfied with her answer, yet was aware he had no choice. He lifted the bucket and poured steamy water into the bowl for her. "Ordinarily, it would take a half score men to hold down de Servian, and they would come away worse for wear, broken noses, bumps to their noggins, mayhap a cracked rib or two. While men enjoy a good fight, I cannot risk my friend wiggling about. If he remains still this will go quickly and can be handled without peril to him. Drugging him would be one way, but that can be unsafe. A pinch too much . . ." He shrugged.

"We could tie him down, my lord," Skena suggested.

"Aye, but he could still flinch. A jerk while under the knife puts him in hazard. Another way is to prick a man's pride. Ten men to hold Noel down." Guillaume smiled, as he placed her pallet on the floor at the end of the bench. "Or one woman."

"Beg pardon, my lord?" Skena stared in confusion.

"A trick we witnessed in the Middle East when we served King Edward. A man's pride will see him accept great pain before he reveals weakness in front of a woman." Guillaume took his sharpened knife and stuck the blade into the fire. "So call the old woman or that dour man to pass me things as I need them. Your task will be to sit on the pallet and aid him in keeping still."

"I will call Jenna. The course of treatment will take a long time. First, bringing the corruption to the surface, then lancing and drawing the remainder of the poison out, before sealing it again. It will go easier on her young legs." Going to the door she found Galen there sitting in a chair. She frowned at him, and then asked him to fetch her maidservant.

"Very well, we start." Guillaume took her arm as she returned, and led her to the pallet. "Sit there on the pillow, Lady Skena, facing Noel." Taking Noel's right hand, he placed it about her lower arm, and then did the same with his other hand and arm. "Do not fear he will hurt you. Our Noel is an arrogant man and will want you to see how brave he is."

"Someday, Guillaume, I shall return this favor." Noel chuckled, but then his expression turned serious as he looked to her. "Please, do not be scared. I would never bring harm to you, Skena."

Jenna came in as Guillaume placed a hot poultice to Noel's side. Instant agony racked de Servian, but Skena saw him fighting against the mind-searing pain. Skena knew the longer the padding remained on him, the more intense his suffering would be. She felt the muscles of his whole body tense, yet his grip on her arms did not grow tighter. It was as Guillaume claimed: Noel held perfectly still, ever mindful of his grasp on her arms. Sweat beaded across his forehead from the intense strain.

"Would you disapprove if I made one of those wishes you dismiss so blithely?" Noel nearly forced the words out.

"'Tis your breath, but wishes are worth naught. If wishes

were carrots, rabbits would have a full belly this night." Skena tried to match his bravery, but tears welled in her eyes. "But then, mayhap we would have plenty of meat for hare stew."

Noel gave her a faint smile. "You still set no store in wishes, Skena? Is there aught I can say to change your mind? I once thought as you do, but life came full circle and I now have hope."

"Wishing never brought me a single thing in my whole life. Not once did it lighten my burden, bring me a chest full of gold, nor fill an empty larder. People spend too much time wishing for what they cannot have," she countered.

"What robbed you of the power to believe?" he asked, searching her face for the answer.

I was forced to marry a man I did not love, and wishing changed naught. But Skena kept those words locked inside her. Unable to meet his soul-stealing eyes, she lowered her lashes.

"Your children believe. They told me they wished for a knight protector to come and care for you and them."

"The children merely chanced upon you in the snow. You were already coming to claim Craigendan. Just happenstance." Her shoulders lifted in a faint shrug. She did not want to admit his words reached her.

"So determined to doubt magic in all forms? 'Tis truth, I was headed to Glenrogha first. I wanted to see Julian, pay my respects to his new bride, see how married life suited them. I met her last August, envied the way she looked at Challon. Instead of reaching Glenrogha, Brishen was spooked by a huge flock of ravens and sent by sheer luck—or fate—on the road to Craigendan. I was knocked from my horse by a low-hanging limb, and lay there, finally becoming covered with snow. I wished for someone to find me before it was too late. Your children came. They were out on a stormy night chasing after an old crone—I believe they called her the Cail-leach, the lady of winter. Had they not found me I would have died. Either the snow or the wolves . . ." He left that thought dangling in the air between them. Lifting her right hand to his face, he rubbed it against his cheek. "So you place little faith in wishes? What about Christmas wishes? 'Tis believed that miracles come at this time of year. That when one opens his or her heart anything is possible."

Guillaume removed one poultice and replaced it with another. Each time the pain would be worse for Noel. Skena felt her throat tighten, her vision blurring with unshed tears. Torn, she fought the passion he provoked within her and a sense of duty to her people and Craigendan.

As another poultice was placed on his back, his whole body vibrated with a torture beyond enduring.

"Open your heart, Skena. Let me in. Walk in my mind . . ." Noel whispered through his pain, "become one with me."

Chapter Fourteen

Become one with him.

Skena could not draw air as she stared into de Servian's silver eyes. The rare inner ring of amber fixed in her mind and lured her into their mysterious depths, invited her to let loose the kenning and become a part of him. To embrace his soul. She knew the risk of allowing herself to freely touch him on this darker plane; the enormity of this sort of bond was terrifying. Their souls would weave together in a way that even the joining of the flesh could never attain. She would give away a piece of herself, forevermore leave her heart unshielded to this man who was barely more than a stranger. There would be no severing this tie. Not even death could stop its sway. With nary a protection against him, she would hand de Servian the power to destroy her.

As Skena stared into Noel's face, she felt the link already forming of its own accord, as if she had no free will to resist his entreating. With little thought to the possible dire consequences, she opened her mind and her heart to this special man.

Instantly, her mind flooded with images—*his images*—of Noel laughing and training with four men very much alike, of his beautiful mother. Deep sadness seized Skena as she stood in his place, watched with his child's eyes as they carried his lady mother's cold, lifeless body into the castle. So many shards of de Servian's past were there in flashes before her. Banquets in a king's hall, sly looks of desire from various women, the ugliness of the battlefield; the jumbled patchwork of memories rolled through her senses so rapidly that she was dizzy from striving to focus upon each, to understand their meaning to him. In the end she gave up trying and simply allowed the scenarios to explode within her aching head.

So much. Too much.

Everything swirled around her, buffeted her, until she was tossed upon a stormy sea of blackness. She floated, carried along in that velvet, almost soothing quiet within the embrace of the cool green darkness of Annwyn. As she began to relax a wall of fire exploded about her, then a scream tore through her mind. Noel. Summoning the dark words, she whispered a charm to take his pain, turn it. She sought his presence, reached out and wrapped her arms about his strong warrior's body and held on with every fiber of her being. The flames hungrily lapped at them, crawling up their bodies.

"Noel." His name fell from her lips

He was her anchor. She would be his. Skena closed her eyes and leaned her head against the curve of his neck, inhaling the wonderful scent that was de Servian. The *right* scent.

Chaos spun them about. With vertiginous force, Skena was yanked away from his protective arms and tossed back into the impenetrable darkness. As she opened her eyes the aroma of a balefire filled her nostrils. For a long moment she panicked, unable to see, then gradually she grew aware her eyes were clouded with tears. She blinked to clear her vision, setting droplets to stream down her cheeks. Slowly, forms assumed shapes and colors.

Drawn onward by the flickering yellow glow, Skena forced her way through tall ferns. She started to push free of the lush woods, but hesitated before stepping fully into the clearing. A huge bonfire shot sparks high, spiraling into the night air, while men and women joyfully danced in wheels around the huge blaze, singing and moving to the rhythmic strains of the lute, pipes, and bodhrán. Confused, Skena stood watching. It seemed to be a Beltane celebration. People whirled around her, past her, almost as if they did not see her. With the smoke from the fire wafting about her, she began to wonder if she was naught but a wraith, merely summoned here to observe this festival of May.

A feral war cry filled the clearing; at the same instant flames of the balefire were split by a man leaping through the fire. He landed before Skena with the grace and power of a catamount, lean, sensual, and all sinewy muscle. A mythical beast come to life, the creature, half-man half-stag, stood before her—the man-stag symbol of life reborn from the fire.

His bare chest glistened with sweat. He was clad in doeskin breeches; they molded to his legs by the lacing of leather thongs up to his mid-thigh. He wore nothing else, though upon his head sat a mask with the antlers of a large buck. Although his face was completely covered by the antlered mask, she recognized him by the thin scar on his upper arm, one she had seen on de Servian that first night when she fought for his life. For several moments he stood perfectly still, causing her to wonder if he, too, failed to see her.

Then with a magician's turn, he held out his hand for her to come to him. Skena vacillated for an instant, still assailed, bewildered by how she was at a May Day celebration, how de Servian could be wearing the mask of the king-god sacrifice. This was an honor that went to a high ranking male within the clan. Never to an Englishman, an outsider. She stared at his upturned hand beckoning to her and then at the bizarre mask with tall antlers.

Nothing made sense, thus she feared trusting the vision before her. She grew anxious that her mind was merely playing tricks, offering her what she so desperately wanted; she feared this man was not really de Servian. Trepidation died as she looked up into the eyes of liquid silver. No one had eyes like his. Once their stares locked there was no resisting the summons of his outstretched hand.

Something about this man drew her, made her want to believe that Christmas wishes could come true.

Noel lifted off the mask, and for an instant stared at the thing gripped in his hand, as if not understanding why he held the bizarre headdress. Allowing it to drop to the ground, he offered her a faint smile. "Skena," he whispered, half welcoming, half in puzzlement.

She placed her fingertips to his lips, stopping the questions. Her intent had been to silence the endless riddles with no answers, yet as her eyes narrowed on her fingers touching his sensual mouth, envy flared in the pit of her belly. An endless, gnawing hunger unfurled within her, and for once in her life, instead of standing by holding unfulfilled hopes in her heart, she acted, raising up on her toes as her hand fell away.

Noel's eyes widened as he grasped her intent. His hands clasped her upper arms, squeezing as if he needed to make certain she was real. Urgency seizing him, he yanked her up and against his chest, his mouth meeting hers with the same burning need. He was not gentle. The kiss was as wild and as pagan as the music that flowed through the night air. This was elemental, primitive.

Skena held nothing back, nor was she terrified by the unchecked feral nature in the way his mouth devoured hers. De Servian was not wooing. He was claiming. His lips were bruising, but she accepted it. Wanted it.

She little cared they stood in the midst of the revelers. Her hands reached out and clung to his waist, fearing her legs too weak to support her. Not close enough, she let her arms slide around him, pressing her body against his, greedily caressing the strong muscular columns of his back.

Finally breaking the kiss, he gasped, "Come with me. . . . Be one with me," and took her hand in his.

Skena's feet felt rooted to the moist soil. This time the appeal to be one with him held a different meaning. As this bond of their minds now sealed their fates, weaving their paths together, what he asked would take them to another level, forge them in a union of Annwyn, the Other word. Yet, knowing the enormity of this step, she could no more resist what he wanted of her than she could cease breathing. For better or worse, Noel de Servian now led her on the shadowy path to the future.

With sure steps he drew her away from the crowd; the haunting notes of the music seemed to follow behind them into the lush, warm darkness. A gust of night breeze rose up from the ground, carrying upon its current the sweet sensual fragrance of apple blooms.

"Where do we go?" Skena could not help but voice the question as her feet rushed steps to keep up, blindly following where Noel drew her.

His laughter was musical. "Ah, beautiful Skena, we go to make wishes come true."

That stopped her in her tracks. He gave a small tug. When she held fast, he turned back to her.

Bathed in the pale moonlight, he appeared more dream than flesh and blood. He stared down at her. "Nothing is ever won without risk, my valiant warrior."

Her eyes drank in de Servian, the body of a warrior king, hair a riot of waves and curls framing his handsome face. With his pale eyes, he almost seemed at one with the silvery light of the moon, as if he drew power from it. Once again, she questioned what was real and what was spun from her mind, her dreams. Reaching out she placed the palm of her hand over his heart, wanting the reassurance that it beat. It did, thudding strong, erratic.

His hand covering hers, he caged hers against his chest. "It beats for you." A sly smile spreading over his lips, he reached out with his other hand and placed it between her breasts.

"Feel it? They sound in the same rhythm. As one. Come with me, Skena."

She nodded, perceiving that she had no will to resist. Whatever he wanted she would grant. No conditions. Nothing held in reserve.

Taking her hand in his, he ran. Skena trailed after him, until she had no sense of direction. He could be leading her to hell and she would follow. By the telling scent of apple blossoms, she knew where they were. The ancient orchard at Glen Shane.

Noel stopped, held his arms out, and spun in a circle. White petals of the blooms rained down on him. "Is this not magic?"

"'Tis so heavy it looks like snow." Skena's heart nearly cramped with the painful realization she was falling in love with this wonderful man. What a foolish, foolish thing to do!

He slowly walked back to her, so assured, so arrogant. "Snow? What else could you expect to be conjured by someone named Noel?" He reached out and gently took her neck with both hands, allowing the thumb of one to stroke her jaw. "Are you scared of me, Skena?"

"Yes." Her whisper was so small she was not sure if he heard her.

The corner of his mouth twitched mischievously. "Mayhap a little scared is well and good. Open your heart, Skena, and wish."

He lowered his head, brushing his lips lightly to hers, so soft, almost reverently. The perfection of the moment made Skena close her eyes to savor it, memorize the scents, the sounds, the feel. On cold wintry nights when she was old and gray, she wanted to be able to conjure this instant out of time and savor its rightness, its perfection.

Sliding his hands down to her shoulders, he allowed them to rest there. With the lightness of a fluttering butterfly, Noel kissed one eyelid, then the other. "Open your eyes, Skena. See me."

She did as he invited, no pleaded, looking into the face of

a man who robbed her of the ability to protect herself from the disappointment that could come from loving him. He disarmed her completely. Left her heart vulnerable.

He moved her loose sark aside, allowing it to slither off her shoulders and down her arms. His breath sucked in on a hiss as the material fell from the crest of her breasts. Wordlessly, he moved toward her, backing her to the apple tree. Placing an arm above her head, he leaned to her and took her mouth, roughly, savagely. It was hard to breathe as his hard warrior's body rocked against hers, allowing Skena to catch the rhythm of his thrusts. Her hips curled up against his groin, relishing the friction against her sensitive flesh.

His sword-toughened hands roamed over Skena's shoulders and then down to slowly gather her skirt to her hips; he rubbed one hand along her outer thigh and back up the inside along the more tender flesh. She almost clamped her thighs on his hand as he continued the upward path. She trembled, but held still as the fingers moved over her, then in her, a small invasion preparing her for a larger one. Two long fingers pushed in, then slowly withdrew, causing her breathing to come in gasps, as she allowed him to touch her as no man ever had.

Fumbling with the lacing on the front of his leather chausses, he stepped into the V of her body. Skena slid her arm around his neck, anchoring herself against the coming plunge. Instead, he joined their bodies in a maddening, leisurely fashion, the fullness causing her to give an exhale of unease. He caught it, kissing her over and over until she forgot her faint resistance. As her body re-conformed to accept him inside, he started rocking. Her leverage on his neck allowed her to meet his thrusts, taking him deeper within her narrow channel. He cradled one arm around her hips, arching her higher, while his mouth closed over the side of her neck, drawing until he would mark her.

He had no idea he would mark her soul as well.

"Skena," he gasped. "Make a Beltane wish. . . ."

* * *

"Lady Skena, 'tis done."

Skena blinked confusion as her mind gradually returned. Guillaume had hold of her arm and was removing Noel's hand from about it. Gone was the orchard, the warm spring breeze. Gone was the heady scent of the balefire mixed with the tangy sweet flowers of apple trees. All naught more than a dream brought on by the potion she had ingested to prove to Lord Challon the brew was safe.

And a woman too foolish to resist wishes.

Her gaze jerked about as she tried to come to grips with the shift. She almost wanted to run to the window, toss back the coverings, and look out to assure herself it was a landscape of deepest winter. She stared up into the hazel green eyes of Guillaume and saw his deep questions. Alarm filled her. What happened while he tended Noel? Had she said aught aloud to permit him to know what she experienced in her mind?

"Are you all right, my lady?" he asked softly.

Instead of concern for herself, she looked to Noel. Touching a hand to his forehead she saw he showed no response. "De Servian?" she managed to say.

"He passed out. Do not fret. 'Tis only a combination of the pain and the poppy. He merely rests from the ordeal." He held up a tiny piece of bent metal. "This was left in his back, a partial link of mail carried into his body by the sword. 'Tis strange about flesh. Sometimes it will accept bits of metal, tolerate them for years. I saw one man have a link of mail buried in his thigh from a tournament accident. Stayed there most of his life. Then one day suddenly it festered and had to come out. Well, this is out of him. Noel's wound is made pure and sealed. He will have an ugly scar. But I do not think it will matter much, eh?"

"Hardly a concern." She felt she should be doing something

to care for Noel, but could only brush the curls off his forehead with trembling fingers.

"Julian has spoken of Tamlyn's abilities," he said from behind her.

Skena turned. "Then you have heard of the kenning?"

"Let's say many things have altered in my way of thinking since I came to Glen Shane."

"Have you not seen such in Rowanne?" she asked, finally pulling her hand back from Noel. "She is not as powerful as Aithinne or Tamlyn, but her Ogilvie blood is true. Stronger than mine."

"Stronger than yours? Mayhap." The word contained doubt. Sir Guillaume helped her rise to her feet. "What I witnessed this day shows you are very keen. At least . . . at least where Noel is concerned."

Ducking his pointed remark, she turned the words back to him. "You failed to answer me about Rowanne."

"You are perceptive, lady. Nay, I have not seen this in Rowanne, but then . . ." He shrugged. "Methinks our match will be a good one. I have hopes of this. I am forward looking to wedding in the spring. Julian permitted me to gift her time to adjust to a new marriage, to come to know me. Mayhap I erred in permitting her this time and space. Rowanne is a lady given to shadows. She hides so much from me, closes herself away. My lady guards her secrets closely. Never once have I touched the closeness that you shared with Noel today. I can only hope someday to share the same magic with my lady."

"You are a good man, Guillaume Challon."

"For one bastard born?" There was challenge to his handsome face.

She shrugged. "Scots set little store in such things. I have a bastard half sister, and wish she were half as good as you."

"You took his pain, did you not? I do not understand how, but saw. He never felt the knife or the hot iron because of you," he spoke his amazement.

Skena's head ached, so intensely, she just wanted to crawl off somewhere and rest. "Should we not shift him to the bed?"

"Aye, I was waiting until he rouses."

"Let us see if we can move him whilst he still feels the pull of the potion. I can get him to drink another tansy, and then he should rest through the night." She softly touched his bare shoulder. "Noel, can you awaken? Noel?"

His eyelids lifted, the poppy's effect clear in the unfocused eyes. He gave her a weak smile. "Skena . . . I dreamed—"

Fearful of what he might say, she cut him off. "Can you go to the bed?"

Guillaume aided him to his feet and in walking, while Skena scurried to the table to mix another potion to ease his sleep through the night. Her hands shook as she carefully measured out the concoction and then carried it to him.

Sliding under the cover, Noel leaned on one elbow. Accepting the cup, he sighed in resignation. "One last time. Tomorrow sees the end of mud and stump water. I need to be up and about."

And assuming control of Craigendan. Skena heard the words as clearly as if he had spoken them. Reining in, she forced herself to show no reaction to the statement as he drained the cup. He was the new lord here; it was only natural he would want to quickly set about to stake his possession. There would be no opposing it. This was something she would have to accept. The uncertainty, nonetheless, left her scared where that would leave her and the children.

"Rest. Your body has been through a lot the past few days. Allow it to heal," she managed to say as he handed the empty cup to her.

As if sensing her reticence, he caught her wrist as she went to turn away. "Everything will work out, Skena. Trust me."

Skena did not want to, but her eyes lifted, compelled to meet his. As she stared into the spellbinding depths, she wondered had he shared her visions? If so, did he recall them?

She gave a short meaningless nod, too confused and fearful to say more.

Going to the fireplace, she added a peat to the fire. She paused, the scent of the flame evoking the images of the bale-fire, making the dream suddenly stronger in her mind. Odd, she knew fantasy was naught more than mists shaped from her desires, and yet, images remained as vivid in her memories as if they had really happened. Her body thrummed as she recalled how he had touched her under the apple tree.

Tired, shaken, Skena went to unroll her pallet in the corner near the fire. She only wanted to lie down and try to gather the pieces of herself, repair the devastation that the kenning and Noel de Servian had brought to her heart.

Guillaume, at the bedside checking on Noel, glanced up and frowned. "What are you doing, Lady Skena?"

Skena paused, putting her hands on her hips. "Lord Challon, I am not feeble witted, a serf, or a child. I have lived a score and six years without having Englishmen question my every move."

Instead of taking umbrage at her challenge, he flashed a grin. "Ah, if you Ogilvie women think we men of Challon are vexing, can you not imagine how troublesome we find you ladies? I assume you plan to seek your rest on that pallet like a servant? Noel would not like that you humble yourself so in order to care for him. Surely, there is a small bed that could be brought in for you?"

Skena gave him a tired smile. "You will find Craigendan is a very poor fief, my lord. Your king did no boon in granting it to de Servian."

"Edward never meant it as a boon. Our lord monarch punishes the men of Challon for daring to raise rebuke against permitting the madness that took place at Berwick," he informed her.

Skena's heart nearly stopped. So Noel was being punished along with the other Challon men. A bubble of hysteria rose within her. She tasted oily bile in the pit of her stomach. "Punishment? Does de Servian ken this?"

"He has not spoken such, but I am sure he is aware. He saw Julian and Damian in August at Berwick." Guillaume read her disheartened expression. "Please, do not perceive disappointment that this was the reason for Noel's coming. Julian has never viewed his being sent here as anything but a blessing. We are not young men, my lady. We have long wearied of war and its aftermath. The beauty and remoteness of Glen Shane and Glen Eallach provide a haven for tired dragons to lick their wounds and heal, find something of value worth living for. As to this fortress being poor, Noel was granted funds by Edward to refit it with all it needs. Whatever else might be required, well, Julian is a very wealthy man. Having the Earl Challon for an overlord can see many things to Craigendan's betterment. As soon as Noel is up and about, he will quickly see to the refitting of supplies and men."

The arched eyebrow told Skena that Craigendan's defenses were not fooling this man. Skena was unable to meet his direct, challenging stare, so she turned back to fixing her blankets. Despite his arrogant highhandedness, she was coming to like Guillaume, respect him. Howbeit, for now she would appreciate it if he just went away and left her to her tattered emotions. Holding it all in, pretending there was naught upsetting her was getting a bit beyond her control.

"About the pallet—" Being a hardheaded male, he started in again.

Skena closed her eyes, fighting the scream of frustration begging to escape. "Lord Challon, please, let me have my distance. This has all been very grinding for me, caring for de Servian for days, fighting for his life, treating his old wounds, and then learning he is the new lord here. Worse, 'tis a punishment. Grant me the ability to ken my own head. I regret if I sound short, but I am bone weary and need rest. Let me seek it without being told how."

He nodded. "Very well. It was not my intent to make things more distressing for you. Thank you for the care you have given Noel. By your leave, I shall go seek my bed as well. You are right. This day has been grinding." With that he left the chamber.

Skena picked up the tangled covers and tried to straighten them out, but could not. Too upset, she was barely aware of her actions. Shaking them vigorously, she finally gave up. Overwhelmed by the hopelessness of the situation, she tossed the blankets down to the pallet in defeat and then fell down on her knees. Scooting until her back was in the corner, she half-heartedly dragged the *plaide* to her chest.

Great sobs of anguish welled up inside her, but she could not let them out for fear of attracting de Servian's attention. Instead, she allowed the silent tears to stream down her face.

She whispered aloud, "Oh, what have I done?"

Chapter Fifteen

"Skena," the soft whisper came, reaching through the dark oblivion.

She jerked awake, instantly fearing it was Noel and he was in pain. But as she opened her eyes, she saw Owen leaning over her. Stiff from sleeping curled up in the corner, she stretched out her numb legs and yawned. "What hour is it?"

"A ways to dawning yet. Sorry to break your sleep. The wolves scratch at the gate again. The run is finished as you wanted. Everything is in ready. Do you wish to start the killing of the wolves this night or wait?"

"Never again say the word *wish* to me." Skena stood up, trying to shake the sleep from her body. "If we wait the chances increase they will find a way in when we are unawares. Go waken Galen."

"Aye, I will do as you bid," the lad said and then scurried off.

Skena went to the bed to check on de Servian. He rested partially on his belly and seemed so peaceful. Placing her hand to his back, she smiled when his flesh felt cool to the touch. He was a strong man. He would heal now the poison had been purged from his body.

She was not sure how love could grow so strong so rapidly, when she scarcely knew him, but as she caressed his hair, she

ached with the emotions rising in her. "Oh, what a stupid fool
I am," she whispered, before turning away.

Skena untied the lacings at the side of her kirtle and pulled
it over her head just as Dorcas entered the small room off the
side of the kitchen. She rarely welcomed dealing with Dorcas,
but she particularly lacked enthusiasm for a confrontation
when Muriel's daughter wore that expression. It boded ill.
Since Angus's death, Dorcas was dissatisfied with her lot in
life and spoiling for a fuss; she reveled in vexing Skena at
every turn. Skena paused to exhale resignation. Offering the
woman a cool look of dismissal, she laid her gown neatly on
the bench.

"Off to play little soldier?" Dorcas asked in a snide tone.
She strolled closer, her eyes judging Skena's appearance,
finding fault as always. "You have lost weight, Skena."

Skena did not stand on manners. Dorcas never did. Why
should she? "And you have gained it. *Plump* is the word that
comes to mind."

"You—" Dorcas's brown eyes widened, but then she reined
in her temper. "You grow more haggard with each passing
day. 'Tis hard to believe, Skena, you are only three summers
younger than I."

"Only three? I always assumed you were *much* older. I figured that is why you are getting a second chin, eh?" She
chucked her under the jaw to add to the insult.

Dorcas slapped Skena's arm away from her. The wild look
in her eyes said she was considering slapping Skena's face, too.

"Go ahead, Dorcas. Hitting the lady of the keep is a flogging
offense. Of course, I will not wait for that. Do it, and I will
knock you on your *plump* arse. I am thinner, aye, but it has gone
to muscle, while your weight has gone to fat. So just try it."

Dorcas's eyes narrowed. "You think you are so wise to
curry favor with this English lord."

Skena shrugged, refusing to defend herself. "Lord de Servian is the new baron of Craigendan. You best soften your tone when you speak of him."

Dorcas sucked in her belly trying either to appear thinner or stiffen her spine. "You will be sorry, Skena."

"And how, pray tell? You have no sway here. I do not toss you out into the snow simply because you are Muriel's daughter. The limited protection afforded you as my lord husband's leman is gone. Angus is dead," Skena reminded her bluntly.

"Is he?"

Skena's laugh of disbelief popped out. "What nonsense is this? Angus is dead. I ken you cared for him, grieve for him, but that part of your life is over. I plan on making a marriage for you come spring."

"Marriage?" she gasped. "Angus will not like that. He will be displeased you dared try to wed me away to some swine herder," Dorcas spewed in rage.

"Do not get fanciful. Talking like that people will think you have gone soft in the head because of Angus's death," Skena scoffed.

"I am not daft. Cipher on it, Skena. How did we hear Angus is dead? Word brought back by Duncan Comyn, a coward who—by his own confession—never made it to the battle. No man from Craigendan has returned to say they saw Angus dead. 'Tis naught, but Duncan's worthless word. If a Comyn put forth the night was black, Angus always said he would go check for himself," Dorcas argued. "Why have you not gone and checked for yourself?"

"I could not leave Craigendan, you ken that."

"You did not even send a messenger to make sure, or see if his body could be brought back for burial here." Dorcas moved closer to press the point.

"Who was I to send? Galen? He is too old for the trip. Owen or Kenneth? They are little more than children." Skena went back to pulling on the worn, woolen kirtle and then the short mail habergeon over that.

"Methinks you do not want Angus to come back. Why you little mind if he is dead or alive." Dorcas stepped before Skena, blocking her from reaching for the surcoat.

"He is dead. He would have returned long before now if he were alive."

"Would he? To you?" Dorcas sneered. "A woman who could not care less? Who already has another man in her bed?"

"Dorcas, I am sorry you still grieve for Angus, but do not allow it to rot your mind—"

"Oh aye, I grieve. I was more a wife to him than you e'er were. You were naught but wife in name only."

Skena was tired of this. It was always the same in dealing with Dorcas. She went for the throat to put the matter to end. "True, but name is what matters most, does it not?"

Dorcas flinched, her body vibrating with fury. "Go ahead and waggle how fate has favored you instead of me from birth. But Angus is alive. Mark my words. I'd ken it in my heart if he were dead." She clenched her fist to the center of her chest. "They say William Wallace is hiding out in Selkirk Forest, gathering men to him. You ken how set Angus was to ridding Scotland of the English. I am betting that he and the rest of our men that survived Dunbar went to join Wallace."

"You waste time with wishes, Dorcas. Angus is not coming back. Ever. Learn to make the best of it. When the weather turns, I will seek to make a marriage for you."

"Angus will be furious to find you married me off while he was away. You do not have the right."

"Aye, I have that right and there is little you can do about it," she countered. "I took you into Craigendan when you were in need because Muriel asked it."

"I have as much right to Craigendan as you—" she started with the old argument, only to be cut off.

"I permitted you to interfere in my marriage to Angus,

because that was what he wanted. And whilst I did not love him as mayhap he sought, few marriages of the nobility are made because of love. But respect, honor, trust—those are things people live by. You and he did me a wrong, but I put up with it. No longer. I have had enough of your selfish ways, your constant attempts to undermine my authority here. It ends now. Angus is dead—"

"He is not! You will regret this day when he comes back." Dorcas's voice rose as she issued the threat.

Skena went on as if Dorcas had not spoken. "We must get on with our lives as best we can."

"Get on with our lives? Is that what you are doing? Trying to win the attention of this English lord? What makes you imagine you could please him any better than you did Angus? Think I could not turn his head? Then mayhap you will not be able to arrange a marriage for me because the Lord de Servian will want me here. Why would he want some frigid, skinny woman such as you, when he could have a young wife without bairns hanging to her kirtle's tails? One who would do more than lie in bed like a stick of wood?"

Skena slowly sucked in a breath to prevent Dorcas from seeing her words had hit target. Had she not fretted over the same problem? Only, the concern was magnified now because the bond was in place. To watch as de Servian took a wife, placed her as lady of Craigendan, would be too hard to bear. She would not survive.

Skena tightened the belt around her waist with a hard jerk. "Well, you best start learning about herding swine, lass, because if I am too old for de Servian, you being seven summers older are near hag."

"Seven!" she gasped. "'Tis only three."

Skena shrugged. "Sorry." She picked up the mantle and swung it around her shoulders. "I tend to forget. Mayhap you should wash your face in the morning dew on May Day. 'Tis spake it makes you appear younger." Picking up the quiver with arrows and the bow, she headed for the door.

"Skena, beware. Angus is not dead," Dorcas called to her back.

Skena did not slow, refusing to give her the satisfaction that the words sent a chill up her spine.

Outside, snow crunched under her boots as she made her way to the postern gate. Galen stood holding a torch, waiting with Owen and Kenneth. Sparing them little thought, her eyes skimmed up and down the run they had hastily constructed. Over the height of a man's head, the structure was a scavenged mix of boards and woven tree limbs, yet appeared sturdy, adequate to hold two wolves long enough for her to loose arrows into them. Skena gave the interior a quick inspection, noting the enclosure they created for her to hide in near the door. She could open the gate to let in a couple wolves, then lock herself into the blind. From its protection, she should be able to fell the beasts with ease.

The horses in the stable were fussing, one or two even trying to kick their way out of their stalls, alarmed by the scent of the pack. She glanced up at the bright, full moon overhead. A killing moon. She inhaled a deep breath and held still, attempting to quash the fluttering inside her stomach. Facing the wolves would not be simple. Only, Craigendan was still hers . . . for now. She could do this. It would be a straightforward chore of just letting them in and picking off one at a time. She still needed to know she had some measure of control in her life.

"Let us make done of this." She opened the end of the pen. "You poke at them with the spears. Keep them from jumping over the fencing."

Galen frowned in disapproval. "Skena, mayhap you should go seek help from the Lord Challon."

"This will be over in a thrice. On the morrow they will take Craigendan away from me. This land is mine, my heritage, and 'tis being given away to another without a 'by your leave' from me. I am lady here still. And no Englishmen, no Dorcas, nor a pack of thieving wolves will rob me of it. I may have to give up Craigendan. So be it. But it will be in a time of my choosing and in my own way. Until that breath, I am lady here and this keep runs by my will, my command."

Galen gave her a crooked smile. "Brave talk, Skena lass. 'Tis that damn Ogilvie blood in you."

"Let us see end to this." She lifted her chin to reinforce her order.

The old man gave her a nod. "Aye, my lady."

As she entered the pen, she pulled up abruptly. From the outside it appeared larger, mayhap even too big for her purposes. Inside it seemed a lot smaller. She choked back the sudden rise of panic, feeling the crude walls close in on her. Facing the wolf in the open with a sword had been one thing. Bringing down two with a bow and arrow in a pen where she stood behind protection was an entirely different matter, a simple matter. So she told herself. Reaching for that confidence, she strode the length of the run going to the postern door.

As Skena neared the end, she saw that Galen had already removed all the swords but one. The door rocked from at least two wolves digging on either side of the remaining broadsword. The blade vibrated from the force of the wolves' constant pressure. She considered if she could not just stand and watch until they finished digging their way under and then drive a sword into them when they pushed through. But that would leave her out in the open. Conceivably both could shove under at the same time, and she would have to deal with two half-starved animals. Memories of the wolf's teeth snapping at her throat, the scent of his blood, flashed to mind. So real, she could almost taste the coppery scent.

Forcing back the recollection, she set the quiver of arrows and the short bow inside the trap, and then went to remove the sword. Taking hold of the hilt she rocked it back and forth in the frozen ground until it loosened. The wolves jerked back, but the yipping not far away said they were still near the curtain wall. Their hunger was driving them to be bold. A quick release, which nearly sent her tumbling backward, saw the blade pull free. She leaned it inside the trap next to the quiver, ready should she need it.

All she had to do was unbolt the postern gate, swing it open, and allow two wolves in. Once they were inside she could slam it shut, then step into the blind and close the crude door over it. There were two slots through which she could aim the arrows.

"Simple as mincemeat tarts." Taking a deep, steadying breath, she yanked the heavy bolt back.

Just as it was all the way to the side, her eye was distracted by someone standing at the top of the stairs to the boulevard. Though moonlight was to their back, it was clearly a man, not one of her women pretending to be a soldier. As she stared, almost held in thrall, a chill shuddered up her spine. Little paying attention to the postern door being hammered by the wolves, she stilled and her heart stopped. He started down the stairs, then paused as he stepped into a silvery shaft of light, just enough to cast his face in half shadow.

The world about Skena spun.

Angus.

Chapter Sixteen

Noel jerked awake when his shoulder was prodded. Struggling to focus, he finally saw Guillaume stood at bedside. Giving him a grumpy frown, he labored to sit up, moving his stiff, aching body. He glanced around, looking for Skena. Flashes of dreams lingered, so intense they worked to suck him back into their velvet embrace. Truth be told, he wanted to escape to their seductive lure, return to the happiness and perfection he found there. As he worked to hold on to the shards, to remember their importance, this world was already intruding, vanquishing them. Forced to return to this cold reality, his heart felt hollow.

"Sorry to waken you so early, especially after what you went through, but figured you would want to know something odd is happening," Guillaume said, watching Noel as he rose from the bed and went to the pitcher on the far side of the room.

Noel poured water into the large bowl and splashed some onto his face. "What is so urgent you awaken me before dawnbreak? Is it not enough you tortured me yestereve?"

"You are lucky I 'tortured' you. Likely, you would find trouble awakening this morn had I not put the knife to you." Guillaume studied him closely, judging his condition. "How do you feel? You look none worse for the wear, considering what you have been through."

"How do I feel? Tired. 'Tis been a rough few days. Damn coughing bruised my ribs, methinks." He rubbed his side, flinched when the wound instantly set to throbbing. "The searing naturally burns, but 'tis small compared to the pain I have suffered through for the past sennights. Happily, I seem on the mend. Thanks to Skena and you." Noel flexed his right hand and for the first time in two months failed to experience even a trace of the numbness that had so troubled him. "In June the sensitivity began. I would get a tingling in my thumb if I moved too sudden. Then it grew to be the whole hand. Each time it was worse. Each time it lingered, taking longer to go away. This past fortnight, at times I had a hard time gripping my sword. All the feeling of deadness is gone. A burn I can handle. I know that will pass. I was truly concerned I might lose use of the hand for good."

"No, you would have lost your life. The poison was already spreading from the wound site. We would have come in one morn and not been able to awaken you. I have seen it happen before. I have grown accustomed to your pretty face and would hate to lose it over this. . . ." He held up the half link of broken mail. "A memento to remember the former baron by."

Noel took the twisted piece of black metal from Guillaume's fingers and held it to the candlelight to study. "Odd what a bit of nothing can do to the body. That would have killed me. Most surprisingly, outside the first few poultices I felt no pain. Mayhap it was too much for my mind and it shuttered in some manner."

Noel puzzled over the matter. The hot poultices had been distressful, and the agony intensified with each new one, pain building upon pain. He simply could not recall much after that. Just Skena . . . and the strange dream, which now faded into mist. In this other realm, he recalled staring at her; the longer they remained unblinking in that match of wills, the more cat-like her eyes became. His body bucked as a fragment of that vision bubbled up in his thoughts, suddenly so clear, of his making love to Skena. After endless weeks of reliving the horrors of Berwick each night, that had been a most agreeable way to pass the dark hours of sleep. It pushed him to want to claim Skena so he could spend the coming nights discovering the pleasures of her flesh, not just dreaming about her.

"Mayhap . . ." Guillaume allowed his thought to trail off, the vivid hazel-green eyes watching for Noel's response to what he was about to say.

"Speak your piece." Noel soaked a rag in the bowl and then placed the cold cloth to the back of his neck to speed the wakening. "I have never known you to be reticent in saying what bites at your mind."

"Very well. Mayhap you felt so little pain because Skena took it for you," his friend suggested, caution touching his voice.

Noel snorted a scoff. "What silliness? No one can take pain for another."

"I mentioned this to you before, and Damian has spoken of it time and again. I have come to the belief that these Ogilvie women are able to do things you and I would first dismiss. For the better part of a year I have watched them. The experience tends to open my thoughts to accepting they have gifts beyond most mortals." Guillaume shrugged. "The Highlands are a queer, moody place, Noel. Once you are here for a length, you forget about the world outside of these glens. 'Tis a spot unto itself, far from the boundaries and perceptions of what we have kenned before."

"Kenned? You begin to sound Scot?" Noel pointed out.

Guillaume turned his palm up. "What can I say? I find I am starting to feel Scot. Feel we belong here. Oh, we must still make token obeisance to Edward to retain what we were given here. But this land, the people . . . the women get under your skin. They have changed me in the few months I have been here. A change I embrace. 'Tis my sincere desire that Edward bends his mind to the campaign against France, sails there, and leaves the men of Challon alone and forgotten in this valley. Permit us to enjoy this peace we finally discover within these glens. Peace that we deserve . . . we earned."

"Peace? Were not Julian and Damian attacked by Scots on the way back from Parliament?"

"Oh, aye. Only Scots—Grant Drummond and Duncan MacThomas—came to their aid. The people in Glen Shane and Glen Eallach accept Julian and Damian. I find them accepting me at Lochshane. Methinks that approval stems from the people knowing their ladies effect change in our hearts." Guillaume gave him a knowing grin. "Tell me you have not already started to feel it. You know Lady Skena but days, and yet already you are in love with her. That same immediate power was there between Julian and Tamlyn, but she is a hellcat. She had to hiss and spit until Julian soothed her. I wish . . ."

"Wish?" A shiver rippled up his spine as a fragment of his dream spiked through his blood. *Make a Beltane wish.* Tossing the cloth into the bowl, Noel dismissed the fey bit of nonsense. He moved to his clothing folded upon the bench and began to dress. "Skena insists we waste time upon wishes."

"And what think you? Has not your deepest yearning been answered in Craigendan? A home of your own, a family . . . if you so choose? Deny you are in love with the lady."

"I am not sure of this thing love, a word balladeers sing of so profusely. An elusive creature, at best. Nonetheless, I do feel a bond, a sense of purpose in coming to Craigendan. Fate. Skena is everything I could want in a lady wife, and taking her as such would see me assuming the title of baron on a more level path. As you say, the people shall accept me easier if their lady approves of me. Only . . . there is more," Noel ended with a shrug, unable to express how deeply his bond with Skena grew already, how time had little to do with its strength. The specter of fear arose in his mind, concern that this newfound link between them could be shattered like fragile glass if she learnt Angus Fadden had died by his hand.

"I envy that bond. 'Tis the same with Julian and Tamlyn, and now Damian and Aithinne," Guillaume said wistfully. "Did Damian tell you how he and the Lady Aithinne first met?"

"We did not have much time to speak at Berwick. Hard to find a moment of privacy when all of Scotland was crammed into the castle. Julian and Damian both kept a distance from the women whilst they were in the presence of others. Only someone who knew them well would have been aware they cared for their ladies deeply."

"They kept wise council. Same as you should remember if you ever come with Lady Skena before Edward. Never allow Edward to see she is valued by you. She then becomes a tool to use against you. You must ask Damian about his 'courtship' when you next see him." Guillaume's eyes twinkled with mischief. "You can also ask him about dreams and wishes. You might find it enlightening."

"Now that I am awake and my head clear, what is so urgent you broke my sleep?"

"I failed to find my rest so decided to tour of your holding, assess what you need to see it secure here. I walked up to the top of the donjon and happened to catch sight of your lady heading toward the stables. They have built some sort of a pen near the postern gate. She and the old man are down there. The horses are raising a racket, trying to kick down the barn."

Noel had no time to question him further, as the door burst open and the old woman called Muriel rushed in. Her eyes widened as she saw them both. She did a small dip of deference and then gasped, "Oh, thank our Lady! You are up. You needs must come! Quick! 'Tis Skena . . . that cork-brain *òinnseach*—"

"*Òinnseach?*" Noel questioned, reaching for his shirt.

Guillaume chuckled. "A female fool. You hear it spoken about Ogilvie women now and again."

"What is wrong with Skena?" Noel's heart rocked with urgency as he searched around for his baldric and found it hanging from a loop in the corner.

"Wolves . . ." the woman gasped. "The silly female is trying to deal with wolves digging to get in. Fool, she thinks she has to do everything herself. The only help she has is that daft old man and two boys. I have a bad feeling about this. You must hurry."

Noel started to ask where, but then remembered. Looking at Guillaume, he said, "To the stables."

"Angus?" His name fell from her lips in a whispered gasp.

Skena's mind snapped back as the wolves crashed against the postern door, which in turn knocked into her, throwing her off balance. With the door all the way back, she was trapped against it and the opening for the blind. She shoved, trying to slide into protective cover, only the wolves jumped against the door's plane, again and again, slamming her head to the stone wall. The last time was so hard that pain lanced through her mind. Reaching up, she felt moisture. When she drew her hand back, blood covered her fingers. It appeared black in the moonlight. *Just like that dead wolf's had in the snow.* Biting back the sense it was an ill omen, she grew aware of voices yelling, but with the wolves snarling and yapping she could not hear what they were shouting.

"Simple, eh?" Skena fought the dizziness brought on by her head hitting the stones. Looking at her trembling hand with the blood smeared on her fingers, she forced herself to take slow breaths to regain control. "I refuse to panic. First, get the door back enough for me to get inside the trap, and then I will continue with my plan. . . . Just kill a few more wolves than I bargained on. More meat for Cook's pot."

Galen and the lads were calling, but she was unsure if that was to lure the wolves away from her, or if they endeavored to drive them out of the pen entirely. One animal screamed, mayhap from catching the end of one of the spears. The growling and barking only increased tenfold after that. Still, it saw an ease of resistance against the metal door.

By pushing with all her might, she was able to rock the door enough for her to see out. The scene petrified her. There were at least seven wolves, but she could not be sure, because they were jumping around, fighting, and attacking the spears. Grays, blacks, and one white, but she took no time to count them as she shoved herself through the narrow slot and into the blind.

As she was almost inside the safety of the blind, the white one turned and lunged at her, his massive jaw clapping on her lower arm. She screamed, seeing blood poured down his neck from a spear wound, soaking his thick fur. *Never leave a wounded animal alive . . . sometimes, not even a man. 'Tis when they are most dangerous.*

While the bite hurt, the mail shirt she wore stopped his sharp teeth from penetrating and reaching her skin. The jaws remained locked on to her arm like a vise. She frantically kicked at his hind legs, but the creature snarled deep in his throat and jerked his head from side-to-side savagely, the force nearly causing her to lose her footing in the snow.

In desperation, Skena grasped at the broadsword, but the strong beast began to drag her out into the pen. As a big black wolf ran foward, preparing to launch toward her, she cried out again, knowing she would not be able to fight off two of them. They would drag her down into the snow. As she struggled to reach the sword, realization hit her that she had no room to wield it since she was up against the doorway. Instead, she clutched at the arrows, finally coming up with two. Jabbing upward, she caught the second wolf in the throat at the last instant, not a deep enough wound to kill, but sufficient to slow his attack. It shrieked and howled, causing another one milling about to turn on him.

A sword descended, slicing downward on the wolf with the arrows protruding from his neck and then the other one fighting with his packmate. *De Servian.* His booted foot slammed into the ribcage of the one hanging on to her arm, causing it finally to release its hold.

Noel grabbed her upper arm and flung her into the blind. "Stay there!" Then he slammed the door shut and turned his attention back to the wolves.

Guillaume tossed Noel a spear, and they began to force the pack to the outer door. Some of the beasts ran, escaping into the predawn darkness. Wounded ones continued to fight. Slowly, the two men backed the animals up enough for Skena to push out behind them. Notching an arrow in the small bow, Skena followed them, careful to nudge the dead wolves on the ground to make certain they had no life in them still.

Half the pack or better was running away, but at least seven were down or dead. One reared up and tried to snap at her booted foot as she pushed at him. She did not hesitate to loose an arrow into his chest.

Noel prodded at one wolf's snout, driving him out the door. Since the crazed animal was attacking and refused to stop, he could not lower the spear long enough to close the door. He tried once, only to have the animal charge again. Noel was forced to follow the vicious animal. With a strong thrust, he caught the furious beast in the front of its chest and used all his strength to force the animal completely out of the gate.

The creature's boldness saw two others flanking him move forward, hoping to drag the man down with the pact's tactics: one would go for one arm, the second the other, leaving the third wolf to lunge for Noel's throat. Guillaume, seeing what the wolves were doing, pursued Noel, quickly killing the small grey on the right by hurling the spear. Only the pike embedded deep in the animal, and Guillaume was having a hard time pulling it out. He had to put his heel to the wolf's body to remove it.

While the pikes had been ideal for fighting within the pen, outside the spears were cumbersome compared to wielding a sword. Skena screamed as a wolf launched itself from the shadows at Noel's back. Not hesitating, she loosed an arrow which flew into his neck, and then another into its chest as it hit the ground.

Noel brought down the black wolf, which finally sent the other fleeing. Both men looked around them to be sure no lurking beasts lingered. At last, lowering their spears, they turned to each other.

"Well, what shall we do for the rest of the morn?" Guillaume laughed. "Let us get within the wall before they grow bolder, drawn by the scent of the blood." He kicked at the small one he had killed last. "This one is hardly more than skin and bones. The bigger ones seem to have fared better. We need to get someone to come pile them up and then burn them."

"Nay, we must drag them inside." When both men stared at her, Skena slung her bow over her shoulder. She rushed to one of the wolves, grabbed his tail, and began dragging him through the snow.

Noel grabbed her arm. "I told you to stay in the blind."

"If I had stayed in the blind, the wolf would have jumped you from behind, my lord," she countered.

"You will learn when I give an order I expect it to be obeyed, my lady." His gaze narrowing on her in anger, he started to pull her toward the entrance.

Guillaume put an arm out to gently restrain him. "Sage advice—which shall serve you well, my friend—never deal with a female when your blood runs hot."

"I am not going to deal with her—I am going to bloody well beat her," Noel threatened.

Skena backed up several steps, crashing into the stone wall. Angus had never beaten her. She knew some men beat their wives; few had ever tried in Clan Ogilvie and not felt the strong hand of retribution. She kenned naught of the ways of these Norman-English. Mayhap they felt they had the right to do such to a woman. It brought clear just how little she knew Noel de Servian, despite this growing bond they shared.

Guillaume shook his head and muttered, "Knave. I warned you to wait for a cooler head."

Noel dropped the pike and moved toward her. "Ah, Skena, lass, I would never lift a hand to you." His hand reached out and stroked her hair. Trembling, she did not trust her voice to answer with strength, so she looked away from his handsome face. His bent finger lifted her chin, forcing her to look at him. "Tell me you do not tremble because you fear me."

Guillaume picked up his sword where he had left it just inside the pen while he used the spear. He nudged Noel's arm with the pommel. "Let us drag *her* wolves inside and then return to the *dun*. She is shaking from the cold and the excitement. You need to get her warm. I need to get *me* warm."

Skena, still traumatized, was in no mood to deal with arrogant males. Ignoring them, she looked to Galen who had rushed in when he saw her backing up from de Servian. "Have the bodies dragged to the tanner. He will deal with them. Tell Cook to go there. Secure the gate with the swords as we did before so they will not try to get in again," she told the elderly man.

"Skena, as soon as we are done here we needs must talk." Noel stared at her.

So the new lord of Craigendan assumes command of her fortress. She nodded in resignation. "Aye, my lord."

Chapter Seventeen

"Meat?" De Servian echoed as he slammed the door to the lord's chamber. Rounding on Skena, he glared at her. "You were serious. Of all the stupid, half-wit—no, *quarter-wit*—notions! I still have a mind to turn you over my knee." He waggled his finger before her face.

Skena glared back at the fuming man despite his formidable presence. Tall men always held an advantage when they wanted to appear menacing, and de Servian was calling upon every measure of his fierce warrior mien. Still, his words instilled less alarm now he had vowed that he would never raise a hand to her in anger. She believed him. In spite of knowing him only a few days, she sensed honor in this man. Her inner voice spake she could trust Noel de Servian; he was a man of his word. Right now, regardless of the flashing eyes and set jaw, she little feared him. Oh, the man clearly had a temper.

Well, after all these years she was discovering she had one as well. Putting her fisted hands on her hips, she said, "You would not dare."

"Watch me." Noel reached out to grab her arm, only to have her duck away from him, putting first a tall stool and then the table between them.

"Actually, my plan was well thought out and would have worked," Skena defended her actions. "Except . . ."

Noel rounded the table's corner, closing in on her. "Except what?"

Skena hesitated to say she had been distracted by Angus, standing on the landing of the boulevard. Though she knew what she had seen, she still had trouble accepting it. De Servian would naturally assume her feeble-minded, or as she accused Dorcas, allowed her grief to make her hope for things that would never be.

Not that she was grieving, which tweaked her conscience. Despite all the trials, tribulations, and sheer panic this year had brought her, there was a sense of freedom from the stifling marriage and the humiliating situation foisted upon her by Angus and Dorcas. For the short span of these past months, no matter how dire things grew, she had been master of her destiny. She made decisions instead of waiting for Angus to rule how matters would be. The faint spark of her young girl's dreams had continued to live in her heart, despite Angus's spirit-crushing notions of marriage, which relegated her to little more than a servant or brood mare. That small hope had fanned to life with her thinking there might be a future with Noel on the horizon. This handsome man with the bespelling eyes provoked her to almost believe wishes could come true.

Angus's return would shatter all. She would be pushed back into a loveless marriage, a union where her only value had been the land she brought him and the son she bore. A marriage where he arrogantly thought he had the right to keep another woman as a lover, regardless of the humiliation it heaped upon her. Before, she had existed in a situation that sapped the life out of her, shredded her self-respect, and nearly killed all her dreams. Now it would destroy her.

"I planned to open the door and quickly step into the trap. . . . Something distracted me. My fault. I should have kept my mind on what was happening," she admitted, skirting around the other side of the table, about three steps ahead of the bedeviling man.

"Something?" Noel kept stalking her. "Pray, what was important enough to pull you away from protecting your life? Those wolves could have killed you, Skena. And for wolf meat? Is this some odd Scottish custom like your haggis?"

"Nay. . . . 'Tis desperation, Lord de Servian." She tossed up her hands, fighting the helplessness rising in her. "'Tis doing what I must to survive, to see my people survive. I fear your king did you nary a boon giving you Craigendan."

"Edward Plantagenet oft fails to see the worth in things. I am not so foolish as to repeat his mistake. Craigendan is my wish fulfilled, Skena." He stopped before her, his eyes meeting hers with a plea for understanding. The unhealed pain of a scared little boy flickered in the shimmering silver depths.

Emotion clogged her throat as she understood what he was telling her. Edward Longshanks had given him the chance to have something he had lacked his whole life. Skena hurt all the more. Noel de Servian craved a family, a home to replace what he once lost. Instead of a place worthy of this man, he was given a rundown fief with dire prospects if they did not receive aid to get them through to spring.

"'Tis you who are blinding yourself. Craigendan has few men. Only elderly, lame, or boys remain," she confessed. She owed him the truth. He would find out soon enough. Better that he be prepared before he assumed the mantle of baron in front of her people.

Noel frowned. "Who has been protecting the keep?"

"Sleight of hand and mummery. My women don the armor of men and patrol the walls. I do not send them out to ride the boundaries as that would be too risky. Most have never been upon a horse anyway." She sighed. "The ruse served us well, else trouble would have already reared its head from Duncan Comyn or Dinsmore Campbell."

"How long—" He paused, understanding hitting him. "Since Dunbar?"

Skena nodded. "Aye. Angus took all the men who could fight, foolishly thinking they would return in a few weeks. Well, they never came back." She sat down on the bench. So tired of the struggle. "Summer saw one of the worst droughts scorch the land, drying up crops. We worked from dawn to dusk trying to save what we could, but the effort was wasted. Quickly, it became a fight to keep the livestock alive. Stores are down. 'Tis why we make use of silverweed and wolf meat to fill out the supplies this past sennight."

"Why did you not go to Challon? He would have supplied soldiers and food."

Skena gave a feeble shrug, feeling imprudent for not having done as he said, ashamed for being selfish. "Fear, I suppose." She looked up at him and attempted to smile at her folly. "I was scared what would happen to me and the children. If I made the situation known to Earl Challon, then he would set his own man here as lord, mayhap force me to marry him."

He sat down on the bench beside her and took her hand. "Well, Skena MacIain, whether you believe in wishes or not, your children do, and they wished for a knight to come care for you. I am that knight. I have long hungered for a home and a family. I believe my wish was answered in my coming here. Allow me to save you from the fate of losing all. I know the taste only too well. Shortly, I need to face your people, tell them that I am the new lord here. Mayhap . . . we should also inform them that on a day of your choosing you and I shall wed. You will not be forced to marry, mind. I ask your consent."

Skena could hardly breathe, his words so filled her heart. De Servian was asking her to wed him? "Marry?"

"Aye. 'Tis sudden, I know. Only our short time together tells me all I need to know I would be most pleased with you as my lady wife. Methinks your children already see me as theirs." He gave a soft laugh. "Cipher upon your response before you tend it. True, we are but strangers. This winter can be spent learning about each other. Come spring, we can start to build a life here."

Despair slammed into her, pushing Skena to jump to her feet and blindly walk to the fireplace. She leaned her head against the stones and silently allowed the tears to come. More than anything in the world she wanted to give Noel de Servian her troth, to look upon the bright promise of the future he offered. Only her mind was tossed back to seeing Angus standing on the stairs, just before the wolves pushed through the postern door.

"Skena, what is it?" Noel came to stand just behind her. He placed his hands on her shoulders, then slid them down to her upper arms. "Did I say aught to upset you? Tell me I am not wrong, that there exists this special bond betwixt us, something very rare. Did I misspeak?"

"Nay, there is bond, rare and pure," she admitted in a pained whisper.

He turned her to face him. "Then you will plight your troth with me? Mayhap on the eve of Christmas? Do you not think it a good omen to marry a man named Noel on that day?"

He pulled her into his arms, those strong arms, holding her against his body. Mayhap, it was too soon to know all about this man, yet Skena sensed this is where she belonged, the only place on earth she wanted to be. She was already falling in love with Noel. Time would only serve to strengthen their connection. Though they were strangers, she had no doubt this man was that part of her heart that had always been missing.

"Skena, trust in wishes. Say yes," he pleaded.

Skena stared into his handsome face, into the gray eyes that sparkled with magic. She would kill for Noel de Servian. She would die for him. But she could not marry him. It was a dagger to her heart.

"You do me an honor in the asking . . . but I cannot wed with you." She was barely able to force the words out.

He stared as if not believing her answer to be true. "Why? You know we would suit. You feel it. I know you do."

"Oh, aye. You are all I could wi—" She started to say wish, but changed it, "want in a husband."

His frown deepened. "Then explain, Skena. I want you for my lady wife. You say I am what you would wish for in a husband. Do not avoid the word. Guillaume says the people of Glen Shane and Glen Eallach already accept them as the lords there. I can win the approval of your people . . . my people . . . our people."

"I have no doubt you will make a good lord for this holding."

Skena's heart broke, as she knew it would be a life without her. She could not marry him. She could not stay here. If she remained she would fall into being his lover. There would be no resisting him. He would have to marry to father a son, an heir. She would be forced to watch him with another woman. Worse, she would be cast into the same spot of shame that Dorcas had filled in her life. She would never do to another woman what had been done to her.

"Unspoken thoughts haunt that statement. You say you cannot wed with me. Then explain." The muscle in right side of his jaw jumped, signaling his refusal to accept her answer.

She closed her eyes, fighting against the burning anguish. When she opened them she gave him the truth. "Angus," was all she managed to get out.

De Servian's head lifted slowly. "Skena, sorry I am for your loss, but life marches on . . . for us all. What has he to do with your answer?"

"Everything. . . . He has *everything* to do with my refusal. I cannot marry with you, Noel de Servian, though it might be my heart's desire, because I am already the wife of another man."

He frowned. "And that man is dead, Skena. Your vows to him ended when he drew his last breath. The practice of the widow following her lord husband onto the funeral pyre went the way of the Vikings."

Skena shook her head. "Nay, he is not dead. I saw him on the boulevard stairs. 'Tis what distracted me when I went to let the wolves in."

Sympathy clear in his silver eyes, Noel's tense muscles seemed to ease. "Ah, lass. I understand only too well letting go is hard. Grief pulls at the heart. Sometimes the mind plays us for a fool. We see what we want to see, not what is real."

"'Tis not what I wanted, but what I saw truly. I spotted him on the boulevard, and then he descended the stairs. Moonlight hit half his face. I saw him, Noel."

Noel shook his head to the side. "'Tis not possible. You simply mistook another man for him."

"Did you not listen before? There are *no* men here young and fit enough to pass for Angus."

"Likely, it was one of Guillaume's men then," he suggested.

"Nay, they are clean shaven like you and Baron Lochshane. This man wore a beard and the braids of a chief."

"Then where is he now? If Fadden had returned, do you not think the man would come through the front gate and announce his arrival?" His right hand gently stroked her cheek. "I am sorry, Skena. Your husband died on the field at Dunbar. There is no shred of doubt. There were witnesses. Edward gave me Craigendan because he was made aware of the man's death and knew the fortress would need a knight to hold it. Edward conferred the title on me in April. I had been wounded in the battle and was slow to heal, which is why it took me so long to come claim the holding. Originally, plans were for me to accompany Damian St. Giles to Glen Shane. He was to assume command of Lyonglen and I Craigendan. Since I am already sworn to Challon, Edward knew it would only cement Julian's control here to place me as baron."

The quiet logic of his words made Skena feel childish. He was right—Edward had sent Noel as new lord here because Angus was dead. Even so, she could not banish the dark image from her mind. Mayhap guilt preying upon her caused her to see a man who was dead? She would never wish Angus harm; even so she did not want him back as her husband. Instead, she wanted to be the wife of this man who believed in wishes, wanted to believe dreams could come true for her.

Reaching out, his large hands cradled her face as if he held the most rare and precious treasure. "Skena, I can make you forget him. Just give me time." He was so close the words fanned across her face, just before he lowered his mouth to hers.

Skena's breathing was shallow, rapid, as his gentle lips teased, giving her a taste of pleasure . . . making her hungry for more. Dizzy with anticipation, she closed her eyes and pushed up on her tiptoes, craving more of the sensations he conjured within her. Eager for all he could show her.

Most vexing, he pulled back. "Open your eyes, Skena." That probing gaze raked over her features, almost as if he were memorizing every curve, every shadow of her face. "You know naught of the ways of kissing, do you, lass?"

She heard the puzzlement in his voice, felt ashamed he found her lacking. Unable to meet his stare, she glanced down. "I am sorry. . . ."

He laughed. The bloody man laughed at her! She felt like punching him.

"Do not look angry or hurt, my sweet Skena. It will be my honor to show you these wondrous pleasures." Noel tilted her chin up a little. "Open your mouth slightly. . . ." The corner of his mouth crooked up as a wicked twinkle flashed in his eyes. His lips, ever so lightly, brushed against hers.

Pulling back he watched the reactions playing across her face. Skena knew she could not hide them from him. What she saw reflected in his eyes robbed her of the ability to think, to draw air, made her want to believe in wishes. This time he tilted her head back slightly and then pulled her chin down to open her mouth. This kiss sent shivers down the backs of her thighs.

As Noel lifted his head, Skena's hands grasped his upper arms, flexing tightly about his hard warrior's muscles, relishing his strength. "There seems to be more to the ways of kissing than I knew." She leaned into him, wanting to feel her body pressed against his.

The door pushed open and chattering children rushed in. Annis and Andrew. Her son said triumphantly, "See, I told you our knight would be awake."

Stepping back with a disappointed sigh, Noel chuckled. "We shall continue our lessons later, my lady."

Skena hummed lowly as she finished changing into one of her better kirtles. After getting out of the mail shirt and cleaning up, she had brushed her hair and added a simple, thin circlet across her forehead. Noel would assume the power of baron shortly, and despite his avowing he wanted her to continue to be the lady here, this would be the last morning she would go before the people of Craigendan as their mistress. Another would soon be deciding their fate. She wanted to face the change appearing every inch the baroness. While the gown was not new, she had always loved the deep blue. She shrugged. It had been a while since she had made a kirtle for herself. Always too busy with other things. She recalled a wine-colored velvet gown her cousin Raven wore last Yuletide. Skena envied that rich shade, but knew she could not afford the material. Well, she had never been one to wear finery such as Raven and Rowanne did. Tamlyn was like her, more comfortable in a sark and skirt of tartan. Only now, with Noel here, she suddenly wished she could put on a kirtle closer to what the women wore at court, what he was used to seeing.

Feeling a quickening within her blood, she was suddenly forward looking to seeing how her people accepted de Servian as their new lord. She put a hand to her belly and took a deep breath, hoping Noel would find her pleasing in blue, be proud to have her standing alongside him.

"Well, I am what I am, no changing it." She spoke her anxiety to her reflection in the bowl of water, and then turned to leave the room.

As Skena approached the lord's chamber she heard voices chattering. Discerning a female one, her steps slowed. The door was not locked, but left open just enough for a body to squeeze inside. She could see movement within, but not a clear view. The voices were too low to hear what was being said. Fearing the worst, a frisson crawled up her spine. Since she was still mistress of this holding and the door was not closed, she put her hand on its plane and slowly pushed it open.

As she suspected, the feminine voice belonged to Dorcas. Her heart dropped, then slammed back up in her chest, making her light-headed. "What are you doing here?" Skena snapped.

She told herself not to give Dorcas the reaction she wanted, yet it was impossible to contain the rage, the hurt . . . the jealousy. Before, with the situation between Dorcas and Angus, she had been humiliated. Angus had allowed Dorcas to flaunt her position in his life, permitted her to openly defy Skena when she gave orders. Still, she saw that it was only a wound of her pride. She had never loved Angus, so she had not been jealous, just resentful. This was a thousand times worse! She vibrated with fury, nearly out of control. She could not think, barely remembered to breathe. Desperately, she tried to rein in her temper, reach for that calm spot in her soul.

Noel, still drying his face on a cloth, turned around. Lowering it, his sweeping glance took in Dorcas, who was straightening the bedding, and then Skena in the doorway. His expression did not change.

Dorcas looked over her shoulder at Noel and gave him a sly

smile, as if sharing a secret meant only for the two of them. "Why, I was seeing to Lord de Servian's needs, my lady."

The way Dorcas said 'my lady' set Skena's teeth on edge. Dorcas's intent. Skena wanted to rip her red hair from the woman's head and force feed it to her. Skena had taken umbrage that Angus never gave a pretense to hiding that he had taken Dorcas as a leman, and in some ways she believed he had flaunted it to shame her. The situation had proved difficult to live with. That offense was only a faint echo compared to what coursed through her blood now. Violent shaking threatened to manifest itself. Skena moved to the fireplace and pretended to warm her hands, in an effort to cover her distress. She quickly saw she was failing. She did not want to fake being calm. She wanted to claw Dorcas's eyes out!

"I need not remind you, Dorcas, that you have chores elsewhere. In the future, please recall you no longer have access to the upper levels of the fortress. Keep belowstairs where you belong." Skena was proud her voice sounded calm.

Dorcas paused, her hand on the top coverlet. Her jaw tightened, but then she continued to smooth the *plaide* of its wrinkles, ignoring Skena. She turned back to Noel and asked, "Is there aught else you would want, my lord?"

Noel put down the cloth. "Nay. Not unless you can do the chores of a bloody squire."

She stopped before him, curling a strand of her long red hair around her finger.

"You will find, Lord de Servian, I am able to do many things. . . . Help a man dress . . . or undress. And you must admit I am easier on the eyes."

Noel laughed. "But can you put an edge to my sword? After last night, it needs care."

Dorcas's laughter bubbled forth. "An edge? Mayhap not an edge. Howbeit, I am quite capable of polishing your *sword* to a *hard* sheen."

Skena thought about picking up the fireplace poker on pretext to fix the fire, instead of watching Dorcas attempting to fix Noel's interest. She decided against it. Her hand wrapped around the length of metal might prove too strong of a temptation. Besides, this was a test of de Servian.

He gave the woman an impassive face. "I am sure if I require anything I merely have to ask Skena."

The lines at the corner of Dorcas's mouth said she strained to keep her comely smile in place. "You will find, Lord de Servian, that our Skena is oft too busy to tend all the baron's needs."

"Enough, Dorcas!" Skena's temper snapped. "You should be on the wall patrolling. See to those duties or I will presume you lack work to keep you busy. The garderobe could use a good cleaning, most likely. Shall I set you to doing that?"

Dorcas shot her a smug expression and shrugged. "Mayhap you might think to do such." She glanced back to de Servian. "Mayhap not."

As Skena watched Dorcas saunter out the door, she wanted to throw something at her. Oh, she would deal with her later, and it would not be pretty. She had planned on waiting until spring to marry Dorcas off, but she would send word sooner to the Campbells and Comyns both. First man that offered could have her. Spending the winter with Dorcas trying to seduce de Servian for spite would be more than she could stomach.

Noel picked up the dark blue shirt folded on the bench. "I will be glad when my men and wagons can get through. This is my last shirt until they do. Can you help me get it on? It pains me to reach over my head. I did not take notice of it when I was killing the wolves, but after the fear burned away, simple movements start the wound to aching all over again. The warrior in me tends to blot out pain when I fight. You must to stay alive."

Skena took the shirt and helped ease it onto his arms. The surcoat came next, also blue, but a shade lighter and trimmed with silver braiding. The dark blues and silver only seemed to highlight his arresting eyes.

He glanced up from buckling his belt loosely about his waist. "Will I do?"

She nodded. "Aye, you are every measure worthy to be the lord here." She started to reach out and brush the curls that spilled carelessly over his forehead, but then pulled her hand back, not feeling she had the right.

Noel caught her wrist. "You are quiet, Skena."

"Sometimes 'tis wiser to travel the road in silence," she replied softly.

"You are angry?" He pressed. "The woman upset you? Why?"

"One of those times when being mute is the lesser of evils."

He pulled her closer. "Holding back will not aid us in coming to know each other better. Why did she upset you?"

Skena sucked in a steadying breath and slowly released it. "Very well, she is not merely an insolent servant. Dorcas was my lord husband's leman."

De Servian's brows lifted. "Ah, I can see where you have a right to be distressed by her presence."

"If you mean your words—"

"I mean everything I have spoken to you, Skena. Everything. I want you for my lady wife. We are but strangers, but marriages have been made between men and women when they have never seen each other. We have a better start, and both recognized the strong liking, the rising feelings betwixt us. I mean for us to marry as soon as it can be arranged. I would prefer if we can dispense with the crying of the bans."

"Then ken this. I married young and learnt there were little choices with an iron-willed, and often uncaring, husband. As such, I abided one husband bringing shame to our marriage by taking another woman as his whore. I do not want to face that again."

Noel's hands took her waist and pulled her toward him. His

mouth caught hers, kissing her, not roughly but thoroughly, quickly taking her anger and turning it into a ravenous hunger. Her whole body ached with the need he stirred to life within her.

Breaking away, he pledged in a harsh whisper, "Never give me reason to doubt you, Skena, and I shan't offer you any reason to question my devotion. Craigendan and you are my deepest wish come true. I will fight to protect that dream."

Skena stepped back to distance herself from the potent magic Noel wove around her. He made it difficult for her to be logical. The closer she was to him, the more the effect took possession of her will.

"Shall you accept my word, Skena, that I honor you above all others?"

Her spine stiffened. "Angus gave his troth with me, spoke words before all, about forsaking all others and keeping only to me. His words were hollow."

"I have come to the belief your dead husband was not an honorable man. When a man of Challon gives his vows, you can place your faith it will be kept." Noel held out his arm for her to take. "Now, shall we go belowstairs and greet the people of Craigendan?"

Had she not just a short time ago pondered that she instinctively trusted this man, saw the nobility within him, recognized Noel de Servian was in all measures more than Angus had been? Mayhap she deluded herself because she wanted Noel to be the perfect warrior of her dreams. Only, as she stared at him, forcing herself to examine him with a jaundiced view of men in general, she still sensed deep integrity in him.

Trusting that inner voice, she placed her hand on his arm and allowed him to lead her out of the room.

"I take your silence as a yes." He placed his other hand over hers and gave it a squeeze of reassurance. "Trust me, Skena, and we will rub along well."

"You are a stranger, yet I feel as if we have kenned each other for longer. I trust you. I just do not like how I felt when I found Dorcas in the chamber with you. It was painful," she admitted.

"If she is so insolent and such a constant thorn in your side, why have you not married her off to some distant clansman and been done with her?" Noel asked as they descended the stairs. "Then she would be out of your hair and not a constant reminder to you."

"Complicated reasons. At first, there was the expectation Angus would return. Then, there was Muriel to consider. Dorcas is her daughter." Skena paused before the Great Hall's doors, looking at him with wary eyes before adding, "There is also the fact that she is my half sister."

Chapter Eighteen

Since all within the keep had been ordered to show themselves before fast was broken, the people of Craigendan anticipated change rode on the cool morning air. Aware of the English presence, they surely suspected a new lord was the next order of business. What was left—how it would affect their everyday lives. Skena smirked when she heard one of her ladies chime, "Well, so long as it ain't no bloody Campbell or Comyn, cannot be too bad." Skena glanced at the solemn faces filling the Great Hall, searching each to judge their moods. Stark uncertainty was upon most countenances. The biggest portion of her clan members kept to the shadows of the far walls, observing as de Servian entered with Skena on his arm and Guillaume Challon just behind him.

She glanced to her side, seeing what her people did. Men of power. Handsome men. She noticed the wistful looks of the younger women in the keep. Even the elders like Muriel watched the Englishmen with guarded admiration.

Her stomach tightened. There was no mistaking it. Noel strode with the mantle of power resting upon his shoulders. This Englishman was assuming command of Craigendan, and none failed to see this. Life here would be forevermore changed.

Well, so be it. In some ways Craigendan had been in suspension these past months. First, the waiting for the men to return, for everything to pick up where it left off. Then news came of Dunbar; mourning and sorrow visited the women who had lost husbands or betrotheds. On the heels of the tides, the drought hit; the summer and autumn of struggle followed. And more waiting.

Noel strode to the trestle table and put his hand on the back of the lord's chair. That simple act sent a ripple throughout the whole chamber. The words that he'd speak were naught but a formality. All understood Noel de Servian was the baron now.

His gaze circled the Great Hall, silently marking what she had warned him of—except for those belonging to the Challon cadre, the only males were old or lame; the rest were barely more than little boys. Turning to Guillaume, Noel arched a dubious brow. The other man merely gave a faint nod, in a way which bespoke a familiarity that they understood each other's thoughts.

"I am sure rumors are rife with my coming, curiosity about the English stranger," Noel began. "Speculation ends now. I am Sir Noel de Servian. Edward Plantagenet has granted me title and charter to Craigendan. I am your new lord. Already I pay homage to Julian Challon, your overlord. We were raised as brothers. I have heard Scots say that between foster brothers the bond is stronger than that of brothers of blood. I agree. Though not a brother by birth, I am a man of Challon by choice. Come nightfall and chores are done, the men amongst you will come bend knee and tend your oath to me. In time, you will find I am a firm master, but one with a soft hand. Serve me well, and I will do all in my power to see you prosper and are protected from any danger that threatens Craigendan. I will shield you with my very life."

Skena's vision roved to her people, trying to fathom their reactions to the news. Resentment was seen on a few faces, mostly those of the small number of males. Some of the women looked relieved. Skena suppressed a smile, knowing they were sighing at the prospects of not having to do the many chores which belonged to men. With a new lord, new men would follow. Come spring, she figured there would be several weddings. Life would gradually return to normal.

Also not escaping their notice—her hand on de Servian's arm. She was nervous despite feeling confident they would accept de Servian as their chief, especially when it was clear he held her approval.

As her line of vision wandered past Guillaume, a little behind and to the left of Noel, Skena tensed when she caught sight of Dorcas in the half shadows of the Great Hall's archway. Her heart jumped, another surge of resentment hitting her blood. She had specifically ordered Dorcas back to the wall; as usual, the woman clearly ignored her rule. Since the dimness hid her half sister's face, it was nearly impossible to see the expression she wore.

"I am also pleased to inform you that the Lady Skena has consented to soon speak her troth, not only accepting me as lord here, but as her husband as well," Noel said, lifting her hand from his arm to kiss it in front of all gathered.

Skena started to turn her attention back to Noel, but then a man entered the hallway and came to stand behind Dorcas. Torn, Skena needed to show how happy she was with Noel's pronouncement, yet her eyes were pulled back to the shadowy figure, leaning toward her sister, as if he were whispering in her ear. Dizziness spun through her. Even so, she had no time to focus on the couple on the far side of the room, for Noel moved closer and kissed her cheek, blocking her view.

"Is that not so, Skena?" he asked.

Skena struggled to hide her confusion with a smile. She saw he wanted her response, that it was important to him; she gave it, having no idea to what she was agreeing. "Whatever my lord wishes, I want as well."

Noel gifted her with a grin, pleased by her answer. He pulled out the lady's chair for her, allowing her to sit at the position that would remain hers—lady of the keep. She slid into it, and then nodded to Muriel to set the servants fetching the food.

Everything had changed. Another man now sat in the lord's chair, soon she was to wed, and this time by her choice. Oh, she had the good of her people in mind, but that had little to do with her joyful acceptance of Noel's offer of marriage. In her heart she felt Noel would be good for Craigendan. Good for her. Though he had tried earlier to intimidate her in the chamber, he had not dictated to her how things would be, never been overbearing as Angus had throughout their marriage. The only time she had managed to bend his will was on the matter of keeping Andrew at Craigendan instead of sending him to the south, to Angus's younger brother, Daragh, to begin training.

Thinking of Angus, she turned her eyes toward the far archway, to see if Dorcas remained, if the man was still with her sister. The doorway was empty. A shiver crawled up her spine, as she recalled how his silhouette had the same shape as Angus. Noel had assured her Angus was dead, and that assurance had not been given lightly. Still, her first impression was that the man had been Angus. There was something in the way he had leaned toward Dorcas that bespoke familiarity, a lovers' closeness she had been forced to observe for the past five years.

Skena was distracted from her thoughts as Annis and Andrew entered, Jenna herding them to the table. Her son took one look at de Servian, sitting in the lord's chair, broke away from her maidservant, and ran to Noel. Without asking, he clamored up onto Noel's knee and hugged him.

"You are better," Andrew exclaimed. "Jenna told us how you battled the wolves with *màthair*. Oh, I wish I could have seen you swinging your sword. See, Mama, I told you he was a valiant knight, just like I asked the Cailleach for."

Annis stood, half-hiding against Jenna's leg, her brown

eyes watching her brother sitting upon Noel's thigh, same as the boy had done numerous times with his father. *Just as she had never been permitted to do.* Her daughter had tried to crawl onto Angus's lap several times when she was younger, only to be rebuffed. She stopped asking after a time. Skena wanted to go to her and hug her, kiss away the lingering hurt. The little girl could not understand why her father had never loved her.

Noel noticed Skena looking behind them. He turned to see what had captured her attention. "Come, Lady Annis, I fortunately have another leg." He patted his thigh and then held out his hand to the child.

Annis backed up, startled by his offer. Jenna gently took hold of her shoulders to steady the skittish child. Poor Annis. Outside of Galen or some of the servants, no male had ever called her by name. Skena's heart squeezed, watching Annis's frightened expression. Oh, she was not scared of de Servian. Like her mother, Annis was too afraid to believe wishes could come true.

Noel plucked a hulled hazelnut from the bowl just placed before him. He gave one to Andrew and then took another and held it out to her little girl. Annis loved hazelnuts, but even the promise of the special treat was not bribe enough to lure her closer to the Englishman.

"What bothers the girl?" Noel asked, then popped the nut into his mouth. Reaching into the bowl, he took another and once again presented it for Annis.

Skena's hands shook as she sliced the bread and then put a piece for Noel on his plate. "Do not call her that."

The words came out harsh, too harsh for a man who had done naught to earn them. The sin was not his. Still, it was difficult to hear this man refer to her daughter in the same manner Angus had.

Noel watched her, puzzled by her strong reaction, unsure

what he had done to summon the rebuke. Again, he ate the nut that Annis refused.

Pretending to be engrossed in cutting cheese and meat and placing the food on his plate, Skena ignored him. Or tried. She felt his stare bore into her, willing her to look up. Unable to resist, she lifted her eyes to meet his. Those damnable silver eyes held the power to pierce her soul, as if she could hide nothing from this man. Vexed, she picked up a piece of cheese to take a bite. When Noel continued to watch her, she instead tossed it down to the metal plate.

"You are a patient man, Noel de Servian," she said, but from her tone it was apparent she did not currently rank the characteristic as entirely positive.

He inclined his head. "I have had much practice. I am not a young man, Skena, as you know. I burned out a lot of my impatient ways in my green years. One also learns to control your words and temper when you serve King Edward. He has more than enough of both to spare. They speak his Angevin rages rival those of his great grandsire."

Skena fixed on the information. "A fearsome man, your king. His deeds this past spring and summer reached all ears in the far corners of the lands. What sort of man wages war to bend people to his will? Destroys towns, slaughters men, women—even children—by the hundred score."

Noel exhaled, then took another nut and held it out to Annis. And waited for the child to snatch it. At length, he answered. "Edward Plantagenet is a complex man. I oft found myself liking the man, but misliking the king."

Skena picked up a slice of bread, but found she had no appetite, so passed it to Andrew. "You were at Berwick?" she asked.

Noel avoided meeting her probing stare. His long, graceful fingers wiggled the nut back and forth to lure Annis. The silence lengthened until Skena presumed he was not going to answer her. Then, he dropped his hand, closed his eyes, and leaned his head back. Grim emotions etched the corners of his sensual mouth.

"Aye, I was at Berwick. To my everlasting disgust and shame." He slowly raised his head and looked at her. "One of the times I *misliked* the king."

She swallowed hard. "Then it was as bad as the tales spoke?"

Noel's expression was hard, level. "Worse. You cannot imagine how horrible. I would have you never to know such ugliness."

Her eyes raked over the handsome man, taking in the ashen shade of his skin. What he had witnessed left deep scars on Noel de Servian's soul. She lived in this sheltered pocket of the Highlands, protected by her uncle, the powerful Earl Kinmarch. War had never come to the gates of Craigendan. Oh, the keep was smaller than the mighty fiefs of Kinmarch, Glenrogha, Lochshane and Kinloch, but all the lesser holdings of Glen Shane's *honours* had been safe as well. Still, Skena understood men sadly were oft ugly to other men; greed, desires, hatreds could push them to do terrible things. Only, she had never witnessed such barbarity firsthand.

"'Tis why you awaken covered in sweat?" Skena asked, but the question did not need his reply. "I first thought your body still fought the cold or the poison from your wound. Each night you awoke, your heart pounding, so hard it vibrated your whole body, speaking odd words. It made no sense to me then. I understand now."

"The things I saw at Berwick are some of the foulest images the mind could be forced to endure. It sorrows me people are capable of such atrocities." He paused, despair tempered with resolution flickering in his pale eyes. "I will fight to protect what is mine, but I hope to God I shall never go to war again. I am too old to face the ugliness."

Skena reached out and touched his arm, hearing the sadness, the weariness in his words. The long years of emptiness. "You keep calling yourself old."

"I am." Hunger was clear in his countenance, in the timber of his voice.

"Not in my eyes." Skena felt that shortness of air he always brought to her, and forced herself to draw a calming breath.

Two souls, each needing the other so much.

Their focus on each other was broken as Annis shyly took Noel's hand and uncurled his fingers from around the nut. Her huge eyes, for once not dimmed by the fear of rejection, sparkled with anticipation. Popping the treat into her mouth, she chewed it slowly. Her pale cheeks crimsoned with a blush, but then she timidly slid upon his knee. De Servian's arm curled around Annis and pulled her back to a firmer seat upon his thigh. Her daughter looked up at the tall man, adoration in her gaze.

"Would you like another, Annis?" Noel asked.

Emotions overwhelming her, Skena put a shaky hand to her mouth in a hope to stop the tears from flooding her eyes. If she had not already been in love with Noel de Servian, she would have lost her heart completely over the way he cradled her daughter, that he had granted her child the one thing long denied Annis—her name.

Mayhap wishes at Yuletide did come true when they were brought by a man named Noel.

Chapter Nineteen

"Why must you go?" Skena wanted to stomp her foot to emphasize her frustration, but knew it a wasted effort. "Men! None of you ever listen! Worse, you always assume you ken best. Though you are prettier than most, de Servian, you remain just as pigheaded."

He cocked his head and flashed a wicked grin. "De Servian? What happened to Noel?"

"Nodcock." She did stomp her foot. It felt good if naught else. "You have been ill for days, and with what you went through in opening the old wound, 'tis unwise for you to venture out into the cold so soon. Guillaume is to blame for this. He should have more sense than to encourage you to ride with the Challon men to hunt game."

Leaning close he whispered, "Prettier than most, eh?"

Skena refused to yield to his charming ways. A comely man was dangerous to a woman's peace of mind. Her head whipped around looking for something to brain him with. Short of the poker, she could not spot anything suitable to fill her need.

"The day wanes. With night coming early to your land, we shan't be out long." Noel merely continued buckling his baldric about his hips. "I am lord here now. I must do lordly things. Besides, I have a yen for something—anything—besides wolf meat stew for my sup."

"Do not dare laugh at me, de Servian." With a disgusted sigh, she straightened the mail grommet about his neck, knowing he would not be able to reach it with his side still tender.

"If I give you kissing lessons when I return may I be Noel again?" He placed a peck on her cheek.

"Save your wiles. You have me playing at squire because it pains you to lift your right arm. You were sick for days with fever." Her mouth pressed into a frown. "And you are old, remember?"

Noel laughed loudly, then leaned over and caught her mouth in a bruising kiss, then ruined it by pulling back too soon. Oh, she wanted to keep kissing him! Clearly, her yearning was upon her face, for his eyes flashed arrogantly. Reaching out, he ran his thumb over her lower lip.

"If I stay, my love, I will end up giving you those kissing lessons, and if I do I shan't stop with kissing." As if he could not resist, he brushed his lips briefly against her stunned mouth. She did not return his kiss. Leaning back he frowned. "Already you tire of kisses from the old man?"

Skena put her quivering hand to his lips to stop him talking. "You are *not* old. You are the most beautiful man I have ever seen. More importantly, you are beautiful inside, Noel de Servian. You make children believe wishes come true. Make *me* believe."

He kissed her fingertips, then took her wrists and pulled her to him. "Then why did you not want me to kiss you?"

"I want your kisses . . . and more." She blushed at her boldness, almost looking away, fearful she would spot reproof in his eyes.

"Then why—"

Skena rose up on her tiptoes and kissed his mouth softly. "You called me *my love*." Her heart stopped and only beat again when she finally drew a small, ragged breath. Like Annis, she was snatching that 'treat' he offered. She recognized she was in love with him, the feeling only strengthened with every passing hour, but dare she hope he was coming to care for her?

Noel's grin faded and seriousness formed his handsome face. "I do—love you, you know. I have never spoken the word to anyone before." When she opened her mouth to talk, he did as she had, put his fingers to her lips to silence her. "Trust me. You say I use the word 'beautiful' too often and thus it has lost value. You are beautiful, no matter how many times I say it— outside and within, Skena. You give me such hope. 'Tis true we are but strangers yet, still, I feel Fate brought me to you. My life was empty ere coming here. I need you. You are that piece of my heart, which has been missing my whole sad life. I am sorry the journey to finding you has taken so long."

"Oh . . ." was all she managed to say. Noel spoke the very words that had long ago formed in her heart—the sense a part of her had always been missing. Mayhap Fate had brought them together, for it would be too cruel for them both to live their lives needing the other and never having that spot filled.

Noel leaned to kiss her, but the door pushed open and Andrew came in, followed by Annis, who was pulling Guillaume along by his first finger. Skena had to smile. Already Noel's early attention toward her daughter saw Annis accepting this other Englishman as well. Her darling child would never before have been so trusting, so bold, as to lead such an imposing warrior around by his finger.

"We caught a dragon, mama," Andrew announced, patting Lord Challon's thigh.

Guillaume rolled his eyes at the children's antics. "I hate to interrupt, but we dragons needs must ride. Winter daylight here lasts but a wink, you will find."

Skena glared at them both, then threw up her hands in exasperation. "Fine. Run along. When de Servian sickens because he is out chasing game, instead of resting in bed—where he should be—then you may nurse him, Lord Dragon!"

Noel's foster brother smiled at her flair of temper. "I warned you, Noel, these Ogilvie women are no end of trouble. Lady Skena, I promise to return him to the keep at the first sign he is unfit to be out."

Noel tried to kiss her, but she turned her cheek, furious he was ignoring her concerns. The side of his mouth crooked up. "The woman is in need of kissing lessons, Guillaume. Methinks I shall have my work cut out for me." He quickly pressed his lips to her forehead, then patted both children on the heads before leaving the chamber with Lord Challon.

"Noel, I love you," she called after him, but the words were drowned out by the men's laughter echoing in the hall.

With a lightness of heart, Skena threw herself into preparations for the Yuletide celebration while the men were off hunting. Her time had been tied up tending Noel since they found him, thus her daily chores had been left to wait. The tally of things needing attention seemed endless. Distracting her from mundane tasks, the sight of holly and evergreen boughs, tied with red yarn around the posts and hung on the doors, lent color and cheer to the gloomy hall. Everything seemed so festive and happy. For the first time in months, Craigendan thrummed with hope instead of fear.

Elspeth rushed up, lacing her fingers together before her to contain her excitement. For a change, color had returned to the girl's cheeks. Not since the news of Dunbar and David's death reached them had Skena witnessed the shine of life in her cousin's eyes. "Skena, might I trouble you for sprigs of juniper for the fire? It would be a promise of new beginnings if we burned some in the fireplace to cleanse Craigendan of evil shades."

A shiver rippled up Skena's spine at Elspeth's speaking of lingering ghosts. Instantly, that shadowy image standing at the top of the stairs filled her mind. No matter how firmly she told herself that it had not been Angus, she failed to accept the conviction. A last shred of doubt refused to be banished.

She squeezed Elspeth's upper arm. "Grand idea, lass. You appear well. Might the twinkle in your eyes have something to do with that handsome squire of Lord Challon?"

Elspeth lowered her gaze and blushed. "Is it wrong, Skena? I loved David, but . . . he is not coming back. I wanted to die for so long." Her voice choked on the words. "Now, my heart beats again."

"What is this handsome squire's name? He has not been made known to me."

"Emory Maynet. He is old enough to be knighted, but does not have coin to maintain that station. Lord Challon suggested that he might wish to stay and become Lord de Servian's man, since he will need to import soldiery to protect us." Again, she lowered her lashes as if afraid to hope. "If things come to pass . . ."

Skena smiled. "The old broch?"

Elspeth's head bobbed in answer. "It comes to me through my Ogilvie blood when I wed. David and I had hoped to refit it with the Earl Challon's blessing. It just . . ." Her cousin shrugged, confused by the ties to the past pushing against the yearning for a future.

Skena understood those emotions only too well. "Times change, Elspeth. Life sometimes allows us no choices. Seize them with both hands when they do come to you. Nay, such wishes are not wrong, dear heart. 'Tis life going on."

"I have seen the way Lord de Servian looks at you. Methinks he will make a good lord here, Skena. More important, I sense he will make you happy. Angus was a good man, I suppose, a good provider, but he never made you blush. Sometimes . . . he hurt you not really meaning to."

Skena sighed at the truth. "De Servian is gentle with Annis. That touches my heart. For so long she has stood in the shadows, cringed when Angus bellowed at her." Skena brushed her thumb over the small dip in her cousin's chin. "You open your heart to Emory Maynet, if it feels right. Bring him to meet me. Mayhap by spring's bloom you will start work on the old broch."

Impulsively, Elspeth grabbed Skena in a tight hug. "'Tis good to live again. Scary, but good."

As Skena headed down the dimly lit hallway, she spotted Ella coming in the opposite direction. She almost steeled herself for their passing. A strange woman, Ella was in charge of the geese and the pigs, and mostly kept to herself. Her pale hair was chopped short, unlike that of most women, not even touching her shoulders, and so coarse and straight that it held no natural softness. Her neck was thick and short, her features almost gnomish. Skena knew everyone could not be pleasing to the eye, but it was not merely Ella's appearance that was off-putting; there was a baleful air about her that caused Skena to distrust her.

There was plenty of room for them to pass without touching, but as they did, the squat woman's shoulder knocked hard against Skena's, causing her to back up a step to brace from losing balance. Frowning, she glared at the strange woman, wondering why she had done that.

"Beg pardon, my lady. Me feets is so clumsy. Got a bad ankle, see. Goes out on me sometimes, it does," she offered in a way of explanation. "I meant no harm."

Skena gave a nod, but failed to accept her words. An odd glint in the woman's hooded eyes bespoke insolence, which in turn set off an alarm at the back of her mind. Skena had never liked Ella, but the woman generally stayed out of the way.

"By your leave," she gave an awkward bob, half-curtsey, half-bow, as if not sure which was proper, and then continued down the hall.

At the stillroom door, Skena paused to ponder what Ella

was doing in this part of the fortress. The woman only came into the Great Hall about once a fortnight; the remainder of her time was spent in the small hut on the edge of the outer bailey. Disquiet rippled through Skena. The peculiar woman had no purpose for being in the back part of Craigendan.

Shrugging off questions, she untied her chatelaine from her belt and sorted through the keys. Just as she found the correct one, her movements froze. Though she could not say why, Skena suddenly felt she was no longer alone in the dark hallway. Prickles crawled up her neck as though she was being watched. Ella? Slowly, she lifted her head and looked down the hallway toward the kitchen to see if the woman lingered, spying on her. No one was in the long corridor. The hall was silent, save kitchen noises and Cook whistling while he went about preparing supper. She watched for a few heartbeats, but no one appeared. Telling herself it had been naught more than a servant going about chores, she started to insert the key, but then hesitated, so strong was the sense of someone's being near. The ring fell from her fingers.

As she stooped down to pick up the keys, Skena turned her head and stared into the long shadows. Since the torchlight did little to banish the darkness, she kept her eyes fixed there to adjust to the heavy gloom. Dizziness whirled through her mind, making her light-headed. She rose, fighting the sense of unreality brushing her mind. The strange sensation did not lessen, but increased with every draw of air. The kenning. That fey sense was alive now Noel had opened her heart, and it was warning her with a strength that compelled her to flee. No fool, she knew better than to ignore the presentiment.

Skena considered her next step. Should she go investigate, or give pretense she was unaware something was off? Urgently seeking the right key, she quietly went through the ring again, but could barely focus on the shape of each.

"Skena . . ."

Gooseflesh rippled up her neck. Yet again, she looked in

both directions. No one was there. Her name had been naught but a ghostly whisper, one easily conjured in the mind when rattled. She held perfectly still and listened. Oddly, she felt like a doe scenting the danger of a human.

Then the dimness shifted.

Her heart stopped, and everything seemed to bend in on itself. Shadows distorted, twisted, and reformed into a man, standing at the turn in the corridor. A force slammed into her as she stared at the silhouette that was only too familiar. "Angus."

Emotions swam through her, too many to sort out. Fear. Pain. Her soul howling, *no!* She would never wish him harm. Yet, for the first time in her life she held hope that true happiness had come to her, seeing Annis embracing that same possibility, instead of growing up beaten down, unloved, and feeling unworthy because she was only 'the girl.' To have that snatched away now would be too cruel.

Willing the figure to be naught more than her imaginings, she closed her eyelids and squeezed them tight. "He will be gone when I open them," she said lowly, almost a prayer to make it so. When she opened them, the dark figure remained.

"Skena . . ." His hissed whisper sent a chill to undulate over her.

This could not be! Noel assured her Angus was dead. Was there some way he escaped the madness at Dunbar? Mayhap they were mistaken. He was not dead, but merely wounded, and it had taken him until now to make it back to Craigendan. Had not Noel's injury taken so long to heal? Angus was older than him by ten years, thus he might mend even more slowly. The kenning swam through her, warning her, but she was determined to know the truth. She refused to have this shadow hanging over her life, her future.

With misgivings, she started down the passageway with slow steps. She did not want to go, but was driven by the need to know if this was Angus, or if her mind conjured his shade out of guilt, simply because her life was moving on. As she neared, he vanished around the corner.

As she reached the bend, she pulled up. The long corridor wound to another turn and ultimately reached a tunnel entrance, which opened upon the bailey behind the stables. Torches were not lit in the sconces, nor were there arrow loops to break the impenetrable darkness. She listened as the man's footfalls carried him farther away. Skena knew every inch of Craigendan, could walk this twisting passage blindfolded, yet she wavered on following him.

At the second bend, he spun on his heel and looked back. "Skena . . . hurry . . . come."

"Angus?" Skena's voice echoed hollowly against the stone walls.

"Hurry . . ."

Putting her hand on the wall, she glanced to the torch behind her, wondering if she should go fetch it. Ahead, there were only the garderobe, a communal bathing area for the soldiery, a hidden outer door to the fortress, and another leading down into the bowels of Craigendan. Just as she decided to collect the torch, a faint light flared behind him as if a candle had been lit.

Keeping her hand on the stone wall, she cautiously made her way down the narrow corridor, the pale yellow glow behind her growing fainter as she turned the corner. Ahead, candlelight flickered from inside the cleansing room. Once more, she hesitated. The sense that something was off about this whole situation increased with each heartbeat.

"Hurry, Skena." The ghostly call came from deep inside the large room.

Frowning, she crossed the threshold and looked about, but failed to spot anyone. The candle and wooden holder were sitting on a table against the far wall. Two large wooden tubs, empty, were before the cold hearth, a long bench on either side. A large wooden privacy screen sat across the corner.

There was only one place he could be—behind the screen. Moving to the table, she picked up the feeble candle by the finger loop, lifting it high.

"Angus, are you here?" she called.

As she headed around the heavy paneled screen, something dropped over her head—burlap—the dust so heavy she choked, gasping for air. The candle dropped from her fingers, as she struggled to get free of the heavy sack. Only it was pulled down, covering her arms. She could not strike out. Suddenly, she was swung hard, sending her crashing against the far wall.

As blackness swirled through her mind, her last thought was that she should have heeded the kenning. "Too . . . late," the words fell from her lips.

Chapter Twenty

Noel loathed to admit it, but Skena had been right—he should have stayed at Craigendan and in bed. His back burned in red hot agony. He remained seated upon Brishen instead of dismounting to investigate the small clearing, fearful of having a rough time getting back in the saddle if he did. The wound throbbed painfully, yet with an ache that bespoke of healing rather than of flesh pushing to putrefaction, which he had suffered for so long.

Swinging his right leg over the pommel in front of him, Guillaume kicked out of his stirrup and then dropped to both feet from his charger. His steed and Brishen were brothers, nearly identical, pure white horses, presents from Julian five summers past. The lead rein in his hand, Guillaume carefully examined the small niche that nature had formed in the thick trees, looking for telltale signs of who had been living on Craigendan land. A crudely erected shelter, a lean-to made of evergreen limbs, had been nestled between the heavy boughs of two tall pine trees. Scratching through the deep snow, Noel's friend exposed the remains of a fire that had been doused before it burned out.

Lifting a half charred branch, he held it up for Noel's inspection, then flashed a look of mislike at the discovery.

"Hard to say how long, due to the covering of snow, howbeit to hazard a guess—this site was abandoned, but not by more than mere days. Mayhap the snow drove him to seek shelter elsewhere?"

Noel gingerly turned in the saddle, searching for other signs that someone had used the tiny clearing for shelter, clues to why anyone would be out here in the dead of winter. Futile effort. The snow had thoroughly blanketed all but recent roe deer tracks. He grimaced from the pain and then asked, "If you were using this as a base, which path would you take from here?"

Guillaume shot him a veiled glance. "You would head out on the trail we came in on." He shrugged. "From there it branches in one of four directions—Gailleann Castle, out on a small isle in Loch Shane Mohr, Comyn land to the north, Glen Shane, or back to Craigendan."

"Who owns Gailleann Castle?" Noel inquired, as he watched Guillaume remount.

"Another Ogilvie heiress, though not by name. Caitrin Bannatyne, Baroness Gailleann. The lady is betrothed to Kerian Mackenzie, second son of a powerful Mackenzie chief near Inverness. Folks in Glen Shane speak 'tis a love match since childhood. He fostered at Gailleann. Child love is vastly different than the love twixt a man and woman. Methinks such familiarity often spoils the passion. And in Mackenzie's case, he seems a bit"—Guillaume shrugged, reaching for the correct word and clearly failing to find it. "Pale? The pair came before me to give oath, since the isle is part of Lochshane's *honours*. I find little comfort in the knowledge he shall be the future baron."

"So he is your vassal?" Noel reined Brishen alongside so they could finish their discussion.

"In a manner of speaking. The isle belongs to the Lady Caitrin. These Ogilvie heiresses hold lands and titles in their own rights, through the distaff blood of their clan. Until

Edward's crushing of the Scottish army last spring, these females controlled their own fiefs because of some ancient ceremony they call *Rite of Line*. They speak such women are descended from witches of the old royal line of the Picts. A strange people, titles, rule, lands, all passed through the mother's blood, not the father's. Thus he shall be my vassal, but only as long as he remains betrothed to the baroness. If he cries off the wedding—no loss for her in my humble opinion—then the man she marries would become the new baron in his stead. The isle is vital, since it watches the comings and goings of both the Comyns and Campbells. I would prefer someone of a less 'pretty' mien guarding the passes at our backs. And speaking of pretty men, did you see Redam or Dare whilst you were in Berwick?"

Noel shrugged, thinking of this other Challon half brother. Darian Challon shared the same father as Julian, Simon, and Guillaume, but he had been born of a servant girl, instead of the high born lady who was Guillaume's mother. "Darian was there, and what can one say, reckless as ever. He plays a dangerous game of tweaking Edward's nose about sending Julian away. He might come to regret it if he missteps."

"And Redam? I fret over him. Always have." Guillaume's face reflected that dark concern.

Redam Maignart, the seventh baron of Raoullin, was a soulless killer, a king's assassin. "Aye, and well you should. He rides at Edward's left hand," Noel answered solemnly, not willing to say more.

Guillaume flashed a grin. "Mayhap we should kidnap our foster brother and hand him over to some Ogilvie female. Might be what his spirit needs."

A horn sounded off in the distance, alerting them game was being herded, driven their way. They both drew their bows and notched arrows waiting as the crashing of a large animal sounded through the thick pines. Two large, red roe deer broke free of the trees, jumping high through the clearing. Arrows were loosed, hitting the animals in vital spots, but still they ran on. Spurring their steeds, they followed, keeping on the deer's blood trail until the animals would finally drop.

Guillaume laughed and then called, "Ah, something besides wolf-meat stew for us this night, my Lord de Servian."

The jarring chase only increased Noel's pain, but they chased the deer until one fell, then finally the other. When his back slammed into the cantle, as Brishen jumped a fallen log, Noel said through gritted teeth, "I should have listened to Skena."

Guillaume pulled alongside and grabbed Noel's shoulder to steady him, as they reined the horses to halt. "Sorry for the manhandling, but Lady Skena would have my hide if you fall off your horse. We would never hear the end of it."

Noel pulled in a ragged breath. "We needs must get these beasts dressed before the meat goes off."

"My lord," Emory called, cantering up from the opposite direction. "Riders come through the lower passes, heading toward Craigendan."

Guillaume's face darkened as he dismounted quickly. "If we take time to gut the animals they will reach there before we can. Help me tie the roes to the backs of the horses. We will have to dress them at the *dun*."

"Did you see the pennon they were flying?" Noel asked of the young man.

Emory shook his brown head. "Nay standard I could see. Safe wager would be Comyns. The Campbells do not venture from fireside when 'tis cold. Besides," he looked from his liege and then back to Noel, "'Tis well known Duncan Comyn has fixed his eye on the Lady Skena."

Forgetting the dead animals, Noel set spurs to Brishen's side, racing back to Craigendan.

"Make way!" Guillaume called. The squires dropped the roe and jumped aside as Brishen leapt over the other fallen animal. "He is a man in love on a mission!"

* * *

Noel nearly vaulted from the saddle before Brishen stopped. The horse was angry for being run so hard, and nipped at his arm as he passed off the reins to the stable boy. He usually took care of Brishen himself, but he needed to find Skena. "Cool him down, curry him, and then an extra ration of oats. Do not look at me wide-eyed. Supplies will be coming in the next few days. Snap to."

"Aye, my lord." The lanky lad nearly hopped in alarm. Noel regretted barking at him, but failed to soften his words. With riders coming he wanted to greet them as the new lord, especially if it was Duncan Comyn, wanting to mark his possession of Craigendan and its lady from the first breath. Quite territorial of him, true, but this was his chance at happiness; he would allow no one to threaten to take it away.

"My bloody back suddenly does not pain me so much. Jealousy takes the edge off it." He chuckled wryly to himself.

He fretted, resentment rising. What if Skena had feelings for this man? Mayhap she had thought to wed with him once she put mourning behind her. Sanity pushed back the savage, unreasoning male and reminded him how Skena looked at him, how she hungered to touch him. Well, he would soon let her caress him all she wanted, which might be half as much as he craved.

"Skena!" Barely into the Great Hall, he bellowed her name. The women were setting up the trestle tables and paused to stare at him. Mayhap their old lord did not run around yelling. Well, they best grow accustomed to his behavior; he had a feeling he would be calling for Skena—and often. "Where is your lady?"

A lovely young woman did a faint bob before him. "I am Elspeth, Lord de Servian. Skena went to the stillroom to fetch boughs of the juniper for a cleansing of the hall. Some time ago. She never returned."

"Has anyone else seen her?" He looked around at the curious faces, realizing he was still new to them. While he had been here for days, this morning was the first time most of them had laid eyes upon his countenance.

The old lady who had helped treat him came slowly forward. "Skena went to the stillroom just after you left. Never came back. Come, I will show you the way."

Noel was not without compassion for the woman's afflictions of age, but the niggling of unease made him want to run instead of follow her slow steps. The disquiet clamored louder when they found the stillroom was locked. "Would she bolt it from inside?"

"Aye, on occasion she has been kenned to do so. Her bolt hole when troubles pressed in on her." Muriel raised her hand to knock, but Noel saw her twisted fingers, and instead rapped on the wood before she could use her poor knuckles.

"Skena?" He waited to hear if there was a shuffling inside in response. Only silence. He rapped again, almost sensing Skena was not in there. "You did not see her return?"

"Nay. Spotted her go down the passageway. Then . . ." Her eyes grew wide in concern.

"What?"

"Mayhap naught. Ella came into the hall from this direction. Thought it passing odd she would be in this area of the *dun*." Muriel's grip on her cane tightened until the fingers, malformed by age, whitened.

"What is at the corridor's end?" Noel asked, looking around. Reaching up he removed the torch from the sconce.

"Garderobe, bathing area for the soldiers after they work out on the lists, outer tunnel door for the fortress—to fetch in meat, goods, and supplies for the kitchen—and another leading down into the bowels of Craigendan where foodstuffs are stored," she answered, trailing after him. "She would have no need to go this way."

Noel paused to light a torch at the corner, and then again,

one halfway down the narrowing passage. He entered the room set aside for the soldiers to wash down after training in the lists. Little was to be seen—two tubs, a wooden screen, and behind it a huge wood trough where they could urinate. The trough sent the liquid outside where it would be collected and used in the processing of dyes. Sighing, he backtracked, as there was nowhere else to go.

Appearing upset, Muriel came toward him. "She ain't in the garderobe."

"Would she have reason to go to the sublevel where the foods are stored?" Noel asked. Alarm setting hard in the pit of his stomach, he did not wait for a reply, but rushed to the door. The cavernous belly of the fortress hungrily swallowed the light to where it only cast the yellow glow halfway down the plank steps. A sense of something not right crawled up his spine, pushing him to descend the stairs. Halfway down, the flickering of the torchlight spilled to the bottom.

"Bloody Hell!" He passed the torch to Muriel, then rushed down on the remaining steps.

Skena lay at the bottom, pale and unmoving. He pulled her onto his lap, fighting back the howl of madness that threatened to erupt from his throat.

Chapter Twenty-One

Noel was not sure he drew a breath until he put his hand to Skena's neck and felt the beat. Faint, so faint he almost feared he imagined it. When he located the pulsing, slow though steady, he gasped in the air denied him. Curling her limp body to his chest, he rocked Skena, willing her to awaken. His heart felt as if a knife were lodged in it. Not since that fateful morning when the servants had carried in his mother's lifeless body had he tasted such deep sorrow.

Muriel gasped, "Oh, by the Lady!" and then tried to come down the stairs.

"Nay! Stay," Noel objected, fearing the frail woman would fall. "I shall carry her up. Hold the torch high so I may have as much light as possible."

"Noel?" came the weak whisper against his chest.

He laughed, trying to shake the panic that had seized his soul. "Ah, so I am back to being Noel? Silly woman, once I can breathe again I might beat you for scaring me. I am not a young man, remember? Shocks to my heart are not a good turn."

Skena reached up and cupped his chin. "You are young and beautiful . . . and methinks just a bit vain. You want me to tell you these things."

"Oh aye, I am an overweening peacock, strutting my fancy

plumage to catch your eye. I am still going to beat you." Noel gave her the toothless threat, closing his eyes as he held her tightly to him. Fear of how close he came to losing her pulsed in his blood.

She managed a small laugh. "Very well, but first, will you kiss me?"

"Reward you for falling down the cellar stairs? Sorry, no kisses for scatty wenches who try to break their necks," he grumbled, pushing the strand of hair away from her cheek.

"I did not fall." Arms and legs akimbo, Skena tried to find purchase to stand.

Noel wanted to carry her up the stairs, but she seemed determined to get to her feet. He finally helped her. "Not fall? Pray tell how did you end up at the bottom of the steps? Fly?"

Skena finally looked around her and frowned. "How did I get down here?"

"Love, you had a fall—"

"I did *not* fall," she stated with vehemence, then winced. She put her hand to the side of her head. "Och. What a goose egg."

Noel nodded in sympathy. "'Tis what happens when you go clanging about and give yourself a knock."

"I did not give myself a knock. Someone else did." She glared, witnessing doubt upon his face.

"What mean you—that someone else did?" he asked, fearing her thoughts had been muddled by hitting her head.

Skena bared her teeth at him. "Someone—else—as in *not* me."

Noel took her upper arm firmly. "A bump to the noggin oft scatters the mind. Let us get you abovestairs and ascertain if you are all right. Then you may tell me about your adventure."

"I am not hurt, Noel, nor did I take a headfirst tumble down these bloody stairs. I went into the washing area, and someone dropped a burlap sack over my head. Then I think they flung me against the wall. How I got from there to the cellars I have no idea. I surrendered to the blackness."

Noel's brows lifted in skepticism, but Skena's expression only grew more resolute. Beginning to believe her, he looked around for the sack. No empty ones were about, the light only touching the barrels and few sacks that were full, sitting atop them. "Where is the sack?"

"Fine. Do not have faith in my word. I ken what I ken, Noel de Servian." She started to stomp up the steps, but he would not let go, forcing her to slow her pace to match his.

At the top of the stairs Muriel waited, concern clear in her lovely eyes. "Ah, lass, are you unharmed?"

Skena kissed the old woman's cheek. "Aye. I sport a proper egg on my pate, and I will have an ache come morn. Other than that I feel well enough."

"What happened?" Muriel pressed, as she closed the door to the root cellar behind them.

"I am unsure." Skena glanced down the long hallway. "I was on the way to the stillroom to fetch juniper boughs for Elspeth, then I—" She stopped speaking and glanced up at Noel, her face confused.

"You did what, Skena?" he asked.

She swallowed hard, but went ahead despite clearly knowing what his reaction would be. "I thought I saw Angus and followed him."

Noel straightened his spine, fearing she had injured herself more than she cared to admit. He reached out intending on taking her into his arms to carry her to the lord's chamber, only she jerked away from him.

"Save that pitying expression, Lord de Servian," she snapped.

He attempted to make light of the tense situation, concerned upsetting her would only aggravate her state. "Sigh, I am no longer Noel once again."

"Do not play folly with my claim." She stomped down the corridor toward the door of the cleansing room, leaving him standing there. "I was at the stillroom door and saw a man at the junction. He called my name. I followed. When I reached here he had vanished, so I entered."

Noel went into the large chamber, followed by Muriel, both trailing after Skena. She strode to the table where a candle had melted onto the tabletop. The wax on the surface was hard.

"A lit candlestick was on the table, the only light when I entered." Her steps carried her toward the screen in the far corner. "When I failed to espy anyone, I picked up the candle—thinking the only place someone could be in here and remain unseen was behind the screen. As I turned, a sack came down over my head."

Noel carried the torch closer so they could inspect the floor. Skena knelt on one knee and picked up the small wooden holder, holding it up with a triumphant smile that said *told you.* Cold wax streaks were visible across the stone slabs, showing a candle had fallen there whilst still burning.

"The sack was dusty. I remember having trouble breathing. Methinks I sneezed, then it felt like someone hurled me against the wall. Hard."

Noel found Skena's injuries distressing enough. Only, to see evidence that she had not simply fallen down the steps sent his temper nearly out of control. Someone had deliberately stalked her, dropped a sack over her head, and then slammed her to the wall. One was an accident. The other was someone intent on malice. Then what?—they arranged her at the bottom of the staircase to appear she had tripped? Why? Such dark actions contained no rhyme or reason. Only pure evil.

"You say you followed a man here—" Noel began, only to be cut off.

"Not a man," she corrected. "I followed . . . Well, I thought it was Angus."

Noel exhaled in frustration. Angus again. "This is the second time you claim to have seen him."

She nibbled on the corner of her lip, but finally admitted, "Nay, thrice now."

"Thrice?" It came out in a roar, so he moderated the word into a soft question. "Thrice, Skena? When else?"

Skena glanced to Muriel to judge her reaction. "I saw him this morn . . . at least I thought it was him . . . when we were presenting you as the new lord. For an instant, he was standing in the far archway in the shadows. He spoke to Dorcas."

"HA!" The snort of disgust popped out of Muriel. "Aught to do with that shameless strumpet who calls herself my daughter only bodes ill."

Noel's stomach twisted into knots. He could end Skena's concerns that Angus was hiding in Craigendan by giving her the truth—that he killed Fadden at Dunbar, drove a sword through his body. There was no doubt of the man's death. Only, if he told her how Fadden died, he might lose the first and last hope of love and happiness ever to come to him. There was no way he could risk saying those words. Someday, he would tell her, when he was assured she could bear his words without turning her heart against him.

"I saw Angus." Skena waited for a response from Muriel. When the old woman looked sad, Skena turned back to him. "Dorcas said he was alive."

"Lass," Muriel shook her head sorrowfully. "Ne'er place faith in what comes out of that lying bitch's mouth. 'Tis ashamed I am that I gave birth to the faithless creature. Better had I strangled her with her natal cord at birth, and saved us all a cartload of hurt and trouble. I watched what she did to you. She turned a deaf ear to me, laughed at the insult she paid you. If Dorcas said the moon just rose, I would expect to see the sun on the horizon. She spake evil words to spoil your new happiness, Skena. 'Tis killing her you might actually find love."

"I ken that well, Muriel. Matters not. I did see him. First, on the stairs to the boulevard when I was going to fight the wolves, again this morn, and just a short time ago in the passageway. He called my name and kept telling me to come, hurry."

Noel pursed his mouth, trying to decide if she held on to Angus's memory, conjuring his shade, because of misguided devotion, or mayhap morsels of guilt at going on with her life. "Skena, Angus is dead. You must accept that—"

"Skena!" Galen called from the doorway. "Riders come. 'Tis Duncan Comyn."

After finding Skena, Noel had forgotten about the riders coming to Craigendan. Now he wished them to Hades. He wanted to take Skena upstairs and cosset her until his fear of losing her finally quieted. Instead, he would be forced to play host to a man he little knew and trusted even less.

"Skena, we brought down two roes. Guillaume and his men will be bringing them shortly. Emory spotted the Comyn party coming through the draw, so I spurred Brishen back to reach Craigendan before they arrived. Come help me out of my mail and let us see ourselves presentable to welcome our guests." Noel turned her toward the door.

Muriel clucked her tongue. "Guests? Ha! 'Tis letting a red fox in with the geese."

"It will be my pleasure," Skena laughed, "to present Craigendan's new lord to The Comyn."

As the women started off down the hallway, Noel allowed his steps to slow. Lightly taking hold of Galen's arm, he pulled the man to match his slower pace. "Show the Comyn chief into the Great Hall and have him made comfortable. Since they likely plan to stay the night, they may be escorted to their rooms if they wish. Tell him Skena and I shall be down presently to greet him. Set guards from Challon's men at the doors so they do not leave the hall. Once Skena and I arrive, I want you to make a quiet search of every cranny and nook in the whole fortress. No corner spared light. We found evidence of someone living in the pines, about a league away from Craigendan. The site has not been used since the snow fell. I am of a mind he is sheltering within the *dun*, mayhap with Dorcas hiding him. If so, I want him found."

"Aye, Lord de Servian. It shall be as you wish." Galen gave him a solemn nod.

Scowling, Noel paused to look back to the cleansing room. He knew Skena had not seen Angus. That much was a certainty. He was coming to fear that the man who had been using the woods for shelter had come to Craigendan to hide after the snow started. But why? Who was he? What did he want? These questions seemed magnified in the light of someone's having thrown a sack over Skena. He believed Skena after seeing the wax on the floor. Only why? Was someone attempting to harm her? His mind returned to the watcher in the woods. Surely, the unknown man was connected to Skena's misadventure. Howbeit, had the knave been trying to scare her, or had the intent been more sinister and something had interrupted the scheme?

From now on, he would be sure Skena was never alone.

Fighting impatience, Noel stood still while Skena finished fussing with his appearance. Though it rankled a bit, he wore a sark of deep gray and a surcoat the color of the sky at midnight, items sewn by Skena, originally intended for Fadden's Yuletide presents. Not entirely happy with wearing the articles intended for a man who tried to kill him, he had little choice until his own belongings arrived. Since he wanted to put on his best appearance as lord of Craigendan before this Comyn chief, he swallowed the objections when Skena had offered these raiments.

"Are you sure you are well enough, Skena? Mayhap you should be resting," he fretted.

Skena chuckled softly, the sound sending a shiver up his spine. "Those words oddly echo ones I spoke earlier to you."

Putting his hands about her waist, he pulled her slowly closer. "And I should have listened. I admit you were right."

Her smile spread as her brown eyes roved over his face. "I could love a man who is wise enough to admit he was in error."

He felt the muscles of his face contort into seriousness. "Could you? Could you really come to love me, Skena?"

She reached up and gently traced the curve of his jaw, her smile fading. "Aye, I could. . . . I do. Had you not been so busy laughing with Lord Challon as you left, you would have heard me calling the words after you. As you said, we are little more than strangers, but there is a rightness when I am with you, Noel, something I have never felt before."

Lowering his head, he brushed his lips to Skena's, tasting her, gently savoring her rare sweetness. His blood surged, the primeval urge to mate roaring through him, overwhelming his thoughts. He wanted to shove her up against the wall and take her hard and fast, an echo of the dream where he had made love to her. Wanted to drag her to the bed and kiss every inch of her body until he was satisfied she was not harmed in the odd attack. Forcing those strong desires back, he tried to set her away from him.

Bold wench, she threw her arms about his neck and arched her body against his, deepening the kiss. He smiled against her mouth, knowing she wanted him as strongly as he craved her, only at this moment he had one poaching Scottish chief to deal with, waiting belowstairs for their appearance. Still, he was but a man, and Skena tempted him like none other; he gave in to her female demand and kissed her with the full passion boiling within him.

A knock at the door caused them to pull apart. Galen pushed his head inside and arched an eyebrow at them straightening their clothing. "Beg pardon, my lord, my lady, but the bloody Comyn demands his audience immediately, else he threatens to storm up here to assure himself Skena is not being held hostage and . . . hmm . . . tortured."

Noel held out his arm to the blushing Skena. "My lady,

shall we go show the Comyn knave the one being tortured in this fortress is me?"

She shyly placed her hand on his arm. "I beg to differ— you are not the only one tortured—but aye, let us deal with this aggravation so we can have done with him."

Noel felt like a king entering the Great Hall with Skena at his side. While he would rather stay abovestairs and give Skena kissing lessons, the male in him relished having this vibrant woman as his betrothed. He watched her with equal measures of pride and hunger.

Her hand squeezed his arm, slowing his steps. "Be careful of this man, Noel. The Comyns are a changeable lot, cutting their raiments to suit how the political clime blows. They are powerful, controlling vast lands and own the fealty of many, better than half of Scotland. Despite the humiliating defeat at Dunbar coming under their command, you can bet they will land on their feet in the way of a cat. Though Duncan is a lesser chief, he still holds strong connections to the powerful Earl Buchan. Craigendan is a small holding, hardly worth a second look from a Comyn, howbeit its position is such that it would be a sword to Julian Challon's side if the wrong man holds it. Duncan fully expected to see that happen. He will not be happy that you are lord here. Trust not a single word from his mouth. His brother Phelan was a knave and a liar. When he lied he could stare you in the eyes and never bat a lash. Duncan is cut from the same weave, but seems to lack the spine. When he lies he cannot meet your eyes. He shields this by some action—reaching for wine, watching a serving wench pass, cutting a piece of food—all done carefully to cover that he is spewing untruths through his teeth. Remember this well for it serves you in dealing with him."

"I heed your words, Skena, but please do not fear. I am apt at reading men. Having spent years dealing with Edward's mercurial mood shifts and his Angevin tempers, I have learned to

do more than hear mere words, but also what is left unspoken."
He lifted her hand and kissed the back of it to reassure her.

As he did so, his eyes spotted the man at the trestle table, rising in preparation to greet them. Noel's movement stilled. Comyn was dark-haired, neatly bearded, not too tall, and rather stocky of build. Women would likely call him a handsome man.

"Is there aught wrong?" Skena asked lowly.

He gave her a slow grin. Already she was sensing his moods. "Nay. All is fine, my love. Duncan Comyn, I presume?"

She nodded. "Have you met him before?"

"Nay, I have not held the *pleasure*." The way he spoke the word let her know he failed to mean it. "I was merely taking note how men in beards appear much the same."

Noel had a deep suspicion he stared at Angus Fadden's *ghost*. "Ah, the answer to one riddle."

Chapter Twenty-Two

Noel knew some men provoked an instant trust within him. Others slowly earned his faith. A few did the exact opposite. Without their saying the first word, some primeval instinct would set him to despising them. Noel experienced no hesitation in counting Duncan Comyn in the latter group. Oh, he recognized that he was already hardened against ever finding favor toward the man. Two reasons. First was that his brother, Phelan, had led men to ambush Damian and Julian back in August, and had died for the fool's effort. More damning, at least in Noel's eyes, was the second—the Scotsman desired Skena. Jealousy flared as Comyn's dark eyes went to Skena, coveting her in a hungry fashion that caused Noel to recall the wolves they had fought. When the man's stare shifted to tally his opinion of the new lord of Craigendan, Noel watched this man of Clan Comyn with veiled hatred.

"So be it," Noel muttered under his breath.

In the manner of a dear friend, Duncan came forward, holding out his hand for Skena to take. She did not accept it, instead leaned closer against Noel's side, and merely offered Comyn a faint incline of her head. The muscles in the man's jaw flexed at her response. Comyn's hand dropped, but steeled determination covered any other reaction.

"My lady, I came as soon as it was safe to travel—"

"'Tis kind of you to be concerned about Craigendan's well-being." Noel deliberately cut him off, taking control of their meeting. "So comforting to learn our neighbors are of such a caring nature. I am Noel de Servian, new baron of Craigendan. I do not believe I have ever seen you at the English court. Not even in Berwick August past, hum?"

"At the time of Edward's Parliament I was no landholder, thus never called to sign the Roll or take oaths before Long-shanks." Comyn met Noel's direct stare, even offered a faint smile, skirting around who his brother was and why he only recently became a landholder. "So the mighty leopard sends yet another of his pet dragons north to lay claim to a piece of Scotland? Though not a Challon by blood, just as true, eh?"

"A fair adjudging. I count myself most fortunate to have been raised with the Challon men," Noel answered, not ran-kled. "The closeness is not unlike your clans here."

Duncan's eyes swung to Skena, lingered, and then finally went back to Noel. "Ah, then we already are finding a com-monality, Sir Noel."

Noel wanted to ram the word *commonality* down the Scots-man's throat. Ignoring the urge, he led Skena to the lady's chair and seated her, then took his place to her right. He smiled when Muriel deftly slid into the place to Skena's left, preventing Comyn from sitting there. The Highlander recog-nized the maneuver for what it was, glared at Muriel, and then grudgingly accepted a seat on Noel's right.

"I am pleased to know the tracks are passable. That means I can safely send for the priest at Glen Shane, permitting Skena and I to wed without delay." Noel wasted no time in declaring his claim clearly.

"Wed?" Duncan Comyn jumped to his feet, nearly knock-ing his chair backward, his stare fixed over Noel's head to Skena. The flash of calculation, which had filled his eyes, turned bitter cold. "Word of this event had not reached my ears, Skena."

Noel lifted Skena's hand and placed a kiss on the back of it. "We only announced the tides to Craigendan's people this morn. Gossip tends to travel fast, but not in winter, I suppose."

"Has Skena suddenly been struck dumb that she cannot speak for herself?" Irritation apparent, Comyn rounded on Noel.

"Nay, Skena has not been struck dumb." She laughed. "There, thus far, has been little calling for me to say aught. But for your peace of mind, aye, I agreed to wed with Lord de Servian as soon as possible."

"You simply accept the will of Longshanks without a fight?" Comyn's derisive tone and words branded her a coward. Snatching up the cup of ale set before him, he nearly drained it up without stopping, as if washing the distaste from his mouth.

Skena threw the ire back into Comyn's face. "I am unsure why you assume I, a lowly maid, should fight the mighty leopard when so many of my countrymen fail to act in the same vein. In this matter there was no command from Edward Plantagenet. 'Tis my will. I wish this marriage with my whole heart."

At her forthright statement Noel's pride swelled. There could be little doubt this lovely woman spoke her words with the pure force of truth. He turned to see Comyn frowning. Even he heard Skena's resolution.

Noel gave her a smile. "I count myself a lucky man indeed, given Craigendan and Lady Skena's consent to plight her troth."

"Any man would consider himself rich in both," Comyn replied tightly.

Not quite the felicitations one might expect upon announcement of a betrothal, but then Noel hardly expected well wishes from this man. He had just stolen two things Duncan Comyn wanted very badly and that would see them bitter enemies. From this point forward, the Highland chief would be set against him in all. Well, he anticipated little more from the Scotsman whose brother tried to murder men close to Noel, hence the reality held little surprise to him. Beyond this, his mind harkened back to the fact that Comyn could so easily be mistaken for Angus Fadden in shadows and at a distance.

"Tell me, Sir Knight, was the former baron here your kinsman?" Noel noticed Skena's head snap back at the question, but he kept his eyes fixed on Duncan, wanting to witness his smallest reactions. Mayhap, make use of that bit of proofing Skena had imparted, which would say if there was truth in his reply.

Duncan looked straight at him in mild curiosity, naught more, not even batting an eyelash. "Nay, Angus came from a Lowlander clan, down near the Marches. Unawares I am of any blood connection betwixt us, none through marriage either."

Noel's hand tightened around the goblet as he raised it to his lips. Well, bloody hell, the man was telling the truth on that much. Still, it did not rule out he played evil games, trying to scare Skena for some dark purpose. Being practical minded, he refused to believe Angus Fadden's ghost was haunting Craigendan. The dead did not rise and walk.

Comyn might have come from his stronghold to the northwest. But if so, that left the burning question of who had been taking shelter in the woods of Craigendan and why?

Just before dark, Noel entered the cleansing room and pulled off his sark. Picking up a bucket of warm water, he poured the contents over his head. He allowed it to rain down upon him to dilute the roe's blood, which had splattered him and soaked through his clothing to his skin. Shaking his head in the manner of a wet dog, he relished shedding the coppery scent and sticky feel.

His head lifted as he spied Skena coming in with the stack of cloths for drying and the Yule raiments for him to change back into. He had not intended that she would attend him, which was why he chose to bathe down here instead of having the tub in the lord's chamber filled. Some ugly things could not be avoided in life, but the stench of butchery he would have spared his lady.

Guillaume sat down on the bench to undo the lacings around his boots, and then untie his chausses. He was a fine figure of a man in only his braies, a man to draw the eye of any female, but Skena barely noticed. Her eyes were only for Noel. His Skena. A half smile formed on his mouth and in his heart. Skena placed the stack of linens on the table and then started toward him.

Noel shook his head. "Keep back, Skena. I am covered in blood. I would not have it getting on you."

Skena gave him a shrug. "I donned a worn kirtle so I can attend you."

"Still, I would rather rid myself of the stench of guts and blood before I touch you." He closed his eyes and fought the waves of emotions flooding through him. "Reminds me too much of battle."

"You did this to see Craigendan's people have meat. If I get blood on me due to caring for you, then I am honored," she said simply.

Guillaume picked up a bucket and poured the water over his black head. Snorting, he wiped his face with his hand. "Lady Skena, can you send for the old woman to help me with washing my back?"

Skena crinkled her brow. "Muriel?"

"Aye, 'tis the one," Guillaume laughed. "Three score if she is a day, has a tongue like an adder, and no respect for Englishmen."

Skena was puzzled by Baron Lochshane's odd request. "Whilst I am sure Muriel would enjoy the task, her fingers are not as nimble as they once were, her joints going bad. One of my maidservants would be willing to aid you, Sir Guillaume."

"Nay, 'tis the old woman or none." Using the long tongs, he pulled the bucket back from the fireplace and then folded a rag around the handle to lift the pail. He poured half of the steaming water into the tub, dropped his braies, and stepped into the water.

Skena looked back to Noel in question, but he lifted his shoulders in a shrug to say he had no idea why Guillaume made the odd request.

"Nay, I have not lost my wits, Lady Skena. My squire is busy paying court to your doe-eyed kinswoman, one Elspeth by name, thus I have no hands to aid me. I am betrothed to Rowanne of Glenshane, and I would have no tales carried to her ears that I was making free with your maids," he explained.

"Then as befitting your rank, I shall tend you. 'Tis your right as baron—"

"Nay!" Noel barked. The word came out before he knew he had spoken. While Guillaume was as a brother to him, he did not want Skena stroking the man's bare flesh. He was unsure his teeth could stand the pressure from his grinding them!

Guillaume's eyes flashed knowingly as he watched his friend. "As I said, send in the old woman."

Skena nodded with a grin. "You are an honorable man, Baron. Not many men keep to their betrothed and respect them in such a fashion." She started to head to the door, but then recalled the tales whispered about the death of Rowanne's first husband, and turned back. Mayhap he was concerned over that. "My lord, you should not give ear to ugly rumors about my kinswoman. Black slurs which come from his family."

"Oh, I do not listen to such bilious tales. These past months, I have slowly come to learn my lady's mind. She is not an easy woman to know, not one to let you near and share her secrets. Whilst I put no store in such gossip, I fully believe my betrothed capable of taking a knife to me should I dally with some maidservant and it reaches her ears. The females of Ogilvie blood are warrior women, unlike any I have faced before. Hence, please call Muriel." His laughter filled the chamber.

Skena noticed the baron did not sound as if he were truly frightened of the lady of Lochshane. The man's tone held a faint hint of amusement, even admiration. She was coming to believe the new lord of Lochshane was a good match for Rowanne.

Noel smiled when Muriel tottered in, and then Skena came back to help him out of his clothing. She hissed in a breath as she spied his wound when he climbed into the water. Two red spots on her cheeks were visible even by firelight, as she lifted the bucket to dump in hot water.

"I do not ken why we bothered to try and heal you, de Servian. You work to see it fester again, mark my words," she fussed.

Noel leaned to confide to Guillaume, "Notice I am de Servian, not Noel. I might be forced to give her kissing lessons to earn my way back into her grace." He jumped as she poured the water into the tub. "Whoa, lass. Watch where you dump that bloody stuff. It might be injurious to parts of me you might find useful in the near future."

"Likely it will not matter, de Servian. You seem determined to rot before next spring."

Noel reached up and stroked her cheek. "'Tis nice, lass, to have someone caring about me. I promise to do better on the morrow. You may give all the orders you wish and I shall obey."

Muriel laughed when Skena snorted her disbelief. "Aye, you are smart not to let a pretty man turn your thoughts, especially with promises of obeying. Methinks our Rowanne will have a handful with this braw one." She worked the rag up and down Lord Challon's spine.

Skena sat down on the stool and looked at Noel with sad

eyes. "Noel, you must have care of the wound. Allow it to heal in the proper fashion." She reached up and wiped the splatters of blood from his face.

He felt bad that she fretted over him. "For far too long I only had myself to consider."

Muriel clucked her tongue at Giullaume. "Why the hurry, my lord? 'Tis been a few days passing since I was able to enjoy scrubbing such a bonnie back as yours."

"The honor is mine, but I just wanted shed of the blood. A warrior comes to hate that copper smell. Hand me the sheeting. I thought I would allow Lady Skena to tend Noel at her leisure since she will need to dress and bandage his wound." Accepting the length of linen, he wrapped it around him as he climbed from the tub.

Noel waited until Guillaume had dressed and left with Muriel, saying he would see them at supper, before he brought up his suspicions about Duncan Comyn. "Skena, I know you told me how to watch Comyn for lies, only what are your feelings toward the man?"

She paused from soaping his back. "Feelings? I have none outside I have never trusted him. His brother I trusted less, I suppose. I am not sure I can explain the difference between them. Phelan Comyn paid court to my cousin Aithinne, and for a short time she feared her guardian might favor his suit. 'Tis why I respected Guillaume's asking for Muriel. Phelan never paid such respect toward Aithinne, thus she was relieved when Baron Lyonglen refused Phelan's suit. There was something evil about him, in a lazy fashion, as if the world was there to serve him. Duncan is unworthy of trust, but I never saw the same evil. He hungers for land, power, and titles, as many second sons do throughout the realm. He keeps his eyes on what he wants. I believe him capable of much to achieve those aims. I always felt one day Phelan would meet with an *accident*. His attacking the Challon party and getting himself killed likely saved Duncan the effort, methinks."

Noel breathed a little easier with her assessment. "So no feelings? Did you expect one day to be his lady wife?"

Her eyes widened in surprise, and she shook her head. "Nay, the mummery of the women pretending to be soldiery upon the wall was to fool him into not acting against Craigendan. Had he understood how few men we have he would have laid siege. We could never have held against his men. Why do you ask this?"

"He put forth an air of familiarity—"

She nearly growled. "His presumption, naught more. Trying to tweak your nose, mayhap see you jealous."

Noel reached out, cupped her neck, and pulled her to him. "Well, it worked. I am territorial, Skena, likely more so where you and Craigendan are concerned. I have wanted a home, a wife, family for too long."

He kissed her gently, slowly, worshipping her with the devotion she deserved. The effect of Skena hit his blood with the power of mead and sent his heart racing wildly. All the blood lodged in his groin, cramped with needing her. He wanted to touch her, stroke her, taste her, endlessly, but now was not the time. He reluctantly pulled back. To save his sanity.

"Oh, lass, let us pray Sir Priest grants dispensation in the calling of the banns." He lightly touched his forehead against hers, relishing their closeness. "If our presence was not required for the evening meal, I would pull you across my lap and let you share my bath."

"There is not room enough for two in that tub." She laughed, picking up a bucket to rinse suds from him.

He grabbed a handful of her kirtle and played at pulling her into the bathtub. "Want to put that to the proof? It shall be my pleasure to teach you how well we will fit in this bloody thing."

"Methinks this will cool you off, Lord de Servian." She dumped the bucket of cold water over him.

A deep shiver racked his body and instantly his manhood

shriveled. "You have no idea, you wicked woman. Hold up the sheet and help me out. Then we can talk whilst you dress my wound."

"Of what do you wish to speak?" She held the linen length for him until he was out, her eyes hungrily taking in his naked form.

He chuckled. "You keep looking at me that way and we shan't be talking at all."

"Very well. Sit on this stool whilst I dress your wound with the salve," she said, then added impishly, "I will look and you may talk."

He sat, straddling the wooden bench. Skena touched the silky ointment to his wound and he jumped, but soon it had a calming effect on the pain. "'Tis soothing."

"Aye, the worts will ease the tenderness and promote the healing. 'Tis angry, but so far shows no signs of a bad healing."

"To be expected, the wound pains me. Howbeit, I failed to experience any of the numbness in my hand this day." He flexed his fingers testing it, glad not to feel the deadness. "Before, it grew worse. I lost feeling in it and then could not use it. It caused me deep concern."

"Poison invades one's body and will slowly kill even the strongest warrior. There. 'Tis covered well. Stand by the fire and warm yourself. Then I will wrap it so it will be comfortable for you."

He stood and allowed the sheeting to drop lower on his hips, though he kept it gathered about him, lest Skena see how aroused he was, despite the dumping of the cold water. Even her prodding on the wound had not slowed his flesh's growing insistence. She carefully rolled the bandage about his waist, snug, yet not too tight. It brought her close. He could not resist. As she tucked the end in, and then raised up, he brought his arms down to encircle her.

Male power rose within him, as he enjoyed how Skena's full breasts pressed against his chest. By damn, he wanted her here and now, cared little about the Church's blessing. No words of man or God could give blessing to what he already knew—this woman belonged to him. This was right, so special, he simply knew to his deepest soul that Skena had been created for him. The emptiness inside him, that corner of his heart was no longer cold, dark—Skena brought him warmth and light.

"Your heart hammers against mine, lass." His words were whispered in awe. "You sense how rare this is? We have been blessed in our meeting one snowy night."

Her trembling hands reached out and clutched his upper arms. "No, I was blessed when I found one snowy knight. My knight. A very special man named Noel who came to me at Christmastide."

Chapter Twenty-Three

The fire had burned down, allowing winter's chill to creep into the lord's chamber. Notwithstanding, more than the night's cold prevented him from sleeping. Restiveness crawled under his skin, a burning hunger summoned by Skena's absence. His wanting her was raw, primitive. Noel flung back the covers in mounting irritation and stalked to the fireplace, absently tossed a couple peats into the flames, then used the poker to prod the fire into life. Like a caged beast, he sensed his mate was near and yet could not get to her. An edginess within him refused to quiet.

Despite still finding burning dirt an oddity, he enjoyed the rich aroma. Staring into the flames, Noel sighed. The whole bloody night had been vexing. He had intended to speak further to Skena about Comyn, question if the man could be mumming as Angus's ghost, what aims he might hope to achieve in tormenting her in this way. Mating instincts had caused him to become sidetracked in the cleansing room, so utterly lost in the magic of love and Skena. He was a breath away from skipping the promised kissing lessons, putting her on that rickety table, and taking her with all the force thundering in his blood. Much to his frustration, he had been thwarted by Cook's sending in Kenneth and Owen to empty the bathwater from the tubs.

They had to hurry to dress for supper. Later, there was no way he could question Skena about Comyn with the man sitting at his elbow. The roasted meat was delicious, and he made sure that Skena ate well. She finally cried off, saying if she partook one morsel more of the wonderful roe he would have to carry her upstairs. Despite his back's aching from being up all day, he would have gladly endured the pain to have that privilege.

They lingered belowstairs, out-waiting Comyn until he finally had given up and sought his bed. After the scare of finding Skena at the bottom of the cellar stairs, Noel had not wanted her to retire to a chamber alone, aching instead to hold her all night, to know she was safe. Only then could he rest. Skena stubbornly refused, saying she would not want to have Duncan going back and speaking of her sleeping with Noel before they were wed.

Noel jabbed at the peat, venting his irritation through the iron rod. "Enough of this." He tossed the poker aside.

Picking up his heavy mantle, he swung it around his shoulders, and stomped off down the hall. His steps slowed as he passed the room where Guillaume was quartered; he did not want to awaken his friend. The door was cracked open—Guillaume being his cautious self. Without doubt, he was sleeping with only one eye closed due to a Comyn's being under the roof. Skena might think the man less a knave than his dead brother, but bad blood tended to run in families. There was no question Phelan Comyn had wanted to murder Damian and Aithinne, would have also killed Julian and Tamlyn in the ambush, just four months past. Neither Guillaume nor he would rest peacefully until the younger brother was far away from Craigendan.

The door creaked as it was slowly pulled back. Guillaume, still dressed in shirt and hose, held his sword in hand. The corner of his mouth quirked up when he saw it was only Noel.

"I am not the only one failing to find my rest this night. Where might you be heading, my friend?"

"If you wish to take that pretty smile back to your Lady Rowanne, you might wisely keep your taunts behind your teeth," Noel warned.

"Not that I fear you besting me in a fight," Guillaume rested the flat of the sword's blade against his shoulder, "but 'tis nary a taunt. I am happy for you, pleased to see you finding something you have long wanted. Happy the Challon men are finding treasure beyond measure in this pagan land. I only hope someday Redam and Dare may be so fortunate."

Noel nodded. "The men of Challon have long served Edward with a devotion sometimes unearned. His acts have seen his dragons tested and hardened in the crucible of war for too many years. The king is not young. Three score comes soon for him. He should hunger for fireside and comfort instead of living from the seat of a war saddle."

"Edward will die on the back of his charger whether he be five score. Go find your lady fair. I keep watch on your unwanted guest this night. Late on the morrow, men from Lochshane will come with your men and wagons, and then stay to man Craigendan. The day after, Julian will send more from Glenrogha. We will take steps to see Craigendan secure through winter. Come spring you can instigate further measures to make safe your *honour*." Guillaume's voice softened in admiration. "Your Skena held this place together for nearly eight months in dire circumstances. Think what the two of you can accomplish together. Keep her close until Comyn is gone. I mislike her being attacked this morn, and then his appearing soon after. Damian heals still from the arrows loosed into him by the hand of Duncan's brother. That alone would see me mistrust aught from this Scot."

"Aye, his looking much like Fadden troubles me as well."

"My men are posted. We can sleep when reinforcements come." Guillaume's green eyes flashed over him. "You must be losing your touch. I would expect you to have Skena close by your side."

"She wants Comyn to carry no tales back to his people about her. I was trying to be honorable." Noel shrugged.

"I tried to be so with Rowanne, though 'tis been damn hard on me. I have since come to the conclusion that being honorable is for priests and saints, and the wrong tack to take with an Ogilvie woman. Learn from my misstep."

Noel nodded. "Methinks I shall take your sage advice."

Guillaume smiled and turned to go back into the room. He called over his shoulder, "I thought you might."

As Noel continued down the dimly lit corridor, he muttered at his stupidity for not insisting Skena stay the night with him. "We could be tucked up, warm, instead of me traipsing about this drafty place."

He pushed open the door to the smaller room and frowned. Noel stared at the empty bed. The covers were rumpled and half tossed back. Even in the deep shadows, it was clear to see Skena was gone.

In measured steps Skena walked the length of the boulevard, counting each step in her path to the turn—the middle point of the walkway around the curtain wall and then back. Many times, these past months of summer and autumn, she had taken her turn at guard duty. She oft selected the late watch because it was one of the few times in her busy life that she found complete solitude. She enjoyed the lure of the night, the mysteries the moon created across the landscape as it played games with shadows and shapes.

She lifted the hood of the fur lined mantle closer about her face. It was cold, but not as bitter as it had been. She worried. Sometimes it grew warmer for a short spell before another heavy snowstorm descended. Still, for the first time this year, she breathed in some measure of hope, her burdens lighter because Noel had come.

A loud crash sounded behind her. She jumped. She was not a coward, yet she froze, through some primeval animalistic instinct that said to stay perfectly still until you knew where the threat came from. She remained motionless, barely breathing, waiting to hear if more noises followed. Only silence. After the first fright, her heart slowly began to beat again, and she felt safe to stir. Pulling her small sword from the sheath, she hurried in the direction of the disturbance.

As she turned at the far right corner, hurried steps came from the opposite track. She pulled up, getting a good grip on the sword's hilt. A man moved through the shadows, coming toward her. She tensed, almost expecting the worst—to come face-to-face with Angus. Instead, warm relief flooded through her as the man passed under a shaft of moonlight, breaking from behind the clouds, and she saw it was only one of the knights from the Challon cadre.

"My lady." He gave a respectful nod. "'Tis naught to fear. No evil invader uses a ram against the walls in a sneak attack. Look for yourself. 'Tis only one of the massive icicles formed by the overhang. It grew too heavy and crashed to the ground below."

Skena leaned through the crenellation in the wall to see a man-sized sheet of ice half shattered directly below. "I suppose there will be more of those crashes."

"Most likely. The wind shifts, coming from the southwest. Air is warmer off the big seas." He eyed her. "Should you not be inside? Whilst the wind is more pleasant, 'tis still too cold to be on the wall. I am certain Lord de Servian would not wish you out this time of night."

"I am used to being up here the wee hours of morn. 'Tis peaceful. 'Tis rare you find true quiet in a fortress." Skena could see the young man was not going to leave her be, so she added, "I will go back inside shortly. The smoke from the fire-place gave me an ache in my head. I came out for fresh air."

"Then I leave you to your thoughts, my lady. If you need aught, just call out. I will hear you. I am Stephan . . . Stephan Mallory," he said.

Skena studied the tall, fair-haired knight in the blue rays of the moonlight. "You are not of Norman blood, but English?"

"Aye, I come from the Cornwall area, my lady. I swore oath to Guillaume Challon because I wanted to fight for none other than the Dragons of Challon. I am honored he accepted me as his man."

"Keep well, Stephan Mallory." Skena turned away.

"God keep you safe, my lady," he called after her.

Skena slowly retraced her steps. If she went inside, she would go straight to Noel, pulled to him as if he were a lode-stone. He had wanted to take her in the cleansing room. He would have if Kenneth and Owen had not come in to empty the tubs. She would have let him. Her body ached, thinking on how hot his flesh burned, how the muscles of his arms tensed under her hands. His scent. His taste. She paused to look out through a crenel across the dead zone, allowing the breeze to buffet her.

Noel brought so many things to her—hopes, that dreams could be more than just wishes. He could help her make them come true. Love. Oh, how she wanted his love! She wanted to belong to this very special man. Yearned to have him need her in the same fashion. Only, she never anticipated that love could affect her body to the point of agony.

As she had lain in her small chamber, her blood had run hot. She craved to go to Noel, slide into his bed, and awaken him as her hands stroked his firm flesh. Never had she wanted to be touched in such wantonness, but she wanted Noel to touch her, to teach her the mysteries of his love. She closed her eyes and summoned the dream of him, from when she walked in his mind, how he touched her under the apple tree. So strong were the images that the scent of apple blossom seemed carried on the night breeze. Drawing hard on the vision, she allowed her body to pulse and burn, experiencing all the feelings of Noel's hands upon her flesh, squeezing her breasts, of his sword-roughened palm gliding up her thigh.

"Skena . . ."

For a heartbeat the discordant whispering almost became a part of her fantasy, but then she felt its icy, alien intrusion. She kept her eyes closed, squeezing the lids tight to give pretense that she did not hear the call. The first time she had seen Angus, she feared her guilt was summoning his shade back from the dead. After this morning when she followed him to the cleansing room, and the dusty sack was dropped over her head, she quickly dismissed this notion. Human hands had pulled that sack over her head and then slammed her against the wall. Hands—strong hands—had carried her to the bottom of the cellar steps. If it were Angus, he was—as Dorcas insisted—very much alive. Only, Noel was adamant Angus was dead, that there was no room for doubt. She knew Noel would never lie about this. The more she tried to unriddle who the man was and his purpose for showing himself only to her, the less she could untangle the questions.

She reached out with the kenning and sensed only blackness, a swirling, seething darkness that terrified her.

"Skena . . ."

Her hand tightened about the small sword hidden under her heavy mantle. This time she would not face the threat defenseless. Her heart rocked heavy in her chest, but she tried to control her alarm's quickening with slow steady breaths.

"Skena . . ."

She gave a small jump, as the summons was closer. Opening her eyes, she saw the shadowy form of a man slowly walking toward her. Since she refused to heed his call, he was stalking her.

"You are not Angus," she muttered under her breath, and

took a hesitant step backward. Then another. Her right foot came down on a pebble, causing her ankle to twist painfully.

If she kept going to her right she would run back to young Mallory on patrol, or she could go back to the entrance, run to Noel, and awaken him. She would not be so foolish as to confront this man as she had done before. The last occasion she ended up at the bottom of a staircase. This time she might end up at the bottom of the curtain wall along with the sheets of icicles.

She kept retreating with shaky steps, her ankle hurting each time she put weight on it. The corner was near, and then it would only be a few paces to the tower entrance. Not far. Yet, it seemed a furlong away.

His footsteps quickened. She matched them, finally turned to run. Skena glanced over her shoulder to see him gaining. She ran. She screamed, but the rising breeze coming strong from the southwest nearly threw the sound back in her face. Surely, Mallory on patrol would still hear and come to her aid.

Looking down the long boulevard, she saw no one. Where had the English soldier gone? The entranceway was just ahead, but she heard the footfalls closing behind her. Panicked, she reached the door and pushed against it. It refused to give. The door was never locked and could only be bolted from the inside. She had left it cracked open when she came out just a short time ago. Pounding on it with her fist, she kicked at it, but then gave up as the dark figure rounded the turn.

Again, she ran, hoping to reach the stairs where they descended into the bailey. Instead of coming on fast, he slowed, moving in deliberate steps, as if confident she had rushed into his trap and he now had her cornered. The moon broke free, sending rays to shower him with the pale light.

Dizziness sprung through her mind. Aye, she trusted Noel to tell her the truth; even so, she stared at Angus. She knew this! He seemed leaner, but then months of hardship could do that to a body. Had she not lost weight? She did not stop to consider why she should fear Angus. The kenning buzzed within her, driving her onward, to flee in fear of losing her life. Whatever had been between them before his going away had changed. She accepted what the inner voice told her—and ran.

The sword tangled with her skirts and mantle, causing her to drop it. She quickly glanced back, but left it where it lay. Coming down off balance on her right foot, her ankle violently jerked to the side, nearly causing her to stumble. She cried out, but kept going. Picking up the heavy material of her clothing, she hurried her gait.

"Skena . . . wait!"

The turn was ahead, the steep steps just beyond. Pushing herself hard, she flew around the corner, not slowing, and slammed hard into the chest of a man. She tried to strike out, push away from him, but he was immovable. Catching her by the upper arms, he held tight and refused to let go. Tears streaming down her face she fought the blackness threatening to claim her.

She had been right—she ran straight into his trap.

Chapter Twenty-Four

"Skena . . . Skena." His calling her name did not instill calm; instead she struggled even more. At length, Noel shook her faintly to stop her from striking him. "Hush, lass. You are safe with me. Stop this now."

His words at last reached her, for she almost crumpled in his embrace, leaning against his chest and weeping. "I saw him," she sobbed.

"Be calm, lass. Let us get inside by the hearth and warm, then you may tell me all." The muscles around Noel's mouth tightened into a deep frown; he suspected who Skena thought she had seen. Irritated, he glanced around for the sentries, yet saw none. "Guards! Guards! To me!" he shouted loudly. His voice rang out against the fortress walls, but drew no response. "Damn their hides. There shall be hell to pay on the morrow."

Taking hold of her upper arm, he started toward the tower entrance. Skena stumbled. Crushing her billowing mantle to her slender body, he easily swung her up into his arms. "I may chain you to the bed. I warn you, soon-to-be-wife, I shall endure no such nocturnal wanderings in my domain. Am I understood?"

She gave a weak nod, so unlike his rebellious lass. Skena was such a brave lady that it hurt him to see her shaken. As he neared the entrance, she lifted her head. "'Tis locked. I tried and could not get in that way."

Noel pulled up, seeing the door rock in the rising wind. "I am going to set you on your feet. Do not move. Disobey me, and I shall beat you."

She hiccuped and then bobbed her head. "I will obey, but not because you threaten me. You will never beat me, Noel."

"Ah, 'tis Noel again now you are in my bad grace." Snatching the long dirk from his right boot, he cautiously moved to the door. The air stirred it to swing only a small measure. He cautiously put his splayed hand on it to stop the creaking movement. Waiting a breath, he finally slammed his foot into the wood, sending the door to crash back against the inner wall. There was only darkness. Soon, flickering light slowly illuminated the spiral staircase, growing brighter as at last Guillaume's head came into view.

His friend scowled, seeing Noel standing in the doorway. "I heard you call for the guards."

"Hell's fire! Aye, I called. Find them! Find out why they abandoned their posts. Now!" Not pleased by the events, Noel allowed Guillaume to feel the sharp edge of his temper.

Guillaume nodded that Noel held that right. "First, allow me to escort you both safely to the lord's chamber. I shall then set about to sort matters with my soldiery." When Skena stepped forward and her ankle almost buckled under her, he offered, "Want me to carry her?"

Noel spared no answer, just a glare, causing Guillaume to chuckle at the possessiveness. Sweeping Skena into his arms, Noel followed Guillaume down the staircase. So alarmed was he by her state, Noel feared he might never let her out of his sight again.

"It was bolted," she insisted quietly.

"Hush, wench. We may speak about why you were on the boulevard once we are in the chamber. After we talk, *then* I shall beat you."

They neared the room occupied by Comyn, and Noel did not want the man overhearing any of their hushed words. He pulled up short when Guillaume raised his hand, then moved to the door in silent steps to check if Duncan were still within. Confirming this with a quick nod, he dropped his hand, and they proceeded forward again.

Once inside the chamber, Noel placed Skena on the bed and lit the fat candle at the bedside. Taking off his heavy mantle, he swung it across her. "Stay under that 'til I get the fire stirred."

"I am off to round up my missing soldiery," Guillaume announced.

Noel looked toward him. "Send in her maidservant with some mead—"

"I do not want—" Skena chirped.

"Hush, wench. Do you want me to beat you?" Noel threatened again, though it was clear Skena failed to believe him. He was having a hard time controlling his wild emotions.

"One maidservant with mead coming shortly." Guillaume closed the door after him.

Noel tossed three peats onto the hearth, then jabbed at them until they caught and burned brightly. Temper rising, he took several deep breaths to rein in the spiraling anger and sense of utter helplessness. He glanced up as Jenna came in, carrying a goblet. The woman looked to him. He tilted his head in Skena's direction. It pleased him the maidservant sought his direction, already accepting him as lord here. Jenna's presence also allowed him time to calm down before he spoke to Skena about what happened.

"I do not want this," Skena protested.

Finally, something Noel could focus upon. "Drink it, you rebellious wench—"

"Do not bother with dire threats of beating me, de Servian. They are toothless as we both ken."

He arched a brow. "Back to de Servian?" Noel took the cup from Jenna's hand and held it out. "I recall the night we met.

You forced me to down some horrid potion that tasted like mud, stump water, and ground twigs. All I ask of you is to drink mead. You were scared up there. I would like your spirit soothed. Once you drink it, then I promise we will speak of what happened."

Skena glowered, but took the cup. "I drink the mead. But you are still de Servian."

Noel smiled at his small victory. "Ah, you forget that I am a warlock and with magic of kissing lessons I can become Noel again." He turned to Skena's handmaiden. "Thank you, Jenna. Please stay with Andrew and Annis the rest of the night."

Skena's head snapped up at the mention of the children, just now considering they might possibly be at risk.

"Do not fret, love. Jenna and Nessa shall stay with them, and Guillaume will set a man at the door with orders to let no one in. They will sleep secure this night," he assured her.

"Do not fash, Skena. The lambs will be safe." Jenna took the empty cup and then left them alone.

Noel sat down on the bed, reaching out to take Skena's hand. "What were you doing on the boulevard? I thought you had retired? I went looking for you and found your room empty. You were not patrolling? I will not stand for it, Skena. You did well in keeping this fortress together and protecting your people until my coming. Now 'tis my responsibility to see to Craigendan's safety."

She pursed her lips while he spoke. When he finally stopped she asked, "Are you done? I cannot answer your questions if you do not take a breath now and again."

He gave her a faint smile. "You sound more like yourself. What happened, Skena?"

"I was not patrolling. I guess I am used to being up at this time of night. When I grew unable to find my sleep, I went for fresh air to clear my mind. I was not out long. I spoke with Stephan Mallory for a few moments—"

"So you saw him? Did you espy the other guards?"

"Not sure how many were on duty, but I saw two others at each end of the far turns. I never approached them though. After I left Mallory, I walked to the far corner of the main boulevard, and I heard someone call my name—"

"Of all the thoughtless things—"

"Oh, hush, de Servian. If you are going to fash without listening, then I am going to sleep. The mead is making me drowsy," she complained.

"Very well, speak. I listen now and beat you come morning."

"So kind of you," she teased. "I ignored the summons this time. I did have my sword, though."

"You did not have one when I found you," he pointed out.

"When he started for me, I dropped it and did not pause to pick it up. I ran to the tower entrance, but it was bolted." She saw him open his mouth to say that it had not been locked when they returned later and stopped his words. "I ken it was open when we used it. It was not when I ran to it. I kicked and beat on it. After seeing it was barred against me, I kept on running, thinking I would find Squire Mallory. He was not there. I screamed. Methinks even with the rising wind he should have heard me."

Noel nodded. "Guillaume is off seeking answers to where the guards were. He will get to the bottom of their where-abouts." He reached down and unlaced his boots, allowing them to drop. "I want no fussing about you staying in here with me this night because Duncan Comyn may carry tales back to his clan. I care not what the man has to say. You had two frightening experiences this day. I want you close."

He slid under the woolen *plaides* and bear skin throw, pulling Skena's trembling body alongside his. She sounded calmer, even traded jests with him about beating her, but she was deeply shaken by this newest incident. He had seen the fear in her eyes. Someday he would kill the man who put it there.

"Noel," she said softly, "thank you for holding me."

"Noel, eh?" He leaned his forehead against hers. "I hope to hold you every night like this for the rest of our lives, lass."

A dreamy look swirled in her dark eyes, the mead hitting her blood. "Is that a promise?"

"Aye, a promise, Skena."

"Good. I plan on holding you to that oath." The trembling lessened as she drew on the warmth from his body. Her eyelids slowly lowered and her head lay on his chest, while he cradled her in his arms.

Noel held her tightly until her faint quaking stopped. At length, she slumbered quietly in his embrace. Skena was a precious gift Fate had given to him, and he would allow no one to threaten her. Someone had dared. Well, he soon would put a stop to that, once and for all. He would make them pay.

"Aye, Skena, I keep my promises," he whispered, his eyes staring into the fire.

The rap upon the door caused Noel to rouse from the blackness of sleep. He blinked several times, and then with a sigh, carefully slid out from under Skena, still half draped across his chest. Despite his body's near constant complaint of needing to do more than just hold her, he had experienced a deep sense of contentment cradling her against him. A feeling of completeness filled his heart. Together they were snug against the room's chill, and though he really would prefer to stay with her now, he recognized the sharp knock as one of import.

For the longest time, rest had evaded him. Too many questions crowded his mind. A clear pattern should be obvious, keys to what was happening to Skena and why. Someone planned to benefit from terrorizing her. He had stared at the flames and gone over every detail, but still the riddles refused to give up answers. At some point, he had drifted off.

Glancing back at Skena resting peacefully, Noel stepped into the hall and pulled the door shut. He lifted his eyebrows and waited for Guillaume to speak. From the hesitant expression on his friend's face, he knew the answers would not please him. "So? Did you find where the errant guards were? They should be whipped, to a man. Their laxness saw Skena's life in peril. If I had not been restless and gone looking for her, she would have been left alone to deal with this menace. Why was no one there to help Skena?"

"I found one at the stable, a knot on his head. He said he heard someone moving around down there and went to investigate, and does not recall what happened after he entered the stable. Another guard was lured away by someone opening the postern gate and going outside. He went after them, only they disappeared into the woods. By the time he returned to his post everything had already happened. Possibly two different incidents. Or it might have been the same person mucking about in the stable left by the postern gate."

"And Mallory?" Noel pressed. "Skena said she spoke with him, but when she ran back for help he was gone."

"He reported that a redheaded woman had gone down the north stairs and tripped near the bottom. He went to her aid. She had twisted her ankle, and he had to carry her back inside."

"Dorcas, no doubt." Noel glowered. "Simple coincidences? I will eat my hauberk if they were."

"The specter of mischief afoot, I agree. First, Skena seeing Fadden's ghost, then someone staging that accident yesterday. The watcher in the woods. Now, half the bloody fortress was up running about as if it was Twelfth Night. Most niggling of all—a Comyn under the roof." Guillaume made a sour face. "His presence only sets hackles to my back."

"'Tis nary a ghost. Someone carried Skena from the cleansing room down to the cellar. A man. Only why leave her there?"

Guillaume asked, "Did you consider that by coming back early you stopped their intended devilry? I mean, did you search the cellars?"

"Bloody hell! I never stopped. . . . I was too upset and wanted to get her upstairs warm and safe." In frustration, Noel ran his hand through his hair, pushing it back from his forehead.

Guillaume's brow lifted. "No purpose, eh, was served in simply putting her there unharmed. Someone knocked her out and carried her down there. What if they were going to place her at the bottom of the stairs, mayhap break her neck and leave her like she fell? They could not kill her in the cleansing rooms. Someone might happen upon them carrying a dead body. It follows they knocked her out and moved her safely to the cellars. If anyone came along, they could say she fell and they were merely carrying her to her chamber. You were out hunting with me and half the men. Only you rushed back, and mayhap stopped them? The cellars run into caves, I am told. You have no way of knowing. . . . Someone could have stood in the shadows watching you."

"By the bones of saints, such never occurred to me. I should have ordered the cellar searched. I was too upset. Mistakes like that cost a warrior his life." Noel wanted to hit something to vent the growing fury.

Guillaume patted his shoulder. "Love has a way of muddling a man's thoughts. Well, if last night's misdeeds were all part of a plan, then clearly you are dealing with more than one person in this keep meaning harm toward Skena, possibly her children." Guillaume's exhale held a deep portent. "I had planned to return to Lochshane this morn, but I am staying now. You need someone watching your back until we unravel what is happening here."

Noel shook his head. "Nay, you will miss Yule and Christmas if you stay. Lady Rowanne will not be happy to find her betrothed away. Perchance she might view it as an insult. 'Tis the first time for you to spend the two holidays together."

"My lady can well do without my presence, much to my wounded pride. And sadly, I welcome the excuse not to be around her. Having to keep my distance is wearing on my honorable intentions." The truth of Guillaume's words was written on his face.

Noel gave him a lopsided smile. "I appreciate you at my back, if you are sure it will not cause sore feelings with Lady Rowanne."

His friend shrugged. "I would delight to know Rowanne missed me and was upset I was not there. I suspect she wishes I just would go away and cease to bedevil her. Mayhap absence will make her heart long for my return." He raised his brows in doubt. "Mayhap not. Go seek your rest. 'Tis early still."

Noel nodded. "Excellent suggestion."

As Guillaume walked away, Noel turned to look back at him. He felt sorrow in him that his friend believed Lady Rowanne harbored resentment for his coming to Lochshane. Later, he would ask Skena about the woman, her cousin. To Noel it was easy to see that his friend was in love with the distant lady, and he hoped they would find a bridge over their differences.

Loving Guillaume as a brother, he wanted only happiness for him. Guillaume, too, had been a warrior for so long. His friend needed peace, a place of his own. Since finding love with Skena, he would wish the same joy to all the battle-weary dragons of Challon.

Chapter Twenty-Five

Entering the chamber, Noel walked to the fireplace, picked up the poker, and prodded the flames into life. Plagued by the troubles stalking Craigendan, his mind could find no peace. Since quick answers to the dilemma were not rising in his thoughts, he was relieved Guillaume had offered to stay for a spell longer. The men of Challon had survived enemies and warfare all these years by watching each other's backs.

"This will be yet another time when brother stands with brother," he whispered to the flickering fire.

Staring intently into the yellow and blue flames, as if the answers to his questions lay in the dancing lights, he failed to notice Skena had awakened until she slid her arms around his waist from behind. He gave a faint start, surprised his warrior's sense had not detected her presence until she touched him. Dismissing that unease, he smiled as she leaned along his back and hugged him. Skena pressed flush against his body, allowing the fullness of her breasts to mold to the columns of his back. The baize chemise did little to shield her softness from his flesh.

Taking hold of her lower arms, he unwrapped her hold about his waist. Not completely, just enough to pull her around to face him. "I wanted you to sleep," he said, then kissed the side of her forehead.

Skena looked up, a drowsy expression in her brown eyes. "You went away and took all that wonderful heat from our bed. Now I feel chilled. I recall you saying there were other ways for a woman to warm a man's blood. Faster ways. Do those tricks work for a man to warm a woman's blood?"

He smiled and tugged her tighter to him. "I believe 'tis the same for a man or a woman."

She rubbed against him like a cat, as though she could not get close enough. "Show me, Noel," she whispered, tilting her mouth up to his.

Skena ignited a blaze in his groin, the sensation flowing outward like molten iron within his blood, a ravenous, clawing need, a force the likes he had never experienced before. Craving pounded through his mind, blotted out reason, leaving it hard to focus on anything except how soft her lips were, how he wanted to taste them.

"'Tis taxing to be honorable, lass, with you against me like this. 'Tis different for a woman. A man's blood rules at such times. Age old instincts drive us, push us. The quickening in the blood turns animalistic. Once the beast within us slips the leash, 'tis not easy to remember soft words." Noel struggled to hold on to the last shred of his sanity, as the scent of her skin filled his mind with intoxicating Skena.

"And you tell me this to say 'tis a bad thing, my lord?" A playful glint reflected in her huge eyes. She pushed up on tiptoes to brush her mouth lightly against his. "And when am I to get my much needed kissing lessons?"

"You play with fire, lass," he nearly hissed when she put her hands on his waist and slowly snaked them up his bare chest.

He tensed, every muscle rigid as though he were turning to steel. The desire was too strong in him, overpowering any sense of control. A smart man, he wanted this first time with the woman he loved to be special, to brand Skena so that she would never want another man's touch. Still, he needed more. He was determined to sear the memory of Fadden from her soul, rid her of the old memories and replace them with images of their being together.

"Fire warms. . . ." She pressed her lips against his again.

He grinned. "Nay, fire . . . *burns*."

As he lowered his head, his mouth took hers. No more playful kisses. He let loose the rapacious force tearing at his insides. No gentle lessons as he had planned to share with her.

He wanted. He took. And took.

He feared shocking her by the near violence of his hunger. Undeterred, her fingers curled around the back of his upper arms as though seeking purchase to hang on. His embrace dropped around her lower back and arched her body against his, letting that soft curve at the apex of her thighs feel the throbbing need she provoked within him. Not frightened by the intensity of the kiss, or the blatant demand of his body, she twined her arms behind his neck and then used the leverage to rub against his groin.

Breaking the kiss, she panted out, "Then, my love, burn me."

Noel felt he was the one burning! "So be it. I want to make all your wishes come true."

Kissing her again, he itched to reach down, grab her thighs, and wrap her strong legs around his waist. Though he was lost in the raging passion, he knew better than to do so; after carrying her down from the bastion earlier, the slightest movement saw his back remind him not to be so foolish again. The wound ached despite the unyielding mating drive taking the edge off the pain. Instead of following the impulse, he spun them toward the bed, nearly dancing her across the floor until her hips made contact with the high frame.

He paused, staring down into Skena's face, held enthralled by her pagan beauty. Not perfumed or bedecked as the fancy ladies at court, yet she was worth a hundred score of them. Skena was simple, honest, and loving. That love shone in her luminous brown eyes.

The way she stared at him humbled Noel in a fashion he

could not put into words. He wanted to fall to his knees and worship her, honor her for giving him something he had never had. Still, the awe of his love pulsed as a fever in his blood, expressing itself in a desire that was near blinding.

As he put his hands around her waist, her mouth turned down at one corner. Troubled by her expression, he asked, "Skena, what upsets you?"

One shoulder gave a small shrug, then she looked down to avoid meeting his questioning stare. "'Tis naught."

"We are betrothed. We should begin as we mean to go on our journey together, thus speaking truths between us is a must."

Her chin lifted. Skena being brave. "You spoke I was too skinny. Worse, if I am in dire need of those kissing lessons, I fear what you will think of the . . . rest."

Noel could not help but laugh. It was soft, not mocking, a simple expression of his happiness bubbling forth. Her frown deepened. She looked to one side, then the other, ready to burst into tears. Instead, she lifted her fisted hand to his chest as if to pound on him; it fell with only the faintest of thuds.

"De Servian . . ." His name came out with a choked sob. "You are an insensitive swine."

"I choose to ignore that. You are thin because you went without supping to save food for others to survive. Now there will be plenty of rations for Craigendan, I shall spend the winter plumping you up. And I pointed out the slightness of your body not because it was unpleasing to me, but simply because I was scared that you might be ill. I have promised you lessons in kissing. As for the *rest,* that tends to be a result of the kissing lessons. Lass, lass, oh lass . . ."

He brushed his mouth tenderly against hers, savored the sweet taste with the hint of mead still on her lips. Lifting his head, he watched the reactions play out in the brown eyes, the awe, the wonder. He tasted her again, deepening it just a bit. As he felt her hunger rise from the contact, he once more pulled back.

"Teaching you the ways of pleasure will be my greatest joy. Howbeit, it will require many lessons, long lessons."

Skimming his hands down to her hips, he squeezed the firm roundness of her buttocks, relished how his palms cupped the curves of her flesh. Then with a quick jerk, he lifted and gave her a small toss onto the bed's plane. "Lay there, do not move, or I shall beat you." He sat down on the bed and began unlacing his hose.

"What if I wiggle my toes? That is moving. Will that require you to beat me?" She pushed the point by tickling the side of his thigh with her foot, toes squirming.

"It might." His eyes danced over her body caressed by the shadows. He climbed upon the high bed, moving to her on his hands and knees. Placing a knee on either side of her thighs, he loomed over her. The primitive male in him relished seeing Skena under him, hungered for her surrender. In the gossamer chemise, nothing was hidden from his hungry eyes. The darker tips of her breasts drew his desire to where he could hardly look to anything else.

Finally raising his head, he said softly, "The first law of kissing is that kisses are not just for the lips." He nibbled gently at the edge of her small, full mouth. "But can be placed anywhere."

"Anywhere?" she chirped.

He nodded slowly. "Any . . . where."

To prove his words, he shifted down her body to reach the tip of her left breast. He kissed the stiff point, nuzzling it, then watched her eyes widen. Leaning back, he took the tip into his mouth and sucked hard. Even through the worn night rail he could feel the changes, signaling the depth of her arousal. As the tiny bud jutted more, he raked the edge of his teeth over the sensitive flesh, pushing her responses higher.

Giving rein to the wildness pulsing within him, he took hold of the garment and ripped it from the neck down to her belly. Her full breasts lay bare before him, the deep shadows flowing around their perfection. Her breasts grew tighter, heavier, evidence of her deep desire for him; the dusky areolas were tight, pushing the nipples into tight nubbins.

In stunned awe, he uttered, "Oh . . . so . . . beautiful."

His hands around her neck, his thumbs lightly stroked along the column of her throat, moving downward. Skena sucked in a ragged breath of anticipation, knowing where the path his hands were taking would end. They slid across her square, proud shoulders and finally to the upper slopes of her smooth breasts. Once again, she drew in sharply, her spine arching, almost as if offering the pale mounds to him in a silent plea.

"You wish something, Skena?" he tormented.

She swallowed hard and then nodded. "Touch me. Put your hands on me."

He smiled deviously, then leaned to her and touched his mouth against hers, then asked, "My hands? Or my mouth?"

"Either . . . both." She trembled with the need clawing its way through her body.

"I intend to grant all your wishes, my lady." His tongue swirled out and around the stiff peak. In response she shivered and then closed her eyes, obviously riding the crest of the conflagration he set loose within her flesh. He drew heavily upon it, suckling until her breath was harsh, raspy. Before moving to the other one to give it the same attention, he commanded, "Open your eyes, Skena. I want to share this joining with you, see the emotions reflected in your haunting depths."

Her long lashes raised, showing her eyes shimmered with unshed tears. The warmth in her gaze bespoke of love, of a soul-deep need for him, almost as if her mind reached out and touched his, whispering to him with this kenning. He had not considered that until now. When his wound had been lanced, he had invited her to walk in his mind. Would that ability increase the pleasure threshold for her, as she could also feel what he experienced?

His lips closed over hers once more. Slanting his angle, he worked her mouth, giving her those lessons of pleasure, how enjoyable it could be between them. His control shattered as the kisses went on. And on. Noel felt a low moan echo within his chest, then another, yet was unsure if the second sound came from him or Skena—little cared as he kept kissing her, she kissing him. Her hand came up and fisted in the curls at the back of his neck, as if she needed an anchor not to be swept away on the storm of emotions.

Heat rolled off their flesh, blistering them, as the kiss deepened, more demanding. His tongue pressed along the seam of her lips, compelling her to open for him. Skena's body flexed in shock, then desire, as she quickly learned the rhythm, the play.

Leaving them both breathless, his mouth moved along her jaw, then down the side of her neck. He paused to lave his tongue against the spot where her pulse jumped in a pagan rhythm. A tattoo as old as time. Her heart slammed against her ribs, the force felt against his chest. The power of this magic between them was beyond measure.

Sliding down the bed, he dragged her under him, his solid weight pressing her into the soft feathered bedding. Her body conformed to his solid planes, rounded softness meeting his hardness in perfection. He was heavy, he knew, yet she seemed to want the sensation, the total surrender.

For an instant out of time, he paused to stare at her face. Then his fingers splayed over her belly and then snaked lower to shift through soft curls at the apex of her thighs. Damp from her body's desire. Preparing her for his invasion. Kissing her, he moaned as he slid a finger into her, then two, then her hips bucked in reaction as he stretched her body.

Almost an echo of the dream.

"Please . . ." She seemed unable to gasp anything further.

Taking Skena's hands, he interlaced his fingers with hers and pushed them up beside her head, while aligning his body to hers. His throbbing erection nudged against her opening, moistening the tip with the silken honey flowing from her body.

He tried to speak, but found the muscles of his throat would hardly work. "Look into my eyes, Skena," he ordered, his voice rough. "You *are* my wish. I want you to see my face as I join with you."

His male hardness stretched her. Both agony and ecstasy, he pushed into her scalding heat. The fullness caused her to take short breaths; he kissed her over and over, easing her mind until her body accepted his blunt presence within her. Slowly she relaxed, and her slick channel allowed him to slide in even deeper.

"Fire magic," she gasped. "You indeed burn me."

"'Tis just the start, lass."

Lifting his hips, he set his swollen flesh to stroke inside her again, going even deeper. Each thrust strengthened, quickened. Her hands clung to his back, her fingernails biting into the flesh of his shoulders. Then clinging did not seem enough. Skena picked up his rhythm, arching to meet his frenzied thrusts. Their mating grew as wild and furious as a summer storm.

Skena cried out at the same instant that Noel's body exploded into a thousand white-hot cinders, nearly blinding him. Grabbing her tighter, he pulled her into a maelstrom of their passion, the scorching heat of his seed pouring into her body.

It took many labored breaths before the racing of his heart slowed. To Skena's surprise, he rolled again, taking her with him, until she was sitting astride his hips. He laughed at her befuddled expression.

"Noel, your back?" she fretted.

"At this moment I feel little other than the need of you." He smiled as she blinked, confused until his hips bucked. "Ride me."

His sensual mouth curved into a grin as he pushed upward within her again. It caused Skena to reach her pleasure that quickly.

She shuddered. "'Tis like . . . shooting stars in my mind. Have . . . mercy."

Her internal muscles rippled along the length of his flesh, fisted about him. "Aye, sweet mercy," he agreed.

But mercy was not what he had in mind. He reared up and wrapped his arms about her back, driving relentlessly into her again and again, each explosion building into another. His back bowed, as his body slammed against hers, harder, more frantic, until she could only obey his command and follow him into the dark storm.

Skena held back nothing, yielded everything to him. It was not enough. He demanded more and she gave. He wanted her physical release . . . but he wanted to burn her heart, brand her. Dark words of love he whispered to her, weaving his own magic.

He kissed her. No gentle kiss of worship, this kiss was full of the passion, born of the fire of their coming together. Skena wanted to burn. And burn her he did!

The perfection of being within her, knowing their joining was done with love, moved Noel so profoundly that he could hardly draw air.

He rained kisses over her face, gasping. "Oh, sweet Skena, I love you. . . ."

Chapter Twenty-Six

"Do I still get my kissing lessons later?" Skena asked as she tugged the kirtle on over her head.

Lacing up his hose, he leaned to slap her on the arse. "Greedy wench. 'Tis not enough you have made me a late riser this morn, already you beg for more kissing lessons. Never satisfied."

Taking hold of her hips, Noel pulled her close. He intended to give her a proper kiss good morning, only the knock at the door caused him to groan in frustration. "'Tis not the children. They never knock," he teased. Going to the door, he opened it to find Guillaume holding a pail of water.

"I am reduced to playing squire for you. I ordered you hot water to shave and told that sour faced cook to have it sent up. He told me to take it myself."

"Leave my cook alone. He knows the art of seasoning." Noel took the bucket. "My thanks, Squire Guillaume."

"Do not tarry. I am most eager to enjoy this morning's work." With a wicked grin, Guillaume sauntered off down the hall.

Noel closed the door and went to the table in the far corner, pouring hot water into the bowl.

Skena set to straighten out the bedding. "And what is this

morning's work? You are not going out hunting again? You said you would rest and allow your back to heal properly."

"No venturing outside the pale this day. We plan to boot Duncan Comyn out the gates of Craigendan, then we shall have done with his mumming at being a ghost. I little understand what he hopes to achieve, but enough is enough."

Skena picked up his mantle from the foot of the bed and folded it carefully. She paused, fascinated with watching him lather and scrape his face with the razor-edged knife. "I have never seen a man do that before. Does it hurt?"

"Only if the knife is dull or the hand is shaky," he chuckled.

"I like seeing your face, mind," she reached out and ran two fingers over his newly clean shaven cheek, "but why do you do it?"

"I mislike a beard. Itchy. Hard to keep clean. In winter, where the vapors from your nose hit it, they can actually form icicles. In summer they are hot. Besides, 'tis better, more pleasurable for kissing lessons." His thumb stroked her chin, which showed dark abrasions from their loving. "Also, 'tis easier on your tender skin. From now on, I shall shave before you get to enjoy kissing lessons."

"I will put some of Bessa's healing salve on the marks." She blinked away her rapture, her mind returning to their former topic. "I wish Duncan to perdition, if that is possible, but what is this about him and ghosts?"

"I would think it obvious. Have you noticed men of similar coloring, build, and wearing beards oft appear very much alike? Especially in poor light. I believe Duncan is your ghost of Angus, Skena. I have not figured out what he hopes to achieve, but he showed up around the time you started seeing Angus. Too much of a coincidence." He wiped the knife on a cloth and stuck it back in the sheath, then leaned over the bowl to wash the remaining soap from his face. "I never had a moment to tell you what we found yesterday when we hunted. Someone has been sheltering in the woods. There was clear evidence of crude refuge. Of course, there is the off chance it might be a runaway serf, who has taken to the woods to live off the land rather than under the hand of his master. Only, I find it telling someone was lurking about Craigendan right before the sightings of your ghost started."

Skena exhaled impatience, mayhap laced with fear. "I keep telling you that it is Angus. Duncan would have no reason to scare or harm me with the pretence of being my dead husband come back to life. It makes no sense."

"He wants Craigendan—and you," he stated flatly.

"Listen to yourself. He cannot gain possession of Craigendan if something happens to me. The property would go to Andrew. . . ." Her words trailed off as panic flashed in her eyes.

"Andrew is too young to hold the fief. Who would shoulder that responsibility?" He wiped his face with a cloth and then stared at her. "Well?"

"I am thinking. Generally, it would go to the closest male to hold for Andrew. Since there are none, I would assume it would fall to Julian Challon to foster my son, to set a protector for Andrew if something happened to me." Skena went to the bench and sat. "I still do not see what all this has to do with Duncan."

"Men oft lose reason when their pale aims are thwarted," Noel insisted. "Ponder upon his brother, Phelan. He set an ambush to kill Damian and Julian as they returned from Berwick. His greed, his taste for revenge pushed him to madness. What says this taint does not also fester in Duncan's mind?"

She stared at him, her large eyes haunted. "I have no leaning to defend Duncan, for I would put little past him, only I see little purpose for his tormenting me as a means to win him Craigendan. 'Tis Angus. Not his ghost. Dorcas insisted he was alive. Surely, it was him living in the wood?"

"Why hide? Would he not just return here openly?" he countered.

"Mayhap he heard Edward had given you Craigendan. This was no sudden thing, you said. He awarded you the charter months ago. The wound kept you from coming to claim it. Perchance Angus heard of this whilst he was healing and hid in the wood to spy, find out what the situation was at Craigendan before revealing himself to anyone. If that is so, then he would contact Dorcas first. She would aid him, sneak him food and information. Ask her. She is a terrible liar, worse than Duncan. She gives you this blank stare and does not bat an eye if she lies. Foolish woman thinks that makes her appear innocent. Force her to tell you where he is."

"Skena, cease this foolishness. Angus is not hiding anywhere. He is dead." Noel dumped the water from the bowl into the slop bucket.

He wished he had some logical reasons to offer as to why Comyn was playing this evil game, so Skena's mind would accept it. Her believing it was Angus only put her in danger. The more he argued it could not be Angus, the stronger Skena insisted it was. He could end her suspicions once and for all. Three simple words would stop all concerns of Fadden's having risen from the dead. *I killed him.* And with that declaration he would destroy the hopes that had taken seed in him. Shatter Skena's tender belief that wishes could come true.

He would ruin all. In that same breath, she would lose everything as well.

Noel's eyes shifted to Guillaume, exchanging a silent message as they waited for the woman to enter the solar. "Comyn went away too easily," he complained.

"You sound disappointed. What did you expect? He had little reason to tarry. His only excuse for coming was to assure himself Skena was all right. She now has a valiant knight protector and is betrothed. His presence was made redundant, and he knew it." Guillaume moved to the fire, warming himself.

"In truth, I had hoped to vent my frustration by rearranging his face." With a predator's focus, Noel watched Dorcas coming down the hallway. "I shall have to settle with confronting Skena's half sister. Notice, she is not limping after her fall."

Instead of being intimidated by a summons from the new lord, Dorcas entered with a languid gait meant to show off the sensual sway of her lush body. That alone set Noel against the woman, even if there were not already a list of reasons to dislike her. Skena had gone without a normal ration of food for sennights, judging by her body's thinness. He saw no such self-deprivation on Dorcas's frame. The haughtiness in the way she carried herself lent credence to Skena's assertion that Dorcas fancied herself above others.

"You wanted me, my lord?" she asked, coming into the large room and stopping only a few feet away. The tone of her words carried an implied sexual meaning. Her hazel eyes flicked to Guillaume, hardened with calculation, and then finally she nodded to him in deference.

"I wanted to speak about your claims to Skena." Noel spoke softly, but only a fool would not hear the steel to his words. He pondered just how much an idiot this woman was. Well, he was about to find out.

She stared at him, eyes wide and unblinking. "Claims, my lord? I am unsure of what you speak."

"Skena spoke that you claim Angus Fadden is alive," he said flatly.

"Alive? I have heard no such tides." She tried to sound shocked, but failed. And once again, she failed to blink. "I have no idea why Skena would say such lies."

"Lady Skena," Noel quietly corrected.

Finally, she batted her eyelids in surprise. "Beg pardon, my lord?"

"I said call her *Lady* Skena—"

She fleered. "But Skena is my—"

"I am aware of who you are and what position you have filled at Craigendan. Do not hope to continue in that vein. You shall address her as Lady Skena. Am I understood?" The pitch of his voice made it clear he would brook no opposition in showing disrespect toward Skena.

Tension was reflected in the woman's jaw, but she gave him a faint nod.

"Good. Now I would like to know why you think Fadden is alive," Noel exhaled in impatience, ignoring her previous assertion.

Yet again, she offered him that wide-eyed expression that Skena had cautioned him to expect. "I cannot give the answer you seek. I have no notion why Skena would say Lord Fadden is alive. All ken he died in April. Duncan brought back the news in early May, mayhap a sennight after Beltane."

Noel targeted the fact that she spoke of Comyn by his given name, but allowed it to pass. For now. He stepped toward her, using his height to intimidate her. "Skena said you told her Fadden was alive."

"Mayhap losing her beloved lord husband has caused her mind to turn inward." One shoulder gave a small shrug. "Skena was never very strong, my lord."

"Lady Skena," he snapped.

"Beg pardon, my lord. 'Tis hard to change the patterns of a lifetime." Her attempt to sound humble failed.

Noel gave a bored wave of the hand. "You are dismissed."

"If there is aught else I can do for you, my lord—" she started almost to purr in sensuality.

"I said dismissed. Do not make me repeat my orders," Noel cut her off. He was rarely brusque with servants, but he wanted Dorcas to understand her place. Crossing his arms, he watched her walking away, something niggling at the back of his mind. "She little resembles Skena, nor Muriel, for that matter. Odd."

"They are only half sisters. Skena favors the Ogilvie line,

so mayhap the woman gets her looks through the father." Guillaume pointed out, "Did you catch her slip about Duncan's telling her Angus was dead? How she also called him by the familiar?"

Noel frowned. "Skena has this ability to pinpoint when people are lying. Told me both Comyn brothers lied, but Phelan would stare you in the eye, whilst Duncan always looked away, guising the action. She warned me Dorcas gives you the wide-eyed innocent look when she speaks untruths. And that is what she did when she mentioned Duncan's telling her about Angus's death. She lied. Again, she uttered falsehoods when she said she never told Skena he was alive."

"So she is involved. We assumed this already after last night. She also is comfortable enough with Comyn to use his Christian name. What shall you do?" Guillaume asked.

"What can we do? Watch the postern gate well. Put one of your men to following Dorcas. Warn him to keep his arse in his braes and three arms distance from her, or I shall skin him alive with a whip."

Guillaume laughed. "Methinks that will convince him to resist her charms."

"It damn well better. She lied. Had last night's mummery of falling not convinced me of her involvement, her lies removed any question in my mind. Comyn is away from Craigendan. He will have to come back if he hopes to keep up his games."

Guillaume tossed the dregs of his ale into the fireplace. "Mayhap, he will give up the plan, after coming face-to-face with you, with the Challon might at your back. His branch of the clan already has one black mark against their name for Phelan's stupidity. He might not want to incur Edward's wrath."

"A possibility. We shall see." Noel's gut told him not to count on that.

* * *

Noel watched Skena pull the kirtle over her head and then wrap the *plaide* diagonally about her. She had been fidgety during supper, her eyes often straying to the children; it was clear she worried about them. She was also a bit irritated with him for not accepting that she had seen Angus.

Sitting on the bench, he pulled off his shirt and unlaced his boots, tasks done absentmindedly. He hated that the foul truth stood between them. Aye, Angus Fadden's ghost loomed near, but not in the fashion Skena believed. Someday what happened would come out. Just not now, not until he bound her to his heart and soul, until she could not breathe without him.

"Has Craigendan been searched?" she asked, pacing to the fire.

He nodded. "Thrice. But now Comyn is gone—"

She tossed up her hands in exasperation. "'Tis Angus I say. He means to kill me. . . . Last night, I felt it with the kenning. . . . I feared he would toss me over the bastion wall. I know it was him in the cleansing room."

He fought clenching his jaw. "Angus is dead, Skena. Accept that. Even if he were alive, how would he benefit from your death? I would still be baron here, by Edward's decree."

"If you were still alive. If. If. If. Do you not see, if you were dead along with me, he could return and claim Craigendan?" she pressed her argument.

He shook his head. "No one is deviling me. Why would Fadden wish you dead?"

She shrugged sadly. "Before, you said there was no end to what men would do to possess a thing, that madness, obsession can grow? Same can be said of some women. Dorcas. With me dead, she believes she could wed Angus and finally become the lady of Craigendan."

Noel shook his head. "She is a mere serving wench—"

"But my half sister. We had the same father."

Noel leaned forward to toss another peat to the fire. "I

thought Craigendan came through your Ogilvie blood—your mother's blood, in your Pictish ways."

She hugged herself against the chill. "I am not an Ogilvie heiress like Tamlyn or my cousin Aithinne. You must not recall my telling you on the first night you came that I took my father's name to inherit this land. King Alexander gave me and Craigendan to Angus. If something happens to me, and Angus is alive, Dorcas might figure he could take her to wife, since she is of Diarmad MacIain's blood. She has always believed she has as much right to this land as I do."

"She is not stalking your shadows. You are seeing a man. Who would help her?"

Skena rolled her eyes as if he were a simpleton. "Angus!" Grabbing his arm, she nearly wailed. "My children are in danger, Noel. That bitch will not let them live if I am not here to protect them."

Doubling over on herself, she clutched her middle and howled in anguish. His heart aching at seeing her in such distress, Noel pulled her close. "Hush, lass, I shan't permit anyone to hurt you or the children."

"You will not be there to protect them. They will kill you, too." She choked out the words through her sobs.

"Skena, Skena . . . your mind turns inward upon itself. Fadden is dead."

"You are wrong!" Another moan racked her body.

When he first came, he feared Skena loved Fadden and still grieved for him. Only, he now pondered just how happy she had been in the marriage with the Lowlander Scot, especially with her half sister as Fadden's leman. One that wanted to be raised to be baroness.

Noel took her by the upper arms, pulling her to stand. "Skena, danger is close at hand. This we both know. Howbeit, I give warrant that Fadden is not the source. He is dead, Skena. I saw his body myself."

She blinked her tear-filled eyes, confusion filling her face. "Saw him? You never said that before."

Noel steeled himself. He treaded upon treacherous ground. "Horrors of battle are not things men speak of to a gentle lady. The savagery, the brute ugliness deeply scars the soul. Talking of such matters only keeps them alive in the mind, permits them to haunt you. I find it repugnant what war does to men, how it robs them of honor and caring. It hardens you, Skena, in a fashion I do not like to see in me. 'Tis what I did to survive. Even in the worst of it, I desperately held on to my humanity, to my basic sense of honor. Many men do not."

"Did you ken Angus?" she asked, trying to focus her thoughts.

He shook his head. "Nay."

"Then how can you be sure? As you said, men of the same build, coloring, and wearing a beard oft appear similiar. Mayhap you only saw a man who looked like Angus."

Damn her, Skena refused to accept his half truth. She showed a good grasp of logic. With nothing solid from him to refute her fears, she remained convinced Angus was still alive.

Three words could knock the legs out from under her. And damn his hopes for a life with her in the same breath.

"It was not Fadden, Skena. Please trust me on this. There is no question. Let it go. There is some other answer."

"Of all the pigheaded men! You, Lord de Servian, rank as King of Fools. By ignoring what I say you condemn me, condemn my children." She tried to shove away from him.

Noel held firm. "Skena, damn it, listen to me. Fadden is dead." She kept struggling, fighting him, as much in her mind as with her physical efforts. She would not listen. "By all that is holy, I know he is dead. I killed him."

"You . . . killed . . . him?" She stilled. The words were barely more than a whisper.

She no longer cried, but looked at him in horror. She finally glanced down to see his hands holding her arms. The look she gave him made him remove them. Noel held them up, palms to her, saying he was not trying to hurt her. Sucking in a deep breath, he tried to find the words to explain.

Instead, she moved fast, shoving him and running; she only slowed long enough to knock the stool into his path, causing him to trip. "Skena, wait!" He grimaced as his back screamed a plaint from his twisting to keep from falling. "Goddammit! Curse saints and sinners alike. Skena, let me explain. 'Tis not what you think."

As he rushed into the hall, he paused to look in both directions.

Skena was gone.

Chapter Twenty-Seven

Noel ran to the staircase, meeting Guillaume coming up the steps with Stephan Mallory behind him. "Did Skena come this way?"

Guillaume shook his head no. "What happened?"

"I told her about Fadden," Noel said, calling himself a thousand kinds of fool. "She has it fixed in her mind he is alive and has come back to kill her. Would not listen to anything else."

Guillaume lifted his eyebrows. "Someone might have that aim in mind, but certainly 'tis not her dead husband. We will go look for her while you get your boots and a shirt on." As Noel turned to go back to the lord's chamber, Guillaume cursed. "God's teeth, man, you are bleeding from the wound."

Noel reached back to the bandage, his fingers coming away with blood. "Small matter. We can deal with the wound once we find her and she is safe—"

The sound of the children talking drew Guillaume to their chamber door. Slowly pushing it open, he looked in. Swinging the door wider, he showed Noel that Skena was with Andrew and Annis. "Stand easy, friend. Your lady is with her children. I was just fetching young Stephan here to set him as guard for the night."

Noel moved to the door and looked inside the room. Skena

sat in the middle of the bed with Annis cuddled in her lap. Andrew hung playfully from the crosspiece of the footboard, jabbering about giants, warriors, and how he would grow up to be a fine knight one day . . . *just like Noel.* At the boy's declaration, Noel felt his heart tighten.

Guillaume's deep voice broke the soft family sounds. "Lady Skena. Noel is bleeding. He needs you to tend him."

"Jenna can—" she began.

Only Guillaume swiped his hand across Noel's back and held up his bloody fingers. "Jenna will care for the wee ones. Squire Mallory has come to stay with them as well."

Skena nodded resignation. Slowly, she slid off the bed and came forward, quickly wiping her tears with the backs of her hands. Without looking at Noel, she swept past him.

Noel watched Skena flitting around the room, preparing worts, cutting the length of material for a bandage—and avoiding looking at him. Her movements were jerky. To be expected, he supposed. She was still grappling with the enormity of what he had told her.

Damn him, why could he not have hid the truth from her? There were too many changes in her life to deal with, plus the threat of someone menacing her and mayhap the children. She little needed to reconcile herself with news that the man she would plight her troth with was also the killer of her husband. He sighed. There was something about how Skena made him feel that saw it hard to keep matters from her. He wanted no shadows between them. Starting off a marriage with truths unspoken would be an ill omen to the path their lives would take.

The damage was done. He could give her time to come to an understanding and want to speak of the circumstances of Fadden's death. She was a smart woman, and wisely realized the gravity of her situation, grasped that in battle men killed. He hoped she was coming to know him well enough to sense he was honorable and would only have taken a life with just cause.

The key was, he knew she desired him. Her own body would be traitor against any stubbornness. She was falling in love with him. Skena was a kind woman, a caring woman. Her heart would listen to him in time. Howbeit, a deep sense of honor was woven into Skena's character. She took vows and bonds seriously. She had owed allegiance to Fadden for many years. That left her in a bad position.

She picked up the knife to cut the length of material. Her hand fisted around the hilt and something dark passed behind her eyes. She glanced over at him, watching him in a way that saddened him.

He held up his arms so she could cut the old bandage away from his waist. Almost daring her, he stood there, knowing if she wanted to plant that dirk in his heart he was giving her the opening. Oh, his warrior's instincts would stop her if it came to that. This was her trial. Would she embrace the future he offered, or cling to the past and a man who did not deserve her? Skena's grip tightened about the bone handle.

"Do you wish to hear the whole truth, or would you prefer just to kill me now?" he asked in resignation. "You tread a dangerous road, Skena. Ugly thoughts flow through your mind. You are a fierce warrior, stronger than even you ever believe, but this is a conflict you should back away from. Do not make this a struggle between us. You will lose. I will lose."

She said nothing, her head lifting to meet his stare. Unshed tears glimmered in her eyes.

He gave a sigh, wanting to grab her and shake some sense into her, wanting to kiss her until she forgot past loyalties to a man who had failed to earn such allegiance. "Very well, if you desire to use the knife on me, your grip is all wrong unless you plan to gut me." His left hand took hold of her wrist tightly. She could not break free, yet he was not hurting her. "The upward thrust is good for slitting the belly. 'Tis a slow, ugly death. A man stands there holding his innards, knowing his death is coming. Pain unendurable. Perchance that is what you wish? Methinks you likely would rather plant it in my heart. In that case, you need to grip it thusly."

His words were ugly, brutal. He wanted to shock her. Curling her fingers slowly from the ornate dagger, he then forced them around it again, until she held the knife for striking at a downward angle.

Clearly Skena was unsure what to make of his present mood. Likely he did not fully understand what was driving him either. He was not giving up Skena's love without a fight, and by damn, he was not going to have her look at him in loathing for the rest of their lives. If she could not let go of the past, let go of a misguided fidelity to a man who did naught to deserve her trust, her devotion, then mayhap it was better she plant the knife in his chest and have done with it. He was leaving it up to Skena which road their lives would travel. She could embrace vengeance or put aside imagined duty and open her heart to him. He hoped for both their sakes she would put her faith in him and their growing love.

"You come at your enemy with a downward arc, like this—" He pulled her arm toward him until the blade touched his chest above his heart. "Your choice, Skena. I am making it quite easy for you. I shan't fight you."

She grew a shade taller as her spine stiffened. "I was going to cut away the bloody bandage instead of unwrapping it, naught more. The linen might be stuck to the wound. If I pull it away it might bleed more."

"You are valiant and willing to fight for what you feel is right." He reached out and lifted the knife between their faces. "This is not the way. This is not right. You saved my life. Twice. Would you prick my heart with this long blade because I was forced to take a life in war?"

Her lower lip trembled faintly. "You speak a fool's blethering."

"Do I? Then tell me you did not consider planting this pig-sticker in my chest? Or was it your intent to strike a blow when I turn my back? 'Tis much easier to do than face a man and look him in the eye. If Fadden were alive he could tell you all about cowardice. Tell me that thought does not linger in your mind even now."

Her head dropped forward, eyes unable to meet his stare.

"Your lack of denial tells the story, Skena. Is that what you really want? Or is it what you believe you should do? Why? Out of misguided loyalty to a husband, a man who took your own sister as his leman and little cared your pride was dragged through the muck in doing it? A man who lies dead and in the ground, food for worms. " His words were harsh. He meant them to be.

Her head snapped up. "You are ugly, de Servian."

"My words are ugly. I am beautiful, according to you." He lifted his brows in challenge, daring her to deny she had said those words to him.

"Bastard," she hissed between her teeth.

He gave his head a small shake. "Nay, my parents were the Baron and Lady Darkmoor. I told you a little about them. Both were beautiful people, and they were very much in love. Rare for the nobility. A true love match. Can you say the same of your marriage? Were you and Fadden a love match? Or did he allow you to sleep in your cold bed each night, while he lay with another?"

Again, no response came. Her mouth pursed, then trembled, as if holding back thoughts that could cause more damage than a knife. He knew Skena well enough already to comprehend that Fadden's taking her half sister as his mistress had deeply wounded her pride. It was why he had used that detail against her. Reminded her how the man little honored her and their vows.

Noel released her hand, leaving her the knife, still testing. Part of him hoped she would drop the blade and seek pax between them. The warrior side of his nature anticipated—feared—she might foolishly push the impasse into a confrontation. He knew Skena had not faced an easy time here at Craigendan since Fadden's death. She worried too much, these past months taking their toll upon her. Even so, war had never touched this glen. Out of the way, Skena and her people had been spared the revolting brutality of war, never forced to bend their will to that of another.

He was sorry such a lesson would come at his hand, should she choose the more treacherous path. But then, mayhap it was better to taste this hard reality so they could move past it.

"I assume your silence means your marriage was not a match born of love." He sounded just a bit smug. Could not suppress it. Secretly, though he felt for the bruised pride she had endured, he was pleased Fadden had not been such a paragon in her eyes. It would be one less obstacle to overcome. He prodded to see her reaction. "He was much older than you. You were—what—ten and six when he took you to wife? Nearly a child bride?"

Skena vibrated with emotion. "I suppose being close enough to kill a man allowed you to judge his age."

"Aye, I killed him, Skena. Do you now want to hear how and why, or have you decided to stick that dirk in me without a proper trial by ordeal?"

She shivered. She was not cold, but scared. Too bad. He was not giving her an out. She had forced his hand. Now she would deal with the repercussions.

"What can I expect from any man but lies?" she finally managed to get out.

"Do not paint me with the same hues as Fadden. He was unworthy of you, Skena. I speak words you already heed within yourself."

When she stood resolute in her fury, anger spurred his temper. He took a step closer, letting her feel the heat off his flesh. Most women would have backed up in fear. He was an intimidating man, tall, powerfully built. Smart women learned at an early age not to provoke any man, especially a knight. And his dear little Skena was smart, so bloody smart. Only she did not flinch. Whether she comprehended, it spoke so much about her. About her fearless nature, about how she trusted him not to hurt her.

The corner of his mouth twitched up. Mayhap he should give her space, and let her see the difference between Fadden and himself, allow her to understand the choices made in war could still be done in an honorable fashion. Fadden had not been respectful of Skena in taking Dorcas as his leman. He had shown only viciousness in killing a lad, not even ten and six summers old, just to get his sword. When the man attacked Noel while he dismounted, Fadden had not been a soldier fighting in war. He tried to do murder. There had been no scrap of honor within Angus Fadden on the moor of Dunbar that ugly April morn. Skena was too smart not to come to this understanding.

Nevertheless, Noel perversely wanted Skena's unconditional acceptance. Wanted her to trust him because her heart did. "You speak of the kenning, these powers in women of Ogilvie blood. Can you not touch me, walk in my mind, and know who I am? What I am?"

Her lower lip trembled. "The kenning was never strong in me. I oft feared because I forsook the Ogilvie name that mayhap I paid price by the power's failing to rise within me. Yet Tamlyn took her father's name, and she is one of the strongest in the clan, so I finally assumed it was just me, that I was lacking. Until . . ."

Her eyes lowered as she turned the knife to carefully slice away the blood soaked bandage. She swallowed hard as she stared at the wound with a dawning realization. The deep gash had been inflicted by Fadden. How close it came to the man's robbing Noel of his life.

"Until?" he pressed.

Her shaking fingers cleansed the wound and then dabbed the soothing salve across it. He heard her breathing hitch. She was too close to him. His scent, his heat was affecting her physically. Their making love would only see this reaction heighten. Poor Skena, she now faced a clash between the logic of her mind and the desires of her body.

He understood the problem only too well. Each brush of those fingers caused his body to buck. So many emotions pumped through him—anger, resentment, hurt—yet he could not sort them out and act according to what would heal this breach between them, simply because his body ruled. He needed her. As he needed his blood or air to survive. Skena was a craving that clawed at his skin, destroyed all reason, thus he struggled against the mating drive pushing him to act. But then, he recalled Guillaume's saying how he committed a mistake in giving Rowanne the room to adjust to their coming marriage, that he should have pushed for matters to be settled between them.

Mayhap it was simply the excuse he offered himself to take what he wanted. He little cared. There was no other choice.

As she tied off the bandaging, he lowered his arms and trapped her against his body. She gave a squeak of surprise. He took advantage to kiss her, thoroughly, and with no mercy. His mouth moved roughly on hers, opening her to his tongue delving deeply, provoking the responses she fought hard not to give. His valiant warrior. Her lips tasted of the wine they had for supper, but it was no more intoxicating than the taste that was all Skena.

She whimpered, pushed against his chest, but with only the faintest of efforts. She tried to lean back, but his hand fisted in her long hair holding her firmly against him, allowing him to kiss her with all the passion driving him. Just as her resistance relaxed, he lifted her and threw her down on the huge bed. She did not resist, did not try to scamper away, just watched with her huge brown eyes while he skimmed off the hose and then climbed onto the bed.

"You have a chemise on again. I want you naked, Skena. Take . . . it . . . off," he demanded in a tone that said he would do it for her if she refused to comply. Only, he wanted her to do it. He wanted her complete submission and would settle for nothing less.

She must have understood him, for she sat, scooting into the deepest shadows and then reluctantly dragged the worn garment up her body. Pulling it over her head, she dropped it, and shook her long hair to form a veil around her. Well, he would have none of that. Noel reached out and grabbed her ankle and yanked her down onto the bed and back into the light from the fire.

Placing a knee on either side of her hips he straddled her. He had a feeling she just planned to accept whatever he wanted of her, allow him to take the burden of choice from her. Take the burden of her wanting him out of her hands. "Sorry, love, passive surrender will not suffice with me."

When she remained silent, Noel shrugged and leaned forward cupping a breast with each hand. He squeezed their firmness. Pushing them up high, he took the crest of one breast into his mouth and sucked hard as the fingers of his left hand rolled the tip of the other. Skena's hips bucked slightly, but again she fought her own body's response. She turned her head to the side and closed her eyes. Little coward. She relished the attention he gave to her body, only tried to hide it. Well, there was no hiding some things, how her nipples were swollen, distended, how her pelvis made little twitches, moving against him restlessly as though she could not suppress the natural urge.

"Skena . . . touch me." He meant it as a command, but the hoarse whisper came out as a plea.

The tone seemed to break through the reserve she was desperately clinging to, for she opened her eyes. For the longest spell she just looked at him. Finally, she lifted her left hand and slowly laced her fingers with his. A simple gesture, but the meaning seemed so profound. Not taking her eyes from his, she repeated the action, this time linking her right hand with his left.

His body slid down hers. His legs shoving her thighs apart, he aligned his body to hers and slowly pushed into her silken heat, nearly scalding his flesh. She fisted around him with the fit of a glove.

"Burn me, Skena. Brand me. Take me," he whispered as he pushed their hands over her head, arching her to him, and sending them to madness.

Chapter Twenty-Eight

With misgivings in her heart, Skena looked across the room to Noel, standing before the Great Hall's fireplace. He feigned attention to the festive start of the celebration of Yule. Merely a pretense. As if he felt her eyes upon him, he glanced up and met her gaze, their eyes locking. His expression was haunted, accusing.

Two days had passed since he had told her how Angus died. Two long days. At an impasse, little had changed between them. During the day he was polite, even supportive in anything she brought up concerning the fortress. He had toured the cellars to take stock of the meager supplies stored below the frost line, and went over the tally books for Craigendan, showing a clear interest in every aspect of its running. Only, he kept himself at an emotional distance from her.

At least during the day.

After the first day, she had started to retire to the small room down the hallway from his. His expression livid, he stormed in, sending the door flying against the wall with a loud crack, swept her into his arms and carried her down the hallway. He dumped her in the middle of the huge bed in the lord's chamber, then warned in a voice that brooked no opposition, "Do not contrary me, Skena."

Both nights he undressed quickly and then pretended to go to sleep. Later, in the hushed darkness, he had turned to her and silently taken her. She offered no resistance, even welcomed his loving as a means of bridging the distance between them. What hurt—no words of love passed between them, just the mindless, blazing passion that left her sweaty, wrung out, and clinging to him, helpless against needing him all the more.

Noel taught her pleasures she never imagined, how he could bring her to that pulsing black magic with just his hands or his mouth. They had come together in near violence, yet turned around and loved so slowly, so exquisitely that tears formed in her eyes. When the morning light came, he rose and prepared to face the day as if nothing had happened in the long hours of the night.

The abrupt switch left her confused. Noel seemed to be waiting, wanting some response from her, yet she remained unsure what that was. Fearful of making the situation worse, she breathed in dread of losing his love.

She had never known love before. Oh, she realized there had been a hunger for the elusive feeling, a sense her life had been lacking without it. Noel had showed her the reality, the bonding of their bodies, minds, and souls, so much more than the dreams of her young girl's heart. Now, she understood just how precious and rare the emotion was. To lose him would be too much to bear. She could not imagine how empty her life would be without his gentle magic.

Noel made her believe in wishes. Yet, with the deft pass of a wizard's hand, he could destroy the fragile, divine spark of hope. Destroy her.

She inhaled, trying to think of something to say to the stubborn man to end the stalemate, but no words of healing came to mind. This night was Yule, the longest night of the year, with the hours of daylight being scant few. A season of endings and renewals, a time for fresh hopes. Time to leave old regrets behind. She had to reach past the confusion and embrace the new life he was bringing to her. Staring at his silver eyes, all else about her faded to mist. She needed to mend this breach, explain to him that she had overreacted on learning of how Angus died. While he had not given any more details, she recalled the vision of Noel taking the sword to his back, how close he came to dying, and now knew Angus had wielded the blade in a cowardly fashion. Noel was obviously leaving it to her to come to him, to say she trusted him to be an honorable man in all.

Covered in snowflakes, Squire Emory Maynet came rushing in. "Riders and wagons come, my lord—under the pennon of the baroness of Lochshane."

Guillaume's hazel green eyes reflected a mix of emotions. He put down the tankard of mulled cider in a show of indifference. "I suppose 'tis Rowanne's way of reminding me that she still rules Lochshane and the wagons come under her largess." He said lowly to Noel, "I am naught but the bastard knight forced upon her by Julian and an English king."

Noel patted Guillaume's back. "Methinks these long nights are grating on your soul. Come, let us go offer well-come to your lady." They started out of the Great Hall, but then Noel swung back to Skena and offered his hand. "My lady?"

Once again, the pale eyes bore into hers. Demanding. Begging. Angry. Hurt. Swallowing the tears clogging her throat, Skena came forward and placed her trembling hand in his.

Flakes fluttered down as Skena stepped out into the winter gloaming. The short day was quickening toward night, rendering the snow-covered landscape a magical blue. She breathed in the air, not too cold, but moist, carrying with it the promise of heavy snow. The renewal of Yuletide slowly filled her. Mayhap on this magical of nights, all things were possible.

By Guillaume's guarded expression, and Noel's grin and nudge of the elbow directed at him, Skena assumed the rider at the lead of the convoy had not been expected. The falling snowflakes covered the pale blue mantle the lady wore. She rode sidesaddle, the massive cape half-covering her legs, hidden by a robin's egg blue kirtle. Her long, pale hair flowed out from one side of the hood lined with white fur. Like a princess of the Snow Fae, Rowanne of Lochshane reined the dapple grey palfrey to a stop and merely sat, staring with an aloof air. Her beautiful countenance reflected serenity, though the brown eyes flashed with a banked fire as she stared at Guillaume.

She waited until he came to help her down. His hand gently touched her booted foot, lingered on her leg as he gave her ankle a squeeze. Then he unwrapped her legs from the horns of the sidesaddle. Seizing her about the waist, he lifted her to the ground. The regard in which Guillaume held her cousin was clear to Skena. Harder to judge was Rowanne's reaction to the handsome Englishman, who would soon become her lord husband.

A knot of envy formed in Skena's throat. Rowanne MacShane was a woman men called beautiful, and they truly meant it. Always attired in rich fabrics and jewels, she could present herself at English Court and hold her head high. By comparison, Skena suddenly ranked herself shabby in her best blue kirtle. Well, there was naught to change it. Steeling herself to the sting of comparison, she went forward to greet her cousin.

"Tides of Yule and well-come, Rowanne." Skena embraced the taller woman.

"I have missed you, Skena. Our *duns* keep us too busy to visit as we oft did when we were children." Not sparing a word for her betrothed, Rowanne linked arms with Skena and started up the stairs to the entrance. "Could you show me the room where I will stay? The ride in the cold was not an easy one. I should like to rest before supper and the festivities."

Guillaume spoke from behind them. "She stays in my room."

Red shown on Rowanne's cheeks as she whipped around. "I will do no such thing."

"You shall," Guillaume countered with clear determination. "I shall sleep on a pallet on the floor if you do not trust me to—

what is it you Scots call it—bundle? But you *will* stay in my room. There has been trouble here, and whilst methinks it shan't extend to you, I want to know where you are at all times."

Rowanne's amber brown eyes went to Noel, judging his reaction to the claim, then back to Skena. Skena nodded faintly. "Very well, Baron Lochshane, you may sleep on the floor." With that, she lifted the hems of her mantle and kirtle and swept regally into the fortress.

Guillaume arched an eyebrow at Noel in silent male communication, then said, "This should prove an interesting Yule."

The Great Hall rang with laughter and good cheer, mayhap for the first time in nearly a year. With the meat the men had added over the past several days and the wagons of much needed supplies, everyone had plenty to eat. To the delight of all, Galen spun a tale of olden days, a favorite, of the great warrior king, Fhitich, and his lady love, Anne, one of the *Cait Sidhe*, and how they fought the Norsemen together to save their people.

Seated at the great table, Rowanne leaned forward to look past Skena and smile at Noel. "Have you not heard the lore, Sir Noel, of how the women of our line came from witches who had the ability to turn into catamounts?"

"Damian spoke of it in passing when he was in Berwick last August," Noel answered, making room for Annis to sit upon his knee. He handed her a slice of bread sweetened with honey and cinnamon. "More recently, Guillaume warned me of such after he came to stay. Methinks you ladies of Clan Ogilvie like to rattle men's resolve with such stories."

Rowanne's laughter rang out. "You will find out the truth one day, Lord de Servian."

Skena watched her daughter blooming under Noel's gentle attention. In the crook of her elbow was a puppet, fashioned to look like a noble lady. Noel had given it to Annis just a short time ago for her Yule present. Behind them, Andrew dashed hither and yond, fighting a mock battle with the knight puppet that was now his.

"They dearly love those hand puppets. Where did you ever find such wondrous gifts?" Skena touched his arm, needing to feel his warmth.

He shrugged as if it were a minor matter. "I bought them off a puppeteer in Berwick right before I left. I had a feeling they might please."

Neither child had ever had such a beautiful present. It was merely another measure of the kindness and caring within this special man. Annis wiggled up to kiss Noel's cheek, leaving bread crumbs sticking to it. Andrew and his knight finally stopped slaying dragons and came to get a piece of the bread. Noel shifted Annis to his other leg, so Andrew had space to sit on a leg as well. Annis let her puppet kiss Noel, and then she fed him a part of her second piece of bread.

Rowanne watched the goings on of both children, clamoring for attention from Noel, and each receiving their share. "He is winning the hearts of the twins, especially Annis."

"Aye, already she has stepped out of the shadows with his patience." Skena could barely take her eyes away from Noel.

Rowanne reached out and squeezed Skena's hand. "Judging from that look in your eyes, I would say the Lord de Servian has captured your heart as well."

A blush flooding her cheeks, Skena dropped her hand from where she was touching Noel's upper arm. Finding no words, she merely looked down at her trencher and nodded.

"Guillaume said you plan to wed with Sir Noel in three days' time, without waiting for banns to be cried. Malcolm is down with the ague, or he would have made the journey from Lochshane with me. I did not ken what he meant when he passed me a message for you. Now it makes sense. He said to tell you that he was sorry to miss this special time with you, to speak your words before all, but he expects you and your

English dragon at the church to be given Holy Communion when the snow melts." Rowanne offered a reassuring smile. "Methinks our dear uncle's Ogilvie blood has been whispering to him."

Skena tired as the celebrating went on and on. Since Yule was the longest night of the year, the custom was to keep the fire burning bright in the Great Hall through the hours of darkness, to hold at bay the night and light the way for the renewing sun's return. Galen shared more legends of the Highlands, spoke of the meaning of Yule and the great battle between light and dark.

As she watched the children holding their precious puppets, she regretted she had no gift for Noel. Her mind brightening with a notion, she hit upon a small one—a gift of peace and rebuilding between them. Gathering her sewing basket, she took a small piece of sun-bleached baize and began sewing. In each corner she stitched a runic symbol and in the center fashioned an empty knot circle.

Noel finally took his eyes off Rowanne, who was now telling a story of the Selkies. Noticing Skena sewing, he reached over and touched his fingertip to the designs on the cloth. "Making a handkerchief?"

"Nay, something different. 'Tis your Yule present. I am sorry, 'tis all I have to offer." Skena gave him a shy shrug. "I sew with a finer stitch, but such attention to detail is not required for this. 'Tis a Yule Cloth."

"I have never heard of such. What do you do with a Yule Cloth?" His hand took her right wrist and gave it a small squeeze.

"Each corner has a symbol—a rune. This one is *Wyrd*—Fate. This corner has *Algiz*—the defender. The third one I selected is *Wunjo* for bringer of joy, and lastly, *Inguz*—beginnings," she explained. "Now you must tell me one word that shall give you what you wish for the most."

Noel stared at her for the longest time, as all around them receded to shadows. Then he spoke, "Skena."

She offered him a mysterious smile and then began sewing. But not her name. The needle quickly worked through the cloth to form the letters *l-o-v-e*. Before he could see what she had done, she took his hand.

"Come. I will show you what to do with the Yule Cloth." At one of the Great Hall posts, she paused. "Pick three leaves from the holly branch—careful, as they are prickly—and three berries."

Noel did as she instructed. Carrying the items, he followed her to the fireplace where she opened the cloth, showing the word in the middle of the circle.

"I said Skena was my wish." The pale eyes moved over her, touching her with a power much like the kenning.

She gave a brief nod. "Oh, aye. But this is a spell for us both. You are *Algiz* the protector. Fate—*Wyrd*—sent you to me. Together we have a joyful beginning that brings love. That is my gift to you, Noel—this Yuletide spell."

Forming her hand to make a cup with the word *love* against her palm, she took the leaves and berries from him and placed them on the cloth, then folded the corners over each other. Stepping to the fire, she started to toss it onto the blaze, but Noel caught her hand. The silver eyes locked with hers, stripping away any protection and touching her soul. Together, they tossed the cloth into the flames.

"By the fire burning bright, three upon three, let it be," she whispered.

Noel's grip on her wrist tightened as he slowly pulled her to him. "I once asked if your name Skena had a meaning. You answered not that you ken. But it does. It means love."

He brushed his lips over hers lightly, igniting the ravenous hunger, the need for him. His hands cradled her back as he deepened the kiss, speaking his emotions through this silent bond. Speaking his love while the Yule Cloth burned to cinders, setting the spell.

Finally recalling they stood before the whole of Craigendan, she broke the kiss and stepped back. Though her cheeks burned, she was pleased by the gift she had created for Noel, knew it was the perfect gesture to heal the breach between them. Whether it was the Yule spell working, or simply her love for Noel, joy filled her heart to overflowing.

Seeing Galen bring in the wooden box of apples, she went to pass them out. They were small and fewer in number this year. Everyone would have to share. As she reached for the first one, she accidentally spotted Dorcas in the kitchen doorway. Though she was partially in shadows, Skena saw enough of her sister's face. The look of hatred and envy sent a chill up her spine.

Passing Noel an apple, she said, "If a woman peels one, careful to remove the skin whole, she can toss it over her right shoulder, quickly look back, and is supposed to glimpse the man who will be her husband. The crop was so small we will have to share. Few apples, fewer husbands." She tried to make light of the situation. "Another way apples can be used for divination is to twist the stem. You say the names of eligible men and whichever name is spoken when the stem breaks is the one you will wed. Of course . . ."

Her words died as she saw Dorcas again, speaking to Andrew. He proudly held up his puppet to show her, but then, Dorcas leaned down to whisper something to the little boy. Foreboding crawled up her spine as she watched the two, alarm turning to panic as she realized what her sister was doing.

She ran toward her son, to snatch him away, but it was too late. She did not know where Dorcas had learnt the details of Angus's death, but the bitch knew! The truth was there when Dorcas raised up, a smile on her lips and the light of triumph in her eyes. Blindly, Skena pushed through the crowd, crashing into bodies, barely seeing who they were. One was Guillaume.

She heard him asking if something was wrong. She mumbled a vague reply and shoved by him.

By the time she reached Andrew, Dorcas was gone. Her son stood pale and shaking, staring down at the puppet held limply in his hands. Her heart broke as she saw the slumped shoulders. Skena reached for him, only he jerked away. He looked up at her with wide, haunted eyes. Then his head jerked to Noel, coming up behind her. The blood seemed to drain from his face as he turned and fled.

"Andrew!" she called, but he did not stop.

Noel caught her arm as she started after her son. "She told him?"

Skena nodded, tears burning her eyes.

Noel wanted to strangle Dorcas for her evil deed, but his first concern was Skena's son. "Let me go after him." Noel held her arm firmly, fearing she was not really hearing him. "Trust me to handle the boy, Skena."

She stared up at him, trying to focus through the tears, then her head finally bobbed consent. Noel handed her to Guillaume and asked that he keep a close watch on her, and then went after Andrew.

The boy was not hard to find. The fortress door had been left open a crack, where the child failed to push it closed securely. From there, it was easy to follow the tracks in the freshly fallen snow. Andrew had gone to the stable. His small footprints stopped there.

Not wanting to set Andrew to running again, he moved into the darkened stable in silent steps. Leaving the door open to increase the light within, he took time to allow his eyes to adjust to the darkness of the enclosed barn. Slowly, he began to see the shapes of the stalls and horses inside them. Brishen was in the largest one at the end, the white of his horse standing out clearly.

Appearing so much the little man, Andrew stood before the

stall, looking down at the puppet still in his hands. His chin quivered. Life had cruelly intruded on his happy world, but then it always had a way of shattering childhood innocence. It had for Noel. Andrew was two years older than Noel had been when he lost both parents and learnt just how brutal the world could be.

Andrew had lost only one and had made a reasonable adjustment to that change. In time, he would accept Noel in the place of a father, if he handled this right. If not, he could harden the child against him forevermore. Knowing how tender a child's emotions were, how deeply a child could be wounded, he had hoped to put off telling Annis and Andrew about Angus until they were older. His hand had been forced by that vicious bitch Dorcas. Oh, Noel would deal with her shortly. For now, he had to try to salvage his honor before Andrew's eyes.

The little boy was pretending to be strong, but faint trembles revealed his inner pain. Noel's heart ached for Andrew; he understood life could be scary when you felt so alone. Once upon a time, Michael Challon had come and saved him from the unending nightmare, had given him a new father and brothers to fill his empty world. Now it was his turn to offer the hand of solace to Skena's son.

"When I was five years old my father died." Noel broke the silence. At the sound of his voice Andrew jumped slightly, but he feigned not to have heard, staring ahead at the horse in the stall. "He died in a tournament. A bizarre accident. One day he was there. The next he was buried." His hand itched to reach out and squeeze the child's shoulder, yet he feared being rebuffed. "I was confused, scared. I did not know what would happen to Mother and me. Then I learned those fears were only the start. My mother howled in grief and never seemed to stop. You see, she loved my father very much. My heart hurt, as I could do naught to stop her from crying."

Andrew's head slowly lifted. "She cried for him?"

Noel's heart ached for the small boy, truly knowing his pain.

"Then one night the crying stopped. I awoke and wondered why there was silence. She was so beautiful with her dark hair and big blue eyes, like some faery princess. I often would peek behind her back to see if gossamer wings were folded there. Methinks the silence terrified me more than the endless tears. I went to her room, hoping to find her there, imagined she would pull me into the big bed, cuddle and kiss me, and tell me everything would be fine soon. She was not there."

"Where was she?" Andrew voice quavered as he sniffed tears. Tears for himself. Likely, tears for Noel.

"The servants carried her back into the castle. She had thrown herself into the lake. She did not want to live without my father."

Teardrops spilled down the child's cheeks. He wiped them away with the sleeve of his sark. Andrew looked up at him, eyes troubled. Even in the shadows, those eyes were so like Skena's. "She drowned? You lost your mother and father? But who took care of you?"

"A brave and valiant knight came, a warrior true, named Michael Challon. He told me that I did not have to worry. I would go live with him and be safe."

"And were you . . . safe?"

Noel nodded. "Yes, I had a wonderful home, had brothers. I never had any before, so it was a happy time to have others my age around. We grew up together, and I was loved and protected. Earl Michael was true to his word—I was safe."

Andrew swallowed hard. "Why did you k . . . kill my father?" Noel turned his back to the child and lifted his sark. Shifting the bandage up, he exposed his still raw wound. "Because he tried to kill me." Putting the shirt down, he turned to face Andrew again. "War is hard to understand. Men do very ugly things to each other. Most times they do not even know each other—as it was with your father and me. Simple truth—we were warriors and met on a field of war. Nothing more, nothing less. Either I killed your father or he killed me. That is how a battle is. Why we spend years training to fight. To save our lives, the lives of those we love. It's a hard lesson, but men learn it. 'Tis the way of things. There is no changing it."

Looking down at the puppet, Andrew's head gave a small nod of understanding.

"Many years ago, Michael Challon said he would be my new father, that I had a home with him and his family. I loved him for that. Loved my new brothers. I will always honor my father, but I made room for Michael Challon. He gave me so much. I hope I can make the same offer to you and Annis—to keep you safe. I will protect you with my life. Will you permit me to do that?"

Andrew raised his head again, the brown eyes staring at him with wisdom beyond his years. Skena's wisdom. "My mama never cried because my father was . . . dead. Methinks sometimes he made her sad. Annis never cried for him either."

Noel squatted before the solemn child. "Women are tender beings. They need men to protect them. Will you allow me to help you do that?"

Brishen moved to the opening to stick his head out. Andrew avoided answering by patting the horse's nose. Just when Noel thought the boy was not going to give him a response, he asked, "Mayhap . . . sometime I could ride Brishen again? I rode him the night we found you covered with snow."

The tightness in his heart easing, Noel smiled in relief. "I think Brishen would like that. Come spring I will find a good mare and breed her with Brishen. The colt can be yours. You two could grow up together."

Andrew nodded. "I would like that." He was trying to hold emotions in, but his chest heaved with a sob.

Noel finally allowed himself to touch Andrew's shoulder, gave him a small squeeze for reassurance. It seemed the final straw to the boy's defenses. Throwing his arms around Noel, Andrew held on and sobbed. Noel knelt and took the child in his arms and allowed him to cry. In an odd way, Andrew shed tears of grief, but they were also tears Noel had never permitted himself to cry all those years ago.

"Noel, might I ask something?" he asked, choking back a sob.

"You may ask whatever you want," Noel agreed.

Andrew's face was sad. "Your wound . . . 'Tis in the back." Too smart by half, the child was already making the leap from two men fighting to one almost dying from a wound in the back.

"Men do not always face each other continuously when fighting. I turned, and he caught me in the back because he had already swung." Noel did not precisely lie. It was hard enough for the child to lose a father, the difficulty compounded by having to accept Noel in Fadden's place. Telling him the full truth would serve naught at this point. He could leave Andrew's childhood memory of his father unblemished.

Andrew's head bobbed twice, but he avoided looking at Noel, as if he did not fully believe him. Skena's son was bright, his incisive mind so like his mother's.

"Come," Noel said, rising. "Your lady mother will be fretting about you." Putting a hand behind Andrew's shoulders, he gently steered him from the stables.

Outside, Andrew took hold of his hand. "Soon we will light the *Cailleach Nollaich. Nollaich* means like your name Noel."

"What will they burn?"

"The *Cailleach Nollaich* is a big log with the face of a woman carved into it—the Cailleach, the lady of winter, the hag of night. They will light at middle night and burn it through the night to drive away winter."

"Sounds like we need to be there to make sure they do it right, eh?"

"Noel, wishes do come true?" Andrew asked. "I mean if you wish for something with all your heart it will come true?"

Noel looked to see Skena in her mantle before the door, waiting for them. "Aye, wishes do come true. Especially Christmas wishes."

Chapter Twenty-Nine

"Surely you jest?" Noel paused from buckling his belt over his wine-colored surcoat. Butterflies fluttered in the pit of his belly, thus he was not in the proper mindset for Guillaume's taunt. Fearing this was naught more than a tweaking of his nose, he tried to judge Guillaume's mood.

Since the Lady Rowanne's arrival three days past, to say Guillaume had been moody was putting it mildly. Still, Noel hardly blamed him. The woman was beautiful in a way that grabbed a man's attention and fixed it. This daughter of the earl of Glen Shane matched her sister Tamlyn in loveliness, but then 'twas reputed far and wide the three daughters, heiresses all in their own right, were beautiful beyond compare. Noel might count Guillaume a lucky man indeed, if not for the fact that Rowanne clearly kept a distance between them at all times. His friend had voiced he made a mistake in granting Rowanne until the end of April before they would wed. Possibly, he was right in that opinion. It was apparent that being near his betrothed, and yet kept at arm's length, was grating on Guillaume's generally even temper.

"Jest? Not in the least. When you consider it, the rite was not so different from an English bedding ceremony, with the husband and bride being inspected and then the bedding taking place before a priest and half the family." Guillaume picked up Noel's knife and tested its balance. "Why would you think I am making it up—just to vex you?"

Noel chuckled. "You are in a rotten mood and looking to vent your foul humors. Sleeping on a pallet on the floor does little to mellow your disposition."

Guillaume twisted to rub his back. "Not doing much time for my spine either."

"If allowing the Lady Rowanne too much time to adjust to your coming marriage was such a bloody mistake, then do something about it."

Balancing the knife on the tip in his hand, Guillaume deftly caught the hilt when it started to fall. "Ah, there is the rub. Rowanne is a lady of secrets. Shadows cloud her heart. And unfortunately, I am a man of my word."

Guillaume went through balancing the dagger on end again, only this time when it toppled Noel snatched it away and stuck it into the sheath fastened at his belt. "Fill her belly with a babe, then her heart shan't have room for shadows. And stop avoiding answering me. Were you telling a story about Julian's wedding?"

Guillaume gave him a wicked grin. "'Tis truth. He married Tamlyn in their pagan ways. Methinks you are fortunate to wed with Skena in deep winter. No marriage in the circle of stones for you."

"Ah, well, Julian was always more bold than I. Still, I little care where I marry Skena—or how—I just want it done." He hung the gold chain about his neck. "How do I look? 'Tis not every day a man weds."

Guillaume smiled at Noel dressed in clothes he would wear at court. "A little anxious to be a married man, but Skena will think you handsome."

"Are you sure they will view this as a true marriage?" Noel fretted, admitting he was eager to know Skena was his. "It shan't be before the church, no priest to speak the words. I want no disgrace or question to fall upon our union."

"Scots take marriage as a solemn vow. If you declare before all that you take Skena as your lady wife, and she accepts you, 'tis as binding as any ceremony before a priest. I have heard of handfasting ceremonies, a marriage for a year and a day. I would never be as foolish as to try that with an Ogilvie lass. They carry wicked daggers called a *sgian dubh* and would likely go to cutting on body parts if crossed." Guillaume reached out and took Noel's hand. Turning it palm up, he placed a small object in it. "This ring belonged to my father. He would have wanted you to have it."

Noel stared at the wide gold band with a large yellow stone in it. "I cannot accept this. 'Tis a piece of your father."

"Your father, too, in all but blood. We are brothers, so this goes to you. May you govern Craigendan with the strength, the incisive mind, and the kindness with which he ruled over Challon." He placed another ring beside it. "This one is more from me. My mother gave it to me. I thought one day to present it to the woman I married, but oddly, in my mind the ring little suits my lady. As soon as I met your Skena I thought you might wish to give this to her as your bride's gift."

Noel was deeply touched by Guillaume's gesture. "I experienced a great loss when Father and Mother were taken from me. However, I have never regretted my family, my life at Challon. I could not ask for a better brother."

"True, we were—and are—lucky. Come, let us go marry you off." Guillaume picked up the strip of material from the table, which had been cut from the shirt Noel had worn the night Skena found him. "Do not forget this. You will not be able to 'tie the knot' without it."

"My thanks. I would not want to err in the ceremony."

They started down the steps and toward the Great Hall. "'Tis hard to think of Julian and Damian happy in wedlock. Shortly, you shall be, and come spring, Simon and I will take that step. Methinks we must fix our minds to finding fine Scottish lasses for Redam and Dare, get them to settle close to us. Then the war-weary dragons can truly have peace."

A shiver of foreboding raced up Noel's spine. Was peace truly attainable? Would the Scots accept Edward's rule, or would some Highlander arise to set the torch to the fires of rebellion? Noel dismissed such grave concerns for another time. He was marrying Skena, a start to a life together. He wanted naught to taint the happiness of this day.

As he entered the great hall, Noel searched for Skena. Juniper and cedar branches had been formed into a circle on the stone floor before the fireplace, and Skena—his beautiful Skena—stood awaiting him in the middle of them. She wore a velvet kirtle of deep wine that nearly matched his surcoat. That brought a smile to his lips as he recalled that on the morning they announced him to be the new lord of Craigendan, they both had chosen to wear dark blue. Her dark auburn hair was free flowing and a thin circlet of gold crossed her forehead. His heart nearly stopped at the vision that would soon be his lady wife.

"Yes, wishes do come true," Noel said under his breath, as he strode through the opening left in the boughs, going to her and taking her hand.

Skena could hardly find moisture enough to swallow as Noel came toward her. He was so handsome in the dark colors of wine and black, his attire setting off those pale silver eyes with an unearthly glow. This man looked beautiful, but more important, he was beautiful inside as well. It would have been so easy to fall in love with him, a man who filled her young girl's dreams. Only, the way he reached out to Annis and Andrew and offered them so much robbed her of any resistance to him. He would be a fine father, a good lord for Craigendan, and every wish come true for her. As he took her hand, nothing in her life had ever felt so right.

"My lady, never have mine eyes beheld such a beautiful vision, my deepest wish come true," he spoke lowly as he brushed a fleeting kiss against her cheek.

They stood in the small circle of the evergreens, symbolically enclosing them in the ever-living boughs that purified and protected them, starting their marriage of true hearts. She smiled as Annis and Andrew broke free from Jenna and came running up, giggling and hiding behind Noel and her. She nodded to the maidservant to let them stay; after all they would be a part of this marriage as well. Andrew quieted and stood fidgeting at her side, trying to behave lest she send him away. Annis had gone to stand on Noel's right, and shyly took his smallest finger.

Skena swallowed the knot tightening in her throat. Sometimes life can be so perfect.

Rowanne placed a small bough of cedar and one of juniper on the fire, and watched as they caught quickly and burned bright. As they turned to ash, she came to the opening at the top of the circle.

"In this sacred circle, Noel and Skena gather to plight their troth of love before all of Craigendan. I must ask, who gives this woman to Noel in a bonding of our ways?"

"I do," Andrew said loudly.

Then a "Me, too," came from the other side of Noel. Annis peeked around his hip and smiled.

That drew a laugh from all in the Great Hall. Rowanne held out her hand waiting for the strips of cloth. Noel let go of Skena's hand to reach between his surcoat and shirt and pull out his cloth for the binding. Her eyes widened as she saw it had been cut from the shirt he wore when she had found him. Skena tugged the small piece of tartan cut from her favorite shawl and passed it to Rowanne.

Her cousin placed it atop Noel's cloth and then held them aloft, turning in a circle for all to witness. She tied the two pieces of material together, "With this knot I bind you. May your love endure everlasting so long as this knot remains true." Turning her brown eyes to Noel, she said, "Speak your words, Lord de Servian."

Noel surprised all by stepping forward and snatching the tied cloths from Rowanne. He tossed the joined cloths into the fire. "No one shall undo this knot." Taking up Skena's hand, he slid a ring on her finger and then lifted their hands high so all could view. "I take Skena MacIain, Baroness Craigendan, as my lady wife, from now until death parts us, and may God grant a blessing upon this union that death takes us in the same breath. I pledge to you, her people, my people, that I will honor her and forsake all others. I will defend her with my life."

Rowanne nibbled on the corner of her lip, fighting the emotions summoned by Noel's words. She blinked away unshed tears, and then cleared her throat. "What say you, Skena of Craigendan? Will you have this man, accept him as your lord husband, give over to him the safe keeping of all you treasure and love?"

Skena reached up and placed the heavy torque belonging to the Lord of Craigendan around Noel's neck. "Aye, I will have him, and a good bargain made, for I will have none other for the rest of my life. I will honor him, support and love him with my whole heart. I wed a man whose name means Christmas on Christmas Eve. No greater gift can come to me."

Rowanne's eyes shifted to Guillaume standing to the side of the fireplace, before coming back to Skena. "Then you are blessed, cousin, for I now bear witness that you and Lord de Servian are wed by our ways. Let no man say otherwise. May this union bring you both all the joy you so richly deserve."

Rowanne bent to sprinkle a handful of grain on the floor to cover the small opening in the circle of evergreens. "Come, jump over the grain as a blessing that this marriage will be fruitful, and then let us feast and celebrate the joyous day."

Skena squeaked as Noel swept her into his arms and then hopped over the grain, careful not to disturb the line. Everyone laughed and clapped as he carried his bride to the lady's chair at the trestle table and deposited her with a flourish. She smiled up at him, so blessed that Noel had come into her life.

Her snowy knight had come on the wings of a child's wish and changed their world. Skena could not recall ever being so happy.

"Skena and I bid you to eat your fill of this wonderful feast, and raise your cup to this coming year to be a good one for Craigendan." Noel raised his glass in a toast, and everyone followed suit.

Several raised their mugs of ale or mead and spoke words of blessings. Some from the Englishmen tended to be slightly ribald in nature. All wished them well.

Save one. Skena tensed as she spotted Dorcas, standing in the kitchen passageway, just as she had the morn they announced Noel was the new lord of Craigendan. She held her breath, almost expecting the shadowy figure of Angus to come up behind Dorcas and whisper to her as he had that time. No one came.

Noel noticed the direction of Skena's stare and gently placed his hand over hers.

"She will be gone shortly. Guillaume will take her back to Lochshane and will arrange for a marriage to someone in the lowlands. She's comely enough. With a few coins someone will take her. Then you shan't have to worry about her mischief making ever again."

"But what about—" she started to say, only he cut her off.

"'Tis over. Duncan Comyn is gone and with him the 'ghost' that walked Craigendan. Notice how nothing further has occurred since he went away? He might try to return, but to what purpose? You are mine now, and he is smart enough to know I will kill to protect you," he assured.

As she stared at Dorcas, she shivered, feeling a touch of foreboding. "Mayhap I am scared."

"Of what?" He lifted her hand and kissed it. "There is naught to fear, Skena. Trust me?"

She nodded. "With my whole heart. Only, I fear what the gods give, they may take away as well. I am so happy. Everything is so perfect that mayhap 'tis too much. It will all be snatched away."

"My first order as your lord husband is this, which you promised to obey—let nothing shadow your heart this day. 'Tis our day. The start of many days to come."

He leaned close and brushed his lips against her cheek.

Trying to shake off the fear suddenly gripping her heart, Skena ignored the ripples of the kenning pulsing through her. "I do not recall promising to obey you, my lord husband," she jested.

He laughed. "But you shall do so or—"

"You will beat me?" She finally gave him a smile. "I love you, Noel de Servian."

"Only half as much as I love you, Skena de Servian. Another change I am making as your lord and husband. Any objections?" he asked with raised eyebrows.

She shook her head. "I like that very much, my lord," and leaned to kiss him to express how much.

A small head popped between them. "Us, too?" They pulled apart to see Annis—and her puppet—pushing between them so she could climb onto Noel's knee.

"You want to be Annis de Servian?" Skena asked, so pleased with how the child was accepting Noel. Her daughter nodded, and then snatched the Christmas bread, made with nutmeg, cloves, and cinnamon from Noel's fingers as he held it out for her.

Noel nodded. "Us, too, though I am not sure what you named your puppet."

She held the dolly up and said with a half full mouth, "Lady Muriel de Servian."

Noel hugged Annis, as a pair of small hands came around to cover his eyes.

"You cannot see again until you answer my riddle," Andrew taunted in a deep voice and then giggled. "Who am I?"

Skena reached out and placed her hand on Noel's shoulder, needing to touch this special man who brought magic to their lives.

"I love you, Noel de Servian," she whispered as she watched him with her children, knowing just how blessed they were with his coming.

Chapter Thirty

At a given signal, Noel scooped up a surprised Skena from her chair, and then ran for the stairs. Guillaume, Stephan, and Emory neatly stepped in a phalanx to block the doorway of the Great Hall, thus preventing the merrymakers from giving chase. He had heard Scots oft played mischief, even abducted the bride in an effort to torment the married couple and fore-stall their wedded bliss. While understanding the mischief would be intended in the spirit of good fun, he would have naught of those devilries. Nor did he want to go through any damnable bedding ceremony. He just wanted Skena all to himself.

Once through the door of the lord's chamber, Noel kicked it closed, then stalked to the bed and playfully tossed Skena upon it. Going back, he slid the bolt on the lock to prevent any 'well-meaning' interruptions. His chest filled with the heady male sense of ownership as he slowly returned to the high-platform bed, his eyes drinking in this beauty who was now his. Life felt good. Damn good indeed.

"Smartly done, de Servian. You outfoxed the foxes." Skena laughed, getting up to walk across the bed on her knees to him. Eyes flashing, she unbuckled his belt.

He grinned. "I have my . . . moments."

"Moments?" She ran her hand down the front of his surcoat, setting his erection to throb insistently. "Just . . . fleeting . . . shards . . . of . . . time? I would have thought you capable of more . . . so . . . much . . . more."

As the belt dropped to the floor, his hands seized Skena's waist and pulled her against him. His woman. His lady wife. His life. Finally, after all these empty years, he was no longer alone.

"Of late, I find that I am very possessive. I want no men stealing kisses from you after your maidservants tuck you up in bed, or worse some of them carrying you off to vex me." He lowered his head to take her mouth in a branding kiss of ownership. Suddenly, kissing was not enough. Not nearly enough. He pulled away from her and ordered, "Take off your kirtle, wife."

"You are constantly demanding I remove my attire." She pushed her first finger at his belly. "I want to take things off you, de Servian. You, with your fox ways, foiled the bedding rituals, thus I am forced to perform the inspection on my own. I need to ken if you come to me without flaw before I accept you as worthy to be my lord husband."

He chuckled at her mischievousness. "You already know my every blemish. I have a wound healing on my back, and there is a line on my left arm—reminder never to underestimate the quickness of Julian Challon. As I recall, you little minded either. Then, there is something about my being beautiful?"

"Cease the blether, or I will go call for help with the disrobing," Skena threatened, climbing off the high bed.

"You call for help from those meddling mischief makers, and I will beat you for certain." He turned to catch her, only she evaded him, spinning around behind his back.

"Always with the threats, de Servian."

He rotated after her. "Cease making me go around in circles, or I shall beat you for making me dizzy. No more idle threats—I mean it."

"Then stop turning, and you will not get lightheaded." She

pushed at his chest, until he dropped back to sit on the edge
of the bed. Kneeling before him, she worked at the knots on
his boot lacings.

With Skena on her knees before him, Noel had a hard time
drawing air. He grinned like a king's fool. Someday soon he
would teach her why. "If I kiss you may I be Noel again?"

"I am nay lass to be had for a kiss," she taunted, pulling off
his boots. "Stand, whilst I disrobe and inspect you."

He arched a brow in challenge. "Nay. I require a bribe, wife."

"A kiss?" she asked.

Noel nodded slowly. "Already she comes to know my
thoughts."

Skena wiggled her fingers as if trying to make up her
mind. "'Tis only one problem, de Servian—you have a habit
of not stopping at a single kiss."

"I have heard no maidenly protestings. If my memory
serves me correct, I recall someone gasping, *oh, Noel, do not
stop . . . please do not stop* last night." His hands gripped her
about the ribcage, his thumbs brushing under her breasts.

Swatting at his hands, she lifted his surcoat over his head,
and then loosened the drawstring on his silk sark. Skena
slowly pushed the material up his chest and then tugged it off.

Her eyes glowed with appreciation. "I admit a passing
fondness for your chest." She ran her palms up the smooth
ripples of his stomach to his strong shoulders, then outward.
"As well, I concede your arms are—"

"Beautiful?" he mocked, standing up.

Damn, but he loved this woman. She made him happy.
Skena gave him the bright promise of joyful days to come.
The only regret to touch his life now was that Fate had not set
them on the road to finding each other long before ravens and
a snowstorm brought him to her.

She nodded faintly. "One might say that." Her hand on his
shoulder, she walked slowly around him. Placing a kiss between his shoulder blades, she stopped by his other side to

undo the points of his chausses, where the lacings attached to his braies at the hips. She moved in front of him, and leaned to brush her lips over his, taunting, then hopped away as he tried to pull her to him.

"Enough, Skena. This grows maddening," he growled.

"Cease fashing, or I will scream for help," she teased, untying the points on the other side of his hip. "Surely, the brave warriors of Challon would rush to a maiden's aid and restrain you whilst I complete the viewing?"

"One step toward that door, my love, and I shall stuff a rag in your mouth and lash you to the bedposts," he warned, kicking out of the woolen chausses.

Skena stepped against him, pressing her soft lips to the side of his throat, while she dragged her fingernails lightly up the insides of his thighs. His body flexed taut as a bow when her hands continued across the front of the braies to loosen the drawstring. Small beads of sweat broke out on his forehead.

Eyes flashing, she nipped at his chin as she pushed the cloth down over his hips. Bringing her hand up between their bodies, she wrapped her strong fingers around the base of his shaft and then leisurely worked the soft, burning flesh toward the mushroomed tip. "Is this one of those other ways for a woman to warm a man's blood? Faster ways?"

"Ah . . . aye . . . lass. 'Tis also a way . . . to push him . . . ah . . . to madness." He sucked air, fighting to focus on what she was saying. Unable to stand it anymore, his hand clamped around her wrist, stopping her movements. "Enough, witch, or this will be a short bedding. Have you finished your scrutiny? Am I deemed of worth?"

Skena ran her hands over his arms, then to his neck and finally his chest. She nipped his earlobe and whispered, "I think you will do."

"Good." Taking hold of her hips, he spun her to face away. "'Tis my turn to assure myself you are without fault and fit to be my lady wife."

With trembling hands, he took hold of the ends of the gold lacings up the back of her gown, and somehow he managed to undo the knot. As he slid the golden cord through the eye hooks, he reined in the urgency pressing him to rip open the back of the gown. He had a feeling Skena would treasure this dress, and mayhap one day Annis might don it to wed some handsome warrior. Stiffening his resolve, he carefully drew the cord back and forth, until he feared his teeth would crack from gnashing them.

Finally, the long cord pulled free. Sucking in a steadying breath, he pushed the dark red velvet to each side to reveal the perfection of Skena's back. Noel pushed his trembling hands inside the kirtle, feeling the heat off her flesh. She shivered. As he peeled the gown over her shoulders, he leaned forward and pressed his lips to her back. Trapped by the gown across her upper arms, she could only stand while he chained kisses along the strong slope to her neck. She shivered, the goose-flesh raising as his tongue swiped out to taste her. Pressing his body to mold to hers, he savored the power in him, relished how she trembled.

He craved to push her forward, her belly to the plane of the bed, and take her with one swift plunge. Only this night was for Skena. He had a feeling her wedding night to Fadden had fallen far short of what young girls dream. This night was about teaching her the full meaning of love, how this physical expression would seal their bond, making them one. Instead of releasing the full strength of his yearnings, he carefully kissed his way down her spine until he was on his knees. Turning her around, he slowly peeled the gown from her body. He drew her to him, squeezing her tightly as he placed the side of his head to her heart, listening to the rapid beating.

Skena's hand reached out to softly cup his chin, and then lifted until their eyes met. Her thumb swiped away the single tear that fell from his eye. "Why do you cry? Are you not happy with me?" Her lip trembled as she awaited his answer.

His throat choked with emotions. Speaking was too hard. Finally, he forced out the words. "Happy? Yes. I feel that and more. Howbeit, I am humbled by our love—and more terrifying mayhap because of my child's days—I taste the panic of what would happen to me if I ever lose you."

This time, the tear that fell came from her eye. "I understand for I, as well, tremble with that fear. Love me, Noel. Make me forget that darkness."

Skena reached out and took his face into her hands, her shimmering eyes speaking more than words ever could. She leaned to him, her soft mouth moving over his, burning as fired-iron. The muscles in his arms tensed to steel to prevent him from crushing her any tighter, so moved was he by the power of this rare emotion. Love. A force that could topple kingdoms. Or drive a man insane. He loved Skena with every shade of his soul, to the depth of his heart, a magic no wizard could ever match. It made him stronger. It saw him weak.

Pulling back, she kissed his right cheek, then the left. "I love you my snowy knight. What magic was cast that night which brought me to you! What wondrous, beautiful magic!"

Noel could no longer rein in. Rising to his feet, he took her mouth and let loose age-old mating instincts. He kissed her, holding back nothing, spearing his tongue into her mouth in a rhythm that would echo how his body would soon claim hers. Barely aware of what he was doing, he pushed the gown down off her arms, the soft velvet pooling at their feet. Skena was left in only a thin chemise. He started to remove that as well, but changed his mind, liking how it both shielded and revealed her flesh. Leaning her back to the bed's plane, he followed her down, relishing the feel of having Skena under him.

Running her hands up his arms and to his shoulders, she toyed with the curls at the back of his neck. Skena rasped out a plea, "Show me all the ways to make a man burn."

The mating scent filtered through his blood, setting scorching fire to roll within him. It nearly blotted out all thoughts, so primitive the power. He covered her body with his, pressing down with the heaviness of his muscles, letting her feel his heart thunder a cadence of love. He kissed her hair and whispered the raw desperation born of years of loneliness, "Love me, Skena. Never stop." His hands cupped her neck, his thumbs brushing lightly along her throat. "So many years I have yearned for you. Needed you."

He chained kisses along her jaw, then over her cheek and to her temple. Leaning his head against hers, he closed his eyes and reveled in the overpowering emotions filling his entire being. He never knew love could be so intense, making all that had come before pale shades by comparison. He could tell her a thousand score over that he loved her. It would not be enough. Never enough.

His hand palmed over the side of her hip and then down to her bare thigh until he found the hem of the chemise. Slowly, agonizingly, he gathered the fabric to her waist, the gauzy material rasping over her sensitized skin. Rolling to his side, he drank in the arousing beauty of her body, how the thin material clung to her full breasts, how the shadowy tips pushed against the fabric with each breath. He gently curved his hand around her right breast, feeling the tightness of the soft mound, speaking to him of how she responded to him. It was torture. Finally, he dragged the chemise over her head and tossed it aside, leaving her naked.

Skena was still unsure of the ways of men and women. She trembled, but held still for his gaze to devour her, clearly wanting his pale eyes to look upon her breasts, yearning for him to stare at her with his unveiled desire. In the days to come, she would become more bold. For now, he relished his role as tutor.

Barely breathing, he just gazed at her. "My beautiful lady wife." He did not move for several heartbeats, stunned by the impact of his dreams now being a reality. He wanted to make this last, but feared his body would betray him. The wanting twisted his gut, a writhing, living creature demanding appeasement. The insistent pounding of his groin was agony.

He searched her eyes, allowing her mind to speak to him with the kenning, for yes, he now believed she could reach him in this manner. No longer fearing this power, he opened himself to her. What he saw in her eyes' brilliance was more than any man could hope for, more than any deserved. He was blessed—whether it was by his God or hers he little knew. Little cared. She was his, and he would fight to protect her, kill to keep her.

Lowering his mouth to her breast, he heard the hiss of air from Skena as his lips latched around the tip. His tongue swirled around the stiffening peak, feeling the flesh tighten with each stroke. When he suddenly drew on it her hips flexed off the bed. Her hands fisted in his hair at the back of his head as though to keep her from coming apart.

He moved to press his mouth between the valley of her breasts and then slowly glided kisses down the center of her belly. She tensed when he reached the dark curls, likely afraid he planned to move even lower . . . mayhap even secretly curious about the dark lure. He hesitated, hovering just above her, allowing his hot breath to caress the soft hair. A wicked grin spreading across his lips, he leaned forward and pressed a gentle kiss to her mons, feeling her hips arch in fear . . . in temptation.

"The night is so wonderfully long this time of year," he whispered as he covered her body with his. When her muscles relaxed, he laughed. "Only a reprieve, my love."

He laced his fingers with hers, raising her arms above her head, at the same time his legs spread hers wide. In excruciating torment, the tip of his shaft nudged against her slit, moistening his sensitive skin with the scalding hot dew her body wept. The solid weight of his warrior-honed muscles pressed Skena into the bedding, the deep feathered ticking almost cocooning them in a nest. Her rounded softness met and conformed to his. Perfection, as if she had been fashioned for him alone. He was heavy, yet he could see reflected in her luminous eyes that she relished the sensation. Offered up her surrender.

For a breathless moment, he just stared down at her. He wanted to capture the image of Skena's pagan beauty in his mind's eye, almost seal this shard of time in amber. Years from now he would summon the precious memory, revisit it, and treasure its special glory and power. He wanted to recall his beautiful wife adored by shadow and firelight.

"I have dreamt of this, of a wife, a family, for many long, cold years. Too many. I had begun to think such wishes were naught but a chimera that existed only to torment me with what I could never have. But you are real, Skena. You are mine. Mine."

He kissed her, his mouth ravaging hers at the same instant he plunged into her, forged their bodies into one in the crucible of their passion. Her female heat surrounded his swollen flesh, blistered him, branded him. His tongue pressed along the seam of her lips, and she opened for him with a sigh. His warrior lady did not just accept what he wanted of her, but she demanded, their muscles working against each other, yet straining together in a fervent urgency.

Conjuring a raspy inhale from her, he trailed kisses long her jaw, then down the arches column of her neck. Skena's nails bit into his arms, when he laved his tongue against the spot where her blood sounded a tattoo of passion. In response, her heart jumped, slamming against his ribs. He felt its force next to his and savored the potency of this rare magic between them.

Lifting slightly, he stroked inside her again, going deeper, his body slamming to hers in a dance primeval. Skena moaned. Pleasure not pain. He whispered against her temple, "See, wishes do come true and shall reign forevermore in our lives."

He set a frantic rhythm of plunges that had Skena clinging to him, her sharp fingernails biting into the flesh covering his shoulder blades. Then clinging was not enough for her. She arched hard to meet his frenzied thrusts.

Noel's body went rigid, vibrating with the need of his release. He fought it, wanting to prolong the beauty, the splendor, only her internal muscles tightened around his flesh like a fist, followed by the undulations rippling down the length of his erection. There was no holding back. His mind and body exploded into a thousand score, blue-hot cinders, blinding his sight as Skena pulled him into a maelstrom of consuming fire. She clung to him as the scalding heat of his seed poured into her welcoming body.

His mouth latched on the side of her neck, drawing hard. He would mark her. Noel smiled. She had marked his back with her fingernails. The tracks they had cut into his flesh would quickly heal. The marks she left on his soul branded him as hers.

He would have it no other way.

Waking up at first light, Noel slid from the cozy bed and tugged on his sark. Padding silently across the floor barefooted, he went to fetch his bride's present. When he had been preparing to come north, he heard these Highlands were often wet and bitter cold. Using common sense, he had commissioned two heavy mantles made for him, each a serviceable brown wool lined with wolf fur. He wished Skena to have one. He had seen how threadbare both her mantles were. He wanted her warm through this coming winter. Going to the chest at the foot of the bed, Noel lifted the lid and removed the neatly folded item.

Sitting on the edge of the bed he offered Skena a gentle smile. "My bride's gift to my lady wife."

Skena scooted up in the bed, rubbing the sleep sand from her eyes, and then gave him a crooked smile. "But you al-

ready gifted me with this lovely ring." She wiggled the ring
on her finger.

"Guillaume gave that to me for you. It was his lady
mother's, intended one day for his lady wife."

"Then why is he not saving it to give to Rowanne? Surely,
we must return it to him? The gesture was lovely, but I cannot
accept something that rightfully belongs to my cousin."

"Nay, I spoke nearly the same words to him. He said while
he treasured the ring, that something whispered it was not
predestined for Rowanne. I saw his eyes. He meant it. Still, I
wanted to offer something from me to you." He stood and unfurled the heavy garment. The cloak was a deep brown wool,
lined with fur of wolf killed in summer when the fur was reddish brown. Perfect for Skena's coloring. Holding it up he
said, "Your mantle is not warm enough. I would have you
better protected. Come, try it on."

Skena laughed. "I am unclothed, husband dear."

Noel felt deep happiness filling his heart, his soul. "You
will find, wife, I am very observant of such details."

She shyly slid off the bed, allowing him to wrap the mantle
about her. Pursing her lips she finally smiled. "'Tis strange to
feel the fur against my skin."

"I had two mantles made for myself, fearing the wrath of
this North Country. I did not know when I applied that fore-
sight that one would cover such a beautiful woman. And she
would be mine." When her mouth opened, Noel knew she was
going to protest his use of the word. Taking hold of her shoulders, he jerked Skena to him and kissed her ever so softly.
"Yes, beautiful. I shall hear none of your prattle otherwise. The
cloak suits you well, enhances your striking hair and eyes."

She looked up at him, her expression hungry to believe he
meant his praise. He wanted desperately to make her understand all that she caused him feel, how important, vital, she was
to him now. All that she gave him. Only it was too much. Love
filled his heart to overflowing, the emotions overwhelming

him. Words were too feeble to express the blinding intensity of this magic.

So instead, he let passion say what he could not speak. Leaning to her, he brushed his lips against hers. When she gave a small gasp, feeling the power of their bond, he deepened it. She moved against him, wanting the pressure, the friction of their bodies. The minx slid her knee against the outside of his thigh, rubbing like a cat.

Something in his mind snapped, and he moved so fast she had no time to react. Pushing her against the stone wall, his mouth claimed hers with a hunger that seared his mind. Bracing his lower arm against the wall, he parted the mantle and leaned into her. The stone was cold, but the heat of her body encased in the warm mantle shielded her from the chill. He used his lips, his teeth, his tongue, working her mouth until she gave him what he wanted. He was not rough, yet he devoured her, kissed her again and again with a ravenous need that was frightening.

Part of him was terrified at just how important Skena was to him. It made him vulnerable, and he was not sure he liked the sense, but there was no changing it. Skena was everything he longed for in the dark, empty nights. She was the sun in his life.

These head-spinning thoughts and sensations eddied through his blood until it was painful.

Skena clung to him as if fearing her legs would not support her. Her fingers bit into his upper arms, as she embraced the wildness in his passion. Encouraged it. His left hand snaked over her hip, then the fingers sifted through the soft curls, the middle one slipping over her mound, along the wet crease, and finally into her blistering heat.

Echoes of the dream.

His throat corded with the intense yearning for her. In near desperation, he broke the kiss and lightly nipped her lip. Moving the finger in and out slowly, he spoke low husky words. "I dreamt of you when you worked to heal me. Of me taking you in an orchard, feeling how your body wept liquid heat for me. So real, 'tis like a memory within me." He chained kisses along her jaw, then nuzzled the hair over her ear. "I want to taste your fire. You sensed I did last night."

Her eyes widened as she understood what he meant. "But that is—"

"Forget what anyone has told you about such things. Between us there are no rules, no limits." Noel's voice was husky with his yearning. "My mouth moving on you . . . My tongue thrusting in you." He pushed his finger slowly in and then out, agonizingly, setting her body to tremble with white hot urgency.

In a surreal blending, these moments with Skena now swirled and combined with the memory of the vision. Her hips flexed against his hand as she wrapped her arms around his neck. He could sense her shock in what he was asking of her, but also sense she was yielding to the dark lure. "We have so many delights to explore, you and I."

His hand worked magic on her, and instantly his mind conjured the dark image, of him on his knees before her, doing everything he promised. And she wanted that, ached for that. He could almost feel her thoughts, knew the kenning vibrated between them, allowing her to see the tableau within his mind.

Her thighs clamped around his hand, holding him as lightning arced through her. So attuned, his body throbbed, feeling her release coming. Grabbing her hips, he lifted her high, pinning her against the wall as he plunged deeply into her, allowing her climax to ripple down his shaft. Before she came down from the pinnacle of ecstasy, he backed out of her slick channel, then flexed hard, to the hilt, causing her to shudder all over again. Like a whirlwind the feelings of lust and love spun through him, making him dizzy. His spine arched once more. The world seemed to vanish . . . then slowly put itself together again.

He held on to Skena, knowing she could keep him safe.

Chapter Thirty-One

Humming to herself, Skena guided the shears through the rich velvet, careful not to ruin the lovely fabric. The shade was pale blue with a grey cast, perfect for Noel. With the hurry to wed, there had been no time for her to sew him a wedding gift. Twirling the ring around her finger, she thought of the past few days and how their bond strengthened with each breath. When Rowanne had presented her with several bolts of velvet as a Yule present, Skena spied the grey-blue fabric as just right for Noel and immediately set it aside.

The winter day was drawing in, the hours of light growing few. Soon, Noel would return with the other men from the hunt. She wanted to have the cutting done before he came back, in order to keep it a surprise until she could present it to him on Hogmanay.

Rowanne's mouth pursed while she watched Skena trimming the edge to match the pattern of Noel's tunic that she had borrowed for that purpose. "I thought the material would make *you* a lovely kirtle, dearest cousin," she chided, a note of jest in her voice.

"I appreciate your generous gift and cannot offer you thanks enough. 'Tis been a while since I had a new kirtle," Skena replied, raising up from her bent over position. "Enough will be left from this bolt that I can fashion part of a gown. An insert for the bodice and the skirt, mayhap lining for the sleeves. Then Noel and I will match."

"There is no need for raiments to make Noel and you match. You are perfect together. Such a beautiful pair, and you will make beautiful babes. I thought you both so lovely in deep wine for the wedding," Rowanne complimented. "But 'tis the colors of Noel's heart and his love for you that is important, and methinks it holds all the hues of the rainbow. I have never seen you happier or more beautiful."

"You will put me to pale come Beltane when you wed with Lord Guillaume." Skena offered Rowanne a loving smile. She pondered her cousin's skittish ways toward the new baron, before returning to work on the velvet.

At length, Rowanne said, "If I wed . . ." allowing the words to trail off.

Skena glanced up from the task, permitting her fingers, sore from the shears, to rest. "You are betrothed with Julian Challon's blessing and by king's command. 'Tis not our Pictish ways any longer, Rowanne. Times have changed. Choice is taken from your sisters and you. From what I hear, Tamlyn is happy, and Guillaume says Aithinne and the new baron of Lyonglen suit as well. Lord Guillaume is a fine man. I truly admire him." She could not hold silent her feelings any longer. "He cares for you. It pains me to see you so cool toward him. I saw the hurt in his eyes last night when he went to help you take a seat at the table—and you abruptly shrugged his touch away. 'Tis unlike you to be deliberately cruel. Why do you treat him so?"

Rowanne tilted her chin up. "Edward Longshanks gave Glen Shane, along with me and my sisters, to Julian Challon to do with us as he pleased. He chose Tamlyn, then informed Raven and me that we would marry with one of his brothers. No 'by your leave.' To add insult to the high-handed situation—Simon offered to joust for which sister each brother should wed. The servants overheard, and the jibe was all over Glenrogha before Vespers. It was . . . well . . . insulting!"

Skena's laughter bubbled forth. "Sorry, I do not make light of your feelings, but men oft say foolish things not stopping to hear how they sound to others. I doubt Sir Simon truly meant they should joust, with Raven and you as their prizes. You have had Guillaume under roof for the better part of a year. In truth, I little understand how you can keep your distance. I love Noel and think him the handsomest of men. But no woman could look at Guillaume and not envy you. Cousin, he is an honorable man, in his promise to you and in his deeds. The whole time at Craigendan he has kept to himself, even requests Muriel to help him with bathing so no tales are carried back to your ears. Few men are that careful. Noel thinks of him as a brother. Do you not wish to marry with him? His keeping his promise to you shows just how gentle he is of your feelings. He is a man any woman would be proud to have as her lord husband."

Rowanne crossed her arms as if keeping her emotions held tightly within. "I—"

"Mama!" Andrew half-bounded into the room, Annis trailing behind him. "The day wanes. When is our Noel coming back?"

"Anon, I should imagine. Why do you fash?" she asked, pleased at the 'our' attached to Noel's name.

Annis held up her beloved puppet. "Mama, can you make my Muriel 'nother dress?"

"Oh, I might be able to do that. Mayhap a mantle as well?" Skena watched her daughter's eyes shine with the prospect. "With the scraps from the bolts I should be able to fashion several changes for Lady Muriel de Servian. She will be all the envy when she goes to court."

"Mama," Andrew tugged on the skirt of Skena's kirtle, wanting her undivided attention. "I wish to go wait for our Noel. He promised I could ride Brishen when he came back. Please?"

"Me . . . I want to ride," Annis complained.

Skena patted them both on the shoulders. "You may go

wait for Noel inside the gates. Be sure to keep the hoods up on your mantles. And if you get cold come back inside. I will not have you getting sick. Understood?"

"Yes, mama," they said together, heads bobbing. They started to run out of the sewing room, but turned and hurried back. Each hugged her about the hips, and then clamored out of the room in a flurry of giggles.

"Did we ever have that much strength? They wear me out watching them." Rowanne chuckled.

Skena laughed at the children's antics. "Och, I better go make sure they get bundled up properly. 'Yes mama' does not always mean yes mama."

As Skena hurried out of the room to catch the children, she slammed hard into a body. Her heart jumped as she, once again, feared coming face-to-face with the man who had stalked her through Craigendan. Startled, she pulled up short, but only saw Ella. She tamped down on her customary reaction of dislike for her, suspicious as to why she was lurking in the shadows. Once again, there was no reason for the woman to be in this area of the fortress.

"Ella, what are you doing here?" She wanted the question to sound offhand. Instead it had an edge to it.

"Beg pardon, Skena. Came—" she suddenly gripped her stomach and doubled over, "for a tansy. Aye, need some worts to help me. Got the gripe sumtin' awful, me has."

Recalling how Ella was in this part of the fortress just before one of the attacks, Skena hesitated, leery to be alone with the strange female. "Rowanne, come aid me in mixing a tansy for Ella."

Rowanne's eyes flashed a silent question, but she gave her a brief nod. She then followed them to the stillroom.

As Skena stepped from the fortress, she paused to pull the hood of her mantle about her face. Rubbing her cheek against the fur lining, she smiled, enjoying the warmth and protection that her bride's gift afforded. She had never owned a cloak of this fine quality. The cozy raiment reminded her of Noel's love.

The snow had returned, not heavy yet, though dark clouds hanging low over Ben Shane promised more bad weather would reach them before nightfall. From the steps of the high porch entrance, she scanned the bailey, looking for the children near the gates. They had been outside too long, waiting for Noel. She wanted them to come inside before they took a chill. They could ride Brishen another day.

Failing to spot them, Skena exhaled in frustration. No one stirred within the ward, as if they feared the snow was settling in for the night. Her people had rushed to complete their chores for the day and were already inside by the fire in the Great Hall, some likely also sharing the warmth of the kitchen.

"Annis! Andrew!" she called. No reply. She strained to hear their voices. No sound anywhere, only the low whirl of the wind pushing the snowflakes through the ballium.

The gatekeeper would still be at his sentry post since the riders had not returned from the hunt. Skena glanced up at the sinking sun, its light casting shades of pinks and purples across the snowy landscape. A faint unease brushed her mind. They should be home soon. She wished that Noel was back, and they were all gathered in the Great Hall, snug against the gathering stour.

The wind shifted, colder now, the flakes suddenly swirling thicker. The children needed to come in now. They were too small and could take chill easily. A blast of icy air buffeted her. Going down the steps, she hugged the heavy mantle about her, glad of the cloak's shield against the worsening weather.

The guard had his hands over a small brazier, trying to warm himself. When he looked up and saw her coming, he hastily put them behind his back. "Eventide, my lady."

She offered him a smile. "Go back to warming yourself. I would be doing the same if I were stuck out here waiting for the men. When they finally come back, go straight to Cook and tell him to give you some hot broth."

"You are kind, Skena MacIain," he spoke with a nod.

She clutched the side of her mantle as the wind whistled around them. "Skena de Servian now," she corrected.

"You take his name? But what about clan law saying you must keep the MacIain name to hold these lands and title?"

She shrugged. "Times change. Lord de Servian owns the charter to the lands and title to Craigendan now."

The old man grimaced. "'Tain't right, Skena. This is Scotland. He is Norman."

"True. But he is my lord husband now. 'Tis my will, not that of an English King." Her tone was soft, but spoke she would hold no reproof for her choosing an English husband. She looked around. "Have you seen my bairns frolicking about? They were coming to the gate to await Lord de Servian's return."

"Aye, they were here for a bit. Then they went to the stables to see the horses."

She looked to the barns. "How long ago was that?"

The man frowned. "Sometime back, my lady. They need to be inside. The fury of the storm will hit soon methinks."

"I agree." Skena glanced up at the darkening sky, the storm clouds nearly blotting out the remaining rays of the sun. "Errant children, errant husband, not sure who is more troublesome."

The snow crunched under her booted feet as she skirted along the curtain wall to keep out of the frigid blast of air that went through the ward. At the stable she paused to listen for their voices. Again, only small sounds broke the silence, the horses in the barn murmuring or moving about, a dog off on the far side barking.

"Annis! Andrew! Answer me!" From the corner of her eye, she noticed the postern gate. It was not locked, but moved faintly, pushed by the storm's force. As she headed toward it, she looked down, trying to spot their footprints in the snow.

There had been considerable traffic, thus it was well packed down, too compressed to take an impression.

As she reached the entranceway, she paused, recalling the fight with the wolves. There had been no further incident of the beasts trying to get in. While they had taken down a large portion of the pack, there had been others. She hoped the twins had not been so foolish as to sneak out the postern gate, hoping to walk out to meet Noel. Jerking the door back, she looked out into the gloaming. There were several sets of tracks, but she spotted one small booted one off to the side.

Skena followed. "I will take a switch to them," she cursed under her breath. She was angry, but more so at herself. Had she not stopped to dose Ella, she would have gone after the children, stressing to them that they must come back inside shortly. It had taken time to prepare the tansy, and then Ella ruined her efforts by tossing up the contents of her stomach, so she had to do it all over again. Had she not been engaged in dealing with the irritating woman, she would never have allowed the time to slip away.

She reached the point where she could clearly see the small print belonged to either Annis or Andrew. The size was right. Only she could not understand why there were not more footprints. Another frigid blast of air buffeted her, knocking back the hood of the mantle. A chill went up her spine that had naught to do with the coming storm.

The reason there were so few prints was that someone had passed this way behind the children. The larger ones—possibly two sets of women's prints and one clearly a man's—had come behind and mostly obliterated the child-size ones. She tried not to panic, but she was running before she realized it. She spotted more partial imprints of the twins, leading away from Craigendan. Surely, the children would not be so foolish as to come out here hoping to meet Noel on the return?

Her lungs burned from running and breathing in the icy air. Gathering her wits against the all-out panic, she stopped to consider what was best to do. She looked around to get her bearing and realized she now stood in the spot where she found the children the night they had come upon Noel.

Their lives had changed so since that stormy night. Now she stood in another gathering storm.

She grimaced at the conclusion she drew—the children were either being led away from the fortress, or someone was stalking them. Neither possibility sat well in her stomach. She frowned as her eyes spotted something, just a few paces ahead. Lifting her skirts, she rushed onward, the snowflakes stinging her eyes.

She reached the spot in the path where it forked into different directions. One branch would lead to the road to Glen Shane. Another led to Gailleann Castle and then to Comyn land beyond. The smaller track would circle around and come back to Craigendan. As she stood at the crossroads, she could not discern which way the children had gone. She carefully searched about, but there were no more small footprints. It was if they had vanished. Several paces from where the tracks stopped, there was a deep impression, as though an adult had fallen to his or her knees in the snow.

She started to call out to them, as she had on the night they had found Noel. Only, something warned this was not a wise thing to do. Far up ahead on the path leading to the Comyn land, she saw something dark alongside the road. She hurried her steps to it. Bending over, she picked up the length of woolen material.

Her blood turned to ice as she saw the weave was one worn by Duncan Comyn. Had Noel been right about Duncan after all? Was he responsible for the strange happenings at Craigendan?

Her mother's instinct pushed her to go onward and search for the children. The kenning and logic warned her to turn back. She hesitated, torn by the warring pressure within her heart.

"Noel." The name fell from her lips. She knew she must go

back and get him. He would be returning by now. Allow him
to deal with this. He had Guillaume and the men of Challon
to back him.

With her mind resolute, she swung back in the direction of
Craigendan, urgency biting at her mind. As she rounded the
bend, the snow was coming down so hard she could barely
see ten paces ahead of her. She pulled up short, startled, when
she nearly ran into Ella. Backing up a step, she clutched the
mantle tightly about her.

"Ella, what are you doing out here? Are you following
me?" Seeing the woman inflamed her anger. She forever
seemed to be asking Ella why she was in places where she
had no reason to be. "You are supposed to be sick."

The ugly, squat woman did not appear ill, but stood there
grinning like a jackanapes. The crone was a mystery, but
Skena had little time to fool with her.

"Sick? Been sick most of me life. Sick of them that think
they are better than others," Ella answered oddly.

Skena had no patience with the queer woman. "Well, be that
as it may, I have no time to listen right now. I need to get back
to Craigendan—" She started to move past Ella, who stood
in the middle of the path blocking the way, but Ella slammed
into her, just as she had when they had passed in the hallway.

"Och, pardon me clumsiness, Lady Skena."

Clumsiness, her arse! Ella had deliberately rammed against
her as she attempted to pass. Skena tried not to show affront,
but felt the frown creasing her brow. "Nevermind," she said
dismissively. She misliked the gleam in Ella's dark grey eyes,
but simply wanted to get past. She would deal with her later,
after the children had been found. "It happens. Footing is slippery in this snow. We both need to get back to Craigendan."

As Skena, once again, started to go by the stout woman,
Ella met her, the club-fisted hands shoving at her so hard, it
knocked her back several steps. She had to struggle not to fall
onto the snow. A gentle mistress to her clansmen, Skena had

never taken a lash to anyone, but she feared Ella was pushing her to that point.

"How dare you, Ella! What has gotten into your brain? Maggots?"

"You ain't so high and mighty now, eh?" Ella came onward, clearly intent on pushing Skena again.

Enough of this! Skena was not having some sort of shoving contest with the ugly woman. While Skena had strengthened her muscles over this past summer and autumn, she recognized Ella had a good three stone on her, and not all was fat. The woman had a brutish thickness to her body generally seen only upon a man. Instead of waiting for the challenge, Skena spun on her heels and ran, intending on taking the path that circled around to Craigendan.

Moving fast, she did not slow as she rounded the bend again. This time she crashed into another body. She jerked away from her half sister and then looked over her shoulder to see Ella coming up behind her.

"Dorcas. What means this?" Skena demanded.

Dorcas smiled. "Tide and time, dear one. Winds of change blow. Methinks beginning with this fine mantle. I have never seen anything so beautiful. Take it off, sister."

"Have you both gone mad? Lord de Servian will have you whipped." Skena jumped as Dorcas grabbed at her mantle. Not about to give Dorcas spit if she was on fire, Skena punched out straight and caught her half sister unawares; her fist slammed upward to her sister's chin, the force enough to knock her on her arse.

Skena rushed by the fallen Dorcas, but suddenly another person stepped into the pathway. A man. She staggered back in horror.

Angus.

"Well met, Skena, lass. I have been waiting for you, said the hunter to the hare." He laughed, the harsh sound ringing through the snowy landscape.

Chapter Thirty-Two

Noel was in a high mood, nearly giddy with the joy of Skena filling his heart, his life. Never had he been this happy. He wanted everyone to share this rare feeling, yet as he glanced at his closest friend in the world, he saw Guillaume was far from the same set of mind. Hurrying to tie the fallen roe onto the back of his squire's horse, his friend's face was drawn. Wanting to do something to reach past the darkness clouding Guillaume's soul, Noel scooped up a handful of snow and let go, hitting him square in the shoulder.

Guillaume swung around. "Are you daft? The snow already comes down to soak us. You need not purposely set out to speed up matters."

"Such a sour disposition! Recall how Julian, Simon, Redam, Damian and Dare used to build snow castles with us? Then we would stage mock battles?" Noel asked, hoping the memory of their childhood would lighten Guillaume's spirit.

Finally, a faint smile played around the corners of Guillaume's mouth. "Happy times, true, but then we were young and too foolish to know it was better to be inside out of the weather. I should make you awares, Noel, your continual good cheer is not infectious, and attempts to jolly me are bloody irritating. I am in a foul mood. Leave it go."

"Alas, marriage agrees with me. I wish those about me to share my contentment."

"Cease prattling and help me tie off the buck so we can please get back? Daylight fast fades, and it cannot escape your notice that a bad storm quickens upon us." Guillaume grumbled, running the rope around the roe's hips. "Stupid deer ran too far. We are nearly to Gailleann Castle. That is the stronghold in the distance—far out there in the middle of the loch."

Noel looked off at the fortress, hardly more than a small glimmer in the fading light. "I shall take your word that it is a castle. Belongs to the Lady Caitrin Bannatyne?"

Guillaume nodded. "Oh, aye. And mind, the name serves her well. They call her Lady Cait in jest, and believe me, that is one cat with claws. What she wants with that sop Kerian Mackenzie I will never know."

Noel chuckled. "Mayhap she wishes a weak husband so she can do as she pleases."

"Possibly. She puts forth claim they were destined to wed because of some childhood vow. Bah! Mackenzie looks at her like a sister, not a lover." Satisfied the dead animal was secure, Guillaume went to mount his white stallion. "Shall we make haste to reach Craigendan before nightfall? You, at least, have someone awaiting your return."

"You have someone waiting for you as well." Noel swung up on Brishen and nudged his mount homeward.

"I am beginning to fear that Rowanne would be most happy if I went away and never returned," Guillaume confessed as they moved out. "You saw her last night—jerked away like my touch was that of a leper's."

Noel reined his stallion to fall in beside Guillaume's charger. "I saw. At the time I pondered that her reaction was a little extreme. Mayhap she feigns not wanting your touch because it provokes too much within her. She works hard to keep you at arm's length, but I question if 'tis because she dares not allow you close or she loses her battle."

As they rode along in silence, Noel considered the woman. He wanted to like Skena's cousin. Rowanne was now kin, a cousin by marriage. Toward him the baroness was warm, even charming. The instant she turned her arresting brown eyes upon Guillaume, her mouth set and her whole demeanor changed. Her perpetual coolness toward Guillaume stopped Noel from truly liking the lady.

"My thoughts—stop deferring to her wishes at every turn. Do not allow the distance she puts between you." Noel knew this was already at the fore of Guillaume's ciphers, so he merely prodded to set things in action. "Lay siege to her. You are one of Edward's fiercest warriors. Surely, winning the surrender of a Highland lass would be a simple task for a man of Challon? Oh, mind, I am not suggesting that you force her into your bed. Simply *inflict* your presence upon the lady at every turn."

Guillaume chuckled. "Inflict? I am sure that is precisely how she would view it."

"Ah, while I am more beautiful than you—and I have Skena's word on this, mind—you are still a comely man. All the Challon dragons are bait to lure females. Why should Lady Rowanne be so different? Mayhap you needs must get sick so she would be forced to care for you. It certainly sped haste to Skena's falling in love with me."

"And you with her, eh?" Guillaume pointed out.

"'Tis truth. I highly recommend it as a way to win a lady's heart. Rowanne would have no way to keep up that bastion between you. The touching, the care, it has a way of working on the senses. Very seductive." Noel gave the reins a jerk as Brishen tried to reach over and nip Guillaume's horse.

Cocking a black brow, Guillaume clearly gave consideration to the idea. The corners of his mouth twitched, saying he was of two minds. "I mislike deception. 'Tis not a good footing to start a marriage." Holding his hand out palm up, he allowed the snow to gather on his leathern gauntlet. "Of course, at this rate I shall catch my death before we reach Craigendan. Mayhap I shall not have to feign sickness." He leaned over in the saddle and patted Noel's shoulder. "Not blood brothers, but truly brothers of our hearts, eh?"

"Scots hold belief that foster brothers have a stronger bond. There is not the competition between them that oft is seen in brothers of blood—no younger brothers coveting what the older has. That—" Noel's words stopped as cold fingers of apprehension spread through his soul. "Sometimes I am a bloody fool. God's teeth! I am a king's fool!" He set his heels to Brishen's ribs, causing the stallion to rear slightly in the snow. "Hiagh!"

"Noel! Wait!" Guillaume shouted.

Noel did not slow Brishen, but urged a faster pace, riding through the slippery snow without care. Perchance it was simply the realization within him, but he suddenly had the urgent feeling Skena needed him.

"You are not Angus," Skena stated flatly.

The man facing her was a shade taller and narrower through the chest. At this close range, she judged him to be younger, mayhap by ten years or so. Aye, he was *not* Angus, despite wearing clothing that belonged to her dead husband. Skena shifted her eyes to Dorcas, imagining how he got them. He was the one who had been sheltering in the woods, with her dear half sister supplying him food, clothing, information on the comings and goings of Craigendan, and even opening the postern gate for his mummeries as a ghost.

"Where are my children? What have you done with them?" Skena was terrified, her mind struggling to absorb the details of his presence, and what Dorcas and Ella were doing out here with him. She urgently needed to locate the children and then find a way back to Craigendan and Noel.

"Safe. You will see them soon." He gave her an affable smile. "So few questions, Skena? Surely, you wonder who I am?"

Feeling her blood turn to ice, Skena pulled the mantle closer about her, glad of the warmth Noel's gift provided. *Noel, I need you.* Her mind spoke the plea, hoping their bond was resilient enough to reach out to him. Mayhap Tamlyn or Aithinne might hold that power, but her abilities with the kenning were so weak, only strong when she was touching Noel. Oh, how she wished she were touching him now!

"There is little need for me to ask who you are, Daragh Fadden," she answered with a regal tilt of her head. "I am Skena of Clan Ogilvie, one of the Daughters of Anne—a race of witchwomen, royally descended from the seven ancient houses of the Picts. Their blood flows through my body. You, being a Lowlander, might be unawares of our Highland ways and lore, but Ella and Dorcas ken these truths." She slanted her eyes toward Ella, sensing she was the weakest link. Folk spoke that the women of Ogilvie blood had eyes that reminded them of a cat's. She hoped to play upon the superstitious fears that grew from this talk.

Ella glanced to Dorcas, unease dawning upon her face. "'Tis true, 'tis whispered some Ogilvie females have the power to change into a mountain cat nine times. Witches! Heard the *Seanchaidh* story about it afore."

Daragh Fadden gave a lopsided smile and reached out, his fingers brushing Skena's chin. "Here, puss. . . . Where are your—?"

Skena slapped his hand away, allowing her fingernails to cut into his wrist, deep enough to draw blood. She watched his smile broaden, though the warmth never reached his black eyes. The intense focus reminded her of that wolf she had faced the night she found Noel.

Daragh lifted the inside of his wrist to his mouth and sucked away the droplets of red. "So . . . sweet puss does have claws. Then, I suppose we can dispense with formal greetings."

Dorcas rocked back and forth on her feet, visibly cold. "Dispense with the mummery and be done with this. The weather is not fit for beasts."

Her lips petulant, she made to snatch the end of Skena's mantle, only to have Daragh snag her wrist, his large hand clapping about it hard. With his breath vaporizing in the air, that hungry smile faded as he stared at her. His iron grip held her firm.

"I want her mantle. 'Tis warmer." Dorcas lifted her head defiantly, but there was an unsure note to her voice.

"Make do with your lot, woman, and stop coveting your *sister's* every breath," Daragh snarled. Yanking Dorcas to him, he hauled her up on tiptoes, nearly causing her to slip in the snow. "And never be so presumptuous as to order me about. Am I made clear?"

"Here now!" Ella complained, her gnomish face crinkling in confusion. "You leave her be. Deal with that 'un there—" She motioned toward Skena with a sweep of her arm.

He gave Dorcas a hard shove back into Ella's chest, and saw both women struggle not to fall. Glaring at Ella as if she were an idiot, he snapped, "Did you not hear what I just said to *Lady* Dorcas?"

Skena was unsure what was going on between these three. Obviously, Ella and Dorcas had been hiding him and aiding him all along. Only, she judged that Daragh was suddenly seeing the two women as a liability. Mayhap that would work in her favor. Noel, surely, would have returned to Craigendan by now. Her absence, along with the children's, would have drawn notice. Rowanne would know something was amiss. Noel would come for her; their tracks would be easy to follow in the snow. She glanced back toward the direction of the fortress. Fear mounting, she suddenly worried that was precisely what Daragh wanted—for Noel to come after her. Trying to reason it out, she nearly jumped when he put a hand upon her and gave her a small push.

"Come, we need to get out of the snow."

Skena resisted his guiding pressure. "Where are you taking me?"

"To see your children. Now move, sweet puss, before I lose patience with you as well."

Skena decided, for the time being, she would go along with him. She wanted to see Annis and Andrew, assure herself they were safe. Then, she needed space to know what was best to do, to figure out what Daragh hoped to achieve by all this nonsense. The farther they walked, the heavier the snow came down, and despite knowing this area of her land, she was growing confused about which direction he was herding her. The only thing for sure in the blinding blizzard was that the land had started to climb.

Finally, a dark finger rose against the white landscape, and she realized where he was heading—the old Pict broch, the one that would go to Elspeth when she wed. The place was sorely neglected and had not been used since before Muriel's birth. Elspeth realized it would take a lot of work to restore it to the point that it would be a good home for her and her husband. Still, the master masons of the Picts built structures to last, and built them to be unassailable. For centuries her ancestors had run to this circular stone fortification in times of war.

She paused at the foot of the knoll to glance up at the drystone structure, which dated back to the time of the Romans. Round and slightly tapering, it rose taller than seven men, designed to keep the people above the line of attackers. There had once been an outer defensive wall, but it had crumbled in places and now lay mostly hidden under the blanket of snow. A faint hint of smoke curled from the chimney. Since she assumed the children were within, this brought a small measure of relief about their safety.

There was only one way to enter a broch, and that was through a cramped tunnel-style entrance. Skena felt an insistent shove at her back, so she lifted her skirts and ducked down to go inside. Since her head would just clunk against the top of the opening if she stood upright, she did not have to incline at the same angle a man would. Thus, the height of the walled, inner staircase did not make her feel confined. It was the breadth. The rough stones on either side dragged at her cape as she moved through the tight confines. A smile crossed her lips. Poor Ella would find herself in a fat man's squeeze! She finally passed under the opening channel, ingeniously built so defenders could stand on a platform above and thrust spears downward on invaders, who in turn were unable to raise shields or wield their arms to defend themselves.

Dim light provided by a single torch filled the central chamber, as blocks of peat burned in the ancient stone fireplace. Skena cried out and rushed forward as she saw Muriel huddled next to the hearth on a pile of furs, with Andrew and Annis on one side of her. Protectively, her cloak was curled around them to add its warmth to their small bodies, so they were just barely visible.

Skena rushed to her dear friend, and knelt before her, hugging her. When she pulled back, she saw tears filled Muriel's eyes. At first she thought there was smudge of black on her cheek. As she reached out to rub it away with her thumb, she hesitated, seeing it was a bruise.

Someone had hit Muriel, hard.

"Who—" she began.

Muriel's hand reached out and gripped Skena's wrist with amazing strength. "Never you mind. 'Tis other things more important now. I am fine. Do not fash, lass."

The children looked up with glassy eyes at Skena, obviously so warm in their nest provided by Muriel that they had drifted off to sleep. She patted their sweet cheeks and then put her finger to her lips to silence them, as from behind her, voices were raised. She lifted her eyebrows in question, asking them if they understood and would obey. Both gave a faint nod.

"How much longer, Daragh? Enough of these games." Dorcas harangued in a shrill tone that set Skena's teeth on edge.

Daragh reached out and slapped her. Not hard, but forceful enough to cause her sister to back up, and put her hand to her cheek rubbing it. She eyed him with growing hatred, a look that Skena had witnessed all too often over the years. She remained unsure what Daragh planned, but secretly was pleased to see that Dorcas was not so delighted with Daragh's high-handedness. It might work in her favor at some point, though she would never place trust in Dorcas's deliberately aiding her in any fashion.

"I will not warn you again to shut up, Dorcas." He wagged his finger at her.

"Here . . . Help me," Ella complained, loudly. While she was short enough to move through the narrow passage without stooping, her square body had become lodged between the two inner walls of the staircase.

Skena swallowed her laughter as Dorcas worked to tug Ella loose by pulling on her hand. For a moment, she feared the woman might be stuck, and they would all be trapped here until Noel found them and put a boot to Ella's broad backside. She supposed her distant ancestors never considered they could trap themselves in such a bizarre manner! Then suddenly, Ella's squat body jerked free from the stones, and she and Dorcas, arms akimbo, tumbled onto the paved floor.

Skena could not help it; the snigger slipped out. Under the dim torchlight, they made such a bizarre sight, sprawled in the middle of the floor, like some mythical monster with two heads, and four arms and legs. Ella bellowed in pain, thrashing about.

"Me leg . . . me leg . . . You ungrateful wretch . . . You broke me anklebone." She tried to lean forward to clutch it, but found it hard because of her fat belly and having to oust Dorcas from practically sitting on her.

Dorcas pushed up from the snarl of limbs and mantles and

straightened hers; the tie was almost strangling her neck. She glared at Skena, her mouth compressing in a frown, as she saw Skena silently chuckled at the silly sight. "I will give you something to wipe that smirk off your face, you stupid cow."

Coming in angry steps, she moved toward Skena, only to have Daragh step to block her. He took hold of Dorcas's forearm, looking down on her. Though Skena could not see his face, she sensed a coiling darkness within this man that terrified her. While she had never considered her sister very smart—cunning, yes, but not smart—even Dorcas should have been able to tell this was a dangerous man, one not to trust.

"Daragh, stop dragging everything out and have done with it. Now," Dorcas said, but it was in a suggestive tone, not an order. Yes, while she was none too smart, neither was she stupid.

He shrugged. "My plans have changed."

"To what?" Dorcas braved a clear challenge with her question.

Dropping her hand, he stepped to the fire to warm himself. "I do not need your tongue to decide how things will go. Keep your teeth closed."

Skena did not want to know his plans, but was not one to hide from things. At least, if she knew something of his mind, she could better prepare for what she must do. She swallowed to find her voice, wanting it to sound strong and assured, not slip to reveal the mounting terror rising in her. "And what have you decided, Daragh Fadden?"

He looked up, flashing a winning smile. "Why, to kill Noel de Servian. What else?"

Chapter Thirty-Three

Noel reined Brishen to pause at the crest of the rise. Stamping the ground and fighting against the bit to run, the destrier snorted streams of vapor into the moist air. Off in the distance, Noel could see Craigendan aglow from torchlights, quite beautiful in the pristine snowscape. Contrarily, his stomach twisted into knots as he comprehended what it meant. *Something was wrong.* The whole time he raced homeward, he fought the gnawing fear that trouble had, once more, reared its sinister head. Somehow, he sensed Skena needed him. He prayed these worries were naught more than insecurities brought on by how deeply he loved her. Once he reached the fortress, surely she would be waiting to comfort him and laugh that everything was fine. The torches illuminating the boulevard bespoke his worse fears were confirmed—danger once more stalked Craigendan.

"Hiagh!" Slapping the reins back and forth on either side of the stallion's neck, he drove Brishen onward.

Images of when he had returned to the fortress and discovered Skena at the bottom of the cellar stairs haunted him. Guillaume held the belief that Noel had foiled an attempt on her life. He shuddered to consider the outcome if he had not returned sooner than expected. He told these dark visions *be gone*, but images still haunted him, of what might await him at the *dun*, of him holding Skena's dead body, of him howling his madness to the skies.

"Demon hobgoblins, away with you," he whispered the banishment. "Skena is fine." Noel had to draw heavily on his warrior's training to focus on the here and now and not allow his mind to become his undoing.

The gate rose when the watch spotted him riding hard, allowing Noel to pass through and into the bailey without slowing. His eyes noticed the numerous torches along the boulevard and ballium. It would have been quite festive if not for their significance. He spotted the beautiful Rowanne on the end of the portico, but no Skena. Rowanne's pale blue mantle gently undulated in the wind; her hands were clutched together in a pose of worry.

Vaulting from the saddle, he noticed no one was about to take Brishen's reins. Instead, he dropped the lead to the ground, knowing the horse would stay as he had been trained to do. "What has happened?" he asked, running up the stone stairs.

Rowanne hurried over to meet him. "We cannot find Skena or the children. We looked. I have the servants searching."

"How long?" he snapped.

Her soft brown eyes expressed concern, and mayhap a trace of guilt. "I am not sure. Earlier, we were working in the sewing room. The children came in and asked permission to go to the portcullis to wait for your return. Skena told them yes, but not to stay outside too long because of the cold. She started to follow after them, only Ella—"

"Ella?" he snorted. "I mislike judging a person on their form, as God fashioned them thus 'tis not my place to be critical. Only, she brings tales of otherworldly beings to my mind, evildoers. She is a malignant troll in human guise. If it is wrong of me to harbor such thoughts, I shan't tend an apology. 'Tis my gut's opinion."

Rowanne gave a concurring nod. "She came to Skena and

complained of being sick, had her fix a tansy. Afterward, Skena spoke she was anxious about the children and went out to check on them. I withdrew to my room to dress for the evening meal. It was the last time I saw her."

Noel's mouth compressed into a frown. Taking off his leather gauntlets, he slapped them against his thigh in frustration. "When was that?"

Her eyes strayed past him. "Where is Guillaume? Why is he not with you? Out jesting with his men instead of here when you need—" Her words broke off as Guillaume rode through the gate followed by two men-at-arms.

Noel was standing two steps below Rowanne. Irritated by her harshness toward his friend, he moved up to the same level, allowing his height and breadth to intimidate her. Rowanne was a tall woman, likely as tall as most Scotsmen, so outside of Guillaume she was unused to looking up at a man. He stood close, using his physical presence to rattle her. She lifted her head in a royal mien, trying to show he failed with the subtle pressure. This woman was warrior born, just like Skena. But then her chin betrayed her, quivering. Noel blinked in shock. She was actually scared.

"That man you so blithely disdain is one of the best men you will ever find. If you lack the mind to see that and cannot count your blessings, then tell Challon. He can find you another husband. Set Guillaume free. I shan't have him hurt any more by your cruel ways. Am I made clear?"

She stared at him, refusing to back away, despite trying to shield her female vulnerability. He saw a contrite flicker in her beautiful eyes, but he could spare her no time. This issue was not settled. They would have at it again, but once Skena and the children had been found.

"What goes on?" Guillaume came rushing up the steps.

"Skena is not inside Craigendan," Rowanne told him. "I missed her, looked, but saw neither she nor the children were within the curtain. I have everyone searching."

From across the yard, Elspeth came running. Nearly out of breath when she reached them, she could not speak her tides. Noel knew he would have to wait until she regained it. His hands flexed to prevent him from grabbing her and shaking the words out of the young woman.

"Beg pardon, my lord. Tracks . . . many in the snow." She sucked air again before going on. "Galen follows. Looks as though Skena and the children walked away from the castle. Mayhap Muriel, as well. She cannot be found either."

"Why in God's teeth would Skena be out in this storm with the children?" Noel fumed to Guillaume. "'Tis not like her."

Elspeth looked up at him with worried eyes. "There are others, too, Lord de Servian."

"Others?" He swung back to her.

"More tracks. Galen said to tell you two, maybe three sets belonging to women or boys, but another is clearly a man. He tracks them with Kenneth, and said their trail would guide you. He said hurry."

Guillaume let out a snort. "God's wounds, half the bloody castle is outside the pale in a blizzard? What nonsense be this?"

"Ella and Dorcas are gone also," Elspeth added.

"Perchance they went after Skena, to help her search for the children?" Rowanne suggested.

"If you believe that, Lady Rowanne, then you are a bigger fool than I already suspect you are." Noel did not take the time to hear her answer, but hurried back to Brishen. Leading the horse across the bailey, he headed toward the stables.

"Noel, wait! Take time to prepare," Guillaume called from behind him. "We need torches. Night falls. It will be impossible to follow without lights."

"Fine, gather torches," he called over his shoulder, but did not slow. "Have Rowanne prepare whatever else we need. A wagon full of furs, warming stones. Tell Cook to keep hot water in the ready and warm the stew."

He eased Brishen through the postern gate, pulling up as he spotted a muddle of tracks. "Bloody bleeding hell."

Footprints were upon footprints, nearly obliterating the ones that had passed before. Galen's set clearly followed along one side and Kenneth's to the other. There seemed to be tracks of two to four people, then the children's and Skena's. In the blinding snow, he could not tell if the man and the women were following the twins or leading them away. Neither prospect bode well. Worse, the snow was so heavy it was already covering them. In a short time it would be impossible to tell anything about who passed this way. Even the impressions created by Galen and Kenneth were starting to fill in. Luckily, the old man had set out to follow them when he did.

"Noel, wait!"

Noel heard Guillaume calling after him, but he did not slow.

Skena's legs nearly buckled under her, stunned by Daragh's stating the very thing she had come to suspect—that his purpose was to kill Noel. To avenge his brother's death? Somehow she doubted that, but then she knew so little of the man it made it hard to decide. Angus had once planned to foster Andrew with Daragh for training. Her instinct was to prod, learn the bent of his mind, yet cold dread filled her soul to where she was unable to think. She needs must gather her thoughts. Playing the witless fool could cost them all their lives. When she said naught, he turned away, and set about to poke the fire to give more heat.

He had done nothing to restrain her, judging she would never leave Muriel or the children behind. The defensive design of the broch protected the round fortress from sudden entry. He also saw it would be nearly impossible for them to escape. Plus, how far could she get with two children and an aging woman in a snowstorm?

Skena ran choices through her mind. Noel would follow

their tracks to the broch. If he foolishly entered he would be exposed to attack without a chance of defense. Noel might not know how a Pictish broch was constructed and would be unprepared to face the narrow defensive entry, likely why Daragh chose to use the old tower as a trap with the children and her as his bait. The only weapon she carried was the *sgian dubh*, tucked in at her waist. Fearful he might discover it, she carefully shifted the small knife under the cover of the mantle until it was snug against her back.

Her injury fleeting, Ella moved off to the shadowy far corner of the chamber as large as a Great Hall. She grumbled to Dorcas, their words too low for Skena to hear. Clearly, Ella was upset over Daragh's shift in attitude toward them, yet both were smart enough to keep their distance and not bother him again. He glanced up from where he was sharpening his knife on a whetstone. His dark brow furrowed, but then he shrugged off their furtive murmurings; it was plain to Skena he was going to carry out his plans, and they would have little bearing on his decisions.

"May as well settle down and stay warm, Skena MacIain," he suggested. "We might have a wait because of the snowstorm."

"Skena de Servian," she corrected.

He looked up at her with cold, assessing eyes. "You took his name. That surprised me. You never took the Fadden name. What does that say about you?"

She cuddled the children, seeking to reassure herself they were unharmed. "What does it say about me? Clan law stated I must bear the MacIain name to own Craigendan. We now have an English king as a ruler. He says the charter now belongs to de Servian. Clan law no longer applies to me."

"But that is not the whole reason, eh?" He gave her a lazy half smile. "You are taken with your new lord husband. I watched you. Not that I fling blame, what with Angus flaunting that one," he inclined his head toward Dorcas, "before your very face. A burr under your saddle, you being a proud woman, eh? Goes without saying, Angus was *not* a smart man. Any man who had a lady wife such as you would treat her with the respect she deserves, count themselves blessed indeed."

A shiver crawled up her spine, and it had naught to do with the draft whistling through the broch. Daragh almost sounded like a swain attempting to win her favor. The prospect caused bile to roil through her.

Figuring it best to let him think she was too scared to force any sort of confrontation, she quietly moved to cuddle against Muriel. Shifting the children between them, she whispered murmurs of assurance and told them to rest and be quiet. She kissed their foreheads, then a faint smile crossed her lips. They were not asleep, but scared and smart enough to keep still until they knew what to do. By pulling her mantle across them, she and Muriel could share their body heat and keep the little ones warm. She kissed Muriel's cheek. While she did not wish her friend to be involved in this ugliness, she was glad Muriel had been here for the children. Annis waited until they were settled, and then she rolled and put her arms around Skena, her thin body trembling. At the soothing stroke of Skena's hand over her hair the shaking slowly lessened.

Skena watched Daragh as he prepared for the battle to come, for she had no doubt that was what he was doing—readying himself to kill Noel. First, he sharpened two knives, tucked one in at the belt about his waist; the other he hid in the edge of the right boot; then he pulled out a dirk and set to work on it.

She felt the pull of the kenning ripple through her, as he held the long knife up to study its edge. In a merging of the images, she saw from when she walked in Noel's mind, how close he came to dying because of Angus. Within her mind's eye that scene wavered, shimmering in her vision, so it was now Daragh's hand stabbing Noel in the back. She blinked several times, hoping to banish the horrible sensation that burned at the pit of her stomach.

"Lady Skena, you watch me," Daragh said, then offered

her a soft smile. "Mayhap you see the difference between my brother and me now? Naturally, I am younger by nearly ten summers. Taller as well and not as thickly formed. Angus was the image of our father, where some of that was blunted within me because I took after my beautiful mother as well. Dorcas thinks I am prettier. What say you?"

Skena could see there was a softer beauty to his eyes. So unlike Angus's they must come from the mother. Oh aye, on the surface he would draw women, a handsome man, indeed. Yet, the surface was where the two men's likeness ended. Angus did wrong in attacking Noel; it was a cowardly act, but one of a man driven to the end of his rope in battle. In most everything else Angus never intentionally meant ill toward anyone. He was careless of Skena's feelings, and oft hurt Annis by his indifference, but he had never been malicious in his deeds. He would never scare or threaten an old lady or child. Unlike the brother there was a ravenous hunger coiled within this man, pushing him to acts that branded him a coward, evil.

He reached up with the razor-sharp blade and began to dry shave the whiskers from his face. Pausing with one side done, he wiped the blade on his pants' leg. "You seem to prefer Lord de Servian's clean face." He continued scraping away the dark hair of his beard.

Skena almost recoiled. He was trying to win her approval! The only reason he would bother to do that was if he planned to keep her after killing Noel. She had not realized she was clenching and unclenching her fists under the mantle until Muriel gripped her arm and squeezed, silently counseling to rein in her reactions. Batting her lashes to give herself space to reform her expression, she met his intense stare with blankness. She was not a good enough mummer to feign interest in this man who had terrorized her, and yet now assumed she would be willing to accept him in Noel's place.

"What are your plans, Sir Daragh?" she asked casually, as if it were naught weightier than how was the weather. She had to tamp down on the other words rising in her throat for they would only serve to worsen her position.

He offered her a wolfish grin. "I told you my plans, Lady Skena."

Glowering, Ella prodded Dorcas with her elbow. "I warned you . . . and did you hear me? Nay. She uses them witch ways on him."

Dorcas glanced from Daragh to Skena, mistrust and resentment marring her face. "Why must you drag all this out? You play games that waste time. Be done with this," she harangued Daragh with the sharp edge of her tongue. Even so, Skena saw worry in her sister's brown eyes, fear that Daragh's shifting plans were not going to include her. She wanted him to act before he changed his mind.

"You sicken me, Dorcas. I have no idea how I could give birth to a malignant creature such as you. I curse the day I pushed you from my body and you drew breath. You are naught but a changeling," Muriel said, revulsion and scorn clear in her soft eyes.

Skena slowly reached out and took her friend's lower arm, hoping to restrain her temper. Time was passing. Noel would be coming. Little would be served if Muriel provoked Dorcas.

Ella laughed, the harsh barking sound echoing against the stone walls. "Changeling, you say? You little ken how right you are." Her dull gray eyes held a gleam of triumph. Something else was there as well—madness. "You thought yourself so beautiful, with your long red hair, better than the rest of us because the Auld Ones blessed you with a comeliness that could turn a man's eye. But you were common, not good enough to take to wife, no matter how pretty you were. So The MacIain made you his whore. Why should you look down on Dorcas for doing the same thing her mama did? Except, you ain't her mama. Never were."

Muriel looked to Skena, confusion in her eyes. She, too, saw Ella was not sane. Her hand closed over Skena's, clutching her for assurance. "You have tides you wish to impart, old woman?"

Dorcas seemed just as puzzled. Putting her hands on her hips, she came to stand near the fire seeking its warmth. "What mean you—she is not my mama? Are you daft? All ken I am The MacIain's daughter."

Ella had all eyes on her, and seemed quite happy to be the center of attention. "Time you ken the truth. The lot of you. All these years I kept secrets to my chest. Now I have my say and have my laugh. Dorcas ain't your spawn. She is flesh of my flesh."

Daragh jumped to his feet, coming between Dorcas and Ella, his knife still in his hand. "What are you blethering about, old woman?"

"Truth. Plain and simple. Muriel never birthed Dorcas. I did." She stuck her chin up defiantly and proudly thumped her fat bosom.

Shaking her head, Dorcas recoiled from the words. "You lie! You are a crazy old woman. I should never have trusted you."

"Crazy am I? The night Muriel went into her birthing pains, old Jenny the midwife came to help her. 'Twas not her time, she said, still a moon and mayhap more before the babe were to come. Jenny was scared sumtin' was wrong with the bairn. She wanted to send for one of the Three Wise Ones of the Woods, but there were a fierce gale and it was not safe to leave Craigendan. Well, turned out she were right. Muriel had a hard time pushing the child out, turned wrong it were. Nearly died in the effort. The poor thing lived, but not for long. During the night it drew its last breath. I told Jenny it was the Auld Ones' will. I had given birth scant a sennight afore. My child would have a better life as the daughter of Muriel the whore than as the daughter of the swine girl. So I switched them. Killed Jenny to keep her mouth shut. The one I brought into this world had the thickest red hair, so no one ever suspected Dorcas was not Muriel's."

"You lie!" Dorcas raged, and slapped out against Ella's shoulder. "Say you lie!"

Surprised, Ella fell back a step. "Truth be out, bald as it is."

"You knew this?" Daragh grabbed Dorcas by the arm and spun her to face him. "If anyone has heard lies, 'tis me. How you were the rightful daughter of The MacIain, that if Skena were gone you could claim Craigendan. The whole time, it was naught but a wagon load of shite you were shoveling."

"I never lied to you, Daragh. The old woman is crazy, I tell you. Turn a deaf ear to her madness," Dorcas pleaded frantically.

"'Tain't madness, but truth, say I," Ella insisted stubbornly.

"Och, if this is not a turn of the screw! You knew!" Daragh accused Dorcas, pointing the knife in a playful manner, yet with veiled menace, toward the spot between her breasts. "Never trust a woman. Fool is he who trusts two!"

Skena watched Dorcas knock the knife away, and then the three exploded into a roaring argument. Her fingers tightened on Muriel; she worried how this was affecting her friend. Age had taken its toll on the lovely woman. Muriel seemed stunned beyond reaction. Secretly, Skena wanted to laugh. This meant Dorcas was not her half sister. "Some good comes of even a foul situation," she said under her breath.

Dorcas rounded on Ella, furious. She had always relished being the daughter of the laird, imagining she was as good as Skena. Now Ella had told her she was the daughter of some low born serf and Ella. She had no claim on Craigendan, and it was not setting well with her. Her face was red, Dorcas was angrier than Skena had ever seen her.

"She pukes lies, I tell you." Dorcas's voice grew higher, shrill.

Daragh shot her a disgusted look. "Neither of you would ken the truth if it marched, pennons flying, down High Street and bit you in the fat arses!"

"It little matters, Daragh. Think!" Dorcas was frantic and clutching at straws. "Whether the old woman tells the right of it or not, people ken me to be daughter of The MacIain. That is all they care about."

Skena spoke up, raising her voice to be heard over the din, "Dorcas could never stand giving oath in the ring of stones on Lochshane Tor. She would have to speak her line of ancestors before Evelynour of the Orchard and declare her right to rule this land was true. None can lie to Evelynour. She is gifted with second sight. She would ken the lies and dark deeds in your heart."

"Enough!" Daragh thundered. "You and that malevolent gnome of a woman get to the corner and keep there. Do not push me. Shut your lying mouths and speak not another word lest it go foul for you."

"Do not give me orders," Ella barked, whipping out a small knife. "Everything still goes as planned—"

Daragh smiled and nodded, then moved so fast, Ella did not have time to blink. He twisted her arm behind her, yanking it at an odd angle. Ella screamed out, flaying with her free hand, trying to get some hold on him. Daragh jerked the knife from her plump little hand, and then put his booted foot to her backside, sending her reeling across the stone floor to crash into the wall. She lay there in a twisted lump, unmoving.

Annis pushed her body tighter against Skena's and whispered in a taut voice, "Mama, I am scared."

Skena leaned forward and kissed the top of her daughter's head. "Do not fash. Noel will come soon."

Beware, Noel, beware, her mind whispered, hoping the kenning was strong enough to carry her warning.

Chapter Thirty-Four

At Noel's approach, Galen spun around, then offered a smile of well-come. "Lord de Servian, you have come."

"Aye, I have." Noel almost chuckled at the man's grin and his stating of the obvious. "Never thought you would be happy to see an Englishman, eh?"

The Scotsman nodded, "'Tis true. But I am right pleased to see this one."

"Skena is up there? The children, too?" Noel tied Brishen out of sight by a stand of tall pines.

"Aye, the footprints—hers, the children's, and several others—lead straight to it."

Noel looked at the positioning of the strange, round tower, wondering what was going on inside the stone structure, trying to see it with warrior's eyes and not with vision clouded by the emotions barely contained within him. It was situated well. Attackers would struggle to maintain their footing up the incline to reach the entrance. On the far side, the tor dropped off, leaving it invulnerable to attack from that angle. These ancient people, who had lived here, fought here, had chosen the perfect location to protect, giving all the advantages to the fortress.

Guillaume rode up, dismounted, and tied his horse close to

Brishen. "A wagon and men follow. Any more tracks, other than the ones we know about?" he asked.

Galen shook his head. "Nay, only the man and several smaller sets—either women or young boys came this way. Kenneth has gone to the other side of the tor to check if men wait beyond, toward the Comyn boundary. We found this on the way here." He held out a length of soggy cloth to Noel. "Comyn *plaide*."

Taking the tartan, Noel glared at it. "'Tis not Duncan Comyn up there. My guess this was left to confuse or misdirect."

"Then it must be your watcher in the woods, acting with Dorcas and Ella aiding him, I adjudge," Guillaume said, walking a short distance up the hillside to study the tracks. "Unless Kenneth returns with tides of men on the other side, none cover his back to give us a problem. Nevertheless, we cannot just storm the tower, Noel. These Pict brochs are extraordinarily constructed, brilliantly engineered. Skena's people were renowned for selecting some of the best defensive locations. Then they built to cause all manner of trouble for invaders. There is only one entrance—"

"One?" Noel exclaimed, tossing down the swatch of wool.

"Aye, and it gets worse. The opening forces a man to stoop to get inside. Then you pass under a platform where people can stand and jab spears down upon anyone stupid enough to force his way in. If you get by that, there is a double wall with the stairs winding inside. The passage is cramped. Your elbows will brush the stones on either side—no room to wield a shield or sword, and it turns you so the body is exposed. There simply is not space wide enough to pull up a shield before you. If you go in, 'tis the obstacles you face," Guillaume pointed out the problems presented by the ancient structure. "And for my curiosity—just who is in there? You seem to ken. Duncan? I cannot believe he would be crack-brained enough to do something like this with no men covering his flanks. With backing, a Comyn is bold enough—foolish enough—to risk attacking Challon and Damian. Alone—they run scared."

"I know you want to tangle with Duncan because of what happened to Damian and Julian, but nay, Comyn is not behind this mess. 'Tis Fadden's brother," Noel stated flatly.

Guillaume's face showed surprise. "Brother? Bloody hell. That's why you galloped off when we were speaking of brothers."

"When Edward gave me the charter to Craigendan, he mumbled something about a younger brother who had been wounded and made prisoner after Dunbar. I assume he escaped. De Moray did. And I hear Challon now has a father-in-law underfoot." He lifted his brow to emphasize the point. "English jails do not seem able to hold these Scotsmen. Skena once mentioned the brother; said Daragh never came north when Angus wed her. He was much younger and was currying favor with their King Alexander at the time, with an eye to winning land of his own. I guess with ten years difference between the men they were never close."

"So why the elaborate mummery? He thinks to murder you to avenge his brother?" Guillaume turned at the sound of horses approaching. Riding by twos, men of Challon came bearing torches, reaching them at the same time young Kenneth trotted up from the opposite direction.

"Nothing so honorable. I think he wanted Skena dead, likely me as well. Once we were out of the way he could claim his brother's holding. Bootlick Edward and give a bent knee and the king forgives all. My guess Daragh promised Dorcas she would be the new lady of Craigendan to gain her succor. Stupid wench." Turning to the young lad, Noel asked, "What say you, Kenneth? Any signs of men waiting behind the knoll?"

The redheaded boy shook his head. "Nay, I went all the way to the bottom on the other side of the hillock. My tracks were the only ones in the snow."

"That is to the good then." Noel pulled his sword from the sheath slung crosswise on his back. "Let us be done with this madness."

Guillaume reached out and grabbed his arm, staying him.

"Wait, Noel. You cannot go rushing in. Did you not hear what I said you face by going in there?"

"I heard." Noel looked at him resolutely. "Skena is in there—with some Lowlander vermin that needs killing. Nothing else matters."

"And kill him you shall, but I shan't see you trade your life for Skena's." When Noel yanked to break the hold, Guillaume tightened his grip, preventing him from pulling free. "Skena would not want that either. You rushed off from Craigendan with no mind to what comes next. Such foolishness gets a warrior killed. Your wife is depending upon you to have a knight's head and come after her in a smart manner."

Noel closed his eyes and sucked in a deep breath, knowing Guillaume spoke true. He slowly nodded. "Thank you, my brother."

Guillaume smiled. "Now let us set about fetching your Skena."

Noel returned the sword to its scabbard. Looking to Galen, he asked, "What condition is the tower in?"

"The broch goes to Elspeth upon her marriage. While the outer defensive wall has fallen into disrepair, the clan has kept the tower sound. Folk started to take stones from the top level ages ago, but a witch of the Ogilvies warned it was a mistake, a dishonor of the ones who came before us. She said if the broch fails, then the clan will fail, too. After that, the Earl of Kinmarch had it fitted with a new roof. Even so, it will take muckle work to set it right for our Elspeth. The joint timbers on the lower two levels are there, but no flooring. Planking is in place for the upper level, but I would show care. The thatch is refreshed every few years, but I am not sure how well it holds the weather out."

"Thatch? Then I should be able to cut my way through?" Noel considered.

"How are you going to get all the way up there, my lord?" Kenneth asked with wide eyes.

Galen shot the lad a sour look, silencing him. "Aye, you should be able to do that. I assume you will scale the left side.

Once up there, cut a hole. Face the wall and drop down. Move to your left about a quarter turn of the tower, and you will find the doorway to the stairs that lead to the next level. From the second landing you can descend straight to the ground floor using the crossbeam."

"Such cannot be accomplished in complete silence. What say you? Make pretence of entering. Call him out and such. That will allow me time to make the climb, cut my way through the thatching, and get into position. A slow count to two score and I shall drop."

Guillaume frowned at him. "Nay, I do the climb. Your back is not healed yet, Noel."

"Right now I shan't feel a thing. Until I hold Skena safely in my arms again I *cannot* breathe." Noel stared Guillaume in the face, their warrior wills clashing. "If that were Rowanne in there, tell me you would stand back whilst I rescued her. Skena is my woman. I will fight for her. I will die for her if need."

Guillaume inclined his head, resigned. "Very well. Just see you do not die."

"Not to fash—as Skena would say. I have a lot to live for." He patted Guillaume's arm.

Mallory came carrying a sack. "You will need this, Lord de Servian. The best rope, made in the rope-walk way. No splices. It shan't fail you, my lord. A grapple hook is on the end."

"Thank you." Noel gave Guillaume a grin as he removed his mantle and handed it to him. "Let me have your dirk."

Guillaume tugged it from his boot and passed it to him hilt first. "Be careful, Noel. I have a fondness for your pretty face. We have ridden too many leagues together to allow some mush-brained Lowlander to change that."

"Give me time to circle around and get in position. Then call to him, get his attention, anything to provoke him. He will not dare come out, but do what you can to give noise, a cover for my climb," Noel instructed.

Guillaume clutched Noel's shoulders and gave them a firm squeeze, his eyes speaking his concern. Life had not seen fit to give Noel a brother, but he counted himself a lucky man to have a true brother of the heart in this man of Challon. With a faint nod, he turned and moved off into the shadows.

Flanked by Mallory, Guillaume openly approached the front of the broch. Noel watched, waiting until they drew near the entrance. In the darkness, Guillaume's build was similar enough that he could pass for Noel at a distance. It might be enough to confuse Daragh Fadden and allow Noel to get in position for the climb.

Hunched down low, Noel sped through the shadows until he was out of sight of the broch's front, then ran through the falling snow until he reached the far side. He opened the drawstring of the sack and dropped it like a snake sheds its skin, leaving him holding the heavy coil of rope with the climbing hook on one end, its length more than enough to reach the top. He heard Guillaume call out, demanding Daragh show himself instead of cowering behind the kirtles of women. He began swinging the three-pronged hook around and around in an ever-widening circle. Finally, he let loose, allowing the rope to play through his hands, sending the metal end flying skyward.

Noel breathed a sigh of relief when the hook landed without noise, the combination of the snow and the thatch muffling the sound as it hit. Carefully easing back on the rope, he felt it finally snag; he gave a small, sharp tug to see if the hook caught. There was resistance. To set it, he yanked hard and found solid opposition. Feeling confident, he tested with his full weight, then smiled that it held firm.

Hefting himself a short distance up the wall, he stood leaning out and waved to Guillaume to say he was ready. His friend withdrew his sword and boldly walked to the very opening. While the Pictish entrance disarmed those entering, those same defensive measures would also hamper anyone trying to come out. Fadden could not easily venture forth, thus Guillaume took his sword and tapped the flat side to the stone entry, tormenting. Inside, it would sound like thunder breaking. The perfect cover for Noel to climb.

Despite his back still being sore he quickly ascended to the top. The thatch was densely packed, hard from several seasons, but he cut a man-size hole in it with little trouble. Sitting on the wall's edge, he slid the dirk back into his boot, and then quickly coiled the rope around his lower arm, from hand to elbow and around again, preparing to use it to descend into the black bowels of the damnable tower.

Below, he could hear voices—Ella and Dorcas, he thought—though not clearly enough to discern words. Still, it was obvious they were not happy about Guillaume's banging on the side of the fortress. Their tone was strident, harsh, as they fussed about the racket, one voice in particular rising above the others.

Noel smirked. "You think that is upsetting, wait until you catch sight of me falling from the roof."

Setting the hook again, he slowly lowered himself into the darkness. It was only a short distance until his feet clunked against wood. Keeping a hold of the rope in case the flooring proved rotten, he followed the inside of the wall around until his gloved hand found the doorway. Moving into the stairwell, he listened, seeing if his presence had been detected. Again, he heard voices raised in heated anger, but the way they bounced against the stone walls distorted the words. He waited, his eyes growing accustomed to the dimness; he began to make out the shape of the structure.

Uncoiling the rope, he started down the stone stairs, moving in silent steps. As he reached the second level the voices became stronger, though their words were still too low for him to tell what was being said. Several were arguing, but over them he recognized Skena's mocking laugh.

"Fools—the lot of you. You kenned de Servian would come," she taunted.

Noel smiled at her spunk. He had told Guillaume he would feel nothing until he held her in his arms again. He lied. His heart jumped into an unsteady rhythm at just hearing her voice. God, he loved her! He meant it when he said he would die for Skena. He would rather live for her.

"But I am bloody well going to beat her once I get her safely back to Craigendan," he muttered under his breath, an attempt to lighten his spirit.

He walked out at the second level, and despite the broad crossbeam blocking part of the view, he could see everyone down below. A single torch burned in the sconce by the ancient fireplace, and in the dark corner he spotted Skena cuddled with Muriel, presumably with the children between them. He fought the urge to drop from the center of the beam, where he could reach Skena and be between her and Fadden. Unsure just how sound the timber was, he decided to go with caution. Better to land in one piece than take the risk and possibly end up injured and little use to Skena.

Wrapping the coil of rope a turn around the beam and then passing it under his right thigh and over his shoulder, he pushed away from the stone wall. To slow the rate the rope played out through his gloved hands, he shoved with his feet against the wall, to almost hop down the remaining distance.

Skena saw him when he was partway down; her face lit with happiness. He paused and held up his finger to his lips. Their eyes met in a silent communication, him trying to tell her to be ready. As he made to cover the final distance in one release, Ella, who had come to, looked up and screamed.

"Stupid cow," he said through gritted teeth as he landed on his feet, trying to jerk the rope from around his thigh. He reached up and behind, to wrap his hand around the hilt of his broadsword, but had to stop as Ella flew at him like a berserker, her right arm back with a knife in her hand. Noel had never hit a woman before, but he did not hesitate to draw up his foot and give her a hard shove to the belly, sending her backward.

"To me!" he shouted to Guillaume waiting outside. "To me!"

Pulling the sword, he took steps toward Skena, only to have Ella jump him, latching on to his sword arm and swinging him off balance. The woman was heavy as a man her size and muscular. She slapped out with one hand trying to scratch his face. Forced to keep the crazed woman off him, dodging, careful she did not put out an eye, he had a hard time seeing what was happening. Skena tugged Muriel and the kids to their feet, and was pushing them farther back in the darkened corner, but then Dorcas grabbed Skena by her long hair and dragged her forward, nearly jerking her off her feet. Noel's eyes searched for Fadden; he spotted his head behind Skena, who was still struggling with the redhead.

Fed up with thrashing about with Ella, he flung the woman to the stone floor. Once more, he started to Skena. Only this time, instead of attacking him, Ella rushed toward Muriel and the twins. Muriel stepped to shield Skena's children, catching Ella's arm as she slashed through the air with the dagger. With her hands twisted with age, Muriel was no match for the stout Ella. The knife caught Muriel on the upper arm, rending fabric and reaching the flesh beneath. Ready to strangle the loathsome woman, Noel seized Ella and dragged her away from the valiant Muriel.

The light in the room shifted as someone grabbed the torch from the wall sconce. Then suddenly the room went to darkness, just as Guillaume and Mallory came through the entrance. Noel shoved Ella toward them, letting them deal with the crazed female.

Muriel collapsed against Noel's arm, sobbing. The children clung to his legs, hugging him. He wanted to comfort them, but he had to reach Skena.

"Torches! Bring torches!" Noel yelled the command.

Torches were brought in, the yellow light banishing the impenetrable darkness. Everyone blinked as the light in the tower revealed Skena was gone.

Chapter Thirty-Five

"Where the hell is Skena?" Noel snarled his demand.

Guillaume moved around the circular hall, poking the torch into several openings that obviously had been intended for small rooms. "She is gone."

"Merde! Think me a halfwit? I can see that. So are Fadden and that bitch Dorcas." Noel bit back the howl of madness rising in his throat.

Perplexed, Guillaume glanced around. "Mayhap a tunnel into a cave?" he suggested.

"Aye, could be." Galen added, "'Tis one under Craigendan. Two others on this side of the loch."

Guillaume moved to the fireplace. "Always figured it none too smart to hole up in a tower with no path to escape. You could run out of food and water, not a detail you overlook in finding a place to make a stand. To my way of thinking, people clever enough to devise these brochs and place them so perfectly would never put themselves in a trap. If there was a passage, then they had the choice of slipping away before they were doomed."

In question, Guillaume looked to Noel, who in turn rounded on Ella. "Where is the entrance, old woman?"

"I ken naught. Cut out my tongue for I will never tell you,

English." Eyes gleaming, Ella stuck out her square chin, happy at the turn of events and oddly not comprehending the bad position she was now in. "My Dorcas is with your Skena. Mayhap you will get a dead woman back for your bed, Lord de Servian. Like that turn of fate?"

Noel's hand lashed out before she could blink, wrapped around her thick neck, and squeezed. She strangled, her arms striking out frantically trying to hit him. Ignoring her, he held her stiff-armed, keeping himself out of her reach. The old woman was surprisingly strong, but she could do no more than flail against the arm that held her. "You best get down on your knees and use that tongue, pray I find her unharmed, you swort hag, for if I do not I will snap your neck like a twig and feed you to your pigs whilst you draw a last breath. Now where *is* the tunnel entrance?"

Ella looked into his eyes and saw he stone cold meant every word of his threat. She finally gasped, "He did not tell me, always kept everythin' to himself. I do not ken. He first said he'd take them to the sheiling in the hills, and leave the Comyn *plaide* to make you ride toward his land. But the storm came, and he changed plans. He has been holding up here. Said it was better to fetch them to the broch. Stupid Muriel saw the children going off with Dorcas and followed."

Frustrated, Noel turned back to Galen. "Do you know where the damn thing is?"

He shook his head. "This place was long abandoned before I was a bairn. Such knowledge would be something only the laird would ken and naught any others. Never a servant such as myself."

"Noel," Guillaume called, "the peat is mashed down and has a clear footprint in the middle. There must be a way through the back of the fireplace."

"Find it," Noel barked as he bent over to inspect the stone structure.

* * *

Skena's foot hit something hard, slamming her down onto her hands and knees, a groan forced from her body. The rough, uneven stones on the cave floor abraded her palms, stinging. Just as she started to get up, Dorcas perversely kicked her backside. She struggled to keep from going face down in the dirt again. Fury bubbling inside her, Skena gritted her teeth against the pains. Recalling her *sgian dubh* was still tucked in her belt at her back, she resisted the urge to plant it in Dorcas's thigh.

"Get up, Skena." Daragh came back, tilting the torch to dispel the impenetrable darkness.

"I am trying, lackwit! Your bastard whore, spawn of a pig woman—" Skena flinched as Dorcas delivered another kick to her rump. "If you want me on my feet and walking, call off your stupid bitch!"

Dorcas took a step to kick her again, but Daragh moved between them. The two stared at each other in the flickering torchlight. At length he spoke, his tone soft, but menacing. "Dorcas, you came because you feared staying behind and facing Lord de Servian. Cease contrarying me with your petty jealousies. Let Skena be. Kicking her when she falls only slows our escape and gives the Englishman time to follow."

"But you said he could not find the tunnel entrance. Even if he does, you jammed the boulder against the passage to block them from pushing it open," Dorcas pointed out in a tight, frustrated voice.

"Stupid cow, you think he will give up when he fails to discover the way into the tunnel?" Daragh's look was one of exasperation. "Someone will likely tell him of the caves and then the bloody *Sasunnach* will come after us. I hope for enough time to get away in the boat. If we can cross the loch, mayhap we have a chance of reaching Duncan Comyn."

Dorcas glared. "Leave her. Kill her now. She slows us down."

"Us?" His brow lifted in mocking. "You are what slows us. Skena comes—a shield should de Servian catch us. Moreover, Comyn will give us shelter if we hand him the lady of

Craigendan as a prize. Listen well; you hold little value now since you are naught but Ella's get. Do not make me stop and upbraid your stupidity again." Finally satisfied Dorcas would not cross him, Daragh used his free hand to catch Skena's lower arm and help her to her feet.

To hurry her along as they passed through the dark cavern, Daragh kept a hold on her arm. Steps rushed, her foot came down on something with a loud snap. She jumped, scared. Skena had been in the cave under Craigendan many times, but it was kept dry and clean. No animals ever got into that area, as they kept a wooden fence over the passage into the bowels of the fortress. As she moved through the long shadows, which seemed to swallow the light from the single torch, her nose disquietingly detected a fetid smell heavy with urine. That caused an alarm within her.

"What is it?" Daragh tugged on her arm when Skena backed up.

Taking hold of her kirtle's sides, she raised the hem and glanced down. "I stepped on something." He lowered the torch to illuminate the cave floor littered with sticks of white.

"Awh! Bones!" Skena hopped back, yanking to break free from his grasp. Her eyes searched the tops of the rocks, many overhanging, almost forming a natural ledge on either side, just above their heads. "Wolves! Och, 'tis their lair." Images of both times she had faced the animals flashed through her mind, causing her stomach to knot.

Daragh whipped around in all directions and lifted the torch high to see along the ledge on both sides. "No wolves here."

"This is their lair," Skena insisted. "Look at all the bones. They drag their kills back here and eat them. You can smell their rank stench."

Dorcas, who had been trailing behind, tugged her mantle around her and moved closer to the circle of light. "Let us flee this accursed place before they return. Likely they hunt, but will come back if this storm continues."

"We only have a short distance. Come." He put a hand on Skena's back and nudged her forward.

After two twists through the rocks, cold wind and blowing snow greeted them. They had reached the cave's mouth. Uneasy, Skena glanced back, wondering if Noel had found the passage yet. Was he only steps behind them?

Just at the edge of the cove, an overturned boat was half hidden by some brush. Letting go of Skena's arm, Daragh hurriedly cleared away the pine limbs with his free hand, and then ordered, "Here, help me get the boat to the loch. 'Tis easier to carry if we lift whilst 'tis still right side down."

Forming her face into a harsh scowl, Dorcas stood unmoving. "Help carry the boat? A boat that is made to hold only two?"

Cautiously, Skena shifted her arm under the mantle, reaching behind to wrap her hand around the hilt of the *sgian dubh*. "Och, I hold no desire to ride in that becursed thing on Loch Shane Mohr at night in a snowstorm. You have my hearty approval to leave me behind."

"Skena, whilst my plans have changed—and likely may yet change again—you come. Comyn wants Craigendan and you. You are my ransom. As long as I hold you, I have something to barter with. If not him, then I am sure the Campbells will aid me. They evidently wish a foothold in Glen Shane as well."

"And where does that leave me? There is no room for three in that boat you want me to help you carry," Dorcas fussed.

Daragh gave her a half smile. "I admire your grasp of the obvious, Dorcas. You, of course, regretfully must stay behind. I do not ken your loch well enough to risk overloading the small craft. De Servian will be out for blood, but I seriously doubt he will take it out on you. Howbeit, if you fear his wrath, then hide in the cave until first light; at dawn, make your way to Campbell land. I am sure they will take you in. A *talented* lass such as yourself will always find a bed to warm."

"Hide in the cave where wolves will return? This is the reward for all the help I have given you?" Her voice rose in ire.

"Things change, lass. As The MacIain's by-blow you were an asset. As the daughter of Ella? You are worth a handful of wind. My schemes have come a cropper because of you and that fat old woman. Count your blessings I must press on instead of giving you just dues for that turn. I needs must salvage what I can. You best do same. You will land on your feet—you have the way of the cat about you."

"Then force Skena to carry the boat," Dorcas refused. "I see no reason to help."

Skena took a step back. "I cannot carry anything, thanks to Dorcas's kicking me into the dirt. My hands are cut and bleeding." She held out one palm—her left one—to show she was telling the truth.

"Both of you cease defying me. I'd just as soon split your throats and leave you here for the wolves," Daragh threatened.

Skena forced a laugh. "Clearly, you are used to dealing with lackwit Dorcas and crazy Ella. You will not kill me—your bartering tool. Kill me and de Servian will follow you to the ends of the earth to destroy you. I cannot carry the boat. My hands are raw and bleeding."

Not deigning to reply, Daragh turned to Dorcas. He leaned the torch forward, briefly touching the ends of her long red hair, close enough to singe one strand. The pungent smell of the curling hair filled the air. "Pick . . . up . . . the . . . boat, Dorcas."

With that small threatening gesture, he warned he would kill her, or, worse in Dorcas's mind, set her hair aflame. If she lived long enough to put it out, she would likely be disfigured, a hideous mockery of the beautiful woman she now was. Dorcas swallowed hard. Oh, her eyes flashed daggers of hatred toward the brother of the man she had loved, but she knew now was not the moment to cross him.

"What about her? I care naught if her hands are bloody. She should still help move the boat," she complained.

"Two will manage just fine—"

Dorcas protested, "But she will run off, lackwit."

Sticking the torch into the snow, Daragh pulled out a thin

thong of leather from the small bag tied at his waist. "Hold out your hands, Skena."

"Nay," she backed up another step. "My hands will not stop bleeding. I hold them against my kirtle to staunch them. Tying them will only see it worsen, maybe fester. I shall become a millstone for you if I bleed too much and become weak, useless if I rage with a fever when you drag me before Duncan Comyn."

His frown was chilling. "Fine." He slapped out and caught her neck. Threading the leather under her hair, he secured the loop around her throat. "Mind, do not make me tug on it, Skena. The knot will tighten. Might make you strangle."

Skena's left fingers clawed at the leather where it curled around her neck. "Again, a half choked woman is no asset, eh?"

Furious, Daragh gave a yank on the cord. Instantly, it tightened. She wiggled two fingers under the band, but winced when the thin strip of leather cut into the raw scrapes. In feint, she gave a strangled cough, knowing by the single torchlight he could not discern that she prevented the thong from cutting off her air.

"Now we move the boat. Skena come." He scooped up the torch and gave them a smile, little more than a bearing of teeth. Once more, it conjured images of that wolf as he had dared to venture closer to her standing over de Servian.

Recognizing he would not accept blether from either of them, Dorcas knelt down and lifted the rear end of the boat. "This is heavy," she grumbled.

"Not trusting either of you with the torch, I hold it and Skena's tether in one hand, so I lift with only partial strength with my left arm," he snarled, wasting breath to explain the obvious. "Sorry," he said, clearly not meaning the sentiment.

As they moved away from the mouth of the cave, Daragh gave a stiff pull on the leather cord, forcing Skena to follow them or fall. Using common sense, she had chosen not to put up resistance in the cave. The prospect of being cornered in there if the wolves returned from the hunt was daunting. Also, there simply was no place to escape. The walls were barely wide enough for three people. She had failed to notice any branches off the main one, nor did she relish running down some passage in the dark, with no idea where it led or where her next footfall would land. That left retracing their route to the passage entrance at the back of the fireplace. A bad choice. Daragh could run faster than she could, so would overtake her. Even if she accidently reached the opening with space to breathe, she doubted she could shove the rock back from where Daragh had wedged it. Logic said get out into the open where she might stand a chance of eluding him and possibly hide long enough for Noel to come.

That Noel would come she never doubted for an instant. He would come. She merely needed to buy time until he arrived.

"Set the boat down and help turn it over," Daragh said, dropping his side of the wooden craft. When the boat was flipped, he pushed it into the edge of the black water, and ordered, "Get in, Lady Craigendan."

When she stood there, he gave another sharp tug on the leather, a reminder to obey. "Go ahead and choke me to death, Daragh Fadden; better that than getting in that leaky boat. Loch Shane Mohr is treacherous for people unfamiliar with it. In places, rocks are hidden just under the surface and will rip that boat to pieces." Skena backed up, straining against the leather at the back of her neck.

As Daragh moved toward Skena, Dorcas seized the chance to dart off in the darkness. His head whipped around to his right; he watched her disappear into the snowy gloom. He shrugged. "She must figure to outrun de Servian before he can catch her."

"She will never elude him. Neither will you," Skena stated flatly.

He jerked on the tether to reel her closer. "Do as I say. Now!"

Skena's head turned at noises high upon the cliffs. Riders. The flickers from torches grew brighter, nearly a dozen and moving fast. "De Servian," she said softly as a smile crossed her lips. Her fingers flexed around the handle of the *sgian dubh*. She planned to catch Daragh in the stomach or the chest, and then make a break and escape toward the cliff path.

Just as she started to lunge for him, someone came running from the shadows along the water. Distracted by the mounted men starting down the cliff's trail, Daragh failed to react fast enough. Dorcas ran up to the opposite side of the small boat. Carrying a large rock, she raised it over her head and dashed the heavy stone into the middle of the craft; the wood cracked and splintered.

"You bitch!" Daragh leapt for Dorcas, forgetting he still held the leash in his left hand.

Nearly jerked off her feet, Skena fought against strangling. The only thing preventing it were the two fingers still lodged between the cord and her throat. She grasped desperately at the knife, intending to use the blade to sever the cord. A second hard tug sent her lumbering forward, off balance. The knife fell from her hand and into the snow. She grabbed the taut tether, grappling against the pressure.

"I will kill you." Daragh nearly tumbled into the boat as he grabbed at Dorcas. "I will wrap that red hair around your throat and watch your eyes bulge."

"You black-hearted bastard. Foam at the mouth like a mad dog. He is here! De Servian's here! Daragh Fadden, he who brays like a jackass and will scurry away, a cowering dog." Laughing, Dorcas dashed into the night, this time away from the cliffs, heading down the shore.

Galen leading, Noel and his men descended the winding path down to the cove. So thrilled to see him, Skena half forgot Daragh still had the thong in his fist. She started to rush toward Noel, only to be jerked around by another stiff snap on the cord.

"Let her go!" Noel's voice rang out clear in the night.

Daragh glanced to his left, in the direction Dorcas had fled, then to the boat, now already filling with water. He jerked the cord, pulling Skena backward until she fell against his chest.

"You better hope he values your life, Lady Craigendan. For if not, then we both die here and now," he said against her ear, as he placed the tip of his knife to her throat.

De Servian dismounted and then handed his torch to Galen, never taking his eyes off Skena and the man holding her. He walked slowly forward, flanked by Guillaume and Stephen. As the men with torches stepped down from their mounts, they formed a phalanx, just paces behind them. Noel appeared coolheaded, his movements controlled. Deadly. Skena wished she could see Daragh's expression as he stared into the face of this warrior true, his silver eyes aglow with an unearthly power. An avenging angel come to unleash hell.

Skena stared, transfixed by his striking countenance. Noel de Servian was the most beautiful man she had ever seen. His wavy brown hair was a shade darker, wet from the falling snow, the long curls making him seem more Scot than Norman-English. His clean shaven face showed his sensual chin, not stubborn so much as resolute, a face that reflected strength, character. Surely, a man this perfect had been touched by the blood of the *Sidhe*, for only one blessed by true magic could be so lovely formed, possessed of a craft to lure a woman into darkest sin, with nary a thought of the risk to her soul. A warrior who already owned her heart. A man Skena knew she would gladly die for.

What marked Noel de Servian as special, above all others, was that his physical beauty was matched by that in his heart and in his soul. Staring into those pale eyes, she knew he would set everything right. She loved him. She trusted him.

"I said—let . . . her . . . go. Only a coward hides behind a woman. Fight me like a man," Noel stated softly.

"I cannot fight you, Lord de Servian. I have no sword." He shifted his elbow to show he held a knife at her throat. Daragh jerked her neck back even more. "Of course, a dagger is all I need to end the life of your beautiful wife, is it not?"

Skena felt the cold blade against her throat, tried not to

swallow her panic as it would push the blade deeper into her flesh. Instead, she watched Noel's beautiful eyes, allowed her trust in him to flood her being.

"But then, you would have no recourse, eh?" Noel countered.

"The coin of the realm is your wife's life." Daragh gave a laugh. "Shall we bargain?"

"How interesting. A man with no honor expecting honor from the man he wrongs." Noel walked toward Daragh and offered him a flat smile. "You cannot leave in the boat. It seems to have developed a *small* leak. So speak, what do you want for your *coin*?"

"My freedom, of course." Daragh chuckled again, his false bravado rumbling through his chest against her back. When Noel gave no answer, he pressed the blade closer to her throat.

"You want honor? I give you honor. Release Skena and fight me man-to-man." Noel turned to the men behind him. "Form a circle so the area is lit. Trial by combat—let God be the judge of who walks away from this field."

Daragh demanded, suspicious. "What mean you? The instant I let her go you will kill me. Even if you keep faith with this offering and I fell you, your men will kill me anyway."

"Nay. Set her free. My men will honor my command." He rotated to look at the warriors in a semicircle behind him holding torches. "Swear before God if Daragh Fadden meets me on this field of combat to the death and he wins, he walks away a free man by God's will."

Every man, including Guillaume repeated, "I do so swear, God is my witness."

Skena tried to still the frantic beating of her heart, pull within herself to that quiet spot where her mind could brush Noel's. She needed his touch even if it was with the kenning. *Please do not do this. Do not put your life at risk for me*, she thought in a silent whisper.

* * *

Noel watched Daragh smile, and then the bastard shrugged. "I still say I am unarmed for a fight against one of the English's greatest knights."

Turning to Guillaume, Noel spoke loud enough for the words to carry, "Give me your sword, brother." He removed his mantle and handed it to Mallory, and then accepted the sword that Guillaume passed to him. Under his breath, Noel said, "If I die, kill him where he stands."

Guillaume's eyes spoke volumes. "Aye, he will be gutted and left for the wolves, although I would rather you not die."

"I share the wish." Noel turned and walked halfway to Daragh. Raising Guillaume's sword, he plunged it into the ground. Backing up, he accepted his own sword from Guillaume's hand.

"There, Fadden. Your one chance at freedom. Let Skena go." When the man remained unmoving, Noel pressed. "You are cornered. You have naught with which to barter but Skena."

"But a good thing to ransom, eh? Will you enjoy watching me split her throat, seeing her blood bleed black onto the white snow?" Daragh threatened, clearly hoping to rattle him.

"Do it and seal your own death," he replied with sangfroid. "Only, I will not be so swift in meting out my punishment. I once saw an infidel torture a man. You would be surprised what I learned. Face facts, you cannot escape in the boat. Your whore saw to that before she ran off. You cannot force us to back off and allow you to leave with Skena. I would rather see her dead, here and now, than abused at your hands, which would surely happen if I permitted you to go and take her as your shield," Noel lied. The untruth almost stuck in his teeth, but he figured the stance was one Daragh would believe. "The only chance this side of hell you have to walk away from here a free man is to let Skena go and pick up the sword. Shall I turn my back and give you the first blow? It seems the only way a Fadden can come at an opponent."

"Arrogant English bastard," Daragh snarled.

Noel held out his arms, the sword in his right hand half-raised in the air. "Aye, I am English born. And I am arrogant. Howbeit, my ancestry is exalted, a son of a powerful baron, and my mother was a lady true—I am not some child of a crazed pig woman."

Daragh slowly inched toward the sword, pushing Skena ahead of him. As the weapon came within grasp, he flung Skena forward with all his might so she crashed into Noel. Yanking the sword from the ground, Daragh slashed through the air, clearly trying to kill them both. Barely in time to block the blade's arc, Noel tossed Skena to the ground. A one-handed grip, his hold was not positioned to check such a hard strike, thus the sword vibrated in his hand, sending numbing shock through his arm and into his shoulder. Gritting his teeth, it was all he could do to keep his grip around the hilt. The odd pain radiated down his spine to slam into the newly healing muscles in his back. Only by sheer force of will was he able to step before Skena and protect her. Reaching behind him with his free hand, he helped Skena to her feet, warding off yet another slashing blow from Fadden, this one even more jarring than the last.

"Beware, he has a dirk in his boot," Skena called the warning. She moved out of the circle, going to stand behind Guillaume, leaving Noel free to fight without the distraction of worrying about her.

Wrapping his left hand behind his right on the long, leather grip, he wielded the broadsword with his solid muscle, meeting the third hacking swing from Daragh. With the proper control of the weapon, he was able to take the blunt force, and yet not transfer the power from Fadden's blade into his own. Noel quickly shifted into a warrior's rhythm of parries, thrusts, swings, and counter swings, the weapons singing and clanging in the night.

The Scotsman came at him with sword high, meaning to chop down on Noel's head. Noel stepped to repel it, but the snow was becoming mushy from their moving about; his foot slipped, causing his balance to be off. He opposed the blow, but at the wrong point. The blades rang out, then grated as the two blades slid down each other until the hilts were locked. At that point, it became a contest of strength, each of them pushing to thrust the other away.

Daragh rocked to the side, swinging out to drive his leg into Noel's side, the bastard clearly aiming for the old wound. The pain was excruciating. Daragh slowly forced him back, trying to knock him off his feet.

Skena cried out, but Noel could not look her way.

Daragh laughed, tasting victory. "Where is your arrogance now, Englishman?"

"Right here, you Lowland knave." Noel sprang. Drawing up his knee to his chest, he lashed out with his booted foot, slamming hard into the center of Daragh's chest.

The air leaving his lungs, Fadden staggered back. Fighting to regain his balance, he came forward, his sword raised high with both hands, preparing to chop downward at Noel again.

Noel spun in a circle, his sword catching Daragh in the center of his chest. The man stopped, almost seemed to hang suspended. A stunned expression crossed his face, as if he did not quite believe a sword was protruding from his torso.

"I will be damned." Daragh laughed weakly.

Noel used his knee to shove the Scotsman back off his sword. Daragh fell into the snow with a soft thud. Moving to stand over the man, Noel said, "Aye, you shall."

Daragh stared up at Noel, blood gurgling in his throat and out the side of his mouth. The brown eyes watched him; Daragh knew he was dying, that he had lost. "You . . . were never . . . going to . . . let me go. . . ."

Noel inclined his head slowly. "I lied. You were a dead man from the first instant you put your hands on Skena. This is just putting paid to your dark deeds."

Daragh raised his hand and tried to say something, but then it dropped, and he coughed. He breathed no more.

Skena ran to Noel, hugging him around the waist. Giving a weak laugh, Noel stiffly wrapped an arm about her, hugging her so tightly he feared he might never let her go again. "Ah, easy, lass. Hugging you hurts." He kissed her temple, closing his eyes in thanks, feeling the pain of knowing how close he came to losing her. "You know I was lying to Daragh about rather having you dead than letting you go with him?"

Skena nodded, sniffing against his chest. "Just words I little recall."

Noel tried to breathe normally, to tell himself everything was all right. And for an instant he was almost convinced of the certainty. Then emotions rolled through him, violent, painful. He had nearly lost Skena—his whole world, his life. "Oh, bloody hell." He took her by the elbows and pulled her against him, his mouth taking hers roughly. His lips moved over hers, tasting the sweetness that was Skena, hungrily drawing from her the radiance that warmed his weary soul.

"Oh, God, lass. I love you. I nearly lost you—" He kissed her eyes, her cheeks, her temples.

She put her fingers to his lips silencing him. "'Tis over now. Take me home, my love."

A scream tore them apart, ringing through the night. It was followed by another. And yet another, then deep snarls of wolves. Dorcas. High up on the far side of the cliffs, they could just barely make out her figure racing along the edge, trying to escape the pack. A white one jumped at Dorcas as she pulled up, reaching the cliff's edge.

"Save her," Skena moaned, but it was too late.

Two more wolves leapt at Dorcas, and all went over the cliff. Her scream marked her descent, echoing all the way down. Skena turned away from the horrible scene, and burrowed her face against Noel's shoulder, muffling her protest against his chest, as if he had the power to blot the horrible scene from her mind.

"Bad end," Guillaume spoke from just behind him. "Even for one such as her."

Noel gave a brief nod, but without remorse. The bitch had endangered Skena's life more than once, and risked the children and Muriel. To his way of thinking, God had given Dorcas her trial by ordeal, and her guilt had damned her.

"Send men to check on her. Though I doubt she lived through that fall, we needs must be certain. If not, fetch her body. Though she deserves it not, I will not leave her for the wolves."

This time another scream rang out, one of rage, as Ella ran across the snowy beach, a squire chasing after her.

"Noel!" Guillaume yelled. He was already partway across the beach, headed to check on Dorcas. He turned and came back at a run.

Ella charged straight for Noel. Instead of protecting himself, he turned to shield Skena from the crazed woman.

A knife held in her hand, Ella screamed, "My baby! You killed my baby!"

The knife caught Noel in the lower back. Though the blade did not penetrate the mail shirt, the force of the blow to his wound, reinjured by Daragh, caused him to slump to one knee, still striving to pull Skena out of Ella's range. Ella slashed at Noel again, but Skena blocked the arc of her swing. Noel surged to his feet, slamming his sword upward, catching Ella under her chin with the pommel and knocking her out.

"Tie the bitch up and toss her into the pit until she can be fetched to Challon. He can deal with the crone."

Stephan came running back, frowning at the squire who had allowed Ella loose. "What means this? She was bound."

The young man shrugged. "She had to pee."

Noel growled, half-vexed with the green lad's folly, half in pain. "Pee my arse. Never again fall for such a ploy. It will see you dead, or lashes to your back."

"The woman is dead," Stephan offered the tides. "The wolves with her. You go ahead, back to Craigendan with your lady. We will see to fetching her body back."

Noel nodded, and led Skena to Brishen. "We need to get you back and into a hot bath to warm you. You are shivering."

"Part cold. Part terrified," she replied, watching him mount.

Guillaume scooped her up and deposited her crosswise on Noel's lap. Situating her securely, he wrapped his mantle around her, too, to add its extra warmth. He took a moment to sigh relief. He swallowed hard to keep back the tears that threatened to come. His warrior's mien had not failed him. But he was left humbled and holding his precious wife in his arms, knowing she was safe; fate had not been so cruel, a second time, as to take away his life, his future.

"Where are the children and Muriel?" Skena asked, trying not to cry anymore.

"Safe. I sent them back to Craigendan with a guard of two. They should be in the care of Lady Rowanne by now." Pulling up the hood about her face, he brushed his lips softly against hers. "I am going to beat you when I get you home, wife," he whispered.

"You will not," she said, knowing it to be the truth.

Noel was forever threatening her with such treatment, but he would never raise a hand to her. This she knew as well as that the sun would rise in the morn; the knowledge shown in her eyes.

"This time I mean it. I do not think anything in life has ever scared me more than seeing you struggling with Daragh."

"Then I will have to beat you, as well. For nothing has ever scared me as much as watching you fight that evil man."

Noel gently nudged Brishen with his knees, giving him the command to move forward. Since the horse obeyed his knee and foot instructions, Noel was able to hold her close. So close she could feel his heart beating.

"I love you Noel de Servian. More than life," Skena whispered against his chest.

Epilogue

Noel held a finger to his lips to stop Jenna from greeting him as he noiselessly entered the lord's chamber. Skena's back was to the door, and the maidservant was soaping her shoulders with a cloth. Jenna smiled as she spotted him. He winked at her and then flicked two fingers toward the door in a silent dismissal. Giving a nod, she passed him the rag, and then tiptoed from the room. At the doorway the young woman paused; a wistful smile molded her face before she gently closed the door.

"The lavender and the heat are relaxing," Skena murmured and then sighed as he trailed the cloth over her beautiful shoulders and neck. "I could stay here all night, but help me out before Noel returns."

"Noel has returned," he whispered against her ear, then laughed as she jumped.

Her face alight, Skena turned partially around and gave him a drowsy smile. "Noel."

"I just checked on Muriel and the children, and all three sleep soundly." Leaning forward, he kissed the back of her neck, grinned as it raised gooseflesh. "You are giving me that come hither smile, hoping I will forget that I promised to beat you once I got you back to Craigendan."

She rotated even more and then fluttered her eyelashes. "Come hither, Noel de Servian."

"Oh, you live dangerously, my lady." He dropped the rag and reached backward to tug his sark off over his head. He dropped it on the bench and sat down beside it to unlace his boots.

Skena watched him with hungry eyes as he stood to undo the front of his chausses and then push them off along with his braies. "Ah, my braw husband."

"Braw? Just braw?" He arched his brow. "Not beautiful?"

Her bare shoulder gave a small shrug. "Mayhap . . . hmm . . . a wee bit bonnie."

"Bonnie? But not beautiful?" he taunted. ·

"'Tis said men do not like being called beautiful." Skena tried to play innocent.

"Well, this one loves it." Pushing her forward in the tub, he started to step into the hot water behind her.

"Och, what are you doing, my lord husband?" she gasped.

He gave a low throaty chuckle. "Well, I am *coming* . . . *hither*, wife."

She scooted forward to give him a bit more room. Her laughter bubbled forth as water splashed over the edge. "I am not sure we will both fit. As Muriel said, there is so much of you."

"Trust me. We will *fit* . . . perfectly. I told you I would show you that we could." He slid his legs carefully on either side of hers, and once settled, pulled her back against his chest. "Not too cramped, eh?"

"Mmmm." Skena almost purred as his arm encircled her. "I agree. . . . It might be near perfect. Such a clever husband I have."

Noel nipped at her earlobe as his arms flexed to pull her more tightly to him. "Are you going to proclaim how clever I am after I beat you?"

"You will not beat me. You bray such nonsense—"

"Bray? How dare you compare me to a fool jackass, wench!" He flipped her in the tub, so she was half draped across him, her right hip exposed above water. Feeling devilish, he planted his palm against her backside.

"Och, that stings," she complained, but playfully, telling him that it did not smart too much. "Why did you do that?"

"To prove I am a man of my word. I said I would beat you—so consider yourself properly beaten, wife. Now you will obey me and not run off and scare me out of ten years of my life. I am not a young man. Never again should you trouble me in such a fashion."

"Me? Trouble?" she spluttered as she rotated in the tub to face him.

"Aye, trouble. You go dashing about in snowstorms—" He started to rail at her, but she moved her thigh between his, rocking gently against his groin. "Ah, that is . . . *distracting*."

"Merely trying to help you *come . . . hither*." Skena pressed her breasts against his chest and then nipped his chin. "Seems to me that I was dashing about in the snow when I found one snowy knight. Where would you be had I not been out causing *trouble?*"

Rolling his eyes, he pretended to think about the question. "Hmm . . . I suppose instead of the wolf being in my belly, I would be in his—"

Skena made a mournful face and thumped his chest. "How horrid! Never say such things. You do not know how scared I was that night."

He kissed the tip of her nose. "Aye, I do. I remember most of it. My valiant lady warrior. No one ever fought for me before you." He stroked the back of his hand against her cheek. "I also recall how you faced the pack another time, to protect and provide for the people of Craigendan—another instance of your running about. I will not have it, Skena. Do not scare me like that ever again."

"De Servian, do hush. Give me those kissing lessons to make me call you Noel again." Skena brushed her lips against his. "I love you, more than words can ever tell you."

He hefted Skena so she was sitting astride him, his hands

gripping the firm globes of her derrière, torn between the driving physical desire clamoring within his blood to rule, and the need to make her understand all these wonderful emotions that were so new to him. The emotions won. "Words can mean a lot. I am not sure I will ever tire of hearing *I . . . love . . . you*—or saying it. I do love you, Skena. It scares me how much. 'Tis not an easy thing for a warrior to admit. I have stood before the mouth of hell unleashed, killed to keep from being killed, seen the vile brutality and ugliness that man can conjure. None of it terrifies me with the same depth as the fear of losing you."

She rubbed her thumb slowly over his lower lip, totally mesmerized by the small caress. "I understand, my love. The moments I stood and watched you fight Daragh were the longest of my life. Every breath, I feared one slip and I would lose you. So I know the fear. I suppose in time, when we are old and gray, mayhap the fear will ease."

"I would not wager anything of value on that." He took her mouth in such tenderness that Skena's shaky hand reached up, her fingers brushing his cheek, proclaiming her awe at the profound bond they shared. Still, his blood could be held at bay for only so long. A naked, wet Skena pressed against his body saw his reason melting and his passion taking control. His groin nearly cramped from the blood flooding his flesh, sending its pulsing hot length nudging against Skena's mound.

"I wanted so to tell you of my love, what you bring to me. Will you be angry with me if other parts of my body rule?" he said against her lips.

Her eyes flashing, she slowly shook her head no. "I was wondering when we would get to the 'come hither' part." She shifted so her body was open to him, her hips rotating gently, rocking the mushroom tip into her channel. "Use those other ways to warm me de Servian."

"Noel," he corrected. He bore down on her derrière with his palms, impaling her with a single trust.

Skena nearly purred. "Noel. My snowy knight with the name of Christmas."